MW01268009

Fifty Cents for a

Dr Pepper

Barri L. Bumgarner

Amy-
Thank you for supporting
my work!
Barri L
Bumgarner

Fifty Cents for a Dr Pepper

Barri L. Bumgarner

Fifty Cents for a Dr Pepper

Copyright © 2020 Barri L. Bumgarner

All rights reserved. No part of this book may be used or reproduced by any means, graphic, electronic, or mechanical, including photocopying, recording, taping or by any information storage retrieval system without the written permission of the publisher except in the case of brief quotations embodied in critical articles and reviews.

The publisher does not have any control over and does not assume any responsibility for author or third-party websites or their content.

Mockingbird Lane Press—Maynard, Arkansas

ISBN: 978-1-64871-530-3

Library of Congress Control Number: Control Number is in publication data.

0 9 8 7 6 5 4 3 2 1

www.mockingbirdlanepress.com

Cover art:
Cover graphics:

When I published my first novel, *8 Days,* in 2004, I owed a debt of gratitude to my then-writing group (Brian, Elaine, Heidi, and Margo). They were instrumental in this book as well. I began this story in 1998, when a student in my junior high classroom told me she couldn't finish her homework for our lesson that day. I had that teacher moment. *You mean work for my class isn't your top priority when you're at home every night?* This student rocked my world when she told me that she couldn't do her homework because she and her mom, along with a little sister, had been living in their car for the past several weeks. It jolted me, exposed my own privilege, and it instilled a drive in me to always be aware of the inequity in our society and to use my voice as often as possible to inspire and instill change. I thank her every single time I think about this book.

That injustice is as prevalent today as it has ever been. Be aware. Use your voice. Find your homeless shelter and support it – often. Don't be silent in any fight for social justice. It is through perseverance and understanding that we build a better tomorrow for ALL Americans.

To those who helped nurture this literary baby to realization, thank you, especially those friends who read drafts: Angie Peterson, Aunt Lyn, my mom, and Marsha Tyson. My journey as an author has been filled with love and support. Finding balance as an educator who writes has been tough, but it is always worth the journey when seeing a project finalized.

Thank you to all who have helped me grow, given advice, offered critiques when I needed them, and to all those who've rejected my work. You have made me stronger, more determined, and proud of the voice I've developed.

For my mom, who loved this book in a draft she read twenty years ago. She was and will always be my first inspiration as a writer.

And for Marsha. Because I wouldn't be where I am today without you.

Part 1

Before & After

Chapter One

Timothy Ryan Weaver woke to screaming. When a trembling hand raked across the crusted blood on his jacket, he clamped his mouth shut. With horror, he realized the screams – and hand – were his own.

A moment of *where am I, who am I, what have I done* clamored through his muddled brain. He didn't know how he got in the damp, smelly storm drain, but survival instincts had kicked in. His eleven-year-old brain couldn't reconcile what had happened. Instead, he tenderly fingered the gash on his left cheekbone, so swollen he could barely open his eye. But that was fine with him. He didn't want to look anyway. A blown fuse in his brain had erased the night before. Too scared to risk remembering, he squeezed his eyes shut and prayed for a do-over...or a miracle.

He fell asleep wondering why his family had left him in the muck of the storm drain to die.

Chapter Two

Twenty-Four Hours Later

"Hey, shrimp, get outta my damn trash can!" A stooped-over, haggard woman glared at Timmy.

He froze, his hand mid-search for something, anything to eat. *Bite me!* he almost hissed. Instead, he played tennis spectator with the trashcan and the shabby woman pushing a junk-filled shopping cart. *Run or fight for it...run or fight for it....*

"Did you hear me, you little shit?" She pulled her lips back to reveal green teeth so crooked, the top chompers were in two rows.

"All this is yours?" Humiliation surged through him, but the hollow rumble in his stomach silenced the shame. He hadn't eaten in what felt like days, could barely stand without his head swimming, and the ultimate kick in the groin? He didn't know how he'd gotten here.

"Damn straight." She pushed her cart closer, the wheels squeaking as she closed the distance between them on the St. Louis sidewalk. The run-down city street was empty, except for the two of them and random scraps of paper skittering in the early morning breeze.

"I – I, uh...sorry." Timmy's vision blurred, glancing from her wild expression to the strange assortment of items in her cart. *Did she really own this trashcan?*

"Get out, kid. Find your own crap." Her watery eyes narrowed. "Get," she repeated, exposing the double row rotting teeth again. She wobbled toward him, maybe to intimidate – and it worked. He was eleven – he understood about territory. "I ain't seen you around here. What's that crap all over you?" Her brow furrowed. "Is that blood?"

Timmy pulled his hand from her trash and ran it down the

front of his Nike pullover. The crusted stains resurrected something in his tired brain.

Blood...somebody's blood. He felt the gash on his left cheekbone, just below the outside corner of his eye. A sizzling pain zipped through him as his finger brushed the wound. *It could be mine...*

She snapped her fingers and motioned him back. No matter the circumstances, Timothy Ryan Weaver understood hierarchy. Maybe not the word, but the concept whipped his scrawny butt into reverse. She was old, he was a kid, and that put her in charge.

"...only a block or two that way. The shelter'll clean you up, feed you, and even letcha sleep for a spell. Now get back. You're crampin' my style." She pointed off to his right, her trembling hand knocking into the paper sack sitting in the front of her cart. None of the beer or soda cans spilled, though Timmy didn't think the bossy lady would've noticed if they had.

His head throbbed, dizzying him. Her mouth kept moving, but Timmy had to concentrate to backpedal. His balance had sprung a leak in the last two or three days since...since... Since what? He didn't know, couldn't remember. But whatever caused the nasty cuts and Easter egg of a knot on his forehead had done a number on his balance. The wicked gash on his left cheekbone had begun to pucker around the edges, but still gaped, and yellow ooze had started to seep from it. In another time, the injuries would've been cool – if he'd had a spill off his Huffy or fallen from an unconquerable tree. *My Huffy....* But words cut through the milky fog of remembering.

"Did you say they'll feed me?" His mouth watered, and everything in his gut clenched in agony. The burning sensation wore off after a few seconds, the possibility of food the best medicine he'd had in days.

"Kid, you bein' a smartass?" She never took her eyes off him as she circled the trashcan, swerving her cart away from him, the wheels *ree-ree-reeing* as she went.

He didn't understand her shopping cart full of treasures. A toaster missing its cord, a section of hard, white pipe, and a tattered black leather purse with a giant pink *D* on it sat in the front like a child being chauffeured around the grocery store. Sections of yellowing newspaper lined the sides and lay in piles underneath. A straw hat sat on top of the newspapers, lifting slightly in the breeze, as if it wanted to fly away but couldn't quite muster the strength.

Like me...but I ran like a baby, didn't I? He just couldn't remember from what.

"I have a real bad headache." He took another step backward. *Tell me again about the food.* He hadn't eaten since the lump on his head scrambled his brains.

"That way. Go around that there corner, you'll see the line in a few blocks. Soup kitchen opens for breakfast in less'n ten minutes, so you best get along. I seen quite a crowd a few minutes ago." She shooed him with her hands, and he got a full whiff of her as she did.

The stench gagged him – a mixture of smoke, soured milk, and other foreign odors that brought tears to his eyes. An early morning breeze – cool for a St. Louis August even at seven a.m. – gave him a reprieve from the vapor clinging to her.

"You listenin' to me?" The woman, under so many layers of clothes Timmy couldn't tell where she started and the fabric began, narrowed her watery eyes again. She didn't sneer enough to expose her decaying teeth this time, and he was glad. But she stared hard at his front – the stained pullover – maybe considering whether to clobber him over the head with a cordless toaster and collect some kind of reward.

"Uh, yes, ma'am. That way?" He pointed in the same direction she had. She nodded. He didn't have to look at the blood she kept staring at. *He* knew it was there. He just wasn't sure how it *got* there.

The gash on his cheek throbbed, but it hadn't bled enough to cover his jacket. *It's not mine...* The possibility of whose made him wobble again.

"You get on up there. Get. Go on. Get them sores looked at." She flicked a finger at him while staring into her trashcan. "Look whatcha done to my stuff! Shit. It's all broken." She started moving things around, maybe sorting them or perhaps sizing up what he hadn't ruined.

He scooted backward toward the corner, the wounds and scrapes on his face throbbing the more he considered them. Would the people at the shelter call the police? For some reason, that scared him more than the blood.

"Thanks," he mumbled, and continued his backward quest, toward the open space past the scary, vacant buildings looming over him like a scolding parent. Timmy stared at the woman rummaging, aware how *unaware* she was of him.

She maneuvered her cart around the trashcan, the wheels squeaking *ree-ree-ree* as she did. He finally tore his eyes away and turned the corner, hearing her cuss him about a ripped newspaper. Less than three blocks from her trashcan – just like she said – a long line filled the far sidewalk. Hunched over, mismatched people all stared straight ahead. Most looked like they would be her friends. Extra layers of clothes even in the August heat, hooded jackets and sweatshirts, the same frayed edges to every garment – he'd seen people like that on TV before. He understood the broad concept of homelessness but had never been up close and personal with any – until two or three days ago when he became one of them.

Chapter Three

North County Shelter was a slice of heaven, as far as Timmy was concerned. Old people, some dirtier than he and his friends had ever managed to get, filled the long tables, bantering about baseball, griping about the weather, and talking a lot about nothing. But Timmy got down to business as soon as he reached the front of the line. Forty minutes of waiting had sent his raging hunger almost to a point of nausea, but nothing that two helpings of scrambled eggs, a biscuit drenched in gravy, and three glasses of orange juice couldn't cure. He let out an impressive belch, getting approving grins from several geezers with more age spots than teeth.

"Nice one. But you better slow down, or it'll start comin' out the other end." An old man cackled, but his buddy hadn't let go of his Cardinal tirade.

"Damn 'Birds. I ain't on the LaRussa bandwagon yet. But thank God for Big Mac – that's all I gotta say."

Hey, Timmy! You better get your cards – we might get McGwire's autograph today! His dad's voice sucker-punched him, forcing him to hold his cramped stomach. He bowed his head, willing the food to stay down.

"Hon, you awright? You eat too much? Listen to these boys about how to eat...small bites and some sips in between." A volunteer hovered over him – he could smell the coffee on her breath.

Dad? But the voice was gone. An after-image of Sam in a Brian Jordan jersey, him in his McGwire favorite. The flash faded but left Timmy trembling in its wake. He grasped at it but felt nothing – like trying to grab fog.

Someone beside him burped, and others snickered that it had only been a two point five.

He stared up at the nice lady, tears blinding him. He could

make out the blonde hair and face shape, and for a moment, he melted.

Momma? But the body odor, clanking silverware, and endless chatter of the old men who called each other *bums* and *geezers* twisted the ache in the pit of his stomach. This place was not home – and a sick certainty assured him he didn't have one anymore.

"C'mon. Let's get your poor face cleaned up. Who did this to you? Well, I understand why you're here. God knows anybody do that to their own kid oughtta be stripped and dipped, as far as I'm concerned." The lady whose face Timmy couldn't really see pulled him from his seat. He wiped his eyes so he wouldn't plow into anyone, being led past the tables, through a room crammed full of cots, and into a small bathroom. She had him sit on the toilet and spent twenty minutes, two wash rags, and numerous paper towels cleaning his face.

She whispered to another woman that they might need to call family services, and for some reason, that made Timmy's heart pound. He folded his arms over the dried blood on his pullover, though he had wiped at it enough that it could pass for dirt.

By the time she finished, he could barely hold his head up. She helped him to one of the cots. He wanted to thank her, to give her a great big hug, and tell her everything that had happened to him. But if he thought about it too much, he could see it. It was just past his mental fingertips and he preferred to keep it that way.

As he drifted to sleep, he did his best to *unthink* all of it.

***

"Oh, God, somebody help me," Timmy moaned.

Panic clenched his bladder – they weren't finished with him, he knew that.

"Get your ass out here, kid," the monster of a man barked.

When a hand banged against the car above him, Timmy let out a piercing shriek. It echoed off surrounding houses and bounced back. The crack of a gunshot just over his head ripped through metal, and he let out another throat-scorching scream. Urine trickled down his leg, and in that instant, a rubber band snapped inside his brain.

"No," he whimpered, then wiped the snotty tears streaming onto his upper lip. It left a slimy smear on the sleeve of his Nike pullover. He gingerly touched his left eye, now so swollen he could barely see through it. A deep gash just below it felt sticky and open.

Oh, God, oh God, oh God. A steady thud-thud-thud behind his eyes nauseated him. He could taste metal in the back of his throat. Colors swirled inside his head. Immediately following a second shot, a thunder of fleeing footsteps smacked pavement, then the world fell deathly silent and black. The whir of sirens stirred something inside him. A strange smell burned his nostrils. Timmy grabbed the edge of the car and shimmied out from under it. Terror had paralyzed him and left a black hole in his mind but suddenly sent a jolt of adrenaline through him. And then Timmy did what he somehow knew he must.

He ran. He sprinted like the wind, blond hair flipping wildly across a barely recognizable battered face. An egg-sized knot stuck out on his forehead like a hood ornament. He raced past window-barred houses. He flew by parked cars, hurdled bushes, and jumped ditch after ditch as he crossed shabbily paved roads and then hit open field. Time melted for Timmy as each burst of leg power propelled him farther away. Eleven-year-old muscles finally began to ache and tighten until he had to slow to a jog. His calves knotted, threatened to stop his flight altogether. Had he gone far enough?

He didn't know, but being out in the open made him tremble. The sirens pierced and ebbed, urging him to hurry.

Searching the dark field, Timmy's heart skipped and nearly pounded out of his ribcage.

A storm drain! *It yawned less than a hundred yards away, down a steep slope.* They won't find me there! *He didn't know why the police scared him so much, he just knew enough to hurry. Bad people wanted him and good people couldn't help.*

And maybe I'm the bad one. *He slowed to a trot but willed his legs to keep moving. He was going to get to that ditch. Tears brimmed in bloodshot eyes, fear and pain churning like a blender in his gut. He fisted the tears away, because there was one thing he knew for certain.*

I'm no crybaby. *Timothy Ryan Weaver had turned eleven in March, nearly a teenager now and bordering on manhood. Men don't cry, he had vowed. For some reason, it seemed important, a necessity to growing up.*

Hurry, hurry, hurry, *rambled through his head, keeping pace with a thumping heart and throbbing legs. Just as he topped the incline, Timmy's tennis shoe clipped a rock. He tried to catch himself, but his right palm skidded off rocks and dirt. In a scary moment of strange clarity, the world flipped upside down, right side up then sideways as he sprawled headfirst and landed spread-eagled at the bottom of the ditch. Timmy's forehead smacked a dirty slab of concrete at the entrance to the storm drain and everything went black, sprinkled with exploding stars. He appeared to be making a snow angel on his belly without the key ingredient.*

Timmy tried to sit up, but the burning pain in his head wouldn't let him. So many parts of his body hurt, all he could do was crawl into the safe haven of the pitch-black storm drain and pray.

***

Timmy woke with a jolt, aware he'd just barely fallen to

sleep.

Where am I? His eyes adjusted, sensing someone too close. When he could focus, a face was less than ten inches from his own, sour breath wrenching his already queasy stomach.

"What the – " He jumped, scrambled backward on the cot, nearly tipping it. "Who're you?"

"Hi," an ancient man mumbled, then smiled. He sat in a rickety chair beside Timmy's cot. Had that been there before? It seemed like there had barely been room to stand, but from the way Timmy's head hurt, he wasn't sure of anything.

"Do I know you?" The words gooed in his throat like globs of icing without milk.

"I can't believe it's you." The man shook his head. "My friend Sara said she seen you earlier... I been lookin' everywhere for you, son."

Timmy tried to focus his scrambled brain, not sure who he was much less who this gray-haired, acne-scarred old man was. When Timmy didn't offer anything else, the guy added, "I wouldn't say you *know* me, but you should. It's sort of a long story though. You up for it?"

Timmy stared, measuring the man's wrinkles and not understanding why there were brown splotches and red lightning streaks all over the old guy's nose. *Why was this old man looking for me?* Everything was mish-mashed, from his brain to where he was to why this ancient bum talked like he knew Timmy.

"I got to start from the beginnin', kid, but we ain't got much time. People be lookin' for ya, and well, I guess that's part of what I gotta tell ya." The man's expression darkened. He glanced over his shoulder nervous-like, nodded to the lady who had cleaned up Timmy's face, then sighed like he had just lost his best dog. Rosy cheeks and deep-tanned forehead framed the pale outline of a ghost beard recently shaved. The pale blue button-up shirt, too wrinkled to be new, was tight across the shoulders, and the gray trousers had risen as he sat, exposing white socks and scuffed-up black shoes. *Highwaters...* The intrusive voice of someone familiar had made fun of old men with highwater pants. *Sam?*

Timmy shook the memory of his older brother away, more than a little worried why the mismatched old man staring at him looked so sad.

"First of all, I'm Max. And, Timmy, I ain't seen you since you was knee high to a grasshopper. I ain't seen you since 1989 or 90. You's still a baby."

He knows me? His head swam, and he fought the urge to race out the door. Nothing familiar rang any bells in his addled brain, no urge to hug the guy and say *Take me home!* As if he felt the uncertainty, Max bowed his head and glanced at something scrawled on a piece of paper folded in his age-spotted right hand. Timmy sat up a little, trying to see it.

"How...how do you know me? And how come you haven't seen me since then?" Timmy hated that he sounded like a whiny baby.

"I don't even know where to start." He glanced at the paper again, unfolding it carefully like a winning poker hand, guarding it.

"What's that?" Timmy's heart pounded so hard, he could barely breathe. Something felt *off* about Max. He couldn't wrap his head around it.

"Uh, it's directions. When I ran in to Sara some blocks away, I had to draw me a map to this shelter. I never been here before. But I been lookin' for ya and she knew it." Max frowned, then wiped at the corners of his eyes.

"Why?"

God, I sound like a two-year old. He wanted to know. He *needed* to know. He wasn't sure who Sara was, but he stared at the folded piece of paper that didn't look anything like a map. He could see typed words. Newsprint maybe? There was a picture at the bottom that might've been a map. Or a face.

"Do you know what's happened to you, kid? Why you're

here?" Max held Timmy's gaze this time.

"I – I don't, I mean, I do. This old lady told me how to get here – I was hungry. But I don't remember what happened in – in the street. The other night...it – I..." A lump lodged in his throat, the threat of resurrecting the night he ended up in the storm drain. "I don't wanna remember. Get away from me – I don't know you." Tears welled in his eyes, and he scooted as far into the corner as he could without falling off.

"Not anymore. But you used to once. I'm – you – well, *shit.*" Max's hands shook so badly he couldn't pull the handkerchief from his front pants pocket. He finally managed, and Timmy wanted to scream at him to just say what he came to say and go.

After an excruciating few minutes, Max spoke, his voice so quiet Timmy had to strain to hear.

"Your mom, dad, and older brother are in trouble. They didn't know where else to turn, so they contacted me. We been on the outs a long time, your mom and me. It's a booze thing. Anyway, she said they didn't have nobody else to go to – their friends couldn't help cuz it could get 'em all in trouble. But I guess she wasn't too worried about me. We hadn't spoke in damn near nine years. I guess Sam was five and you wuz just a baby. The whitest hair I ever seen."

Timmy furrowed his brow, his head reeling with what this old man was saying. *Daddy used to call me a towhead, my hair so white it didn't have any color at all.*

"How do you know my mom and dad?" Timmy's cheekbone throbbed, and this old man was unraveling his insides.

Get outta your Es-ca-lade, dog. You ain't no prime piece of shit, now, are ya? Timmy shook his head, refused to make sense of the words someone had hissed at him – two nights ago? Three?

"You okay?" Max leaned forward, worry etched across his bronze forehead.

"No." Timmy continued to stare at Max. Both sat silent for several minutes.

"I'm yer grandpa, son. And it's been a long time comin' for me to see you, I'm just sorry it had to be like this. But I'm here to help now, to do what your momma asked. I think I'm the only one who can help you, and she knew that." Max fidgeted, wadded the piece of paper into his front pants pocket where the handkerchief was.

Grandpa? He shook his head. "I don't have a grandpa. I don't have a grandpa or a grandma. They all died when I was little. Dad told me all about them...I – I –" But Timmy couldn't finish. It was hard to think about his parents. He could see them two months ago, even two weeks ago in his mind, but the last few days were like deleted scenes from their new Gateway computer – gone but an afterimage burned into his tired brain. And thinking about them made him want to bawl – they were gone, but he couldn't remember where. Or why.

And I'm covered in somebody's blood. He fingered his pullover, feeling the baseball cards in the zippered pouch, the rough dried blood all over the front.

"Yes, I know what they told you. Victoria didn't approve of my drinking or the gamblin'. And she said I was a bad influence." Max bowed his head. "Robert tried to punch me that last time, and I was pissed. Sam kept screamin' for them to stop, but they didn't listen. Your brother hugged me before I left, and I never saw you again. Not that I didn't try." A tear streamed down Max's cheek, making Timmy's heart ache.

Victoria? Robert? He knows their names? But Dad calls her Tori... everybody's always called her Tori.

"You – you're my grandpa? But I don't have a grandpa." He couldn't believe it, it didn't make sense. "What kind of trouble are they in? Where are they? Where's Sam? I want my mom and dad." Timmy felt the lump in his throat giving way, but he swallowed hard, trying to stay tough.

But if they're okay, why am I here?

"I know, buddy. They're gonna get in touch with me when they can. Your dad gave me a number to call when I get you safe." Max held out a post-it note with a number scribbled on it.

"If you can call them, you can take me to them, right?" He narrowed his eyes at Max.

"I don't know where they are. That's to keep us safe. I'm just s'posed to call soon as I got you safe." Max tucked the Post-it in the right pocket of his pants, behind the other folded paper. "I know this is hard, Timmy. But they want me to take care of you. I'm the only family you got right now. But I promise I'll getcha back to 'em when I call. Okay? They know the police are after ya – cuz of whatcha done. So I'm supposed to hide you out. They're tryin' to get to a safe place, cuz people's after them, too. Then they'll be able to explain to the cops what happened."

Cuz of what I did? What did I do? Why do they hafta hide without me? He tried to ask the questions, but the clog of emotion in his throat wouldn't let him. And the tears finally came. He flopped onto his stomach and bawled like a baby, sobbing into the flimsy pillow. The swirl of confusion screwing up his insides made him cry harder. He heard the chair scoot as Max got up and left, the fading footsteps followed by a door closing.

Good! Go, you stupid old man! If you were my grandpa, how come you never came to see me like Scott's always did? Huh?

He allowed pity to swallow him as he cried. He didn't believe the stupid old man, and no one could make him.

Chapter Four

Where the heck was his bike?

Timmy stood looking up and down Catalina Avenue like he was following a tennis match. A knot tethered his stomach as thoughts of what his mom was going to say rambled through his head. When she realized he hadn't chained it up like he promised, she would ground him for sure. She had threatened him with bedroom imprisonment for a whole day the last time he had left it unlocked.

"BRENT, SCOTT, YOU MORONS, IF YOU HAVE MY BIKE, I'M GONNA KICK YOUR BUTTS!" His voice boomed up and down the street. The ferocity of his words defied his swirling insides. Tears threatened to betray him. He fisted them away and glanced all around him to make sure no one saw.

Timothy Ryan Weaver was no crybaby.

A noise behind him sent him twirling around. Across the street, a monstrous man sat atop his Huffy. The whites of Muscle Man's eyes shone like marshmallows.

"What'd you do with it, boy?" Right there on the sidewalk in front of Scott's house, big as you please. The bike was swallowed underneath the mammoth body. Timmy edged cautiously toward him.

"That's my bike, Mister." The words limped through the air.

"You took somethin' a mine, I take somethin' a yours. Tit for tat."

"But –"

The massive arms rippled as the thug clenched his fists around the rubber handlebars. Timmy watched the enormous paws squeeze the handles until he thought the black might liquefy. The man stood, barely lifted his foot over the small Huffy and allowed it to tumble lifelessly to the sidewalk. He loomed in front of Timmy, who was fixated on the dagger-in-heart tattoo on the left upper arm. The sinister smile featured a set of heavily metaled teeth. The gold sparkled in the sun.

"Unless you wanna gimme back whatcha took." Hands as big as dinner plates reached toward him, and Timmy thought his earlier declaration that he was no crybaby might be debatable. His knees buckled, his bottom lip trembled, and his bladder threatened to take a few minutes off duty.

The enormous hands continued to close the distance, and Timmy understood the emotions of every movie star at that pivotal moment in a horror flick when something terrible is about to happen to them. The certainty of death washed over him as he retreated then stumbled. His sneaker caught the curb sending him plunging backward to the concrete, landing on a rock. The hands hovered just above him. His world eclipsed into total darkness.

Chapter Five

Timmy bolted upright. "Oh, god..." His head throbbed, and his stomach felt like it had been run through a blender – twice. He surveyed the filthy bedroom, the nightmare dissolving in slow motion, and then it came back to him. Max.

The man – his grandpa? – had come back, a tattered note scrawled on a piece of paper for the volunteers at the shelter. He swept Timmy away, assuring him everything would be all right, and next thing he knew, they stopped in front of a run-down apartment building with "Condemned" signs on every door and quite a few of the unbroken windows.

Sitting on a flimsy mattress, still in his filthy pullover, it was all Timmy could do not to cry. He sucked air, desperate to shake the images of the nightmare.

"Gimme back whatcha took, you little shit."

The nice lady at the shelter promised he'd be okay. *Okay, my hiney!*

"I wanna go HOME!" Timmy shouted at the dismal room, the afterimages still swimming around him. He scrambled to the corner, sending plumes of dust from the stained mattress. He curled up in a ball, inspecting what he hadn't been able to make out in the dark when they arrived late the night before.

I don't blame him for bein' ashamed of this dump...

The walls, covered in what must've once been red roses with thorny vines, now stared at him in varying degrees of fading grays. He scratched at one, just to make himself feel better. Day one - rose one. He sighed. The mattress, shoved into the corner, had rust-colored stains in assorted sizes and shapes. One tiny grime-covered window offered a little light, enough to notice the absence of any other furniture. Who moves into an apartment and doesn't have a matching bed, dresser, and chest of drawers? His room at home...

Home.

The image danced in his throbbing head, the cut seeping and pulsating with each beat of his heart. His brain, now on hyperdrive, could see it. The white two-story house, his Huffy sprawled on the lawn next to Sam's ten-speed.

Sam.

"Stop, whinin', Timmy. I didn't hit you that hard...Christ, you're such a pussy..." Sam grunted. He'd belted Timmy for getting a grimy fingerprint on a rookie Willie McGee ball card. But when? Overlapping with the thought came a vast ocean, a shark suddenly lunging for his brother, eating Sam's head in one fluid motion.

"NOOOOOO!" Timmy shrieked, scrambling away from the great white now eerily similar to Muscle Man. Random images flooded his head, overwhelming him – the smell of burnt rubber searing his nostrils, resurrecting demons that screamed at him to get the hell out from under the bed.

"GET AWAY FROM ME!"

Muscle Man's arms hovered in mid-air, swam out of focus, and even though Timmy knew the monster wasn't really there, he trembled all over. After a few seconds, all of it began to fade, to dim like a weakening battery in his brain. He took a deep breath and tried to remember what Max had said, what their plan was, when he would call his parents.

This is our hideout...we gotta lay low, Timmy, to throw off the wolves. We'll be safe here. I called 'em and they said to stay where we was so they could contact us next.

Timmy didn't know there were wolves in St. Louis, but the city offered horrors he'd never suspected in his previous life. So why not wolves? He was pissed Max had called them while he was sleeping. Why wouldn't the old man let him talk to his dad?

He panted, contemplated screaming some more, then buried his face in his hands and cried. The nasty, run-down apartment building hadn't seemed like a good hideout to Timmy – what looked safe about it? Abandoned, Max had said, perfect for now, then the old man claiming to be his grandpa introduced Timmy to a bunch of Max-duplicates – old men with sunburns, brown spots, and funny sores all over their faces. Even Skippy, Max's mutt terrier, tucked his tail between his legs and growled at Timmy every chance he got. If the boy moved too fast or got up too quickly, Skippy pounced into attack-mode, front end lowered and teeth bared like he meant to launch at any minute. Max would scold the mongrel, telling Timmy it would take time.

Timmy hoped he wouldn't have enough of it to find out.

The night before, all of them sat around a tiny grill in the living room passing around a bottle. They let Timmy smell it, and they laughed as he jerked his nose away.

"That smells nasty!" he cried, and they laughed harder. He stared at them, scowling, as the nine men stared back.

"What're you gawking at, kid?" Cooter asked, his bright red hair pulled back in a ponytail, and his sun burnt skin shimmered in the fire's glow. Skippy lay next to Max, thumping his wiry tail every time the old man patted him.

"How come all you guys are here...I mean, Max said this place was abandoned. It's our hideout. So I don't get why you guys are here."

Max lowered the bottle he'd lifted to his lips and gave a half smirk. Ralph, as close to a hundred as a man could get and remain upright, snickered. Vernon, damn near sixty and proud as hell of it, announced after Timmy's question, "You got your hands full with this whipper snapper, Max. You may be out of your league this time."

This time?

Timmy had frowned. He didn't understand and didn't like being confused, but he was getting used to it. He just wanted his family to contact Max and tell the old man how to reunite with them. Timmy didn't mind hiding, playing this cops and robbers game, but why couldn't he just do it with his family? Why did he have to be the one by himself?

Self-pity and anger, his new emotional cocktail, sent him stalking to his bedroom. *Screw you!* He wanted to yell at every one of them. He wondered what Vernon had meant, where his parents were, why every time he thought of them he felt a cold rush of fear in his stomach.

Why won't they come get me? Why did they take Sam and not me?

The questions kept dancing in his brain like a menacing fly. He'd catch a glimpse of Sam, his mom, his dad, but the faces would disintegrate before he could latch onto them.

The other men, more like bums in Timmy's opinion, had swirled around him last night, asking questions, trying to get the 411, Cooter said. That comment plopped right on top of the confusion pile. It all overwhelmed him to the point of tears, contradicting his vow never to be a crybaby.

Things had definitely changed.

As he lay on the scratchy mattress listening to the old men laugh, clank bottles, and jabber into the night, Timmy let the tears come. He bawled like a two-year old in the middle of a tantrum. Finally managing to get hold of himself and make the ghosts go away, he wiped his snotty nose on the sleeve of his Nike pullover, and then rubbed the smear onto the butt of his jeans.

He dried his eyes with his palm, tried to quiet the rage building inside him, and struggled to his feet. He tiptoed back out into the hall without making any noise. Timmy had no idea what time it was, but the men had all left or gone to bed.

I don't want to wake anyone...I don't want to see anyone... I don't even want to remember their names....

Somehow, knowing their names meant he'd have to be nice to them, and Timmy sure didn't want that. They smelled bad and laughed at things that weren't funny.

Mimicking a cartoon cat burglar, he took careful tiptoes down the hall toward the living room – the apartment was too quiet. He inspected each bedroom along the way seeing nothing except dirty floors and grimed over windows. It was still dark out, so the best light to aid him was the glow from the living room.

When he peered into the bathroom, he gagged, the stench forcing him to pull his T-shirt over his nose. A lantern sat on the edge of the tub, barely glowing but enough light for him to see the cloud of swirling flies. They buzzed over the toilet filled to the rim with dark brown liquid mucked with newspaper strips and cigarette butts. The tub had the same dark brown sludge about two inches deep with as many flies flying routes over it. Before the gags evolved into the real thing, he lurched past the doorway and into the large room.

He breathed a little easier, the bile in his throat sliding back into the safe haven of his stomach – empty enough to throw a wrench in Timmy's plan if he didn't eat soon. These walls, much like the others, had lost their color and had devolved to a grimy slate gray. Had they been that dark last night?

The grill smoldered in the middle of the room casting an orange glow on bottles, cans, and miscellaneous trash littering the floor – all around the nine sleeping men. Skippy raised his head that had been resting on Max's arm and growled – a deep, throaty sound that meant *keep your distance.* Timmy intended to, though it crushed him that the wriggly terrier mutt didn't like him.

Dogs always like me...Trevor loves me, he...

Trevor. Their yellow lab. A vision as clear as Skippy's snarl filled his mind. Had his parents gone to get Trevor? Had Trevor been with them when the rubber band in his brain snapped? He racked his memory, unable to dredge anything coherent, angry at the blank spaces.

The gagging stench of alcohol, smoke, and body odor cut off all thinking. One of the men rolled over, mumbled something, then lay quiet again. All of them were scattered throughout the room asleep on cushions, beanbags, and some just directly on the nasty floor. A harmonized snore would've been funny if Timmy weren't so freaked out by the sight of it. He wondered why his screams hadn't woken every single one of them, but the stacks of empty bottles all around them might have something to do with that. He could hear a faint car horn honking through one barely cracked window.

I wanna go home.

The black hole in his head – his family, his house, his life – sucked all the energy out of him. Unable to keep his throbbing brain quiet, he padded into the kitchen, hoping to miraculously emerge into a real house, with a refrigerator filled with food, and his mom making monkey bread. But from the constant buzz of flies, he doubted anything there would be worth eating.

Moldy food, takeout containers, a multitude of beer and whiskey bottles, and then his eyes locked on the sink. Another cloud of flies swarmed over rusted pans, chipped plates, dirty glasses so caked, they might've been there waiting to be washed since his first birthday.

For a panicky second, Timmy couldn't remember his own birthday.

Spring Break! zipped into his head, splashing Brent and Scott as they chased him in the rec center's swimming pool. His mom harped about not getting back into the water until the cake had settled, which it definitely hadn't. But who could wait?

March 26, that last spring break from his fourth-grade year... *My birthday...*

Hunger motivated him to reach for the ancient refrigerator's handle, even though reason told him nothing edible would be inside. But not looking, not taking the chance made his stomach growl harder, more insistent. He tugged it open, and no cold air wafted out, no light came on – only a sour stench that coiled his insides.

"God," he mumbled, then put his hand over his mouth. Refusing to puke in the nasty sink, he raced to the front door, jerked it open, and yakked up bile all over the hallway carpet.

He wasn't the first – stains dotted the gold shag carpet as far as Timmy could see. When he spat and got the last of the acid from his mouth, he took a deep breath.

Leave, Timmy, get the hell out of this shit palace...

He remembered one of Sam's favorite phrases, reserved for young ears only. Their parents would've been appalled, believing both children to be angels, perfect in every way. Sam once told him it was the way of the world – kids manipulate and parents accept it. Just the facts, ma'am, he'd say. And Timmy would laugh. Lots of stuff Sam did made him laugh. Being almost five years older, Sam had a way with people, with making them laugh, with bringing out a smile on the crappiest day.

Timmy ached for it – for him – now. Sam was starting high school this year – in a matter of weeks, right? What would his parents do? If they were running from...from the bad people, would Sam be able to go to school?

No way Sam misses football.

But how *could* Sam take that kind of chance if Timmy wasn't even allowed to be with them? The jumbled goop of information clogged all reasoning in his brain. It was too messed up to be real – Max was too messed up to be real – this apartment was too messed up to be real.

That's it! I'm dreaming! I'll wake up any minute!

But as Timmy stared at the shag-covered hallway, at the splatter pattern of his own vomit, he suspected he'd never had a dream – or nightmare – as real. He slipped back inside, not sure running was the answer. Where would he go? Skippy had followed him to the door and backed away as he pushed it closed.

"Leave me alone," Timmy whispered, and tiptoed past the campsite of a living room, down the hall, and into the last bedroom. *Mine?* He shut the door and locked it, hoping the thin hollow wood could block out the evil world nipping at his heels. He was sure Skippy was plotting a chance to eat his leg as he plopped onto the moldy mattress, no longer bothered by the stench.

In a world where parents abandoned their kids, dogs hated eleven-year old boys, and old men laughed at them, who cared how it smelled?

Chapter Six

A few scratched off roses later in the week, Max hoisted Timmy onto a wobbly card table one of the other guys said he brought from home. *If you got a home, how come you sleep here?* Timmy blurted. The guy laughed, and told Max, "Dude, you really found yourself a sheltered richie this time." It wasn't the first time one of Max's buddies called him strange names – Posh boy, mall rat, and the most confusing *Baby Gates*.

He ignored them just like he'd tried to ignore the wallpaper over his head that morning. But in the slits of light, he obliterated his seventh flower with the pronged edges of a beer bottle cap. Some of the caps had cool logos on them, so Timmy started collecting them – one of each he could find laying around the trashcan they called an apartment.

Have I really been here a week? As a...a... A what? He didn't know if he was truly homeless since this was sort of a house. And Max kept saying they were on the run, but they sure sat still a lot. He just felt *in limbo*. All he did know was that every time he asked if his parents had called or if Max had called the number again, the old man frowned. Then Max would screw up his forehead, like it hurt him to admit it, and mumble there was no news. Timmy insisted he try the number again, that his parents had to be worried about him. But Max shook his head and said it wouldn't be much longer, it *couldn't* be much longer.

"How d'you know, Max?" A lump filled his throat.

The old man dabbed greasy anti-fungal cream on the reopened gash.

"D – don't they want me back?"

"Ah, kid, sure they do. But I think they're runnin', you know, on the lam. A little kid will sure slow you down in them circumstances. I ain't crazy about this arrangement neither. Think I like livin' in this dump? I might not be no preppie like you, but I got better places to be than in this pit." Max smeared the goop on his finger onto his threadbare jeans and cursed. "Hope this stuff helps – it's not exactly what you need, but it's all we got. That thing needed stitches in the worst way, kid. Wonder what the hell hit you."

"I dunno, I –" For a flashing second, he saw fireworks in his brain, felt the impact of something brutal against his cheekbone and *did* remember. But the memory caved in, and it was gone. Another black spot filled it where his normal world used to exist. "Thanks, Max," Timmy mumbled. "Sorry I've been so much trouble. Y – you can go if you wanna, just leave me here." Tears welled in his eyes, and self-pity swallowed him in one massive gulp. He slipped off the table, ignored Skippy's growls, and hurried past the chattering men in the living room, sitting cross-legged around the tiny glowing grill.

This time when he got to the room at the end of the hall, he curled onto the mattress and didn't have to wonder about anything before he fell asleep, not even sure if it was daytime, nighttime, or dinnertime. It all blurred, like ice cream and chocolate in a blender. Thoughts of chocolate warmed him as he drifted, and for a brief reprieve, he dreamt of it, of swimming in it, licking it from his fingers, and drizzling it over scoops and scoops of his favorite vanilla bean. He plopped a spoonful of ice cream into a glass of Dr Pepper and groaned with pleasure at the blessed treat.

When he woke hours later, the smell still filled his nostrils, warming him and making it hard to remember where he was. A dull stream of light allowed him to inspect the roses over his head – he scratched the eighth one until it disappeared.

I'm not going to ask about them today...I'm going to get that number and try to call them myself. Or call home. He tried to resurrect the number he'd recited more times than he could count, but he suspected his fingers wouldn't have any trouble remembering. Max had taken to grunting incoherently in response to his questions, so he'd do a little calling of his own. He just had to wait until the time was right.

"Hey, nimrods, get your asses in here!" someone shouted as the front door closed. Timmy's heart raced.

Mom? Dad? Sam?

When peering out the door and down the hall, Cooter, Timmy's favorite not just because he was the youngest, but because he was cool, waved a piece of paper over his head. "FOOD!" he bellowed.

Timmy's heart dropped, but his stomach responded with a vicious gurgle. At least if it wasn't his family, it was something good. He hustled down the hall in his sock feet.

"Behold the flyer!" Cooter cackled.

"Unfuckingbelievable." Billy stared at the single page, a smile the size of the Arch spread across his face. Timmy steered clear of Billy when he could help it – not nearly as old as Max, only forty-two he claimed, but by far the meanest. Max had turned fifty-eight last May, and swore Billy was just a few years behind. They both sure had a lot of wrinkles around their mouth, eyes, and forehead. When Timmy told Billy he looked at least a hundred, Billy told him to mind his own shit, clacked his teeth at him, and hissed, "I eat kids for breakfast and beggar dogs for dinner."

Skippy seemed to believe it, because the mutt never came close enough to Billy to give him the chance.

Cooter – barely thirty – slapped his leg and danced in the middle of the room. His ponytail bounced, and it made Timmy want to join in, the thought of filling his belly almost as invigorating as going home.

Timmy weaseled past Billy without the guy noticing him and watched over Vernon's shoulder. He caught a glimpse of the word "buffet". Then he saw *Saturday* in bold print.

Is that today?

"We'll hop on the bus and get there early. Billy, you still got that Chinese container? We'll take us some leftovers for later."

"Hey, smart thinkin', Cooter." Billy grinned, revealing

yellow teeth and rotting gums. It added to the look – wild hair in gray-black wisps that stuck out in all directions, a wet finger in a light socket effect, Sam would say. His bulging dark eyes lacked color, and a sneer kept people at a distance. It completed the image one of the geriatric bums said resembled Animal from *Taxi*. Timmy didn't know the character or the show, but the name seemed to fit. Billy never shared anything about his life or why he hung out with Max and the guys. Timmy suspected he didn't have a home, that maybe a lot of them didn't. *Does Max?* It wasn't the first time he'd wondered.

"Kid, you ain't quite as fresh lookin' as you was a week ago, but that blond hair and them dimples are gonna attract a lot of attention. We don't want too much of it, got it?" Max cocked a scraggly eyebrow. He bent down and rubbed Skippy's head. "You stay and hold down the fort, 'kay, Skip?"

"You're crazy the way you talk to that mutt, Max. How come that dog don't like nobody but you?" Cooter laughed and tried to pet Skippy, but the terrier growled just like they all knew he would. "Fine, you old hateful thing. I'm gonna go eat chicken and mashed potatoes with gravy and green beans, and I bet they even got *cake*. And I ain't bringin' you nothin'!"

To punctuate his true nature, Skippy snapped at Cooter's fingers, missing by inches. The Gerries, their self-appointed nickname because they all claimed their geriatric stage in life mandated more about them than their previous professions, hooted with appreciation at Skippy's scrappiness.

When Timmy asked how the terrier earned his name, Max said the dog skipped out on everyone, only using and abusing people as he needed them. They had a lot in common, Max added, though when Timmy pressed for more on the old man's past life, it was a no-go. Even when he begged, saying it was his past too, Max refused.

"Well, screw you, Skippy. I'm goin' to eat! Hey, Max, you think they'll have beer?"

"Shit, Cooter. Beer? For the needy?" Max pulled Skippy

into his lap, and Timmy reached tentatively toward the mutt. Skippy growled.

"Sorry, Tim. I'm thinkin' some kid's been hard on Skip. You gotta give him time. He'll come around."

Timmy nodded and tugged the grimy St. Louis Cardinal's ball cap low on his forehead, careful not to touch the fading purplish green bruises, his war reminders from the night in the storm drain. Max's lessons on utilizing his cute face and faucet-washed golden hair would apply better when Timmy healed. Bad things happen to cute kids, the old man said, and Timmy believed him. Max hadn't been wrong about much so far, though Timmy had yet to refer to the old man as "grandpa." It just didn't sound right on his tongue.

The day before, Max had spent over an hour teaching him how to handle a knife. The art of holding it, concealing it, producing it only when ready to attack, his grandpa explained. They practiced on a sheet-wrapped box they named Wally. "He's gonna getcha," Max would say, then show Timmy how to poke and cut with the blade.

It felt awkward to drive the knife into an object, no matter how innocent. Thinking about the cardboard being flesh sent prickly shivers down his legs and back.

When the lesson had ended, he'd learned more about knives and his grandpa. Whether the old man showed it or not, he cared about Timmy. Without Max, he couldn't imagine where he'd be now. Certainly not on his way to a picnic.

"Anybody wanna peek at this baby again?" Max waved the flyer and gave a hearty *hoo-raw!* Timmy could see the bold-faced *all-you-can-eat* along the top, and his mouth flowed like the Mississippi. He didn't care that the heading, *Labor Day Charity Meal*, meant it was his first holiday without his family. He couldn't think about that now, not until something put a dent in his excruciating hunger.

"C'mon, guys, let's go. Aren't you ready?" Timmy didn't bother to hide his excitement. "It is today, right?"

"Yeah, it's today, and Timmy's right. Let's get a move on. It'll be hoppin' and we wanna get seats on the bus." Max stood, wobbled a few times before bracing a hand on the filthy wall.

"Anybody hangin' too bad to grab a bite of *boofay?"* Cooter giggled like a maniac.

"Hangin'?" Timmy regarded each Gerrie.

"God, how sheltered are you, kid? Don't richies drink?" Billy shorted a laugh and high-fived Vernon.

Timmy scowled, felt anger build in his chest, and wanted more than anything to smack the guy hard in the face. Just the thought of it gave him a surge. Everything about Billy rubbed him sideways.

"You are green, kid. If you're hangin', it means you're hungover." Max shook his head as the others laughed. "Had too much to drink and feel like upchuckin' everything we didn't eat the day before."

"Why do you do it then?" More laughter followed that question, but he really wanted to know.

"Cuz it numbs the brain, kid. And that's the best thing when you live like this. You'll learn soon enough." Billy turned to the others. "Think Blondie here could handle a shooter or two?" He squawked laughter, making Timmy's skin crawl with each squeal. The sound, and most of what Billy said, was like ten fingernails dragging along his chalkboard spine. The man mocked people and insisted that just because Max was older didn't make him smarter. Except Billy didn't have the guts to say it to Max's face. He picked at a person's scabs just to see them seep but would never admit it was him who did it. Even if there were witnesses.

"Shut up, Billy," Max snapped. "Timmy, you gotta remember to lay low, you got it? Them cops still be lookin' for ya, you hear me? Your mom would have my hide if somethin' happened to you under my watch. Be especially leery of uniforms. You see 'em, you skedaddle. They lock your scrawny butt up faster than a whore slummin' in church. Your luck, you'd end up in some foster home with a daddy thinkin' you're a little too pretty." Max brushed his bangs out of his eyes. Timmy shivered and gave an almost imperceptible nod. He got the *lay low* part, but there was a lot of stuff Max said that didn't make much sense.

A whore slummin' in church? It sounded dirty, like something his mom would disapprove of, and it occurred to Timmy that his mom would disapprove of most things Max said. Yet this man was her father.

Maybe that's why she never wanted us to see him. It made sense, didn't it?

"Thanks for watchin' out for me, Max," he finally mumbled, grateful for how much Max protected him.

"No problem, kid. Couldn't stand the thought of you bein' mistreated." Max ruffled Timmy's hair, a gesture that made him feel like Skippy's sidekick. But the thought came through loud and clear. Grandpa Max cared about him, and there wasn't anyone else left to play that part. His parents obviously didn't give a crap about him. Not anymore. If they loved him, they would come get him. They wouldn't let him live like this. They just wouldn't. Timmy could tell when he was being dumped like a scraggly, unwanted mongrel, and wrote the first of many Notes-to-Self: *if Max doesn't hear from them or if I can't get to a phone to call them, I gotta do something – get out of here anyway. California maybe?* The police wouldn't know him there, would they?

Timmy ran down the stairs ahead of them and then paced until the Gerries caught up. The idea of *all he could eat* swam around his head like a mad goldfish, putting a lid on the dark hole his family had fallen in. The morning sun had risen with sweat in mind, and August clamped hold of them with a suffocating humidity. *Wait a minute...if it's Labor Day, does that mean it's September? School had always started a week or so before Labor Day, right?*

The reality of passing days sucker-punched his enthusiasm

for a minute, but he squashed it. The here-and-now excitement of a real meal forced the calendar out of his head. Food trumped everything, even his parents today.

Tomorrow, he'd find a payphone.

Chapter Seven

By the time Timmy and the Gerries reached the Labor Day charity picnic, scads of people wound a full city block, chattering, shuffling their feet, dressed in varying stages of Maxdom. He caught a whiff of fried chicken, the only smell stronger than the men around him. Between the river of saliva swelling in his mouth and his gurgling stomach, he worried he might not survive the wait. He didn't know how long it took a person to starve to death, but he suspected he was well on his way.

"God, Timmy, you're oinking like a caveman. Rein it in, or Mom's gonna bench you for dessert." Sam shook his head, but the corners of his mouth twitched.

"Huh-uh," he mumbled around a savory mouthful of cashew chicken. "I like it when it runs down my chin. Tastes better that way...c'mon, try it!"

Sam narrowed his baby blues, a tiny smile pushing at the edges of his mouth. Never tearing his gaze away, Sam shoved a bite of oyster sauce-covered chicken into his mouth, too big to fit right, and sauce oozed down his chin. A king-kong sized grin spread across his face as he took a finger and scooped the dribble into his mouth.

"Right?" Timmy nodded appreciatively. He would've clapped except he saw his mom coming, their dad still standing at one of the sections of the buffet piling his plate too high to get to things on the bottom.

"Good God, Sam, what are you doing? Try to show your brother some manners for once, would you?" Their mother plopped down into the booth across from them and shook her head. Sam bopped Timmy on the arm, but every trip to the Great Wall had similar outcomes. As soon as Dad sat down, she would harp that he could go back, he didn't have to get so much the first time.

"Hey! Earth to Timmy!"

"Huh?" His brain reeled from being yanked from one place to the other. A sour stench filled his nose, reminding him where he was and why he stunk like rotten garbage. The sun beat on his back making him sleepy, returning him to days of swimming pools, Chinese buffets, and neighborhoods where kids played whiffle ball in the street or board games under the street lights.

"Christ, kid, why the hell you wipin' your chin like you eatin' ice cream? Your brain's mushier than I thought." Max patted him too hard on the back and Billy grunted.

Timmy scowled at Billy, hating the sleazy bum and wishing Max would recognize it. Billy scowled right back, took a quick glance over his shoulder to make sure Max wasn't looking, and snarled at the boy.

Dropping his gaze to the sidewalk, a signal of defeat, Timmy clutched hold of Max's flimsy army jacket. *Screw you, Billy!* he wanted to scream, but instead took baby penguin steps forward as the line finally inched along. A horrifying thought occurred to him. "What if they run out of food, Max? What if there's not enough, I mean, look at all these people. What'll they do?"

"Don't get your panties in a bunch, Timmy. There'll be plenty. They plan for lines like this – I been here before. Last year..." Max stopped mid-sentence and stared at the kid. "Just stick close to me, Timmy," he barked. The old man acted as nervous as a cat in a dog pound. It put Timmy on edge just to see him so skittish.

"You were here before? How come?" Timmy felt that swimming confusion muddle his brain.

"Long story...and you ain't got the patience for it now anyhow." Max scraped his feet back and forth across the concrete.

"Tell the kid about Taneisha. And Drey. He'll find out soon enough the way you talk in your sleep." Billy gave the sideways wicked grin that made Timmy itch to hide – or run.

"He don't hear shit over your snorin', Billy, you asswipe," Cooter snapped, laughing and telling Vernon about a time Billy woke Skippy and the mutt went straight for the dude's balls to shut him up.

"How long have you guys lived together?" Timmy tried to picture Max in a house letting all the guys crash in his living room. Did Max have a regular house, like the one he used to live in? Hadn't Max said this arrangement – taking care of Timmy – kept him from going home? "Who's Drey?"

"Mind your damn business, Timmy. You got me? Now shut the hell up, all of ya." Max glared dark enough to scare away the sun. It drifted behind a cloud, as if on cue, and offered some relief from the suffocating heat.

For eternal minutes, Timmy stared past the tables pushed together on the grass at the muddy river churning, and the Arch looming on the other side. He'd been on the east side of the Mississippi to visit a giant ketchup bottle once. His parents lectured the boys on how dangerous it could be over here, in East St. Louis, but it confused Timmy. It didn't look any different than the other side. Except for the sea of tables that seemed to go on for miles, canopies over some, people already surrounding most on rickety chairs. Food-piled plates, people stuffing drumsticks in mouths, taking bites while still standing. The random empty seats filled too fast, panicking him.

"Maybe we should get seats and take turns," Cooter suggested, reading Timmy's mind.

"Yeah, sure, if you're willing to wait." Billy sneered, uglier and meaner than ever. Before they could argue, the line sped up, and they were within touching distance. Lining the backside of the park was a mass of trees and to the right a temporary play area with a jumping house that Timmy wanted to check out. After food. Trash cans had been set up everywhere, flies having their own buffet with the already overflowing garbage. A steady stream of people ebbed in and out of a small building between the trees and the playground equipment.

"What're they doing?" Timmy pointed at them.

"Lots of trots." Billy snorted. "We ain't used to heavy food. Ours is a primarily liquid diet." A few of the guys chuckled, but it was lost on Timmy. His mouth watered at the sight of chicken and barbecue and watermelon and corn on the cob and.... His head swooned. By the time he picked up a plate, he was almost delirious.

The past and present overlapped, layers of confusion wrapped around a hunger so complete, he couldn't resist stuffing half a roll in his mouth. For the past week, his meals had consisted of packaged crackers for breakfast, a random cookie here and there, and one evening he'd eaten an entire can of Pringles for dinner. Most of the Gerries didn't bother to eat much – they focused on drinking. Did they even notice he had so little to eat?

Careful to make room for as much as possible, he filled his plate in silence – he was too hungry to talk, and his stomach had plenty to say without his help. Images of his family shimmered like heat waves in his brain – he was growing familiar with emptiness.

"C'mon, kid. Stick close," Max whispered, as they passed the first seven or eight rows of tables. "Let's get a spot near the back."

Most of the tables were full or had hats and various other pieces of clothing on seats to save them. The entire field buzzed with energy, voices climbing over one another, lulls when new groups sat and concentrated first on their meal. The lip-smacking groans quickened his pace, his hunger now a pain knifing his insides. They found a perfect spot with enough seats for all the Gerries, and Timmy took a bite of his drumstick as he was sitting. He followed it with a chomp into a hot dog with everything on it, then shoveled a spoonful of baked beans in his mouth without taking a breath.

"Hey, Timmy. You're gonna get the trots if you don't pace

yourself. Probably will anyway. Eat slow and pocket the rest." Max patted him on the back, but Timmy couldn't hear the old man. Or had no intention of listening. The delectable flavors of his past, of summer, of picnics not so long ago made it hard to focus.

He gobbled the rest of the drumstick, crunched barbecued potato chips, and licked his fingers between bites. No matter how dirty they had been, greasy fried chicken, drips from the burger, and traces of ketchup made them lickable. He sunk his teeth into a wedge of watermelon and knew he'd died and gone to heaven. If only for a bit.

After a much-needed burp, he stared the piece of chocolate cake with red, white, and blue icing. For the first time, he was aware of the others. He managed another belch to relieve the pressure already building in his stomach.

The place was as packed as his plate had been – men milling from table to table, women hovering over children. All of them as dirty as him, their clothes disheveled like the Gerries. Billy, Max, and Cooter jabbered about the Cardinals finally making the play-offs and who would carry them, when some guy tapped Timmy on the shoulder. He dropped his cleaned-off wedge of melon when a beady-eyed bald man told him to fork over the cake.

"Huh?" Timmy didn't understand what the hateful man wanted because even though he demanded Timmy's dessert, he stared the boy straight in the face. *Couldn't he get his own?*

"I said give me your goddamned cake. I ain't gonna ask again. Me and my boys want some dessert for later, and the assholes in charge won't give us doggie bags. Get the picture?"

"Go away, Baldy," Max snipped, standing to let the guy see that he loomed nearly a head taller.

Timmy guarded his plate like a starving mongrel, circling his arms around it and cramming a bite of the chocolate into his mouth. The hunger was gone, but the *mine* mentality reigned. Regardless of how much it gooed in his throat, making him ache for milk, he savored the chocolate on his tongue. Rolling it around his mouth, he decided it beat a snow day in February. He took a swallow of his water and refused to look back at the bald man.

"It's okay, Timmy. Enjoy your cake. You'll be visiting the porcelain god soon enough." Max mumbled something to Billy and turned his back on the bald man. Cooter remained standing. "Damn jockers are everywhere," Max said, patting Timmy as he sat back down, a signal to the intruder that this match was over.

Jockers?

"Like you ain't one," the bald man mumbled, this time aimed at Max. To Timmy he added, "I bet I got more to offer than that old fart." Cooter took a step toward the short bald man until he backed away, retreating to where a group of younger, not-quite-as-dirty men stood. A few minutes later, his gaze drifted Timmy's way. "That, my boys..." Baldy pointed at him and smirked. "...is a *catch*."

The expression on the guy's face goose pimpled Timmy's arms. "Why'd he do that, Max?" He tried not to stare at the guy, but something told Timmy not to let Baldy out of his sight.

"Oh, Baldy's jealous I got me a kid to hustle grub and goods, Timmy. That's all. And we protect ya, we're your jocker."

"Jocker?" He thought he'd misheard the term before.

"An old hobo label from the Depression. Just means it's our job to protect ya."

Billy made a humphing sound, but Timmy refused to look at the mean bum. He wasn't sure what *hustling grub* meant but thought that might be his future with Max. Was that why Billy didn't like him?

"Matter of fact, Timmy, put this in your pocket. It'd make me feel better." Max pulled the switchblade from his pocket and slid it into Timmy's lap.

Timmy felt a ripple of power as he took it and shoved it into his front right pocket. With a surge of pride, he took another delectable bite of chocolate cake, as moist as any his mom would make for Sam's birthday every fall, ignoring everyone around him.

I got monkey bread for my birthday...Sam had chocolate cake...Dad's was ooey gooey butter cake. The images of sitting around the kitchen table...*at home*...danced and overlapped with the massive array of people swarming around him. The past and present meshing made him dizzy.

A slow roll started in his stomach, beginning its slow objection. Before he could even revel in the sunlight on his face, the peace of a quiet stomach and even quieter brain, a bubble started building low in his gut.

Several Gerries lumbered out of their seats to go back for dessert, while Timmy squeezed his eyes shut hoping the pain would pass. He rubbed his bowling ball of a belly and burped loud enough to make his eyes water.

"Sorry," he said, but felt immediate relief.

"That's a seven and a half, at least," Cooter chimed in with an appreciative smile. Several other guys laughed in agreement.

"Naw, just a five. Give me a minute, I'll belt one out for ya." Ralph, God's older brother according to Cooter, sat up straight and seemed to be conjuring beasts from deep in the well of his insides.

For a few minutes, the gurgling settled, and he listened to the guys compare burps, chat about baseball, and the forgotten glory of an ice-cold Bud at Busch Stadium. None of them had been to a game in eons, they said, but hustling shirts outside got them close to the electricity, Cooter insisted. Max shushed him, always acting like Timmy shouldn't be hearing stuff. With the rumble in his gut, he couldn't focus, but later he'd think about all the comments, the shushes, and what it all meant. Right now, he was trying desperately not to upchuck the best meal he'd had in over a week.

The Gerries each wiped their plates clean with fingers or pieces of dinner roll. By the time they each stood and stretched,

Timmy's stomach gave a final thunderous rejection.

"Whoa, that didn't sound good," Cooter said. "You okay?"

"No," Timmy groaned. He stood at the end of the table holding on, the whole world a little tilted.

"Christ, kid, we don't have time for your crap," Billy snipped. Most of the guys headed toward the bus stop, but Cooter stayed with Timmy.

"I gotta go, I really gotta go." He wobbled, the now monstrous bubble in his stomach telling him it was a matter of *when* not *if*. He saw the long line and told Cooter to make them wait – he couldn't.

He speed-walked to the small building tucked near the trees. The pressure was going to force its way out, one end or the other. With a second to spare, he made it into the john, into a stall, and got his jeans down. Even through the pain of diarrhea, the relief was immediate. When he finished, he stood just as the bathroom door opened.

"I know you're in here, pretty boy," a man's voice chimed.

Timmy froze with his jeans part the way up. *The beady-eyed bald man.* Fear sliced through him like ice water. He tugged his jeans up and zipped them as quietly as he could. He felt the knife's weight and considered pulling it out.

"Open the goddamned door, boy." Baldy pounded on each stall door till he got to Timmy's, the flimsy wood splintering on impact. It was all Timmy could do with ten fumbling thumbs to get his belt fastened. Before he could figure a way to escape or pull the knife out, the man banged the door open and yanked him by the arm, pulling him across the filthy bathroom.

"Let go of me!" Timmy screamed. "MAX! HELP M – " A sweaty palm stifled his screams.

"You didn't wanna give me cake, I'll take a piece of what I really want," Baldy hissed, sending spittle into Timmy's face. The man took his thumb and gently traced the outline of the cut on Timmy's cheek, an odd glimmer in his eyes. "I'm gonna uncover your mouth, and if you know what's good for you,

you'll shut your pie hole. Got me?" Baldy stared hard into Timmy's eyes, his expression frost-bitten.

Timmy nodded.

When the grimy hand came off his mouth, Timmy mumbled, "I'm sorry, mister, I'll getcha some cake..."

"Fuck cake," Baldy muttered, his voice husky and odd. But when the man reached down to unbuckle his own jeans, Timmy's eyes flashed wide.

"No," he groaned, not quite comprehending what the man meant to do but the guesses he had weren't good.

Before Baldy could get his jeans unbuttoned, the bathroom door whacked open, and Timmy dove under the sink when the man let go. Before he could even look up, Max had plowed Baldy in the face.

"You sonuvabitch," Baldy growled, popped Max in the mouth, then touched the stream of blood at the corner of his own. Max dropped to the floor with a groan.

No...no... Pure panic welled in his still-uncertain belly as the man reached for him.

"Time someone taught you a lesson in respect." Baldy grabbed Timmy's feet and dragged him out from under the sink. "You're a little shit, you know that?" In less than a second, Baldy had Timmy by the throat, his feet several inches off the floor.

"OPEN YOUR EYES, YOU LITTLE SHIT!"

Timmy blinked. *Who said that?*

"You damn pervert," Max hissed, and slugged the man in the gut. Timmy's feet hit the floor, but despite blood dripping from Baldy's mouth, the grip around his neck didn't loosen. In a wild flurry, Timmy clawed at the man's arms, tugged at fingers digging into his throat, gasping for air as the hands clamped tighter. Before panic could get a firm hold on him, he was free. Max plowed into the guy, slammed him into the bathroom wall, but Baldy doubled his fists and dropped a massive blow across Max's back. The old Gerrie wobbled and dropped to a knee.

"Now, where were we?" Baldy's evil smile didn't touch his beady dark eyes, stalking toward Timmy with an ominous gait.

A sizzle of terror shot through him, Baldy now between him and the door. *C'mon, Timmy...maneuver...* it was a line Sam used when they played flag football.

"There's no way out, shrimp." Baldy sneered, following Timmy's train of thought.

When the man got close, Timmy went low and made a dash around him for the door. He would've made it if the guy hadn't gotten hold of the ankle of his jeans. With a thud, he hit the filthy floor, and he still tried to get leverage on the slippery floor. But it was too late. A hand grabbed the waistband of his jeans and dragged him across the dirty tile floor. Fingernails scraped his neck, the steely hold making him frantic as he was thrust into the first stall. A surge of hope erupted when he saw Max scramble after them, but Baldy opened the toilet's door in Max's face – *Boom!* It knocked the old Gerrie out cold.

"Let go of me!" Timmy screamed, seeing Max fall like a discarded ribbon. True panic gripped him now. He beat at the arm wrapped around his chest, bucking and thrashing like a trapped rat.

"Humph. I'll show you." The beady-eyed man dropped him onto the toilet seat. Timmy scratched at the hand continually grabbing his throat – a split second later, Baldy slammed him face-first into the side of the stall's wall.

Lights exploded and a cloudburst of pain erupted as Timmy's cut reopened. His head lolled as he tried to grab hold of something, anything to keep him upright.

"Squeal all you want, kid. That makes it more fun." Baldy pressed his now bloody face into the side wall of the stall.

What? He heard a zipper, the intent now crystal clear. "MAX!" he howled, bucking, kicking, flailing blindly at the man's arms, hands, and anything else he could reach.

"Shut up!" Baldy pinned Timmy's head with a forearm as

he tugged his jeans open. "You know the drill, pretty boy."

Timmy, light as a feather to the grown man, jerked as hard as he could, but Baldy had him by the back of the neck with a ruthless left hand now. Free to use his right, Baldy shoved Timmy off the toilet and onto battered knees. When he was eye-level with Baldy's crotch, Timmy clawed desperately at the arm and hand gripping his head. Blood oozed from his clawing, but it didn't sway Baldy's intent.

He was no match. Then he remembered the knife in his pocket.

Gripping him by the hair and angling his head to stare at the sleazy man's face, Baldy growled through gritted teeth. "You listen to me, you little shit. You're mine now. Got it?"

On the fringe of giving up or checking out, he heard Max moan and scramble behind Baldy.

"MAX!" he wailed, sounding two and feeling every bit as small.

"Now, Timmy. Use it now!" Max belted Baldy in the back and connected a crunching blow his knee. The guy fell sideways, Timmy suddenly able to kick himself free. He dropped to all fours, dug in his pocket, and gripped the handle.

The tilting sensation returned, but not out of nausea. Fear and uncertainty swayed his world.

"You little shit," Baldy snarled and clutched at his feet.

But Timmy was ready this time. When he flipped around, he glared into the beady eyes and pressed the handle to the guy's gut.

Baldy understood. He let go of Timmy's jeans, but before he could grab the knife, Timmy punched the button.

A whoosh of air erupted from Baldy's mouth. Hands that had been busy with his jeans suddenly clutched at an oozing mid-section.

Oh, God. What have I done scrambled Timmy's brain. The sickening thrill of success and a chest-crushing guilt pinballed through him. Survival instinct kicked in as he scrambled from under a writhing Baldy, smearing a bloody hand on the leg of Timmy's Levi's. Max crawled toward the boy, using Timmy as leverage to struggle to his feet.

Neither looked back as they hustled from bathroom, heads bowed, hurrying toward the bus. The Gerries had waited, the first bus long gone but another about to close its doors. Cooter stood on the bottom step yelling for them to run. Timmy saw Cooter's mouth fall open, shocked either by the blood on his jeans or his freshly battered face. Both had to be equally shocking.

He and Max climbed the three steps past Cooter and the driver without saying a word. Everyone stared, their eyes drifting from his face to his T-shirt to his jeans. Timmy shoved his bloody hands into his pockets along with the switchblade he'd managed to hold onto. He didn't dare breathe or attempt to speak, though he heard Ralph and Vernon ask Max what the hell happened. Max hissed for them to shut it. He sat trembling against Max's shoulder for what felt like an eternal ride back across the Mississippi, his cheek throbbing, his stomach churning, and a searing certainty settling in his soul.

I'm bad. I'm so bad. I'm a cold-blooded killer. Whatever I did before can't be any worse than what I've done now....

"His boys'll rush him to the hospital, Timmy, and I bet he'll be fine. As long as he ain't lost too much blood," Max added quickly. "A few stitches and that loser'll be on the prowl again."

"Is that what happened? He wanted a cute little blondie for his own badself?" Billy smirked, then mumbled something to Cooter that made Max glare at them.

But he could be dead lingered in the back of Timmy's mind.

"Kid, you didn't kill him. I'm pretty sure of that," Max placated. But the possibility hovered in Timmy's mind along with the likelihood that he'd done something horrible that night before the storm drain.

That night festered in Timmy like a pus-filled wound – the

certainty that he'd done something horrible, something *illegal.* He didn't know, but it had been awful enough that it couldn't be brought into focus. Someone had erased it from his brain like a permanent delete key.

The dried blood on my brand-new pullover belonged to someone from that night, didn't it?

Timmy tried to grasp the memory that eluded him like a wispy cloud but whiffed. It haunted every minute of sleep he managed to steal and most in between. When they got off the bus, all of them scuffled toward the apartment building, each hitting a first-floor apartment bathroom. He wondered if not eating at all would hurt less, as another gut-wrenching cramp rendered him to shivers.

By the time he climbed the rickety steps to the third floor, it was all he could do to make it to the flimsy mattress in his room. The Gerries were lighting a fire in the tiny grill and starting their drinking rituals, their stomachs obviously more accustomed to the abuse.

Their voices followed him to sleep but couldn't drown out the demons waiting there.

Chapter Eight

"I knowed whatcha took, and I mean to get it back," Muscle Man insisted, the whites of his eyes too big to be real. Instead of his bike this time, the goon had hold of Timmy's baseball cards, tossing them to the ground one at a time.

"Those're mine," Timmy whined, not sure why he always sounded two around the hulking thug.

"Free exchange...or I'll send that Bald Man after you again." Muscle Man sniggered, then threw the last of the cards to the concrete.

Timmy didn't know where he was – some neighborhood street with unfamiliar houses, unfamiliar cars, unfamiliar happy lives. All he knew was that this giant bully standing ten feet tall on the sidewalk wasn't going to let him pass. And for some reason, Timmy couldn't run any other direction.

Why?

'Because I couldn't that night...'

A breeze lifted his sun-bleached blond hair, rustling the cards and threatening to send them scattering into some other kid's house, hands, life. He took a step forward just as a voice pulled him back.

"DREY!" a man yelled. The voice clawed for purchase on his brain as Timmy turned and fled.

***

He bolted upright on the mattress to hear the scream repeated.

"DREY! GET BACK HERE!"

For a brief, blissful second, he thought he was in his bedroom – *at home* – but the shadows didn't match. No desk, no chest of drawers, no TV or stereo in the corner. None of his clothes tossed about like castaways on a deserted island.

"Shut-up," a Gerrie griped from down the hall, and

suddenly all was wrong with the world. It was the middle of the night in the dismal run-down apartment that reeked of urine, feces, and smoke – all that swallowed the stench lingering in the kitchen.

He fumbled to his feet and slipped into his stiffer-than-usual jeans. When he ran his hands over his thighs and felt the crusty blood, the afternoon washed over him like a Tsunami. He fell back onto the mattress and shimmied out of the jeans as fast as he could. Sitting and trembling, he knew what he had to do.

After several deep breaths for courage, he tiptoed toward the living room, feeling vulnerable in just his underwear. The glow had dimmed, offering barely enough light to make out the men's faces. But a snore and another mumbled, "Drey, watch out!" revealed Max in the far corner on a bean bag, his jeans and Salvation Army jacket, with the Post-it note, lay in a pile beside him. But so did Billy. Skippy was nowhere in sight, or he would've long since growled and sent Timmy's heart hammering. Just thinking about the terrier mutt spiked his adrenaline. Max said the dog liked to go prowling for babes during the night, and thank God for that, Timmy thought, as he weaved his way around the snoring drunks.

When he got close to Billy, the old bum stirred, sending panic slicing through Timmy. If Billy caught him going through Max's things, surely the bum would let him have it for real. Throwing him out would be just for starters. But as he dropped to a squat next to the jeans and jacket, he waited, and all snores continued their strange synchronized symphony. He pressed his hand to the clothes and felt for the crumple of paper. With careful movements, he unfolded the jacket and slithered a hand into each pocket until his fingers found it, wrapped around it, and pulled it free. Without hesitating, he took the Post-it and slinked off to his room. He pulled on a pair of shorts Max had gotten him at Salvation Army, grabbed his pullover just in case, then set off back down the hallway and out the door. Not wanting to be too far from his prized cards, he tied the pullover around his waist and hurried down the stairs out onto the sidewalk. He had plenty of time, since the Gerries always slept till late morning, even into early afternoon some days. Staring at the Hemphill Avenue street sign, he took a deep breath and prepared to retrace the path he'd memorized over the last week.

This is it... He took one last look at the Post-it, the unfamiliar number, and hustled in the direction of the shelter where he knew there was a payphone on the corner. He feared he might get in trouble, he might get his parents in trouble, or they might hang up on him. He didn't know what to expect. He just wanted to hear someone's voice, someone to tell him it would be all right and they would be after him in a jiffy. His mom said that all the time, and if she could just hear his voice, he knew she would come save him.

He'd saved a quarter just for this call, and even with his cheek and head pounding, he broke into a jog. When he rounded the last corner and saw the payphone, he sprinted to it.

He was certain his parents had probably been trying to call for days. It had been a week and two days, hadn't it? Without the roses in front of him to count, he couldn't be sure. *Too long...I waited too long. I should've done this sooner.*

He plunged the quarter into the slot with trembling fingers, punched in the numbers on the Post-it, and waited. He was convinced his family had to be terrified, not knowing where he was. They had probably been hunting for him all week, had maybe even called the police to find him.

Even if I've done something wrong, they've gotta be looking for me. Maybe not with a cop's help, but surely they've been hunting for me.

"Good morning," an automated voice said. "Today is Tuesday, September seventh. The time is 2:42. Current temperature 71 degrees."

Timmy pulled the phone away from his ear and stared at

the receiver. A familiar tug, of his brother and him calling time and temperature, a near obsession when praying for a snow day. On the heels of the memory came pure confusion.

Time and temperature. Then he wondered if he needed to dial a different area code. He assumed 314, since there weren't any other numbers before the seven scribbled on the yellow Post-it. He had one more quarter and pulled it from his pocket, another thought occurring to him. Without hesitation, he tapped the number he'd memorized when he was five years old. No thinking, no second-guessing, no reconsidering.

Punch- punch- punch... punch- punch- punch- punch. He panicked for an instant when no clicks signaled a connection, but then it began to ring. After only two times, it picked up. Timmy's heart catapulted into his throat, but before he could speak, an automated voice monotoned, "I'm sorry, the mailbox for 555-4320 is full."

Again, he stared at the receiver, unfamiliar with the response. *Full? Why would our answering machine be full?* He slammed the phone into its cradle, more frustrated than angry. Too numb to hang it up, he let the handset fall and clank against the frame, dangling from a metal encased cord. He backed away, tears threatening to break the dam, but he couldn't look away from the phone.

They left me...they've gone somewhere, they're hiding, they're running... without me... from me... But why?

Without thinking, Timmy ran. In no particular direction or without a destination in mind, he sprinted down the streets of downtown St. Louis, around corners, toward the riverfront and not caring if he launched himself into the muddy Mississippi. Anything would be better than the confusion scrambling his brain. He ran toward the Arch, a favorite spot when his family would go to Rams or Cardinal games. Even in the middle of the night and no moon, the landmark was visible in the night sky.

"Let's go to the top before the game, Dad, pleeeeeeeeease?"

They often did, and now all he wanted to do was wallow

there, near a place he'd been with his family, a place he worried he'd never go again with his family.

A sick dread settled into his gut that he might not have one anymore.

Chapter Nine

Timmy didn't know why the fury spurred his feet into a sprint or why running always felt so good, but he didn't stop until a stitch threatened to yank his lungs through his ribs. He collapsed on a corner and sucked air in throat-searing gulps, trying to relieve the cramp and hoping a miracle would help him suddenly realize where he was. How long had he run? When had the Arch disappeared behind mammoth hotels and why couldn't he see it? He just wanted to find the giant structure and hug it, lean against it, feel the cushiony grass under his bare feet, between his toes.

He'd sprinted from the run-down district to the upscale world of Tucker's Fine Clothing, Harrison's Jewelers, and a Juice Box. A giant Anheuser-Busch sign loomed over the top of a hotel. The huge buildings, some with mirrored sides, others multi-colored brick, didn't look anything like those he'd seen near the abandoned apartment building. It was still dark out, not as close to daybreak as he'd hoped. Fancy molding, signs in white lights, pretty awnings. Timmy didn't see any condemned signs or broken windows.

I've been here before. A shoe store brought a twinge of familiarity. And another, a sports shoe store, on the corner.

Mom bought me Nikes there before basketball camp last summer.

Timmy's head swam. Turmoil chewed his insides and rolled through him like heavy fog. He couldn't stay out in the open – bloody T-shirt, dark smears on the Nike pullover wrapped around his waist, more cuts on his face than freckles. Absent-mindedly, he double-checked the zippered pouch of his pullover and fingered the square outline of the baseball cards. The new habit somehow comforted him, as he leaned against a building and studied each way trying to figure out what to do or where to go.

I put them in there to show Sam...when we left home. When was that? Timmy slid down the side of the building and laid his head back against the bumpy brick, the stitch in his side letting go in tiny increments. He closed his eyes and remembered something, a vapor hovering just past his fingertips.

Momma teasing Sam about his new haircut.

Hair removal, I called it.

***

July – A Year Earlier

"Oh, shut up, Timmy. It's called a buzz. Your hair's stupid anyway. Ain't even got any color. Rather have no hair than be a towhead."

My eyes bore into Sam, laser beams only a ten-year-old could muster against a God-like older brother. Sam took the bait and smacked the back of my head hard enough to make Mom snap at him to stop it. I worried maybe my brains had rattled loose.

"Kiss my ass, Sam!" I blurted, knowing Momma would punish me for the cuss word. I didn't care. I had to pack a wallop. The soap she made me eat didn't even taste that bad, so the dig had been worth it. He'd always have a four-and-a-half year edge, plus the size and muscle, so I had to fight back any way I could. My current role as Sam's tackling dummy had me bruised in more places than not, and the end wasn't even glimmering on the horizon. It was day three of football two-a-days, another week and a half to go. At that rate, bones would begin breaking, and I suspected I might run out of those. He timed the attacks with the savvy of a special ops expert – Mom never saw, Dad never suspected. And if I told, the repercussions would be brutal.

On some subconscious level, I didn't mind. Sam had a

legitimate run as starting quarterback on the varsity roster. Only a handful of freshmen would make it, but odds, a good throwing arm, and blinding speed put Sam at the top of the list.

Before I could contemplate my counterattack, Sam caught me coming around the corner from the kitchen and launched me like a pillow onto the couch. He pinned me in milliseconds then cast me aside.

"Make like a crack and split, shrimp." He plopped onto the sofa, nabbed the remote, and tried to dismiss me by cranking the volume. But I couldn't go down without a fight – in mere seconds I was on him like spots on a Dalmatian. We wrestled until Mom nearly busted a gut yelling at us to stop it, cut it out, and couldn't we all just get along?

Sam and I laughed until I snorted, and then he started howling even louder. I couldn't stop laugh-snorting and didn't care if I served as his target. Sam ranked higher than Nintendo, the Cardinals, and Rusty Wallace combined.

Of course, I would never tell him – I pretended to despise him. Those were our roles, and we gave our best performances most of the time. It proved pretty lame on my part to think I could keep up, but Sam always managed to make me feel tough enough to keep trying.

***

A blaring horn yanked Timmy back to the St. Louis street. Occasional cars sped through intersections, a faraway voice hollered in the distance then faded. It was still well before sunrise, but he wasn't really sure what time it was. Time had taken on new meaning in the past week.

Life had taken on new meaning in the past week, so what did he care about time? Before pondering the finer points of that concept, he hobbled into an alley and huddled next to a sandwich shop's trash bin. The memory zapped Timmy, sucked the air out of his recuperating lungs and made him dry heave.

Sam. *Before.* His life prior to the storm drain had been swept away like a feather in a hurricane. Life before That Night.

Defeated and too scared he'd be seen, Timmy decided to curl up and try to escape the world he no longer understood. He closed his eyes and didn't care what he remembered or who visited him in his sleep.

In a few hours, he would figure out where to go and not worry about the boogeyman. But for now, it was all he could think about.

Chapter Ten

Timmy heard Muscle Man cackle.

"Open your eyes, you little shit. Remember me?" But the man resembled several people – Billy, Ralph, Baldy, and – and –

"BRENT, SCOTT, RUN!" His voice echoed of the houses on Catalina Avenue like a ping-pong ball.

A noise behind him made him cringe.

"Why do I keep reliving this nightmare?" he moaned.

He turned slowly – he knew what he would see. On the sidewalk, a monstrous man sat atop his Huffy. Muscle Man's eyes narrowed into a sinister smile.

"Give it back."

"I don't know what you're talkin' about, Mister." And it was true, wasn't it?

"You took it, so I take somethin' of yours. But I don't want no lame ass bike."

"So?" Timmy was annoyed at this thug constantly taunting him but never explaining himself.

The massive arms rippled, the dagger-in-heart tattoo stretching with each flex. He stepped off the bike, letting it topple sideways.

"I'll trade ya." Hands as big as dinner plates reached for Timmy.

Not again. "Leave me alone." A flash of a bald-headed man grabbing him by the waist of his jeans overlapped between this nightmare-world and another.

The giant man flexed, and it was then Timmy noticed the pistol – a black revolver with smoke swirling from the barrel. The thug waved it at the boy, like he really wanted Timmy to see it before – before what?

The certainty of death washed over him again as he backed away. When he got the nerve to look behind him for a getaway route, Timmy froze.

A mangled Cadillac Escalade lay in the front yard. He turned and stared at it – the acrid smell of gunfire burning his nose. The chuckle less than five feet behind him didn't scare him nearly as much as what the SUV on his lawn meant.

"I'm earnin' my tag now, you little shit."

When Timmy turned toward Muscle Man, the hands closed the distance while he screamed.

***

"NOOOO!" Timmy slapped air as he sat up. He tried to scramble farther backward, confused by the darkness, but smacked his already thudding head against a brick wall.

He squinted, trying to get his night sight – the dumpster and buildings blocking any light the street lamps had to offer. It took a few seconds to orient himself, to resurrect what had happened – the Post-it note, the full mailbox message, running. Somewhere not too far away, he thought he heard a dog growl.

Are the Gerries worried about me? Maybe Max and Cooter, but Billy and Skippy are probably glad.

He looked around for Skippy, suddenly feeling canine eyes on him. He'd heard soft feet behind him at various times during his escape, hadn't he? But as much as he stared down the alley, out in the open street, around the area in general, there was no terrier mutt waiting to rip his hand off.

Timmy braced himself to stand. Legs as heavy as bricks quivered, joints popped that had stiffened and didn't like the sudden movement. He groped the wall, used the trash bin to steady himself, then wobbled out to the empty street. Open air brushed across his face, chilly but refreshing, as he gazed up at the pre-dawn blue sky. The Gerries had said it had been an unseasonably cool August and Labor Day. *That's why I was wearing the Nike pullover....* Though he had been known to wear it when it was too warm for it anyway, hadn't he?

He tugged on the pullover, wondering if it was always this cool this time of the morning. Not one to spend many nights exposed to it, he shoved his hands into the pullover's pockets now damp with dew. A shiver rolled down his spine, and he shuddered uncontrollably for a few seconds. A car revved a block away, growling like a hungry tiger. Timmy ducked into the shadows of the building just as the clunker raced by. He watched it burn rubber around a corner and suddenly felt vulnerable.

He knew he had a place to go, even if it was a rough one. The Gerries would still be snoring in the living room – would he be able to find his way back if he wanted to? But Catalina Avenue was pulling him like a paperclip to a magnet. He didn't have a clue how to get there, but wouldn't a bus driver? He saw a bus stop sign at the end of the street and headed toward it. Careful to stay out of sight, he hustled to read it.

Monday through Friday, First Stop, 6:00 a.m. Last Stop 10:00 p.m.

He didn't think it was near 6:00 yet, though he couldn't be sure. *I should've slept longer.* With a sense of purpose he hadn't felt in days, Timmy set off toward the well-lit streets a few blocks away to find out what time it was. Surely he would find something in a window, a sign, or even an all-night restaurant.

Before he had a chance to reach the first intersection, the clunker he'd seen earlier squealed to a halt next to him.

"Hey, squirt, whatcha doin' out this time of night?"

"Or mornin," a voice blurted, then burst into laughter.

"It's waaaaaay past your bedtime." Cackling laughter followed, and Timmy side-glanced them. The four guys didn't seem much older than Sam, though the car could've been his grandpa's... *Max's*? Thinking of the bum as his grandfather still felt weird.

"Shit, homie, who did that number on your face? You look like someone gave you a smack-down." Another voice mimicked a wrestling announcer, chanting something about the fighter in the left corner.

The chipping paint, rusted handle, and rumbling muffler didn't mean much to Timmy, but the stocking caps and jewelry poking out of eyebrows, noses, and ears did. Kids dressed like that, like Eminem, used to ride his bus. Sam steered clear of them – *hoods,* he called them. Gang-banger wannabes and whiggers, white guys who wanted to be black.

He lowered his head and walked faster, heading toward the lights. He knew better than to run, but his feet itched to do it anyway. That was fast becoming his M.O. Sam taught him about M.O.s but until That Night, his had been a Dr Pepper with his two other Musketeers, Brent and Scott.

"Ah, c'mon, kid. Don't be a spoilsport. We ain't gonna hurtcha," the same guy whined as the car grumbled down the street beside him. Timmy angled a little more toward the buildings putting as much distance between him and the road as he could.

"Hey, Cameron, slow down, man. This little guy might be just the accomplice we need, know what I mean?"

Accomplice? Timmy knew the word from cop shows but couldn't imagine what they needed one for. Too many things in his brain had disconnected like faulty wires.

The clunker lurched to a stop. The squeal of an opening door startled him. Before he could think, he bolted, beating feet to the intersection, and sprinted to the next and then the next. The car rumbled noisily beside him, with the boys shouting, cheering him on, and then they started calling out offers.

"Yo, kid, there's good money in it for you!"

"Whatcha runnin' from? You don't even know what we want! We can make you rich!"

"We're not gonna mess with you, kid, we just need your help!"

As Timmy approached the next cross street, the car wheeled sharply around the corner and slammed on its brakes, cutting him off. Before he could get around it or turn to head the other way, the doors flew open. Hands were all over him, pinning his arms to his sides, until one of the bigger guys picked him up from behind and bear hugged his small body.

"Yo, squirt, stop kickin'. Just chill for a second!"

But Timmy couldn't chill. A terror had seized hold of him and being held captive didn't do anything to dispel the déjà vu ripping through him. Baldy grabbing his ankles, Muscle Man clutching his throat, a burning memory in his brain that threatened to shut it off for good. It didn't help that they kept bumping the cuts on his face.

"Get offa me!" he yelled. "I mean it, I'll call the cops. HELP!" He squealed with all his might, his throat almost instantly raw. A flash of moments just before the storm drain, of his own earsplitting screams that only died when his voice did. That Night and now last night. The symmetry and the constant chaos had him reeling.

A hand slammed over his mouth. "Jesus, kid, we didn't hafta do this the hard way." A stocking capped boy with two hoops in his left eyebrow, a huge sparkling diamond in his nose, and a tattoo laced across his entire neck held Timmy's whole head and face.

Oh, God, no more tattoos.

Another hand grabbed each of his ankles, and before he knew what was happening, he was laid out flat mid-air being pulled from all directions. He flailed wildly, adrenaline-pumping strength enough to kick one of the shorter guys in the stomach.

"Hold his legs, God, Cam, *hold on!*"

With a *whoomph*, the guy went down and let go of his left foot. Timmy swung his free leg violently at the person grabbing him.

"Shit! Get him!" Cameron ducked the blow. But the instant of shock and resistance allowed Timmy to nearly break free.

"Kid, you're pissin' me off!" the biggest one shouted and

yanked out a switchblade. With a *flick,* the blade came to life, and Timmy's stomach flipped inside out.

Where's mine? Had he grabbed it? Left it under his mattress? *Stupid.* His panic doubled when the hand around his wrist clamped tighter and the knife came to his throat.

"Don't fuck with me," a low voice hissed in his ear. The guy he had kicked in the stomach grabbed him and put a chokehold on him. A strong forearm pressed into his neck and for an instant Timmy could barely breathe.

"I can't br – " His words became a gurgle when the arm tightened.

"Don't hurt him, Cameron," one of the guys warned. "We need him."

"Shut up, Theo," Cameron snapped, but eased the hold around Timmy's throat. "You little punk, you're gonna do exactly what I fuckin' tell ya, you hear me? There's a window you're gonna shimmy through, and then you're gonna open the goddamn door and let us in. And then, if you're lucky, we'll let you live. You got it?" His eyes, cold and mean, sizzled into Timmy. The hateful expression, too Billy-like with a sprinkle of Baldy, stifled Timmy's fight.

His head bulged with the pressure, throbbing as he struggled for air. A strange heat filled his ears, a loud buzz accompanied the pain, and everything started to fade.

"Get him in back," Cameron ordered, releasing the death grip but then other hands gripped him just as firmly. Timmy coughed and then gagged as he was tossed into the backseat of the clunker. Bile rose in his throat and he retched hard enough to make all of them let go.

"Shit, kid, don't you puke on me!"

Oh, sure, no problem, Timmy wanted to say, sitting up, and dry heaving into the floorboard. He clutched his angry stomach and rubbed his neck to make sure his windpipe hadn't been crushed. It was still sore from his altercation with Baldy.

...and Muscle Man....

Tenderly touching his throat, he could imagine the bruise he would have later.

If I have a later.

"Okay, that's enough. C'mon, let's go. We gotta job and you're gonna help us." Cameron and the rest of them piled in the car, a smelly but quiet guy smashed into his right side in the back seat, Theo the other half of the sandwich on his left. The biggest guy got in the shotgun seat and the doors barely closed before Cameron revved the engine and took off fast enough to throw them all back in their seats.

"Theo, you'll hoist the kid to that one window, then me, Derek, and Greg'll go around back. It's dark back there. We'll be able to get in without a glitch now." Cameron stared into the rearview at the guys on either side of Timmy. The boy was older than Sam, but not a lot. A strange flatness in his eyes stirred Timmy's stomach, too much like Muscle Man and Baldy, the two an odd mash-up in his brain.

"Derek's bigger, he should toss the little man in. But I don't care. Whatever we do, we gotta bust ass once we get in. Not like last time, don't go huntin' for shit. Just get the big stuff in boxes. Their stash will be a helluva haul. And remember there's a laptop in the back bedroom we've gotta have. There's also that money jar and some serious jewelry in the front bedroom."

The car whipped around corners, sending Timmy into the quiet one who had to be Greg. The guy had on too much cologne, and Theo had as many freckles as he did piercings. Cameron was the leader – he kept giving orders as he drove. Derek didn't say much either, but his size spoke for itself.

Timmy couldn't speak. Captive in a car with four thugs wondering where they were taking him, whose house they were about to rob, or what bridge they would throw him off of when they finished. The big one that crossed the Missouri River on the highway they took to Wentzville sometimes? Or the one heading over into East St. Louis? Both would do the trick.

His world was disintegrating into a strange state of

weirdness. He had no word for the detached, dreamy fog he was in, but it reminded him of an episode of *Star Trek* when Captain Kirk got poisoned from mushrooms – or maybe it had been a gas of some kind. No memories were safe anymore.

"Hey, crank it! I love this song!" Greg shouted, nearly elbowing Timmy in the head. A sudden boom-boom-boom rattled the windows as some rapper started chanting words Timmy couldn't understand. The four guys could – they sang every line.

He had to be in the middle of a stupid *Beavis and Butthead* nightmare, and any minute he would jerk awake, Sam ribbing him about sleeping away his life.

God, please...please wake up.

Nothing else could explain everything happening to him. From the storm drain to a grandfather he didn't know he had, now abducted by a gang of hoods about to break into someone's house. *And I've gotta help....* This stuff only happened in books and movies, didn't it? Or episodes of *Law & Order*, Sam's favorite show.

He laid his head back against the cracked leather seat, closed his eyes, and tried to will it all away.

Three or four minutes later, the car barreled into a driveway and jerked to a stop. Timmy couldn't believe the change in scenery. Small houses with bars over the windows, beat-up, wheel-less cars sitting haphazardly in two of the yards, kids' shoddy toys scattered everywhere. Weeds towered over the toys, waist high in some parts of the targeted house. They had parked right in front, as big as you please. A street lamp stood at the corner, less than fifteen feet away. They were going to break into this house with all this light? And park in the driveway?

Either these guys are dumb, or they know who lives here. They all climbed out of the clunker, whispering about their plan. Timmy stared at the warped siding, overflowing trash in plastic cans by the garage, and a pile of rolled newspapers in front of the garage door. Two more leaned against the battered front door.

"You're comin' with me, short stuff. I'm gonna lift you to a window around the side, then you're gonna go unlock the back door. You got it?" Theo motioned for Timmy to get out.

"You parked in the driveway already, why not the front door?" Timmy blurted and then immediately wished he'd kept his mouth shut.

"Are you a wise ass or what? Cuz the front needs a key for one of the locks, that's why." Theo grunted, motioning to Cameron. "Kid's got a 'tude."

"I'll take care of the squirt. You go around back with the others." To Timmy, Cameron barked, "Just follow directions, got it?" He grabbed Timmy by the arm and set off around the corner of the house.

I don't wanna do this... His heart pounded in his ears, too loud, pulsating in every cut on his face. As gained his night sight, he watched Cameron stack two wooden crates against the house. When they seemed sturdy enough, the guy hopped onto them.

"C'mere," he snapped. The older boy squatted and motioned for Timmy to climb up next to him. With both feet planted, Cameron grabbed Timmy and hoisted him up. "You're gonna twist that handle. You see it?"

Screw you! But he knew better than to piss off a guy like this, especially as Cameron held him and could launch him twenty feet. So he looked up. Less than a foot over his head was a small window. He grabbed a handle that had been painted to match the house and had rusted since. He gripped it, braced his weight on Cameron's shoulders, and turned. Nothing budged.

"Pull harder!" Cameron ordered. "Jesus, we find a kid small enough, and you gotta be a freakin' wimp."

The insult ticked Timmy off, so to prove the jerk wrong, he used every ounce of strength he had and tugged. Just when he thought it wouldn't, it gave way, and for a scary second, he teetered. Cameron gripped his calves, and the two nearly toppled over.

"Nice! Okay, kid, pull the window out and then up. See?"

Timmy followed Cameron's hand motions without saying a word. The window was no more than a foot tall and maybe just a tad wider with a hinge on top. Once he got it open, he would have to pull himself up to crawl in. What if he couldn't do it? Would they make fun of him, kill him, cut his legs off at the knees like on that new show he watched on A&E when his parents weren't home? None of the guys had guns that he'd seen, but there were other ways, weren't there? Cameron could definitely follow in Tony Soprano's footsteps.

"Okay, up you go," Cameron said, wedged hands under Timmy's sneakers, and thrust him up. Timmy was vaulted through the window and shimmied the rest of the way through the small space landing head first on the cold, bare floor. *And I worried about getting in?*

Then it occurred to him someone might be home. Had the guys checked? It sent his heart into overdrive, like so many things had in the past week. His nerves jangled. With trembling hands, he grabbed for anything to help pull himself up. It was too dark to see. He found a bedpost, groping about like he was playing a strange game of pin-the-tail-on-the-donkey. Feeling his way about the room, he waited for his eyes to adjust until he could see the outline of a doorway. He tiptoed toward it.

I'm in someone else's house getting ready to help four guys rip these people off. The idea sent a chill through him. *Just add it to my list of crimes....*

When he got to the hall, he saw three open doors. The eerie darkness wasn't total like it had been in the bedroom. A clock in one of them blinked *5:38*. Only twenty minutes until the buses would run.

A floorboard creaked under his weight. He froze, anticipating the shout – *Get the hell outta my house!* But he knew better. Even from upstairs, the house felt empty. He crept down the hall, walked silently down the stairs, and understood immediately why they were there. VCRs, CD players, TVs, and stereos lined the living room in stacked boxes, three and four deep. One giant Gateway box appeared to be unopened, with ten or twelve Sony packages that read *The best in palm pilots* on top of them. A smaller pile with Apple on the packaging made Timmy let out a whistle. He stared at brand new iMacs, something Sam had wanted desperately but would never get, according to their mom. *When you have a job, Sam, you can buy your own computer. Until then, you get to use the family one.*

"Hurry up, kid!" a voice shouted from the back door.

I could just plant my butt on the couch and sleep, watch a little TV, see what's in the fridge.... The thought of food made him consider taking a detour.

"Goddammit, kid, you better open this door!" Theo hissed.

Or what? You kidnap me and then expect me to be your gopher? Sam had called Timmy his gopher for years. But the guys would get angrier, and he couldn't stay in some stranger's house forever. He hustled through a tidy kitchen with dishes drying in the sink and a teddy bear dishtowel draped over the handle of the oven.

Several bad drawings of dogs, a tree half-covering a sun accented by a rainbow decorated an older model refrigerator. When he reached the back door, he had to unlock two deadbolts and unlatch a chain. The family obviously thought it was enough. They should've done the same to the windows. When he pulled the door open, the boys nearly ran him over. He saw the opportunity to flee, but before he could do it, Theo grabbed him by the back of the neck and squeezed.

"What took you so long?"

"Uh, it was dark. I couldn't see."

Theo thought about it, even glanced across the room for a second. "All right, but you gotta get outta the way now, okay? By the way, what's yer name?"

"Timmy," he said, before he could think to lie.

"Well, Timmy, you done good," Theo said with a laugh. "Let's see what we can do for you. Don't suppose you need a CD player. With a face like that, I'm thinkin' your folks prob'ly don't give ya much."

"I have an idea. C'mere a minute." Cameron opened a door off the main room, opposite the stairs, and emerged with a Folgers's coffee can. He plucked the lid off and pulled out a wad of bills.

"Hey, don't be givin' him our cut," Theo griped, as he stacked a smaller TV on top of a bigger one.

"Here you go, kid. Your first score, I betcha. Keep you outta them porn shops. Stay away from that shit, those people ain't got no class." Cameron handed Timmy a crisp one-hundred-dollar bill.

Theo and Greg busted out laughing. They immediately started lugging boxes out the door, completely ignoring Timmy. He followed them out into the backyard and stood watching them take trip after trip to the car. The kitchen telephone beckoned him, but he couldn't bear to hear that strange *mailbox full* message again. Instead, he yanked open the refrigerator, thrilled to see cans of soda. No Dr Pepper, but he cracked open a Sprite and took a big enough gulp to burn going down. A bag of apples beckoned, so he grabbed one of those, too.

"By the way, Timmy, you tell anybody about this, even breathe a word, we'll hunt your scrawny ass down and shut you up for good. Got it?" Cameron didn't blink or smile.

"Got it," he whispered, suppressing a burp.

"Well, don't just stand there. Either grab a load or scram." Theo winked at him and hoisted the stack in the corner of the house. Greg walked by him and shrugged his shoulders as if to say *Why not?*

Because I'm not a thief, he wanted to say, but it hadn't made him refuse the hundred dollars. That was already stuffed in his pocket. After sifting through cabinets, pocketing some granola bars, peanuts, and a few packages of crackers, he followed them around to the car and waited awkwardly to say he was going to take off. It felt strange to be ignored by four boys who had kidnapped him.

"Okay, kid," Cameron finally said. "Your part is done. If you ain't gonna help, you can go. But remember what I said. I don't wanna hafta hurtcha."

"Yeah, thanks, kid. No way we could've done it withoutcha." Theo smacked him on the back. "You're the best break-in boy we had in a while. That makes you an accomplice, Squirt, and you're a natural."

Accomplice... Timmy added it to his growing list of crimes.

"Um, how do I get to a bus stop?" he asked, knowing if he didn't, he might end up in Iowa. He didn't exactly have a map with a big star marked *You are here,* like when he went to Six Flags...*with my family.* The memory took the air out of him, made his knees watery.

"Kid, you okay?" Cameron stared at him.

He didn't have the air to mutter, "Yeah." But he managed a nod.

"Man, let's get crackin'. There's a bus stop just down the road." Theo pointed off somewhere behind him.

"But..." Timmy stopped, a little panicked by the area and unsure what to do. "Okay. I just...I don't know where to go or what to do." Honesty tumbled from his mouth. He considered begging but stopped short.

"Tell ya what, you're our partner in crime...can't leave a man behind. As soon as we finish, you can sit in the front, but you'll have to straddle the gearshift. We'll drop you off where we found ya. How's that?"

Timmy thought about it for a minute. He hadn't known where he was then either, but he would have the bus stop. On a whim, he asked, "You know where Catalina Avenue is, in Town and Country?"

"That around Ballwin?" Cameron looked to Theo and Greg.

Both guys shrugged. "Derek, you're a richie...you live near Clayton. That's close, right?"

The guy's head emerged from the other side of the trunk. "Screw you, Cam, I'm not a richie. You ain't exactly thug-central...we play it but we don't live it. But yeah, it ain't too far. We could drop him on Manchester, past that car dealership."

"All right, kid. We can do that. Better'n where we gotcha. I think we can get you near there. Greg lives that direction, too." Cameron shooed Theo and Greg back toward the house to finish up.

"Thanks." Timmy felt awkward waiting for the guys to finish robbing the house, but the prospect of going home offered a strange relief. Maybe voicemail was just full because they didn't want any bad people to call, maybe his parents and Sam were laying low, hiding out in the basement, waiting for the worst to pass. Or maybe he would get there and there would be a note for him. Hadn't Max said something they were hiding out but checking in? The prospect of a note just made him want to go home that much more.

By the time Cameron hustled everyone back into the car, Timmy barely fit. The trunk wouldn't close, but a bungee cord secured it. With Cameron driving, Greg and Theo squeezed into the front seat and had Timmy sit on their laps. Derek squeezed in back with enough technology to open a store. Timmy tried to sit as still as possible, afraid if a bump made him plop up and down on the guys, they might chuck him out the window.

Partners in crime, they'd said, adding, *You'd be a good criminal, kid.*

He squirmed, sure they'd be shocked if he listed the ones he'd committed in the past twenty-four hours. Or last week.

"You did remember to wipe all your fingerprints off, didn't you, Tim?"

Oh, God. For the first time, he noticed they all had on gloves.

"Oh, well." Cameron peeled out and barreled down the

residential street. "It's not like you're a repeat offender. You're not in the system, are ya?"

The boys laughed. They began chattering, cranking the radio to another head-banging song he couldn't understand. They shouted about the beer they would drink the next night, the real celebration. Timmy's mind raced with the realization of what he had done, the newest item on a growing list.

Repeat offender? What would Jack McCoy charge him with for his newest crime? He had no idea, but then again, he knew better than that. Because deep inside he knew he'd done something horrible That Night. And then he'd killed Baldy, he was sure of it. So tonight was peanuts in comparison.

He'd be the storyline on NBC before he knew it.

Chapter Eleven

Please let the Gerries still be asleep...please please please please....

Sitting at the last bus stop waiting, he ran through every scenario possible. He doubted they were even up, but he kept imagining them opening his door and seeing that he had bailed on them. Skippy and Billy would throw a party, and the others would probably be relieved. With his luck, the cops had probably stormed the place to arrest his ass for killing Baldy, and the whole lot of them had scrammed.

Timmy couldn't bear the thought of having no one. The Gerries might not be much, but having somebody to watch out for him felt strangely necessary. Even if they were pissed at him for ditching them, at least they gave him a place to squat, as they called it. It was a home, maybe a crappy one, but he couldn't complain anymore, could he? Not now that a Granville Auction sign screamed *YOU DON'T HAVE ONE!* If Max really was his grandpa, the old man was family.

The only family who gives a shit, sizzled in his brain. He didn't know where his parents were, why they hadn't bothered to find him, but two weeks was its own sign. And not a good one.

Before pity could swallow him, he welcomed the guilt at almost ditching the Gerries and jumped to his feet when he heard the bus rumble a street away. He would show Max, and even Billy, that he could watch out for himself. He'd already marched right in to a McDonalds this morning for a value meal, too tired and hungry to care about the customers who stared at him. He didn't bother to go to the bathroom to clean up. What did it matter? The goal was to fill his stomach and break his hundred-dollar bill. He doubted a bus driver would take it, so why not splurge?

With a full stomach and money in his pocket, he had

climbed the steps for his first city bus ride. He marveled how easy it was to traverse the city, even though he hadn't been sure how to get back to Hemphill. He asked the first driver for general directions and then watched for landmarks. Two rides later, buildings started looking familiar. Now that he knew where to head, he hopped on his last bus. He dropped coins in the slot and didn't bother asking the driver anything. He was a pro now.

He sat with his head against the window and enjoyed the feel of wheels on the road, something he'd taken for granted in his former life. When the bus stopped at a corner he recognized, he hopped off to walk the final few blocks. His stomach jittered with nerves as he turned the corner onto Hemphill.

As nervous as a mouse in a hot dog factory. The Samisms kept resurfacing no matter how hard he fought them.

There it was. The building he'd ditched but now saw through new eyes. The sun glinted off the broken shards of glass around bottom floor windows, sparkling like diamonds. Decaying boards dangled like the nasty teeth he'd seen once in Sam's nutrition textbook, and bars on the lower windows protruded at strange angles, like chicken wing bones after being torn apart and stripped clean.

He hadn't bothered to consider the cool features before. At least there was no auction sign in the yard. Timmy took a deep breath as he mounted the single crumbling concrete step. *Don't be mad, don't be mad.* He knew they could tell him to get lost or beat feet, as Cooter liked to say. What did they owe him? Grandpa or not, Max had admitted having him around made life tougher. And now he'd run away. Getting to his parents or hearing from them had been on his mind 24-7...look where that had gotten him.

"Hey, kid," Cooter called out, startling Timmy as he headed toward the apartment building.

"What's up, Cooter?" His heart raced – had they been

looking for him?

"I saw an ad for plasma and the cops came by. I guess they been lookin' for you for a coupla weeks. You a wanted man. Check out them posters." Cooter head-nodded toward random sheets of paper scattering on the sidewalk and into the street. Before Timmy reached one, Cooter cheered. "Hot damn! I got it!" He jumped up, dropped the pile of newspapers he had wadded in his lap, and speed-walked down Hemphill. "Gonna sell me some plasma and buy a burger!" he called out as he raced away.

You a wanted man. *His heart hammered – and look where he'd been and what he'd done in the past few hours.*

You're the best break-in boy we had in a while. *Timmy cringed. What had he been thinking? Could the police match his fingerprints from the robbery to the – the – the gun?*

He watched the sheets fluttering in the morning breeze, suddenly forgetting he had been worried about the Gerries. Trapping one with his foot, his hands trembled as he picked it up and read.

Missing Child. Reward for any information leading to his whereabouts. Please call the St. Louis Police Department at 314-555-1287 if you know anything about Timothy Ryan Weaver. Child may be frightened, needed for questioning.

Then in the center, blown up and a little blurry, was his school picture from the year before – a cute little fifth-grader without a care in the world. Timmy's heart raced. He gripped the paper so tightly, he crumpled the edge. Granville Auction....

God, I look like a baby. *The year since had added two inches and had thinned his face, though his dimples still left pits in each cheek. The color photo made his eyes look bluer, his blond hair lighter. Or maybe the summer sun hadn't lightened it as much this year. His hands trembled as he let the paper slip from them and drift to the ground like a swaying feather. He watched it fall and had the urge to stomp on it – to smash it into non-existence.*

He stared at the few continuing to blow around the street. Why had Cooter left them on the ground to just scatter with the wind? He trudged through the rickety front door, clomped up the stairs, and stood outside the apartment and listened.

Faint rustlings, though it was early.

Missing child...

Taking a deep breath, Timmy entered the apartment and braced for the lecture. His heart beat a mile a minute staring at the Gerries doing their usual shove-everything-against-the-wall method of clean-up, giving themselves plenty of space to light the grill and not spark a fire. They stacked the few beanbags and blankets as neatly as they could without bothering to fold or roll anything up.

"Hey, kid, you're up early too. Guess we all got our sleep out after the buffet, huh?" Max scratched his head, then tugged holey jeans on over a pair of equally tattered boxers. "I didn't know you'd gone out. Cooter got a hold of some cookies...ain't the best breakfast in the known world, but it's food. Come have a couple." Max motioned him over, and Timmy glanced around for the Post-it note. It wasn't on the floor where he'd left it.

...needed for questioning. He couldn't slow his brain down, overwhelmed by coming back, seeing the flyer, waiting for their reaction to his departure. But they didn't know he'd been gone or where he'd been all night.

So where's the Post-it?

"I – uh, sure." Timmy shuffled toward them, still scoping out the area most people would've used for a dining room. Random shoes the Gerries had taken off, piles of newspapers, empty booze bottles – but no Post-it.

He plopped on the floor next to Max, crossing his legs and never taking his eyes off the old man. His grandpa. Most of the Gerries had upside down buckets of some variation to sit on – they said the farther down they went, the longer it took to get up, so they rarely sat on the floor.

"You look rough, kid. What'd you do, go play in the

river?" Max chuckled and ruffled his matted hair.

Tears swelled in Timmy's throat – two-parts relief, one part resignation that this was his reality. Skippy's tail thumped slightly as the boy sat. Timmy's eyes went wide with surprise.

"Hi," he muttered, waiting for the mutt to growl. But Skippy didn't – before Timmy could second-guess the newfound interest, the terrier-mix was sniffing his pullover, his back where he'd scraped it on the deck, and all the random scents from crawling on the ground.

A wave of emotion overcame him, but no one noticed. Or if they did, no one bothered to tease him for it. The stench in the apartment reminded him of their priorities, of his reality. The night's journey seemed blurry but all too real, and Skippy was trying to get a sense of where the boy had been, who he'd been with, and any other details the high-powered nose could fill-in.

"Seems Skippy might be warming to you." Max handed him two cookies.

As Timmy took them, the mutt sat and waited for a bite.

"Damn dog ain't never paid me the time of day. What the hell's the kid got that I don't?" Billy sneered, tossed a tiny morsel of cookie at Skippy, who raced over with his tail between his legs and snarfed it, backing away before Billy could reach out and smack him.

"Personality," Ralph tittered and Vernon stifled a chuckle.

"Shut-up," Billy snarled, and Skippy ducked behind Max at the tone in the guy's voice.

But Timmy was smitten with Skippy's attention – any diversion from the images swirling in his overloaded brain. The worry at returning was gone, but the sick feeling in his stomach stewed harder than boiling water. He channeled all his energy on getting Skippy to eat from his hand. It took sharing much of both of his cookies to do it, but he'd eaten breakfast. A fact he would never share with the Gerries or that he had over ninety dollars in his pocket. After coaxing Skippy closer, the mutt lay within petting distance.

"Think he'll let me, Max?" Timmy's hand hovered in the air near Skippy's head. The terrier's gaze met Timmy's without moving anything else – no tail wag, but no growl either.

"I think so." Max whispered *good dog* to Skippy as Timmy's hand rested on the dog's head. Gently stroking Skippy, like he always did with Trevor, Timmy felt a surge inside him. Some strange normalcy emerged: abandoned with a grandpa he'd never met but the possibility that he might have a dog.

Skippy didn't tolerate the attention long. He let Timmy pet him for a few minutes, then he dashed out the door the instant someone opened it. It was okay with Timmy – the first obstacle had been cleared, and he hoped it was only a matter of time before he and Skippy could be friends.

Needed for questioning. But what kind of questions? Would it be worth the punishment to get some answers of his own? *Granville Auction.* The images wouldn't let go, but for now, he would enjoy the small victories. The rest just hurt too bad to think about.

"Shitty scotch tastes like piss." Billy spat on the hardwood floor, adding to the montage of stains dotting the nasty living room floor.

"Here he goes," Vernon groaned, as Billy started in on his ritualistic griping about everything that had been done wrong to him in his life.

Timmy would rather eat barf than listen to the hateful man. Who drank scotch for breakfast anyway?

Self-pity filled his head, and he wanted to challenge Billy for the pity prize, as Max called it. The past two weeks could rival any the bully had ever weathered. Instead, he gritted his teeth and mumbled, "I'm tired. I think I'm gonna lay down for a little bit."

He heard their whispers as he shuffled down the hallway.

"...dirty as hell...'

"Where you think he went?"

"...had he pissed himself?"

By the time he reached his bedroom door, emotion got the better of him. He crawled onto the musty mattress, suddenly aware of all the sore spots on his body. His head where he bonked it on the underside of the deck, his back where he'd scraped it, places on his belly that had gotten cut, his fingernails throbbed from tiny rocks being jammed underneath them, and both wrists from Cam and the guys holding him. None of that compared to how bad his face still hurt, the cut under his eye re-opened, and the knot on his forehead pulsating.

An ocean of self-pity swallowed him, and Timmy bawled. Abandoned, the image of the Granville Auction sign permanently etched in his brain. Cameron and his crew shoved him into a car, making him an accessory in yet another crime. Wanted posters littered Hemphill Avenue for the whole world to see how bad he was. *Needed for questioning....* And the plate-sized hands looming, waiting for him to close his eyes. He wiped his snotty nose, dried his face though tears still streamed down his cheeks. Lying on his stomach, chin on his hands, he stared at the once well-loved roses in front of him. He counted the roses he'd decimated.

Fifteen days away from his taken-for-granted life, now sixteen. His fingers were too sore to scratch a new one. Instead, he tried a diversion, to escape the dingy apartment. He imagined who else had lain in this room, before it became home to a bunch of bums with nothing better to do than drink and dig through trash.

Who had slept in the room when it had been beautiful? He considered pulling the dirty knife from under the mattress to mark the new day, but flashes of Baldy, of the blood-covered blade, rolled his stomach.

Is this it? Am I stuck here with...with my bum of a

grandpa?

The sense of relief, of being happy the Gerries weren't mad, had melted quicker than shit on a hotplate. *Wasn't that my third Samism already this morning?* It made him wonder what would've happened if they *had* kicked him out. Would it have given him the guts to go to the police? Wouldn't that be better than this?

He didn't know, and right now, he couldn't deal with expending any more energy. He was exhausted. He closed his eyes and willed it all to go away. But Catalina Avenue tugged at him.

I want my mom. He let the ache swallow him as tears streamed down his cheeks, stinging cuts as they fell. Everything in his body throbbed – tired muscles, bruised neck, battered face. In a world so foreign to Before, this was all that was left.

I'm bad...I hurt Baldy, I robbed a house, and...and...That Night...I know what I did.... He felt the blood on his pullover, ran a hand over his pocket where at least ninety dollars was crammed. For the first time in two weeks, he refused to let daylight fill him with hope. Every time he woke, became aware, he forced himself back to sleep.

Sometime in the afternoon, Max came and checked on him – he felt the old man staring at him, but Timmy kept his eyes closed. Skippy sniffed his face, his cuts, and for a fleeting moment, he thought Skippy might actually lick him. But the mutt scampered back to Max and the door closed. Barriers had been broken, but Skippy was still Max's.

Someone in the living room screeched like a wounded animal, then glass exploded against a wall. Timmy jumped and nearly wet himself – again. "Hootchie Momma!" the same voice hollered, and laughter followed.

"God! Can't you let me sleep?" He threw his shoe at the door and the flimsy wood creaked with the impact. Hours had passed, only dim light showing through the grimy window. The sun was setting, and continual sleep hadn't remedied his exhaustion – it only made him feel worse. *Sleep drunk,* Sam called it.

He slid off the mattress and listened for a few minutes. Sometimes the Gerries spent calm hours in the early evening gabbing, smoking, and flipping cards. Their voices drifted down the hall, but Timmy couldn't judge the mood or alcohol intake by their words.

As the laughter got louder, he tugged on the stiff jeans, then the Nike pullover. He patted the square lump of baseball cards in the front pouch. Thankful it was a cool early September – the bums had repeated it too often not to remember it – he pulled a Salvation Army jacket on over it. Note to Self: clean the damn pullover so there's not a need to cover it up.

He trudged down the hall, braced for the acrid smells of the living room and kitchen. No matter how long he hid in the bedroom, nothing penetrated a stuffy nose like feces and rotting food. He tucked his face inside his T-shirt and jacket, much happier to smell his own sweat. The special blend reminded him of a poor kid whose trailer he'd visited in third grade.

*What was his name? God, I don't remember...*And what else was new? He felt disjointed, fragmented somehow by That Night.

Timmy barely acknowledged the Gerries laughing, playing some game with bottles that resembled checkers. A fresh wet spot in the front room's corner wasn't water or beer. Flies swirled around the area. Billy stoked the coals in the fire and dropped a few pages of newspaper into the grill. Flames leaped into the air sending a wave of warmth Timmy's way.

"NO!" Cooter shouted, as Max tossed a beer bottle off their make-shift board of paper squares.

"Ten to two! Damn, I'm *good!*" Max cackled, smacking palms with Billy.

Ralph and another ancient geezer clapped Cooter on the

back and dropped change onto a box that served as a table. Half-full liquor bottles stood around the men like saluting soldiers. Eruptions of laughter sent Timmy scurrying past into the kitchen. He hated all the noise – it made his head hurt. His belly rumbled – he worried he might be mistaking hunger for another round of the trots, as the Gerries called them. After the buffet, he'd been forced to use various bathrooms on the floor, sick from the massive meal, but the scuffle with Baldy hadn't helped either.

A fleeting image of Baldy dead on that bathroom floor socked the wind out of Timmy. He braced himself on the counter. Something squirmed under his fingertips, and he jerked his hand away. He'd never seen maggots before, but the Gerries had given him his first science lesson on them a few days earlier. He grimaced and rubbed his hand on his filthy jeans enough times to create heat from the friction.

He stared at the kitchen counters, hoping for something to drink other than booze. Occasionally he would find juice, soda, and even bottled water from their dumpster when he went excavating. But he didn't see anything. He knew better than to open the non-functioning refrigerator and refused to look at the sink piled with various carry-out containers, coffee cups, and crusted paper plates. Flies swirled, roaches skittered over moldy food, and the tiny white egg-like creatures oozed over everything. Timmy had never had a problem with bugs. He and the guys played roly poly marbles all the time, but direct contact with maggots changed that opinion in a hurry.

"Ethan," he whispered, as he headed toward the front door and stepped quietly into the hall. He eased the cracked door closed.

The boy's name in third grade had been Ethan, and he went to the kid's house for a birthday party. Brent and Scott went, too.

My best friends. He could even see their faces. *Oh, my god. I had two of the best friends ever...the Three Musketeers.*

Everything Before flitted on his fingertips like smoke. That Night had sequestered portions of his brain, the memories wrapped like an egg roll inside his head. He just couldn't figure out how to untuck the ends to see inside.

Shaking away the surge of emotion, Timmy stepped past the broken top step, then bounded down the three flights. They groaned under his weight, and he hoped nothing would collapse before he got outside.

He welcomed the September evening breeze, the apartment stench whisked away, and for the first time in hours, he could breathe. His Tigger watch, a dumpster find during his first lesson with Cooter, read 7:45. Daylight was fading, but he liked this time of night. He, Brent, and Scott played their greatest games during twilight – army, hide 'n seek, and even hard-fought bouts of kickball.

He reached the end of Hemphill and turned down McCarty. According to a rough map Cooter had drawn of the immediate area, there were endless delicatessens only seven blocks away. Timmy knew the alley dumpsters hadn't been emptied yet – tomorrow was their trash day. Cooter had given him the hows and wheres and other helpful hints in landing nearly fresh meals. The Micky D's value meal was long gone, and the emptiness in the pit of his stomach growled for him to do something about it. He didn't want to resort to his cash if he could help it. That would become his emergency stash.

Right now, the hunt for food was multi-purpose: to satisfy the monster in his gut and to give him a mission. He pulled Cooter's crude map from his back pocket, unfolded it, and located where he was. It only covered a twenty-block radius, but for now, it was plenty. If there was one thing Timmy had always struggled with, it was directions. And now he was left to fend for himself in a city that could make kids invisible.

Teenagers run away and their folks never find 'em, Max told him, warning Timmy what a scary city St. Louis could be.

It worked. But it was time to stop waiting for Max to toss

him cookies for breakfast. He'd master the dumpsters, the routes, the soup kitchens. Whatever he had to do, Timmy was ready to make good. Cooter's crude map outlined a few of the major points, and Timmy would fill it in as he learned the ropes. It would be his mission.

Welcoming the challenge, Timmy set off down McCarty hoping to score something before it got too dark. It took two hours, but he ran across a small pizza shop cleaning up at closing. He watched them toss bags into their back dumpster and thought it was worth a shot to check it out. Lurking around the dumpster, waiting for sounds inside to dissipate, Timmy couldn't wait any longer. The mixture of smells, some intoxicating and others nauseating, squelched the shame as he shimmied over the edge and into the dumpster. He tore open bags, some obviously trash, but then he hit the mother lode. He opened a pizza box of what must've been a screw-up and couldn't stifle a victory whoop.

He froze, waiting for the back door to open, but the alley was silent. He rummaged around, found a bag of garlic toast, a million packets of parmesan cheese and red peppers, and several slices of pizza in a small box someone had boxed to take home.

That used to be me.... A blip of memory, of Sam and him sharing a large pepperoni and sausage. They'd eaten all they could and escaped to the arcade game in the corner. Before leaving, their dad had the pizza boxed up but they'd forgotten it. Later, their mother had chastised them that some starving kid in China could have lived on those four slices for two days.

Not China, Mom...right here in St. Louis...and not just some kid. He tried to swallow the lump that lurched into his throat. *Me.* Tears sprung to his eyes, the smell of his mom so sharp it sucker punched him.

Grabbing a wrinkled sack, he stuffed in his treasure, dropped the other pizza box over the edge, then climbed out. Setting off for the apartment, he knew if this didn't impress the

Gerries, nothing would. A few blocks away, he pulled out a piece and ate it while he walked, chewing slow to let it settle and swell. Cooter taught him about slow eating, all the tricks of the trade to fill up. He flashed to the million times his mom would insist that he and Sam *slow down* while devouring her fried chicken or at the Chinese buffet.

She knew and she didn't even need to.

By the time he got back, he was itching with anticipation. When he burst through the door, the Gerries were doing their morning rituals. Roll up, shove to the wall, replace with buckets, rickety chairs, or anything else that would serve as a seat.

Yawning and stretching, Cooter eyed the bag and box. "Whoa, kid, you score?"

Timmy beamed. "Boy, did I! You guys up for some pizza for breakfast?" He eyed a bum he didn't know, but there was no sign of Ralph, so it still meant two slices for everyone.

Max let out a Richter-tipping belch, they all gave an appreciative *nice,* and he smiled. "That's my boy!" He slapped Timmy on the back and for the time being, Timmy felt *good.*

The guys sat and savored the pizza, praising him intermittently. Cooter added tips on how else to score, more places to consider, and even a couple of spots he might show up that would just feed him because he was a kid.

After that morning, it took less than a week to master lesson number one on dumpster diving – learn trash pick-up days and routes. Part two of that lesson – return to a gold mine on a consistent basis, usually just before trash day.

It was Saturday evening, so he found the block letters *Su* over three different places on the map – those would be ripe for the picking with full dumpsters. He'd already gotten the gang some day-old donuts that morning. His goal tonight was to bring them a late dinner to soak up the whiskey they insisted on drinking every night. *How do they afford that every day?* He wondered. But then nothing the Gerries did made much sense to Timmy.

At the next intersection, he turned right and headed for a sandwich shop on Bingham, only seven blocks away. He folded the map, their work-in-progress, tucked it into his back pocket, then trudged down Wagner, First Street, Two Bridges Avenue, and Second Street. According to his map, he should be nearing familiar stores, but nothing looked right. New to the hunt and no daylight left to really explore, he worried that he had somehow gotten turned around. People wandered past him, way more than on Hemphill but not nearly as many as where the delis were.

I gotta go back the way I came. Timmy trucked back down Second Street but several blocks past where he'd ever been. When he came to the end, he whipped his head left then right and neither appeared correct. An uneasy dread festered, but he sighed and turned right. Three streets later, he pulled out his map, but nothing he saw was on it. He wandered for three or four more blocks and felt a queasy confusion in his gut. Older men rushed by, hats pulled low over their faces. Each corner had pockets of women strolling around, all in high heels, too short skirts, and too much lipstick. They leaned against buildings smiling, and sometimes walked alongside cars that rolled down windows to talk with them. Timmy wondered if they were cold. Late September had turned nippy at night. The days, still warm enough, had gotten shorter, so it made nighttime scrounging tougher.

"Hey, sweetie, you better gitch yoself on home. This ain't no place for you." A lady with a rip in her hose and a bruise on her cheek smiled but hurried to a car slowing to a stop at the curb.

He wanted to oblige, but he wasn't sure which way *home* was. Not his temporary one or his old one.

I am royally lost.

He hustled down the street, past strange-looking stores with XXX in the window, crowded with men, young couples, and a group of guys a little older than Cameron's crew who laughed too loud. Two movie theaters had posters, familiar but with twisted titles – *Snow White and the Seven Whores, Star Whores,* and *Pulp Friction.* Timmy had heard boys on the bus call a girl a ho, and he'd also heard Sam talk about a girl he liked to some of his buddies, but said he couldn't date her because she had a rep for 'whoring around.' So even if he didn't know the exact definition, the references and the naked women on the posters gave him context. He was in an area his parents would call *the slums.*

"Kid, you're gonna get run over if you stand out in the middle of the street like that."

Timmy jerked his head to see a man washing a liquor store window.

"Huh?" He realized he was indeed standing in the middle of the road. "Oh."

"You okay, kid?" The manager dried his hands on a towel and studied Timmy.

"No," he mumbled. He knew to be careful. Max had told him adults would be quick to call the cops or the Division of Youth Services to have him picked up. Had this guy maybe seen his face on those wanted posters?

Chills raced down Timmy's spine at the possibility.

"I – I got turned around. I can't find Hemphill Avenue, um, and I, um, I'm supposed to meet a friend there." *Quick thinkin', moron. Nobody lives on Hemphill. Crap.*

"Hemphill. God, kid, that's worse than this one. You wanna stay away from that area. But it's that way." He pointed down the street. "Take a left, then a straight shot all the way to Vernon. From there, if you gotta go," but the man paused. "If you're pornin', kid, I can help you out."

Timmy froze. *Pornin'?*

Before saying anything that might get him in trouble, Timmy turned tail and ran. It helped in almost every situation, he had discovered, to just beat feet. He sprinted the way the man had said and prayed he would remember the directions that would lead him back to the apartment building. Running felt good in a way that pleased Timmy. He felt free, relaxed, and invigorated. Even if he was lost. How bad could it be to get lost from a place that should never be anybody's home?

But just as he thought he might never make it back, he saw the McCarty sign – the next road over from Hemphill. He slowed to a jog and decided just because he found his way back didn't mean he had to *go* back. He hadn't scored food for them, so the prospect of Billy ranting about not earning his keep didn't appeal to him. *Screw you,* he would think but knew better than to say it. It was late but not late enough. The Gerries would be in full drink mode. He preferred to either be in the bedroom before they got loud or wait until they'd passed out.

"Skippy?" he called out, hoping maybe the mutt was outside. But he didn't hear scampering feet or a bark. The mutt hadn't gotten too chummy with Timmy, but it wasn't for lack of trying.

Chirping crickets filled the silence, making noise in the only tree Timmy had seen in blocks. Night had smothered the city, and broken street lamps gave the block a gloomy feel. A clank somewhere in the distance made him jump.

He sat on his building's stoop and studied the street he now called home. Nothing had color. Garbage littered the sidewalks, clouding the air with putrid smells. Nothing pretty could be seen anywhere – one measly tree, no flowers, no bushes. Empty shells of once beautiful buildings now sported drooping shutters, chipped siding, and shattered windows. The three abandoned buildings across the street were just as colorless as the rest of the street. *Just like the roses on the wallpaper.* He sighed and wished he'd started that stash he'd been thinking about. If he didn't score, having something for backup to keep the Gerries happy was his next goal. But getting lost had thwarted his plan for the dumpster behind an Italian deli. *Note to self: Mark streets as I go and improve that darn map.*

Resigned to a life of no color and too tired to wait for the Gerries to drink themselves silly, Timmy trudged inside and dragged himself up the multitude of stairs. He didn't know why getting lost had wiped him out, but all he wanted now was to sleep and make the yucky feeling inside him go away.

Not that it's helped so far, but it's always worth a shot.

He turned the knob so slow that it squeaked, then tiptoed past the gang as they bantered and banged around in the living room. A haze of smoke from the grill blanketed the top half of the room, blurring faces. They always cracked windows to let in semi-fresh air and to let out toxins, Max insisted, but never enough to eliminate the nasty-smelling smoke.

Halfway down the hall to freedom, Timmy heard Billy bark, "You get us anything to eat, squirt? You know you gotta earn your rent around here!" Some of the guys chuckled, then someone farted, and they all burst into fresh howls of laughter. "HEY!" Billy boomed when Timmy didn't turn around or respond.

The laughing stopped and Cooter snapped, "Cut him some slack, Billy. You got breakfast cuz of the kid."

"Kiss my ass, Cooter. Protégé or not, he ain't good for us and you know it." To Timmy who had halted and half-turned, Billy snapped. "This ain't no Holiday Inn. Juvie's just one call away if you don't start kickin' in regular like!"

Yeah, you and what phone, asshole? He mumbled, "Sorry," but what he really wanted to snap was, "Screw you." He hadn't gotten brazen enough to cross Billy. The urge flashed at least five times a day, and the tension between them only thickened as the days wore on. Timmy hurried on down the hall and slipped into the room. As he shut the door, he heard a bottle break and wondered if it had been dropped or thrown. He made his umpteenth note to self to spend less time around Billy and more time exploring and scoring, then plopped onto the mattress causing a blast of dust to explode into the stale air.

Timmy amended the reason to stay away to include *breathe fresh air*.

He pulled a new bottle cap from his pocket and scratched the twenty-first rose from the wallpaper. More roses disappeared and his bottle cap collection was growing – neither was a good sign.

Three weeks. In another world, three weeks of summer would fly, but three weeks of school would drag. Now time made little difference, wondering if his parents and Sam had been forced to leave the country. Max had suggested it a few days earlier. It all sounded so crazy and like someone else's life. But as he counted the next row of roses, he couldn't wrap his head around what had become his. It didn't take long for him to drift to sleep, thinking about the flowers, the people who might've lived there, the families who'd moved on to bigger, better places, or some kid just like him who might've lost the battle with Billy.

What felt like only minutes later, shouts and crashes rumbled through the apartment.

Someone banged on his door, and Timmy shot off the mattress wondering why his mom was waking him for school before daylight.

Pounding footsteps thundered down the hall, and Timmy's startled heart matched the pace.

"TIMMY!" Max shouted.

My parents!

He jumped up and raced out into the hall, praying this was the moment he'd been waiting for.

Chapter Twelve

"GET UP! NOW! We gotta get the hell outta here! GO, everybody, *go*!" Max shouted. The tone in the old man's voice coiled Timmy's empty stomach. He darted back into his bedroom, snaked a hand under the mattress, and stuffed the knife into his back pocket. Cramming bottle caps into the front pouch of his pullover with the ball cards and cash stash, he tugged it on, bumping his healing cheek.

"NOW!" Voices boomed throughout the apartment, spurring him out the door. Timmy could hear similar cries other places in the building, his own heart pounding ninety miles a minute in his ears.

Hands banged the walls trying to roust everyone. Shouts echoed on the floors above and below. Then Timmy heard it. Sirens! Cops. *Shit*.

"Go, Timmy, get the lead out," Max ordered. Voices sounded like booms of thunder in the hallway, officers slamming open neighboring doors with thuds that grew louder and louder.

"Open the goddamned door!" A bang on their own door gripped Timmy with terror, suddenly sure he was going to pee his pants.

Billy grabbed him by the sleeve and slung him into the kitchen where Ralph and Cooter both yanked on the window leading out onto the fire escape. Max shoved Timmy past him and then pulled the kitchen door closed. That same instant, a splintering crack echoed through the living room, and a massive boom followed. More thundering footsteps filled the apartment just as Cooter heaved the window open far enough to dive onto the fire escape. Billy hoisted Timmy out after Cooter, then Max and Ralph nearly fell on top of him.

All five of them scrambled to their feet and took off lanking down the steps.

"STOP! POLICE!"

Timmy's heart lurched. He glanced above him, through the crisscrossed metal fire escape, at Billy and Ralph battling a cop trying to come through the window. The few seconds head start allowed Max, Cooter, and Timmy to scamper all the way down the ladder. Ralph lumbered after them.

The split-second Timmy hit the street, he took off like a jackrabbit with a Doberman on his tail. Max managed to stay close, despite his age. Skippy had jetted off in the night barking his crazy head off.

Just past the next building, Max whipped into an alley and whisper-shouted for Timmy. "Get over here!"

Desperate to get distance between him and the sirens, Timmy hesitated, turning in time to see Billy drop to the pavement milliseconds before the chasing officer pummeled him. The bum's fists flew, flopping around like a wild animal, swinging and connecting every other punch. Another cop threw Billy onto his stomach and squatted to press a knee in the bully's back.

A vindictive *yes!* surged through Timmy, as he streaked into the alley for cover. He squatted low to the ground peeking around the corner. He'd never tell Max, but seeing Billy on the ground getting cuffed ranked right up there with cashew chicken. He ducked his head back, worried they would see him and come get him when they finished with Billy.

"Are they after me, Max?" A lump in his throat threatened to bring tears with it.

Someone shouted, and he couldn't help but watch as the knee-in-the-back cop wrestled with Billy after cuffing him. The cop was clearly pissed, shoving Billy's face into the concrete. Words volleyed between the two, but nothing Timmy could decipher.

"I don't think so, kid. But if they was, they got somethin' better." Max shook his head as the cops yanked Billy to his feet. "Get down," Max hissed.

Flashlight beams flicked up and down the street, strobes of light darting over their heads and all around them. For a couple of seconds, Timmy held his breath, certain his heart would fly out if he opened his mouth. Ralph tried to swallow a cough, and Cooter stuffed a hand over the old man's mouth and nose. His eyes bulged, his too bushy eyebrows sticking out above them like gray and white wire. Wrinkles so deep, they spider-webbed around the Gerries' eyes. Turning beet red, Ralph's cheeks puffed, the old geezer struggling to breathe and suppress a cough again. Cooter let go so Ralph could get air, and panic rippled through Timmy. *You'll get us caught!* He reached down to hold his privates, too scared to think but knowing his bladder had better things to do than worry about pee patrol.

"You've got the right to remain fucking silent, asswipe. You give up that right, then I'll shut it up for you, got it?" One cop stuffed Billy into the back of the patrol car, another slammed the door. Timmy peeked in time to see the flashing lights go dark and the police car roar the opposite way down Hemphill Avenue.

"Thank God," Ralph gasped, giving in to a tirade of coughs until tears streamed down his craggy face.

Cooter stared at the spot where Billy had just been taken, shaking his head but said nothing. For a few long minutes, no one moved, no one spoke, and the silence scared Timmy.

What do we do now?

Max finally let out a cheek-puffing sigh. "Someone gave us up, for real. Guys have been sick of Billy, like Vernon, where the hell is that old fart anyway? Yep, that's it, it's gotta be Vernon, or maybe – " Max stopped when Cooter let out an abbreviated, "AH! God, Max..."

"What?" Max blurted. The old man turned on Cooter, the two staring one another down, Cooter's face red, furrowed, clenched like he might explode. Timmy still in a crouch, unsure what the guys were saying and even more unsure why they were about to fight. His heart had barely slowed and now his stomach stewed.

"Shut the fuck up, Max. Maybe it was Vernon, but, goddamn, 1-800, for real. Billy's been askin' for this ever since..." Cooter's gaze trailed to Timmy then locked with Max's. "The jerk had it coming. His crap put us in a lot of danger. You know what I'm talkin' about."

"Yeah." Max took a deep breath and let it out so slow it seemed it might last forever. But Ralph and Cooter waited, clearly expecting an opinion or an idea from him.

"1-800?" Timmy whispered.

Cooter laughed, his reddened face relaxing a bit. "Like 1-800-Let-itgo. You know, get over it, let it go. Who gives a shit."

Timmy grinned. *I like that...1-800-Let-itgo. Maybe I should try a bit of that....*

"Maybe it was Freaky Freddie. Think he'd nark on us?" Ralph's deep voice had an edge of child-like fear in it.

"Who cares. We've gotta think. We can't go back there, can we, Max?" Cooter ran a hand through his unruly red hair, the top greasy enough to lay flat, the rest sticking out like an electrocuted cat Timmy had seen in cartoons.

"No..." Max smacked the brick building. "*Dammit.*"

"Welp, I suppose we gonna have to cop a squat in the alley, huh, Max? Boys in blue might be back...*likely* to be back. Which one, though?"

"I don't know, Ralphie. Probably Brookline or Danner." Max pressed the heel of his hand into his forehead.

Brookline or Danner? Who're they? Nothing the guys talked about made sense. He just wanted to crawl into a hole and make all of this go away. A slideshow of images clouded his brain – him shimmying under the McKinney's deck, hiding in the hedge on Catalina, cowering in the storm drain That Night three weeks ago. He squeezed his eyes shut to make it go away.

"What about your house, Max?" Timmy hadn't meant to say it out loud, though it had limped through his head more than once. Every time one of the guys made strange comments about Taneisha and Drey, he couldn't help but wonder where they lived. *And how the heck did my parents find you?*

"Shut-up, kid. I'm trying to think here." Max turned and glowered at him, sending a zip of fear through Timmy. Heaving a sigh, he said, "Let's head to Brookline, especially if the burn barrel is still there, along with them old bucket seats. And just so you know, preppie boy, not everybody had your life. My house ain't my house no more, so quit askin, got it?"

Timmy recoiled, not sure what he'd done to piss Max off. It wasn't a dumb question, was it? How could his parents have contacted Max if the guy lived in abandoned buildings? Where did he get his mail? *I really wanna know!* But Timmy knew better than to ask.

"Yeah, Danner's got all that construction goin' on around it. Cops are liable to be keepin' a closer eye on squatters." Cooter squinted and picked at a scab on his chin until it seeped blood. Timmy dropped his gaze, his already queasy stomach rolling.

Ralph poked his head around the corner to make sure the coast was clear, and all of them wandered out into the street. Timmy followed, wishing Max would explain where the heck they were going. He obsessively patted the front of his pullover – his baseball cards and bottle caps were safe. And then the four of them set off walking without talking.

Timmy scanned the dark roads for landmarks, but too many street lamps didn't work. The quarter moon offered little help, so the farther they walked, the more disoriented he was. The broken-down buildings continued for several blocks, but then they made a right turn into a world of lights.

"Whoa," he muttered, ogling the flashing signs advertising Jim Beam, Budweiser, and more weird movie titles he didn't know. *I think I was here before...*

"It ain't as pretty as it looks, kid." Cooter let out a laugh.

"This is no-go zone, kid. Got me?" Max didn't look at him, so he wasn't sure the old man was talking to him. They even picked up the pace as they passed through the area.

Less than three blocks from the World of Lights, they found Brookline Avenue. Max, Cooter, and Ralph stood at the entrance of a dirty, narrow alley.

"We're here." Max walked over to a rusted barrel and peered into it.

While Timmy tried to process what all of it meant, the Gerrie grabbed a pole he obviously knew was tucked behind a gutter downspout and poked at something inside the barrel. "Grab those papers over there, Timmy."

Timmy swallowed hard, vowing he wouldn't cry. *This is really my life.* Self-pity threatened to consume him when Max snapped his fingers and pointed.

He saw the fluttering news pages skittering down the street and stomped on them. Reaching down to pick them up, he saw Kurt Warner's face on the cover of sports page.

Gonna have a team for real this year! Sam's face, as clear as an NFL crystal ball on Monday, sucker-punched him. Their family had always reveled in Samisms, hadn't they?

Not anymore.

"C'mon, kid, get a move on. It ain't that bad. But we need some heat, so let's get a fire started." Max took the papers from him, minus the article Timmy tore off to read.

He got it now. The names they rattled off weren't people or anybody's home – they were street names and he was officially homeless. Max could sugarcoat and blow smoke up his ass, one of Sam's favorite phrases, but this disgusting alley was really where they intended to stay.

None of the nearby buildings had apartments. Most of the small businesses had long been abandoned, except for a liquor store and a pawn shop a block over. Broken windows on what used to be a tattoo parlor stood directly across the street from the alley.

"We're better off in the alley anyways." Cooter helped Max tip the burn barrel on its side to dump the water. Black sludge hit the ground with a plop. Somehow the sight and sound of it fit exactly how Timmy felt.

"Where do we sleep?" He wandered deeper into the alley to explore, to see if there were cots or mattresses somewhere back under all the boxes.

"I sleep standin' up," Cooter blurted, then grabbed a paint bucket and flipped it over to sit on.

"I got dibs on that U-Haul box, so don't get your grubby paws on it," Ralph ordered, and then let out a ground rumbling belch.

"Nice!" Cooter spouted, and slapped a high-five with the scraggly old man.

"Why don't you guys be useful and help me get this fire started." Max had dropped some sticks and the papers into the barrel but couldn't get his Bic to light.

Ralph pulled a lighter from his pocket and tossed it to Max. He hovered over the barrel to help hold something for Max to light. In seconds, there was smoke billowing from the barrel and a waft of heat Timmy welcomed. He wasn't that cold, but somehow a fire made the alley feel more welcoming. He continued to explore, to pick through the cardboard boxes that littered the alley that couldn't be more than fifteen feet wide. Strange sounds skittered somewhere in the far corner.

Ralph hustled past him shouting, "They're here!" Halfway down the alley, on the other side of a tower of boxes, he dropped onto tattered leather seats that had lost its car. "Hot damn!"

"Ralphie, you're a moron." Cooter shook his head, then instructed Timmy to gather more cardboard, paper, and anything else that would burn. "We gotta keep this fire goin'. But not the sturdy boxes...those are our penthouses. *That's* where we sleep, kid."

Timmy's mouth fell open. Reeling, processing what it all meant, he assessed the alley. The Musketeers would've had a heyday with the piled crates in back, the array of giant boxes –

a cool place to explore, but to stay? "Max? We're gonna *live* here?" He stared at his grandpa – *no, I wanna go home, to* any *home.*

"Sorry, kid, we do what we gotta do. And if I gotta keep you on the down low, then an alley's better than juvie, right? Unless you'd rather give the police a go." Max scowled. The message was clear – *quit whining, or I'm ditchin' ya.* Chills ran through Timmy's bladder and settled around his privates.

Cooter interrupted the awkward moment. "Paper, Timmy, get crackin'. We gotta get a fire or we'll freeze our asses off. It gets damn cold late at night, even in September. A nice fire will make the alley roasty-toasty." Cooter took a piece of paper and rubbed it on the ground, then dropped it in the barrel. "Go!" He gestured for Timmy to get a move on.

I'm gonna sleep in an alley...am...am I homeless? Timmy shuddered, not from the cold but letting his brain think that word. Blinking back tears, he scrounged in the back corner, shifting crates, cringing when skittering seemed too close. It was too dark to make much out, so grabbing in the dark sent his insides stewing. *Yeah, we'll lay low for a few days, maybe a week, then we'll find another place. Or I am bailing. Being in jail can't be worse than this, can it?*

Within an hour or so, somewhere around one a.m., according to Max, flames danced and flickered in the dark alley. The fire gave Timmy enough light to really inspect the area. Just past the dented cardboard boxes and the carless bucket seats, junk was heaped so high two men on shoulders could've reached the second-floor fire escape. Despite his horror at being subjected to living in the alley, the pile promised some adventure after the sun came up. He didn't intend to go near it again until armed with something – anything – and able to see.

He rubbed his Adidas against the slick concrete and wondered why the ground was so slippery. He took a two-step jog and slid to see if it was skateable. It was.

"That's oil, kid," Cooter said. "When one of us can, we nab

some to help us start fires. That's why I rubbed the paper scraps on the ground. It also keeps water from soakin' in to the cardboard."

"Where's it come from?"

"It's freakin' everywhere...in cans, in the street from cars, you name it. When we find it, we want it. It's a hot commodity." Cooter rubbed another scrap of cardboard on the ground, dropped it in the fire, and watched flames leap to prove his point.

"These're the lessons you best listen to," Max told him. He lifted the burlap flap that covered the opening of a huge wooden crate. A tarp had been folded back and lay on top and drooped over the sides. "You get to sleep here, Timmy."

"Hey, why's he get the biggest?" Ralph stood rooted to the spot he hadn't moved from – standing at the burn barrel with his palms as close to the fire as he could seem to stand. The oldest of the Gerries rarely did any work, but made up for it with his griping.

"Because him and me'll share, Ralphie. Did you find this burlap, fasten it, layer it with that crap, and then bitch-slap that woman who tried to swipe it?" Max glared at the bushy-browed man. "Huh? Besides, you dibbed the U-Haul box. We all heard ya. So have at it." Max glared hard. Timmy felt the sizzle of the stare.

"Damn, don't get yer panties in a wad, old man. Seems like I 'member you havin' some help from Retard Rita anyways. God, everybody's all pissy." Ralph rotated around the barrel so his back was to the alley and to Max. "Woman and her damn shopping cart oughta be ticketed for drunk driving." Ralph grunted and continued mumbling things that didn't make sense.

Timmy had a vague memory of a woman rousting him from a trashcan – before the shelter, before Max came to save him. He wondered what would've become of him if his grandpa hadn't come to get him.

"Somebody left this tarp, and that's a nice addition. That'll keep us nice and warm. Go on, get inside. You gotta get some sleep. The first mornin' in an alley, we gotta be on our toes – just in case. And trust me, when that sun comes up, so will you." Max held the burlap, waiting for Timmy to crawl inside.

Timmy guessed from the size that he could probably sit up on his knees and not bonk his head, but he wouldn't be able to lie down without his feet sticking out a little. Max's would stick out a lot, though the two of them could lay side by side on their backs with plenty of room to spare. *Good thing I'm short...* His Musketeer buddies always teased that it was a good thing he was fast, because still shy of five feet, he was the runt of the trio.

"Hey! What about Skippy? How'll he find us?" Timmy felt a strange rush of devoted panic.

"Oh, trust me. The Skipmeister'll find us." Max let out a whistle. "That's our bat signal." He chuckled, and Ralph mumbled something about liars getting what's coming. Timmy started to ask, but the old man had retreated deeper into the alley with his giant U-Haul box, big enough for a refrigerator.

Confusion, questions, uncertainty all hammered away in his head. When was Max here before? Why did he sleep in alleys when there were abandoned buildings everywhere? But the men had other plans, whispering about how to get a bottle and who was making the fly. Not knowing what else to do, Timmy got down on all fours and peered inside. A pungent odor tickled his nose and even though it looked damp, it didn't feel too bad when he touched it. There were no pillows, no blankets, no tiny mattresses, no sleeping bags. The apartment had been skanky, stinky, and run-down, but at least he'd had a bedroom, a make-shift bed, and even a shoddy pillow.

Wish I'd grabbed that...maybe tomorrow I'll sneak back there and get some stuff. But where was *back there*? They'd walked for what felt like an hour. With Timmy's sense of direction, that would be a dangerous trek to take.

He glanced over his shoulder at Max. "Is there anything to lay on, Max?"

The old man bowed his head. Cooter was zipping his coat like he was heading out somewhere, and Ralphie had returned to roast himself over the burn barrel. But Max didn't say a word. He didn't need to. His face said plenty.

Timmy could imagine Billy's response – he'd heard it a few times at the apartment. *Ungrateful kid, nobody's holdin' your ass hostage. Get, if you don't like the accommodations.*

The prospect of no place to go prompted him to crawl inside and curl into a fetal position as far in the corner as he could go. If he slept that small, no one could say he took up too much room or expected too much from him. Max could spread out with the space he'd left.

"G'night, kid. Sorry." Max sounded sad, barely loud enough to hear, and the words brought a lump into Timmy's throat.

Huddled in the corner, Timmy resituated so he could peek through the crack between the burlap and the edge of the box. He watched the men around the burn barrel, warming their hands, whispering, probably talking about what a wimp he was. Timmy tried to see some resemblance, some familiarity with his own face, his mom's, Sam's, but he was having trouble with their faces. When he could picture them, tears blurred the view. When he couldn't, a jolt of panic scissored through him.

Thinking about his brother and his parents filled him with an anguish he couldn't prevent. He buried his face in his hands and cried until he fell asleep. Sometime later, a warm tongue licked his hands, his face. A small body, like a heater, nestled in tight behind his bent knees.

He woke well before dawn, the tiny heater gone, and no Max anywhere. Timmy crawled out of the crate, saw an orange glow in the barrel, and little else. Still dark, he guessed it might only be three or four a.m. Scared and worried the Gerries had left him, he poked his head into several of the boxes. Ralph snored, flat on his back in a beat-up refrigerator box with the side slit open, Cooter lay sprawled on the bucket seats covered with newspapers, and he found Max folded in a washing machine box near the pile of junk, mumbling in his sleep.

Wandering out into the street, Timmy couldn't think of one reason to stay in the grimy alley. His back hurt from the short sleep on the hard ground, and his joints popped as he stretched. The cuts and bruises had healed from That Night, even the gash under his left eye. Still sore sometimes, he touched it, fingered the length of the jagged scar. More than any physical pain, his heart ached from thinking about his mom, his dad, and Sam.

When he set off walking, he didn't know where he was going or why. The stores were still closed, though the sky off to the right showed promise of sunrise. Days would still be the same, it would be the nights he dreaded. Aside from the dark, damp cold, everything was eerily silent. He'd never known how quiet it could be in a big city. What dangers of the north St. Louis streets threatened to swallow him? For some weird reason, the notion didn't scare him. As that sad reality set in, he wandered toward the intersection with another one quick on its heels – he didn't care anymore. But he meant to use a little cash to get some breakfast.

Box in an alley or box springs on the floor didn't mean he couldn't treat himself to some normalcy. It was one of the only ways he knew how.

Chapter Thirteen

Timmy walked without regard for where he was going or how far away he'd wandered. Did it matter? He didn't think so. He rested in doorways of condemned buildings, and then continued his trek to nowhere. When his legs began to throb, he found a dark entryway into what might be a parking garage and huddled as far out of the chilly breeze as he could. As he drifted to sleep, he clutched the switchblade in case someone like Baldy lurked in the shadows. Every so often, he traced the outline of the baseball cards and his stash of cash in the front pouch of his Nike pullover. There was something soothing about the gesture.

As he drifted in and out of sleep, he had flashing images of Cameron, of the cop who threw Billy to the ground, of a giant man with plate-sized hands reaching for him. When he saw the tattoos, he remembered bits and pieces, but then the goon's face morphed into a blend of Baldy's and Billy's.

When the Missouri morning sun warmed his exposed ankles, he woke slowly, confused by his surroundings, but quickly shoved the knife into his back pocket before anyone could swipe it. Beyond hungry, he stretched and inspected the city street. His heart lurched at the sight of the Gateway Arch in the distance, high above surrounding buildings – hotels or companies that reeked of importance. The Arch was still far away, part of the horizon and not close enough to make out the panels. But it was a landmark he understood, and it meant he was far from the alley. *Good.* Energy pulsed through him as he headed toward the riverfront.

I'll never find Brookline again. But he was beyond accepting there were things he couldn't do. First and foremost, he decided to splurge on food. He'd avoided it, knowing he could blow it fast on something as trivial as a meal. But an emptiness unlike any he'd ever felt clawed at his insides.

Just as he kicked a McDonald's cup near a building, a man sleeping on the sidewalk sat up right in front of him.

"Shit, runt, watch where the hell you're goin'."

Timmy jumped away from the old bum lying on the sidewalk near the building. Then the guy sat up on his elbow, and Timmy got a clear enough view of his face, completely unlined except for a gnarly rash around his nose. It was all Timmy could do not to stare.

He's not much older than Sam.... The guy could've been sixteen, maybe seventeen or eighteen tops. Tears filled Timmy's eyes as he took a wide berth, the guy already covered back up and oblivious of him. A sick sensation filled him, sure he'd just gotten a glimpse of his future.

That can't be me...I can't become him. He jogged, then sprinted, bent on finding a McDonald's to clean up and then eat like a real person. They would be open soon or might be open already, from the tinge of light in the sky. His month on the street had taught him a lot, even if he hadn't mastered directions yet. Within thirty minutes, he found one that he made a note to add to his map, and hurried into the bathroom. At least thirty paper towels later, his face was presentable and he smelled almost decent. Standing in line, anxious to order his usual, he tried to blend in. Surrounded by people with jobs, lives, homes, he knew his blending days were passing. All the while, his past continued to overlap.

"My God, Sam. You can't eat two double quarter pounders. Get one and see how you feel."

"But, Mom, I'm starving, for real. Feel this..." Sam placed a hand on his flat, six-pack muscled stomach. His mom refused, a hint of a smile tugging at the corners of her mouth.

"Sam. I'm the mom. You're the son. Regardless of how you've distorted your world, I still have the cash. One for starters, okay? Timmy, what do you want, honey? You want a happy meal?"

"Mom, I'm not a kid...I want a double quarter pounder, too."

Her smile drifted past him like a warm breeze, sucking the present away.

"Oh, God." He braced himself against the counter he'd just reached, aware of eyes on him.

"You gonna order or are you tryin' to hustle me?" A check-out girl with a zit-freckle battle on her cheeks, glared at him. "And I wanna see the cash before you order," she added, nodding like her role as a McDonald's checker included security.

Panic swelled inside him, too many people staring, the check-out agent's eyes narrowing. *She's gonna call the cops...*

Before he could say anything, he bolted, the M.O. of champions.

Flying out into the street – a nice commercial area with people heading to work, maddening smells of food, horns already honking – all he could think about was running back toward the safety of broken windowed buildings and gray silence. Twelve blocks later, he slowed to a jog, and after four more, he doubled-over, clutching at the stitch stabbing his side. He glanced up at the corner. Carolina Avenue, the sign read, but for that split second, he saw *Catalina Avenue*. But he knew what waited there for him....

Granville Auction... Someone selling his stuff, reading his comics, smacking a fist into *his* ball glove.

For one crazy minute, Timmy contemplated standing at the bus stop next to the street sign, telling the bus driver to take him home, and swiping the things that belonged to him. But something tugged at his heart, his head, and he knew that home didn't exist anymore, that his things would be gone, his family gone, his life gone. *But where were they? His family? His things?*

He didn't know, and that uncertainty, that vast hole in his brain threatened to swallow him. So he kept walk-jogging, liking the pain that sizzled in his side, the ache in his legs, the fire in his lungs.

Cleaning up won't make me one of them...I'm homeless. I got nowhere to go and no one to tell me I can't go there. Timmy finally slowed to a walk, street signs starting to ring familiar, some even on his makeshift map. Frowning, he trudged down two streets of broken down apartment buildings, abandoned businesses, and pawnshops. Mickey's Deli, a sandwich shop with busted windows, had a permanent open sign that someone forgot to flip, and enough paper strewn about to pass for tile. He meandered past Adam's Automotive, long since vacated, and a few lounges still running but with few customers. Two massage parlors sported neon signs and provided the only color to an otherwise gray world.

Shattered windows intrigued Timmy. In another time, he would've wanted to play with the shards of glass, pretending to be a swordsman in a Dumas novel. *We loved the short version of 'The Three Musketeers' in Language Arts.* He remembered the fat paperback and how his teacher explained abridged books. Some strange snips of memory came back like fuzzy commercials. Others in long, elaborate nightmares.

Condemned. Closed until further notice. Bank Foreclosure. The signs didn't make a lot of sense to Timmy, but he knew the crumbling, run-down buildings appeared about as sad as the alley. Even if he wasn't in school, Timmy's education continued. As the morning sun rose, brightening the streets and his mood, he had wound back around in giant loop, noting his path on the map. He wandered back a block that tugged at his memory. It drew him like a magnet.

Street by street, the scenery began to change again. *I don't wanna be the guy on the sidewalk...* Dress shops next door to *Ernesto's Café*, teeming with business, then shoe stores, fine pottery places, and office supplies. Whole streets with open businesses and no more condemned or closed signs. People in suits walked with purpose, ladies with shopping bags pushed strollers, and many of them sipped coffee from containers he recognized. A new coffee place his mom loved, with a funny green logo that resembled a lady on the cups. A woman with a bagel smiled at him, a hint of pity in her eyes.

Clean or not, I look like a punching bag. He dropped his gaze to the ground, then darted into an alley far cleaner than the one on Brookline. He leaned against the stones of a fancy bank and caught a whiff of pasta, the smell so scrumptious his mouth watered. A loud clank deeper in the alley made him jump. A man dropped the lid on the dumpster with an even louder thunk and glanced Timmy's way.

"Yo, scram, kid, no loitering." A college aged guy, maybe a tad older, gestured with his hands.

"What?" Timmy understood *scram,* but the young guy's eyes were friendly, not at all the expression Billy wore with a permanent sneer when he meant for Timmy to beat feet.

"What happened to you, kid?"

"Uh, I got in a fight." Nerves made his feet itchy, his M.O. at the ready.

"Are you lost? Or is your mom shoppin' or somethin'?" He wiped his hands on his apron, streaked red from various sauces. The smell made Timmy dizzy with hunger. As if to prove it, his stomach rumbled loud enough to pass for thunder.

"Whoa, now that's a sound I understand. You ain't eaten in a while, have you? Want some pasta?"

"Uh, my mom, she's in that big pottery store, and I should probably be getting back..." Timmy's lies came out faster than he could polish them. The cook held up his hand.

"Hey, kid, you don't gotta snow me. I got some leftovers, and you can have 'em. But no smoke up my ass, okay?" The slight smile, dark black hair, and round dimpled face were comforting.

"Okay," Timmy agreed. "I can pay..."

"Wouldn't think of it. Name's Nathan, what's yours?" The young guy wiped his hands on his apron. The red smears sent a chill through Timmy.

After he told Nathan his name, the guy slipped back inside and emerged with a Styrofoam container. “Here you go, buddy. Enjoy. And when you’re struggling, come back, okay? I’ve been there, broke and hungry. Never homeless but close. So put me on your route, capisce?” He winked and was gone before Timmy could respond.

His first meal as a hustler proved to be one of his best. The small Styrofoam container was filled with spaghetti and meatballs. It made his heart smile. He raced to a spot he had noticed a few blocks back. A bench faced a tiny park – two trees and a patch of grass. Not much, but the best place he could think of for an Italian breakfast.

By the time he got there, his stomach gurgled painfully. He had never known true hunger in his Before life, but he knew now – two weeks on one buffet, a McD’s breakfast, and random samplings of cookies, crackers, and donuts. An emptiness that caused cramps and could double him over mercilessly. Timmy forced himself to chew slowly, rolling the sauce on his tongue, and swallowed bites still hot enough to burn his throat. But he didn’t care. He ached to remember what it felt like to be full – Baldy had ruined that for him at the buffet.

An image flashed of the bald man on that bathroom floor, but Max had to be right – that guy’s buddies would’ve rushed him to the hospital and stitched him up good as new. Probably, Max had added, the lingering possibility haunting Timmy.

Shoving the memory away, he let some noodles and meat sauce settle on his lips and tongue, enjoying the tang of tomatoes in his mouth. He barely got halfway through the meal when his stomach bulged and the rebellion started.

A gurgle similar to the hunger pangs bubbled in his stomach. Then the food rolled, seemed to lump together, and before he could stop it, he vomited most of it onto the mulch around the small tree. And then the worst case of cramps hit Timmy without warning. He doubled over, willing it to pass.

When the first wave did, Timmy got up and walked slowly toward a Starbuck's coffee shop – not the one his mom loved but the parallelisms didn't help his insides.

Restroom, I need a restroom. A new bubble in his stomach wasn't coming north. He raced into the trendy coffee shop and nearly gagged on the overpowering aroma of lattes, cappuccinos, and pastries. He searched the rear of the store for signs and made a beeline for the men's room.

"Hey, kid, this ain't a gas station!" a clerk shouted, as Timmy hit the door and made it into a stall. The first wave hit a second after he tugged his Levis to his knees. Tears streamed down his face when the second attack doubled him over, groans coming from deep within him. Humiliated and tired, he braced himself as each cramp gripped and released. Timmy brushed the tears away with each spurt of burning pain.

He sat so long, his legs began to go numb. But he didn't dare stand for fear a cramp would catch him off guard again. In his eleven short years, he couldn't remember ever having cramps so excruciating or getting so sick – and this was round two.

"Oh, God, make it stop," he moaned, and for the first time since being rescued by Max, Timmy ached for his mom and dad with such severity that he thought he would pass out. The cramp in his heart hurt so much more than any the pasta could create.

By the time the battle ended, he cleaned himself as best he could and flushed. He stared at his reflection in the mirror, splashed water and rubbed away a few more smudges near his hairline. His head itched, and he considered washing it with the hand soap. The ugly splotches of bluish green, tinged with yellow still surrounded his right eye. *Baldy.* The scar under his left puckered a little at the edges. *Wicked,* his Musketeers would describe it. All he knew was that the cheekbone behind the scar ached almost as much as his heart when he thought back to That Night.

Someone jangled the handle, making Timmy jump. He heaved a sigh, gave his reflection one last glance, and fully understood what people had to think when they stared at him.

Slinking back through Starbuck's, the shame followed him as the guy whistled, "Damn, kid, you fall in? Shew-ee."

Timmy took off running. *Don't look, don't listen, just run.* He wanted to get back to the half-meal he had left. When he raced out the door, he barreled into a heavy-set lady.

"Watch where you're goin', son," she barked. Then she held him out from her and studied him, grasping each shoulder firmly. "Are you okay?"

Her judging eyes scoped him from head to foot and back again. He didn't know what her nametag meant, but the Division of Youth Services title below the engraved *Sarah Chapman* renewed the panic.

Oh shit... Sam would call this bad karma. Timmy chalked it up to his new normal.

"I...I think so." He pulled away and mumbled an apology.

"Where's your mom, sweetie?" she interrupted. Her tone and her demeanor softened. He wasn't sure why, but he didn't like that either. Distrust had become his mode of survival.

"Um, up there." He pointed down the street, the direction he had come from. He waited for her to let go of him. "She's shopping. I think she went into that pottery store, but I was messin' around and didn't see." The lie, he knew, could be easily trapped. He just needed a diversion to get free.

"Let's go find her," Sarah Chapman stated matter-of-factly. She raised her eyebrows and turned him by the shoulders, but when he didn't move, she narrowed her gaze.

What now?

"Where'd you say you thought she was? Or are you lost?" She didn't blink when she stared at him.

"I'm not lost." *Short answers.* "She's just down the street."

She furrowed her brow. "So let's go find her. You don't look so great. She's got to be worried about you."

He couldn't read her. She was in a position to help him, and she seemed genuinely worried about him. But she was a little too insistent for his paranoia. "We're going to McDonald's for lunch." The long pause had to have fueled her suspicions.

"Why don't we go there together? If she doesn't show up for a bit, I'll buy you a milkshake. How's that sound?"

"Um, I don't know you." He played the stranger card, knowing any adult would respect that.

"Well, son, I can't just leave you here. And I think she would understand...a nine or ten-year old out here by himself."

"I'm eleven," he interjected, offended by her tone.

"I'm sorry, of course you are. You're my grandson's age. So, Mr. I'm Eleven, what's your name?" Her tone had taken on a teacherly tone that he couldn't help but answer.

"Timmy."

"Well, I'm Sarah." She pointed to her nametag, then offered him her hand. He shook it.

"What're all those letters by your name?" He didn't care, but he had to stall. She could be an asset but Max's voice whispered *you've been bad...don't forget.*

"Um, they mean that I'm a social worker who helps kids like you find their moms. C'mon, let me buy you a shake. Sound good?" Her eyes, sensitive now and almost worried, didn't look mean anymore.

The idea of a soothing shake on his stomach sounded blissful, even at the expense of the half-meal still on the tiny park bench.

They walked the block and a half, while she asked him questions about his favorite Cardinal, which Ram wide receiver was the best, and did he really believe they could turn their season around.

"Which team?" he asked, always loving to talk sports.

"Both!" she said with a laugh, but added, "Don't think LaRussa has the pieces yet to make a run, but Kurt Warner might just be the real deal."

Timmy's impressed-meter spiked. She knew her sports. And no matter what her motives were for wanting to help him, he kind of liked her already.

When they reached the fast food restaurant and took a seat in the back corner, she went to the counter to get their shakes. She wasn't skinny like his mom but rounder like Scott's grandma, though Timmy didn't think she was all that old. It was hard to tell, but he suspected being a grandma automatically made her old. Especially if her grandson was his age.

Sitting twenty feet away, he knew he could bolt if he wanted to. But the lure of the shake was strong, and he let himself feel some optimism that maybe Sarah Chapman might be able to help him find his parents. Besides, if he had a mom coming, he wouldn't run. She stood waiting for the shakes, and that's when he noticed she was talking on a mobile phone.

Oh, crap.

He couldn't make out what she was saying, but he was pretty certain it was about him. She kept casting her gaze his way, as if to remind him she was watching. When the cashier set the two cups in front of her, she hurriedly hung up.

"Here you go!" She slid his chocolate shake across the table, and it was all he could do to control the urge to grab it and suck it down in one brain-freezing slurp. Instead, he took a casual sip on the straw and rolled the glorious ice cream on his tongue. Within minutes, the soothing cream calmed his uneasy stomach.

"So what school do you go to?" It sounded innocent, but his paranoia piqued. Her stare lingered a little long on his scar. He lied, saying Parkway South. If he said Selvidge, she could figure too much out, couldn't she? She followed that with what classes he liked best, did he have a girlfriend, and when he gave a dramatic *ewwww*, she laughed.

They didn't sound like accusing questions, but they made him feel a little uncomfortable. After a few minutes and a half shake, he was letting his guard down. They chatted about Isaac

Bruce and Torey Holt, about the McGwire-Sosa homerun competition, and could Big Mac help them get back to the playoffs. She asked him if he'd gotten a chance to see a game at the Trans World Dome, but he informed her he'd been to two games last year with his dad and brother.

As soon as the admission slipped out, he knew he'd made a mistake.

"So where's your dad and brother now? And your mom?" They were innocent questions, weren't they? And in another world, an easy one to answer.

"I'm not sure," he admitted, and just like that, he was crying. After a month of uncertainty and bad deeds, he couldn't hold it in. He laid his head on the table and the sobs shook him, no matter how hard he tried to swallow them.

"Sweetie, please let me help you. I know something bad has happened, and I can help you. I really can." She reached across the table and patted his shoulder. The touch made him melt, remembering his mom swooping in with as many minutes as he needed. *Minutes...* It was a Weaverism he hadn't thought about since...since he'd stopped being one.

"...and that way we can find out what's going on, how would that be?"

He'd gotten lost in thought and wasn't sure what she'd just said. He wiped his eyes, took a napkin and blew his nose, then took another drink of his shake. When she asked again if he would be willing to do that, he had to look confused.

"My office, it's just two blocks away. Come with me, and we'll sort all this out for you. We'll find someone who can help you. Okay?" Her voice soothed him, even made him more homesick than he thought possible.

"Okay," he mumbled, knowing it could be the worst mistake of his life. But then again, maybe not.

Mrs. Chapman just might be the answer to his prayers. He had no deep ties to Max, grandpa or not. What grandpa let his grandson live on the street, or in an apartment with maggots and roaches?

I don't wanna be homeless.

They finished their shakes and talked a little more about the Rams. She shared where her family's season ticket seats were and she climbed even higher up on his cool-o-meter. By the time he was following her down the street, he almost felt relieved.

He gingerly touched the scar on his cheek, but couldn't get to the agony streaking through his brain. If he could find answers, it would be worth it, right?

"You'll be okay now, Timmy. I promise, we'll take care of you." Sarah Chapman assured him as they walked. She seemed to sense his uncertainty.

He didn't feel okay. But he had let in a glimmer of hope. If he was honest with her, told her enough to find out what happened That Night, she might be able to find his parents. If they were in danger, *really* in danger, wouldn't the cops be able to help?

"Are you hungry?" she asked. "That shake wasn't exactly a meal. I've got some snacks in my office if you are."

"No, I had McDonald's for breakfast," he lied, because that came easier than the truth. But the truth was close. He had tried, so it was a small one. "I have a question," he managed, unsure if he was treading into waters he couldn't swim out of.

"Fire away." They were crossing a parking lot toward a building with Division of Youth Services etched on the front door.

He took a deep, nervous breath. *Here we go.* He was running out of time if he meant to keep escape as an option.

"What if I need help finding my parents because something bad happened, something I...I...don't really remember?" His heart hammered so hard in his chest, it channeled bile in his stomach and up his throat. Panic had his feet twitching.

"Let's just start simple, Timmy. Let's go inside, I'll get you a soda. Do you like root beer or Dr Pepper? That's what my Luke likes. Then we'll see what we can do. How's that sound?" She pushed the right side of the double doors open for him before he could process what was happening. The thought of a Dr Pepper ranked right up there with the shake.

Once they were settled in her warm office, she opened a Dr Pepper and poured it into a small plastic cup for him. The Before life was easy to return to, he found, but then felt a twinge of guilt for abandoning Max so easily.

Mrs. Chapman tapped on a keyboard, staring at her computer monitor, and cut to the chase.

"Let's start with your last name, Timmy, and we'll find some answers, okay?"

Panic zipped through him.

You was bad, 'member what you done to me, you little pissant? The giant goon's hands loomed just out of his grasp. What had he done? What would happen if Sarah Chapman entered his full name and found a police report and had to handcuff him? Did she have handcuffs? Maybe not, but she could contact the police with her computer and he wouldn't even know they were coming. He'd watched *NYPD Blue,* even though his mom didn't like him to. And what if something he said got his parents hurt? They had gone to a lot of trouble to protect him, hadn't they? Even if they were hurt, they had Max come get him so he'd be safe. And he was about to screw that up.

Her hand poised above the keyboard, to possible answers, but to a certain end he wasn't sure he could live with.

"Um, Thomas, my name is Timothy Scott Thomas." The lie came easier than the breakfast fib. And stealing a classmate's last name who slightly resembled him was even easier.

She tapped some keys. "And your date of birth?"

Without skipping a beat, he answered, "October 17, 1988."

A few minutes later, Mrs. Chapman pushed away from her desk and let out a long sigh. "Hmmmm, Timmy Thomas, I'm miffed. Unless the 37-year old who died in 1986 with that name is you, there is no Timmy Thomas your age anywhere in St. Louis. I know you're scared and you're not sure whether to trust me, but I really want to help you. Please...*please*...let me help you, son." She lowered her voice. "Let's find your home, and if that's not possible, let's find you someplace safe you can be."

"I...I, uh, I'd like that," he muttered, trying to be polite. He knew the niceties. His parents had raised him right, had taught him good manners, had even somehow prepared him for desperate situations. He knew how he smelled, how he looked, and what Mrs. Chapman must think of him. It defied his image of himself, the Timmy who had existed Before.

Maybe she really can find my parents. It seemed too good to be true, didn't it? He ached for answers but immediately thought of Max. *I gotta keep you under the radar, kid, it's what I promised your folks...they're in trouble.*

It all felt like a dream, someone else's life. If he talked about his parents or his brother, would he be risking their lives?

"My job's to keep the police from findin' you. That's what your mom asked me to do..." Max's face swam out of focus, nauseating him.

"I don't feel so good," he whispered. "Is there a restroom I can use?" He doubled over a bit, to add to the effect.

"Oh honey, It's just down the hall. Let me show you." She came around the desk and guided him down the hall.

In a few minutes, he stood in front of a mirror, hands on the counter to steady himself. He really didn't feel so hot. He splashed water on his face, cupped his hands and drank a little, then dried both his hands and his face.

What now, Timmy? He emerged from the bathroom trying to decide whether to run or come clean. There didn't seem to be any in between. With a computer, she could disprove any lies.

In an adjoining room, three teenagers sat at a table,

bickering.

"Kiss my ass, Anthony, you don't know shit about shit." A lanky guy about Sam's age shoved his seat away from the table, screeching his chair, and flipping off the guy straight across from him.

"Oh, bite me, Daveon," Anthony snapped and returned the bird.

"It's okay, Timmy. Come back to my office, away from all the hullabaloo." Mrs. Chapman stood outside her office door, gesturing for him to come back to her office.

"Sam, cut that out. Don't tease your brother. You boys and all your hullabaloo, I swear. You weren't raised in a cave. You know better."

His mom's voice boomed loud in his head, a wave of emotion bombarding him. Mrs. Chapman paused, asked him if he was all right, and when he muttered, "No," she walked down the hall toward him.

Then her office phone rang. "C'mon back and let me help you, Timmy. I'll get that, and then we'll see what we can find out, okay?"

As she walked into her office to answer it, Timmy took it as a sign. The minute he heard her answer the phone, he dashed out the last door they'd come through then out the double-doors. His feet hit the grass around the side of the building, and he turned on the jets.

He never looked back.

Dashing across two parking lots, he leaped over a concrete flower garden and sprinted down the street. He pushed past men in suits, women with briefcases, a street vendor holding out a hot dog to a customer.

Free. I'm free. Timmy ran with his face up and arms pumping. His sore legs objected, but he had to make distance fast. He had to dodge a man coming out of a cell phone store and slammed into a blue post office drop box.

"Oh, God," he groaned, holding his injured hip. He limped

across the busy street filled with cars waiting for the light to change. A cab's horn blared as he dashed in front of it.

"Get outta the street, kid!"

Timmy ignored his throbbing hip and took off jogging down foreign streets of St. Louis. By the time his body lodged a full objection and forced him to rest, he knew it had happened.

I'm so lost. But no matter how much that scared him, he knew he'd done the right thing. Nothing good was going to come from Sarah Chapman's office. He didn't know how he knew, he just did. With that certainty came the deeper realization...*Max is all I got.*

Now, he only had to find his way back to Brookline.

Chapter Fourteen

Timmy crawled behind a dumpster in an alley and plopped onto his butt. Middle of the day or not, he was exhausted. Bubbles clenched his stomach, the pain of cramps as close as a finger-snap. His brain untethered, overwhelmed by all that happened in the past forty-eight hours – Cameron, Granville Auction, the panicked exit from the apartment, a pasta meal revolting in Starbuck's, and then Sarah Chapman. A guy could only handle so much.

Close your eyes...it'll go away. Close your eyes...it'll go away... Timmy hugged his knees and buried his face between them.

...go away, go away, go away... *As he drifted, a cell phone in his brain rang.* Mom?

Fleeting images of Before, prior to the storm drain, came in bits and pieces. Cameron reminded Timmy of Sam, and the familiarity added to the thud in his head. His mom's face wafted past his fingertips – *she's pretty...*

As he floated between dreams and the city sounds, he heard Sam, his studly older brother, and Sam was whispering *Timmy*, wasn't he?

"Don't wake up. We're here – in your dreams..." Sam beckoned, lingering somewhere through the fog in his brain. "C'mon..."

***

June – Three Months Earlier

"Hey, Tim, my man. You and your *mouse*keteers can join me and the guys at the swimmin' hole if you want. Won't turn your hair green like that old city pool will." Sam stood broad shouldered in my doorway, his Brett Favre half-jersey a few inches short of his belly button. I envied his stomach muscles, his "six pack," he called them.

"Sure, if the boys wanna. Maybe after the movie. We're catchin' a noon matinee."

"What're you gonna see? Haven't you seen all of them already?" Sam flipped his autographed football, spinning it on one finger like the pros. No matter how much I practiced, I couldn't do it. Sam had been born doing it, because he never went anywhere without a pigskin in his hands. I admired his focus, wondering if I would have it, too. I wasn't quite as athletic, but *give me time,* I'd add. I *had* inherited the same blinding speed. It came in handy when he chased me through the house.

"Um, the new Bruce Willis movie, I think."

"Well, we'll be there around eleven and prob'ly won't leave 'til five or so. Don't be a wuss and wimp out on us."

I grinned. Sam's friends liked us a lot, but what they really wanted was to play chicken with the smaller kids on their shoulders. Every so often, they would launch us, sending us splaying like maniacs through the air screaming our crazy heads off. The older guys liked having groupies, Sam said, and we fit the bill.

Brent and Scott idolized all Sam's friends, so it made me somewhat of the hero link. On only the third day of summer break, life was good. Change meant fifty cents for a Dr Pepper or switching from grimy Levi's to blue-jean shorts. But if the world revolved right, it was the only change we liked. The Musketeers thrived on routine, on living the stories we read in school.

The mission of the day, one I chose every summer to accept, began the same. I didn't bother phoning Brent or Scott – I didn't need to. They each knew their role.

Scott's house stood directly across from mine – 4319 Catalina – while Brent lived a block over from us. My job started by picking up Scott, then we retrieved Brent together. It often took an hour or longer, but the process always ended the same. From there, life knew no bounds. For no other reason than I was the oldest by seventy-five days, six hours, and nineteen minutes, I led our trio.

The Three Amigos, Mom called us. Our teachers affectionately referred to us as the Three Stooges. But we preferred the Three Musketeers. Regardless of Sam's mouseketeer jokes, we took Alexander Dumas' characters to a new level. We had read a shorter version of the book in language arts, and the story hooked us from the first duel. After that, we consumed *Treasure Island, Count of Monte Cristo,* and *Hunchback of Notre Dame.*

I searched for my cleanest dirty jeans hidden in the recesses of my closet. Mom hadn't found the hiding place yet. She didn't understand that I liked them soft and worn but with a little crust to them. Washing took away the ruggedness, so I took drastic measures to avoid it. A tear in the knee christened a pair into denim sainthood. They'd be converted to shorts soon.

I tugged an Aerosmith T-shirt over my bed-head matted hair and feathered my hands through it, amazed at the static electricity making it stand on end. I stared at it in the mirror and licked my fingers to subdue a few strands.

I gave up and prayed for the millionth time that Sam was wrong – this summer it wouldn't turn green. Sam had too many jokes for it, then Mom would tell him to stop. And he would – eventually. Then he would turn his humor on Momma and her smile would span the state of Missouri. Her face and beautiful blonde hair would catch the light and make me dizzy with love for her.

I smiled while I scooped Science Diet into Trevor's food bowl, then filled his water pan. He bounded around the backyard like a goofball after a squirrel who dared invade his territory. Dad's homemade sign hung just over the lab's doghouse.

"No crossing. Squirrels, birds, and rabbits beware." Every "s" was backward, and the sign never failed to crack me up. Dad said he watched Trevor paint it, and no matter how much we mocked him, he never admitted he'd made it.

The lab panted at me, added a feverish wag, canine for hello, and launched in another direction toward sounds only he could hear.

"I'll be back later, Trev. Scare off those nasty ol' squirrels."

Before setting off for the day, I jetted upstairs for movie cash from my cow bank. I hollered bye to Mom and bounded out the front door like it was the first day of the rest of my life. I breathed in the fresh early summer break air then sprinted over Catalina Avenue, through the front yard directly across the street, and rapped my knuckles ruthlessly on the Kruschaven's front door. Scott answered it with a sleepy smile that told me it would be a few minutes before he matched my energy – which neither ever succeeded in doing. Scott's asthma slowed him a little, but Brent and I never held it against him. Scott was too funny to let a small breathing problem hinder his rating on the cool-o-meter.

I plopped onto the Kruschaven's living room sofa, ready for quality cartoonage. But his kid sister trumped my classic roadrunner with some lame talking ponies. Stephie, only seven, couldn't appreciate finer television, so I didn't bother trying to reason with her. She and I didn't see eye-to-eye on much. Gender and her maxing out the snotty-meter hovered between us like Mount St. Helens. Why did a girl three and a half years younger act like Miss Suprema-Donna? I didn't get it, but experience had taught me to steer clear. Her whining wasn't worth it.

"Yo, Scott, hurry up, man. We got an agenda. Chop-chop," I barked down the hall from the couch. No point in over-exerting myself.

"I'm almost ready. You know Brent's still snoozin'. Bonehead never gets enough sleep."

"That boy could sleep till noon if we let him. Heck, I've been up since seven-thirty. I'm still on school time." I twisted so my head hung upside down off the couch, my feet against the wall – I could flip onto the floor if the coffee table hadn't been in my way. Stephie's animated ponies had more giddyup upside down.

I relished the finer points of the morning, only three days into summer. We'd left Woerther Elementary in our wake and now bordered on manhood. Two years until teenagerdom, three months from stomping the halls of middle school. But the glorious feeling that Labor Day seemed centuries away broadened the smile on my face. Sun, swimming, and serious deeds would be had before then.

Stephie zapped the TV off as the show ended and tossed the clicker on the floor in front of me – just below my dangling hair.

"Watch your stupid boy stuff. *I'm* going out to play." Stephie humphed, her declaration so hoity-toity, I wished she'd trip over it. Her *why do boys even bother to live* tone got under my skin worse than an inch-long splinter. She, unlike Sam, wanted nothing to do with her brother or his friends. No one would know we had three years on her – she treated us like miniscule ants she couldn't even bother with stomping on. She had, on occasion, had the nerve to refer to us as immature. *Whatever.*

I grabbed the remote control, pushed myself upright, then flipped one Adidas off at a time. I found an episode of *X-Files* on Sci-Fi, shouted one more time for the bonehead to hurry, all the while aware that Stephie was shaking her head as she tied her shoes. But Fox Mulder gawking at a stream of white light glowing through a window diverted my attention. Mulder and Scully ruled high on my cool-o-meter, reruns included.

Stephie mumbled something about aliens and exited the room like she was storming off stage. She tossed her brown ponytail with a quick jerk of her head, symbolically flipping me off. I laughed but wondered how Scott could have such a cucumber for a sister. *Don't let the door hit you in the ass,* I wanted to call out, but fuel could be ignited both ways.

Twenty minutes later, after Scully zapped a mutating ET and I scarfed a bowl of Cocoa Puffs, Scott and I set off for Brent's house. Scott's speculation about Brent still catching zees would probably be a bull's eye. Half of our summer fun was spent finding creative ways to shock him out of bed.

"Hey, boys, how are you two this morning? You eaten?" Brent's mom let us in and continued offering us food and drinks until we succumbed to a glass of juice.

Sam claimed Mrs. Matthews ranked right up there with her oldest daughter, Morgan, and that both barely nudged out Scott's mom. He insisted that if he had buddies with hot babes lurking in their shorts and t-shirts, he would either move in or install a camera.

I didn't get it and would blurt *yuck,* but Sam said I would soon, adding something about wild horses not being able to tear me away. I just shook my head in disgust. How could having a hot mom be cool? I thought ours held her own, though Mom's homemade cookies didn't hold a candle to Mrs. Matthews *or* Mrs. K's. But wild horses? What did that have to do with anything?

"Is Brent up?" I thought asking couldn't hurt.

"Now what do you think, Timmy?" She nodded toward the stairs. "Help yourselves, boys. But please, don't break anything. Morgan is still in bed, too. And no messes – I mean it." She tossed the kitchen towel over her shoulder, flipped the bacon sizzling in the skillet, checked the biscuits in the oven, and stirred the scrambling eggs. Even though I had eaten, the smells made my glands water.

"Hey, boys. Glad school's out?" Brent's sister shuffled into the kitchen in her Tigger house shoes, hair a little fuzzy, and a shimmery robe wrapped loosely over her pajamas.

"We're great, Morgan, we didn't wake you, did we?" I took

a sip of my juice and wondered if Sam would be as impressed with the seventeen-year old looking like this.

Scott whopped me on the shoulder for answering for the two of us. It was a nasty habit he detested and never missed a chance to hit me for it. He also jumped on any opportunity to interact with Morgan.

Morgan Matthews, the most popular girl at Marquette High School according to Sam, rivaled my brother in God-like status. It wasn't so much her looks, though she was pretty enough. Morgan just had an air about her. She told us once that she intended to blur the barriers between cliques and show everyone how easy it would be to accept people for who they are. I had nodded, and Scott and Brent made some lame comment, but they didn't have any more of a clue than I did. Cliques? We had them in elementary school, but they were as simple as the cool kids and the not-cool kids. But if a not-cool kid was good at something, we'd pick them in a heartbeat. I decided it must be different in middle school. I didn't worry about people accepting me – we were, after all, the three musketeers. What the heck did I care what my classmates thought? I noticed how much people followed us around and tried hard to be our friends, but what for? Didn't they have their own Aramis and Porthos?

Within fifteen minutes, our attempt to make Brent wet the bed failed, but his dash to the bathroom left us rolling on his bedroom floor. Grumbling and changing at the same time, he informed us that our juvenile attempts to disrupt his beauty sleep were childish. Scott and I fell to our knees and begged for his forgiveness. Brent smacked us with his pillow hard enough to knock us both over.

Somewhere in another room, someone shouted, "Scram!"

For a frantic moment, I teetered between the sleeping world and the crappy one I'd woken to in that storm drain.

***

"Scram, kid, no back stage passes for the show tonight." A beefy man with a T-shirt that read *Security* stood holding a door open. The alley shadows had shifted, and late afternoon had ebbed toward sundown.

Timmy scrambled to his feet, too stiff to move with much authority. "I'm goin'," he mumbled.

"Better hurry. There's a band on its way, and their bus is gonna pancake you."

Timmy stared at the guy, everything warbled, muffled by his overlapping worlds. His head still wavered between the Matthews' home and the grimy alley in downtown St. Louis. When the security guy took a step toward him, Timmy understood the body language and hustled out of the alley. He emerged onto the city sidewalk, but nothing seemed familiar. He barely remembered getting there, running from Mrs. Chapman. How far had he gone?

Far enough...

His stomach growled, a *real* growl of hunger, not rejection of a meal. He longed for the half he'd left in that small park before his stomach rejected it.

I got cash.

The desire for normalcy emerged again. Buy some dinner, grab the bus, and get home. Even a crappy alley could pass as a home if it felt safe. He might be homeless but it didn't mean he had to act the part 24-7. Thinking about the only family he had left, the grandpa he never knew he had, Timothy Ryan Weaver set off down the street with his brain swimming.

I was a musketeer. I had a mom, a dad, and a cool big brother. What happened to me?

By the time he made it back to Brookline, it was dark, the Gerries huddled around the burn barrel laughing about stuff Timmy didn't understand, and he prayed they wouldn't interrogate him about his disappearance. Max studied him long and hard, but an enormous grin filled his face when Timmy shoved a McDonald's bag into his chapped hands.

"Where'd you get this?" Max tore open the sack to reveal four small hamburgers and some French fries.

He couldn't tell Max how he sneaked into a downtown McDonald's to clean up in the restroom, then ran away. Or how he landed at DYS, then ran yet again, only to find another Micky D's, marched up to the counter like Before, and ordered himself a quarter pounder with cheese, a small fry, and a giant Dr Pepper. When he had his food and small cheeseburgers for the Gerries, he sat on a bus stop bench and ate like he belonged in the world, not a sidebar or an afterthought.

"I'm cute, remember?" Without another word, Timmy shuffled through the alley to the crate. The Gerries toasted their evening meal, Max taking credit for his boy, while the others moaned around the bites of burger. Ralph licked his fingers, the sandwich already history.

One night sleeping on the hard ground had taken a toll on Timmy, but it was too chilly to fight Ralph for the bucket seats. He crawled into Max's giant crate, overwhelmed with exhaustion – the insanity from the night before, his near imprisonment with Sarah, and the prospect of days without a future.

"That kid's gonna be an asset," Max boasted, and the Gerries grunted agreement around comments about the burger being the best meal they'd had since the buffet.

Timmy listened to them chatter, but he couldn't decipher their words. All he wanted to do was sleep and hopefully conjure Sam, his mom and dad, and his fellow musketeers. Just as he settled in, curling up on his side so he could keep his feet inside the crate, a cold nose touched his cheek. Not daring to move for fear Skippy would run, he waited while the mutt sniffed his face, licked his ear, then curled up behind his legs like he'd adored the kid from day one.

A warmth filled Timmy. No matter how bad things could be, Skippy's attention melted some of the ice that had begun to form around his heart. He let a hand settle on his hip inches from Skippy, and when the terrier's breathing evened, he petted the mutt's scraggily head. Timmy didn't know Skippy's history, but the hesitation to trust, the jaunting off into the night, the me-syndrome – he recognized all the signs.

You and me got a lot in common, Skip.

Part II

A Hundred More of the Same

Chapter Fifteen

Three and a Half Months Later

Timmy sat up trying not to disturb Skippy if he could and rubbed his eyes. He wasn't sure why he tried, because Skippy promptly scampered out of their sleeping bag and into the alley, did his own stretching, and took off for his morning business. No one knew where Skippy went, but Timmy figured the mutt had to have his private time. Or maybe his terrier stud had a girl. Skip would return in half an hour or so, ready to run their routine together. The colder it got, they all noticed, the quicker the mutt returned.

Crawling out from under the covers, Timmy pulled on a tattered sweatshirt he'd gotten from Goodwill and his least holey gloves. The bitter December wind didn't penetrate straight into his box, but he knew that first blast when he crawled out would bite hard. He sat up, peered at the bottle-capped walls of his U-Haul box with pride, and glanced into his tiny cracked mirror. The sores on his mouth had healed a little, but the dark circles under his eyes hadn't diminished at all. He rubbed the gray, wondering if it was dirt. But no, it was months of life in a box that couldn't be erased that easy. Instead of dwelling, he grabbed his Tigger watch from the shoebox table and put it on, then peeled off one of the three pair of socks and replaced them with beat-up hiking boots. He double-checked to make sure his baseball cards were safe and sound in the worn Nike pullover pillow—it was a daily ritual.

"Yo, Tim! Got a coupla cookies for you!" Max shouted.

Timmy crept out into the freezing alley and took several minutes to stretch, stand, and stretch again. His tired joints cracked and popped with every extension of his arms and legs. With sleeping in a box came punishment in the form of aches and pains he once thought only old men got. *I feel old*...Sleeping on concrete, no matter the thickness of the box, cushions, and sleeping bag, took its toll.

The routine started the same every day. Three months, three weeks, and three days of the same routine, repeated like a cruel joke. Timmy replayed scenes from a movie he saw once, a guy who had to relive Groundhog Day over and over again – he wanted to tell the schmuck to stop complaining, at least he woke in a warm bed, even if it was to an annoying song.

"Hey, kid, why don't you score us some grub today. I ain't eaten a good meal in damn near a week. I'm tired of makin' that long walk to one of them kitchens. 'Sides, we been goin' too much anyways. Don't want folks askin' too many questions." Max ran a trembling hand across his gray beard and wrinkly face. His chocolate eyes were so bloodshot, they looked like a fudge sundae with cherries drowning it.

"Sure, Max. I'll see what I can do." Timmy grabbed a cookie from a plastic bag that had clearly spent a few days in the trash. He took a nibble – it tasted a little like cardboard, but he didn't care. By the time they divvied them, he ate four and washed them down with three swallows of bitter coffee.

Mornings had been like this for too long – except for brief reprieves when they landed another abandoned apartment building, once in an old run-down bookstore, and a couple of stints in condemned factories. The bookstore lasted nearly three weeks, but they always returned to Brookline. And no matter where they slept, the schedule was pretty much the same. Morning begging that might or might not pan out, afternoon trash digging and dumpster diving – more so now that it had gotten cold – and long walks to fight the boredom. The only relief was Skippy. Their bond had deepened, especially as Timmy let go of his parents coming back for him. Whatever the plan was for Max to take him in, he understood that this was his life now. At least Skippy made it bearable. They even had a hiding place in the basement of the closest branch of the St. Louis Library during business hours. Timmy would sneak Skippy in through a service entrance, and the two would chill with a book he'd sometimes read out loud to his furry boy. To hang out surrounded by stories of escape, free from the elements, with his best buddy? Both boys, human and canine, couldn't beat that with a stick.

"God, I'm ready for spring," Billy muttered, hobbling over to the burn barrel to warm up. His stint in the county jail, nearly two months, had taken its toll on the caustic bum. Seeing him return had dimmed Timmy's horizon. Billy's sour nature had grown more bitter and his moods had darkened to a permanent charcoal gray. A knife fight with an inmate left him with a stiff limp, and there was more gray flecks in his brown beard. Forty-something looked a heck of a lot older on the asshole than it did on his dad. Timmy knew to steer a little wider and speak a little less around him now that he was back.

"Ah, cold weather's good for you. Cures what ails ya." Cooter hoisted a bourbon bottle. "And a nip of this helps."

Ralph, who had turned sixty-five a few weeks earlier, bitched non-stop about everything, especially the weather. Stunned that he wasn't closer to ninety, Timmy groaned every time the oldest of the Gerries griped about the sub-freezing temps. Vernon added how much harder it was to get a break in the winter.

"Huh-uh," Timmy disagreed with Vernon. "People feel sorry for you during the holidays. I learned that around Thanksgiving. People got more money on 'em, too. They feel more generous."

"Toward you maybe," Max grumbled, kicking at trash around the barrel. "The silly season ain't a walk in the park for some of us, kid. So just shut up for once. Shut. Up."

Timmy snapped his mouth closed. He itched to snap back, but he could tell the old man was hanging in a big way. And he knew when *shut up* meant to shut up.

"Kid, you're just wantin' your freakin' Dr Pepper," Cooter teased. "Christmas is still at least a week away, you know."

Timmy gave a nervous laugh, keeping a close eye on Max. The soda had become his treat on special occasions. Rams home opener, Columbus Day, Halloween, Thanksgiving, and two weeks ago, they celebrated Hanukkah, since it fell early in the month. A taste from his past, something he used to take for granted. Back then change, a piddly fifty cents, bought an ice cold Dr Pepper. Now nothing ever changed except the weather and the begging route.

"Okay, you boys are bummin' me out. Me and Skippy are headin' for the hills. You guys stay outta trouble. You ready, Skip?" Timmy didn't bother studying their reaction to his casual attitude. He didn't care anymore, unless it meant a run-in with Billy. Otherwise, he'd gotten to the point where negativity got him down and he didn't need any help.

After racing off into the morning for whatever business he had to take care of, the terrier was front and center when it mattered. Timmy mapped out various legs of their begging route, each ending at the Arch. The two would eat whatever they managed to scavenge and then lay in the luxurious grasses of Riverfront Park before the leaves and now the snow swallowed them. It meant hours "on the road," as he described it to Max, but it wasn't like he had other pressing appointments. No school bus, no homework, no deadlines.

As they headed off down the street, Timmy called back, "Don't do anything I wouldn't do!" The Gerries laughed, always tickled by the kid's quick tongue – all but Billy.

"Don't forget to get me somethin' to eat!" Max shouted, as Timmy and Skippy trudged down Brookline. "And don't be too late. You need to be back by early evening, got it? I mean it!"

"Yeah!" he shouted and then whispered, "Skippy, do I look like a waiter?"

The terrier smiled with a wag but failed to answer – the mutt sat on the fence and refused to choose sides between his boy and the old man. Max was still Skippy's daddy. But for three and half months, the dog slept with his boy. That had to count for something. Timmy stomped in a mud puddle to see how high he could get the splash. Clear to the inside of his knees, nearly a record.

"See that, Skip?" He grinned at the terrier. "What? Not good enough for you? Well, let's see you do better."

Skippy yapped and turned a quick circle. His tail wagged ninety miles a minute.

"That's it, it's finally happened. You've lost your marbles," he said and ruffled Skippy's head, ears, and scruff.

Skippy barked, even if it sounded like a yap, Timmy knew the mutt wanted more. But the two had places to go. This wasn't the stuff of Norman Rockwell paintings or most kids' lives. Then again, most of them sat trapped at a desk or in some stuffy, over-heated classroom on a day like today. Skippy gave him a lick on the nose, and the two set off to prospect.

Probably some cheesy countdown 'til Christmas on the chalkboard.

Timmy didn't subscribe to all that sentimental crap. That was for babies, and he vowed to do all he could to avoid it. In the back of his mind he wrote a new "note-to-self"—*find out how many days it really is until Christmas.* He guessed about twelve, but they tended to blur.

It wasn't to say that if Timmy had his druthers he wouldn't opt for a desk-chair in some overcrowded classroom. He might even trade this day that he had relived over a hundred times for a boring lecture or even a pop quiz. He remembered taking tests and doing homework.

I used to forget my lunch money.

Days behind a desk learning the state capitals or practicing equations seemed like centuries ago. His past teased him like a steaming cup of cocoa through a diner's window.

If I were there right now, I wouldn't care if a teacher called on me for an answer I didn't know. I'd tell her to teach me, that's what the heck we're here for. I'm a paper towel eager to soak up your knowledge, I'd tell her.

Okay, he had to admit he might not say exactly those words, but the idea of sitting in a warm room with other kids leading a normal life? Wow. A concept so off-kilter it didn't even fit in his brain anymore. Almost four months ago when he had washed up here, that wasn't the case. Timmy would have jumped through rings of fire only to land on broken glass barefooted just to go back to the chores of Before.

He shoved his misshapen blond bangs away from his eyes. The golden hair had lost its luster, like a bright leaf gone crisp and brown. The dull, brittle locks stayed stiff where he pushed them. Cradle cap threatened to set in again if he didn't find a friendly restroom and a bar of soap. It had been weeks since he had washed it and longer since Max used the knife to trim it.

He used to prioritize better. Cleaning ranked right up there with food. But that changed about two months ago. Cleanliness only played a role if begging proved unfruitful. Sometimes being too spotless or too dirty affected the odds – it was a delicate balance. And now that he was street-roughened, as Cooter put it, he had lost the round features, and people treated him differently. Even the dimples had shallowed.

Timmy kicked absent-mindedly at a Snicker's wrapper as he walked the streets he hated but thought of as home. Skippy picked it up and tossed it playfully in the air.

"Hey, kid, wanna accept Jesus Christ into your life? He's our savior and He will help you with all your problems. God gave His only begotten son so that you and I could live in peace, comfort, and tranquility. To perpetuate the spirit and goodwill of mankind. Wanna buy one?" A street vendor, unshaven and as grimy as Timmy, shoved a pamphlet at the kid.

"He's the answer to all your problems, son," the hustler repeated. Something in the guy's voice made Timmy look up. The man stood well over six-feet two or three, at least a foot taller than him, but it wasn't just the height that caught Timmy's eye. The swindler's expression made him shiver. Max had warned him never to make eye contact with street people he didn't know, to steer clear. Hustlers and prostitutes were the most desperate of all.

Save me and **all** my problems? How the hell's He gonna do that? *He blistered the man with a glare so savage, the prophet jerked the flyer back.*

"Then fuck off, kid, and stay outta my scene."

Timmy watched the hustler hassle an old lady who swung her purse at him.

"So much for the spirit and good will of mankind, huh?" Timmy sneered, but the pamphlet-pusher had scored with a handout from a woman bogged down with shopping bags.

His stomach growled, and he knew he had to make good this morning. He hadn't eaten anything but a few cookies in nearly twenty-four hours, and he couldn't handle another day on an empty stomach. A week earlier, he had been forced to eat at soup kitchens three different times, so he had to stay away. The volunteers had asked more and more questions over the course of three and a half months, and Max worried they might connect him to Baldy or the night that landed him here in the first place. But Max assured them that the alternatives were scary. He made up a story about an abusive father who would ultimately get Timmy back if the boy landed in foster care, and most of the compassionate people who worked the charity centers believed them. They'd grown fond of Timmy. They couldn't bear to think of him getting beaten. They remembered what he looked like when they first met him. The jagged scar on his cheek was an ugly reminder.

"Skippy, I'm hungry, how 'bout you?" At the mention of the "H" word, Skippy jumped high enough to lick Timmy's nose, but his aim was off. "Ah, man, Skip, you got my eye, you big goof!"

Skippy wagged so hard he walked sideways. He barked in high-pitched yips that made people turn and smile at him. *Even if I've lost my little boy looks, Skippy hasn't.*

"Hey, I know. We haven't visited Frankie's in a while.

How's that sound?"

Skippy let out a round of yaps that Timmy took for a yes. So, the two set off for Cramer Street, a long walk but worth it for some of Frankie's pasta. Nothing felt better or more filling on an empty stomach than a calm plate of spaghetti and meatballs. As they set off on their mission, Timmy spied a Barq's Diet Root Beer bottle cap laying in a gutter.

"Hey, Skip! Look!" he yelled. He had been searching for that one for over a month. His bottle cap collection was one of the finest in the city, he bet. And his display was the rave of Brookline. So was his box for that matter.

He hadn't spent the past months doing nothing. A boy with an imagination had to focus on something, and his obsession had become bottle caps. At first, he kept them to play with, like a solitary game of concentration. Then he realized the variety and sheer volume of caps that existed. At one point, he told Max he planned to find every bottle cap that ever existed. Now he had two and a half walls of his box covered with hundreds of them.

"Damn. That's so cool." Timmy carefully slid the cap in the one back pocket that didn't have a rip in it. Salvation Army jeans were hard to find without holes in the pockets.

Three hours later, he and Skippy sat behind an enormous trash barrel eating a small plate of fettuccini alfredo and a piece of garlic bread.

"Man, that's good, ain't it, Skip?" He licked his fingers and gave his terrier another bite. For a hungry dog, he sat patiently waiting his turn, but the wiggling tail made him look like a vibrating stuffed animal.

The two sat back, enjoyed each other's company, and curled up for a short nap. Nothing felt better than to sleep with a full stomach. It reminded Timmy of camping trips he had taken with his dad and Sam.

He smiled as he drifted to sleep, feeling content with Skippy as a blanket.

Chapter Sixteen

May 1998

"Hey, Timmy, you got the strap buckled?"

"I got it, Dad! You might check it to make sure it's tight enough though." I examined my work and oozed with pride that I had been strong enough to get the clamp to close. It was the first time Dad had ever *really let* me load the CR-V for a trip. He and Sam usually did all the big stuff, while I carried the bags from the house that Mom had packed.

"Well, men, looks like we're ready. Tori, you sure you don't wanna join us?" Dad's grin told both of us he had no intention of talking Mom into coming. It was an impossibility anyway. His wink sealed it. We understood that he had to at least try.

"When God provides electricity in the wilderness, I'll be happy to come along." She returned his wink.

We all giggled at her classic response. None of us wanted to burst her bubble that we had an electric generator or that there was such a thing as electric campsites, though we didn't go to such wimpy spots. We roughed it in the wild, like real men.

Mom stood with her arms crossed loosely across her chest. *Don't disappoint us, Mom. C'mon....*

"You know, if God meant for me to sleep on the ground, He wouldn't have invented waterbeds."

We all three applauded and ceremoniously hemmed and hawed at how much we would miss her. Truth was, we really would. She told us how much she would miss us, though we knew she couldn't wait to have the house to herself. Her book already sat on the edge of the couch alongside a fresh Diet Coke in her famous can coolie that read *I'll save the planet tomorrow.* She probably wouldn't even turn on the TV.

I couldn't comprehend it. Life in the woods called for music—batteries or electric generators. And at home, TV provided much-needed electrical energy, even if I wasn't watching it. Why in the world did Mom like silence so much?

"Love you, Honey," Dad called to her, and she hooked her finger at him telling him to get his buns over there. Her blonde hair blew gently around her face like slow, rolling waves. I loved how she brushed it back with her hands, and it was always beautiful. Her soft features only seemed more beautiful framed by her golden hair. Dad, on the other hand, already had wisps of gray sprouting at his temples. It didn't help that his light brown hair left them exposed. He had tried a beard once or twice, but Mom said they made him look like a convict.

"You're not going anywhere, Mister, not without at least two minutes." She held up two fingers and flashed a wicked grin.

Needing minutes was an expression we had used since before I could remember. An early memory surfaced, of me falling off my big wheel and racing in to show Mom my cut knees. Blood dripped down my shin, and clear as day I recall whimpering that I needed at least six minutes. It was easier to ask for attention, for cuddling and some serious TLC if all you had to say was how many minutes of it you wanted or needed.

"Take care of the boys, don't go doing anything stupid, and remember to play the adult," she teased Dad. Then she kissed his neck too many times to watch.

Sam and I turned away, gagging at their display of affection. My brother held me in his arms and pretended to kiss me, professed his undying love and misery at the prospect of being away from the woman he loved for three agonizing days. Mom and Dad laughed at us and then gave each other one last kiss. My friends said I was lucky my parents loved each other because many of theirs had divorced. I just wished they could love each other a little less in public.

"Okay, Casanova, let's make like a tree and leave," Sam

ordered. Only he could say such a thing – and it worked. Nearly three hours later, we reached Eminence, the Current River drawing us like a magnet. By the time we reached the campground, Dad was delegating.

"You boys as hungry as I am?" Dad maneuvered the SUV around various spots, and the three of us analyzed them and the woods beyond. What we really wanted was to migrate deep into the forest, skip the sissy plots. "Sam, you and me have a date with the tent. Timmy, you know your job."

Sam and I responded simultaneously, "Firewood!" We giggled, but we knew the truth – camping was an art form – finding the perfect campsite and building kick butt campfires. But sundown smothered us like a heavy comforter by the time we unloaded the coolers and equipment.

"Okay, Sam, you and I are hookin' it up. Tent—twelve o'clock." Dad pointed at a spot dead ahead. "Tim, you best get crackin'. The darker it gets, the harder it'll be to find. Without it, we go hungry."

I swelled with pride. *Tim*, he had said. Not Timmy, but Tim. And the responsibility of dinner wouldn't be lost on me. Sam and I obsessed over finding wood. For days after a camping trip, we would notice any little twigs and proclaim, "Kindling!"

In less than thirty minutes, I had enough wood to outfit every fire we would need for twice the number of days we were staying. I discovered a deadfall only yards from our site, but I didn't tell them that. Let them think I had labored like a fiend.

The fire we built lit the moonless sky so completely, Dad joked that Hillary could've caught Bill sneaking off for a rendezvous clear down in Arkansas. Sam and I laughed like buffoons at that one. Three hours later, we slept with the night sounds serenading us. The chirrups of crickets and other critters Missourians took for granted chased me into the most worry-free sleep, the kind only ten-year olds on a camping trip know. Rattling trash bags didn't even compute in my deep slumber.

I finally woke when something kuh-thumped off the picnic table only inches from my head. Startled and suddenly one hundred percent certain a massive bear intended to eat me in one chomp, I nearly yanked Sam's shoulder off.

"What the heck? Lemme go," he demanded through a fog of sleep.

"Sam, there's somethin' out there!"

"What is it?" He peeked through the mesh window. "I don't see nothin'. What'd you see, Timmy?"

I could hear an odd lilt in his voice, and it took me a moment to identify it. Fear. A sensation clawed into my belly and clenched my privates. I heard rustling leaves, cans from our trash clattered and shifted in the garbage bag. Something clanked on the picnic table again.

"What is it, Sam? Maybe we should wake up Dad."

"I bet it's a bear. You wake him, quick." Sam sounded like my bossy teenaged brother again. "C'mon, Timmy, do it!" He shoved me toward Dad, then thumped me on the arm.

"Huh-uh, you wake him up."

"Whatsup, boys?"

"Dad, there's a bear out there!" Sam blurted.

"There're no bears 'round here, Sambo. Let me have a look." Dad unzipped the tent door, peered out into the noisy night and laughed.

"Coons," he proclaimed. "Three of 'em, look." He pointed to the trash, and Sam and I watched three bandit-faced raccoons drag scraps out of the garbage sack and pick through our gear on the picnic table. One of the larger ones scored the remaining chunk of my burger. I had gotten so full I was sure my stomach would pop, but I had forgotten to wrap it up and put it in the cooler.

The coons stiffened when they saw us watching. They scampered a few feet into the trees to wait us out. Campers provided a mighty service, Dad said, and then told us the opportunists wouldn't hurt us as long as we left them alone. His simple declaration made us feel better. He slipped back into his sleeping bag to leave Sam and me staring into the dark.

"It's okay, Timmy," Sam tried to soothe. His voice didn't have the conviction of Dad's.

We finally laid back down, but I remained awake for what felt like hours straining to hear the slightest rustle. I was on coon patrol, and my nerves twitched with every tiny sound.

"I hear 'em again, don't you?" I listened intently. Sam didn't answer, and the shear idea that he was asleep made me anxious. Just when I thought the jitters would consume me, I drifted off. I never succeeded in fighting off sleep. Not even at sleepovers with Brent and Scott.

A soft bed, a pillow, and opportunity were all I needed.

***

Timmy jerked awake when something rattled a bag behind him. Skippy jumped up and let the intruder have it. A starving cat meowed weakly.

"Oh, God, Momma," Timmy moaned. "I need a thousand minutes." A sob hitched in his throat, the dream memories weakening his resolve. If he could control them, he would shut the power off. But deep down, he liked the sleep visits – it was the only time he felt like Timothy Ryan Weaver, and the only chance he had to really remember his past. The rest of the time, he was Timmy the Homeless, like some Viking warrior searching for his homeland.

"Go away, stupid cat," he snipped. The cat hissed back. He recoiled and then saw the outline of every rib. His anger dissipated, the bitterness at his evasive life melted as the tabby kitten sniffed for any crumb it could scrounge.

"Sorry, kitty, here you go." Timmy rummaged through remnants from his Italian meal. The small yellow cat was too scared to come close enough to be petted but snatched the crust of garlic toast Timmy tossed it. "Hey, kitty. Here's an apple core I found." He pushed it close to the kitten, who tugged it by the stem and started nibbling. Skippy stayed back, understanding fear when he smelled it.

"We better get back, Skip. It's gettin' late. Look at those shadows." He had lost track of time again, a dangerous habit that was recurring more and more often now that it got dark early. Dreaming took him back to Before – it beat the heck out of his day-to-day routine, so he did it as often as possible. But now he knew they would have to hoof it to get back before Max blew his top.

When they made their way to Brookline, he was out of breath and numb from head to toe. Decembers in St. Louis had gotten colder and colder.

"Where the hell you been, kid?" Max staggered the boy's way and patted him roughly on the head. The gesture always made Timmy feel like a Golden Retriever puppy, but he knew it was Max's way of showing affection. He gripped the boy by the back of the neck and whispered, spraying alcohol on Timmy, "When I tell you to be back, you be back, got it? And I guess you didn't get me nothin' to eat?"

"Sorry, Max. Skippy and I struck out today. Found some crusts in a trash bin, but we ate them. And by the way, I'm fine, thanks for askin'." He jerked away, freeing himself from the drunk's grasp. Timmy recapped an abbreviated version of his day, and then disappeared into his box. He wasn't as much exhausted as frustrated with his grandpa, and a little hungry, an all-too familiar combination. The pasta provided plenty of energy to make the long trek back, but small portions didn't go as far as they used to. His growing body had increased its demands, not that Max cared. The old man's worries centered around booze and manipulating Timmy to feed him.

That's all I am to him.... An angry voice hissed that even if his parents had gotten in trouble or had to leave the country, like Max insisted, why'd the guy treat him like a gopher?

Grandfathers were supposed to be nice, right?

He crawled under the army blanket without changing into his sweats. The sprint home had worn him out, but at least the rumbling in the pit of his stomach was only a fraction of most days' emptiness. Timmy hoped the exercise, pasta, and wedging the brand new Diet Barq's cap into the left wall of his box would lead to a full night's rest. Night sleep, now an evasive ghost, found him within an hour of the usual rituals. His nightly ceremony didn't consist of sheep but an inventory of his bottle caps. Three entire walls of his cardboard bedroom sported various tops to sodas, beer, malt beverages, and anything else with a pop-off or screw-off top. The pronged kind stuck the easiest, but smooth-edged ones did fine with a little help from his swiped bottle of Crazy Glue.

Even in the pitch black, Timmy could picture them, staring hard to adjust his night eyes but seeing was mostly mental. He'd start with his right-hand wall, go across the top, and do the left wall if he was still awake. He found the longer he lived on the streets, the more caps he found. The more caps he found, the more he needed to count in search of sleep. And the more he had to have them, the scarier it got that he might run out of space. What then? But on this night, a one-wall inventory was all Timmy needed.

A cramping calf wouldn't wake him again for hours, sometime in the middle of the night. He gripped the seizing muscle, rubbed it savagely, then counted tops in hopes of drifting back into the safe haven of sleep. It was a vicious cycle.

Flashes of caps he had seen in convenience store coolers punctuated his light sleep. A lavender Grape Crush bottle top was number one on his Wish List.

He tried to turn his head as it rested on his left arm, but a stiffening cramp limited any movement. A sliver of concrete had edged its way beneath his box and now blossomed into a boulder-sized pressure under his left shoulder, even through the thin sleeping bag.

Hadn't I just been dreaming about something wonderful?

He couldn't remember, because the memory had slipped away like a flimsy fog. The sensation in his arm and shoulder prickled the numbness like dotting an *i* with an ice pick. He knew he needed to get up to shake off the tingling shots of needles that came with every muscle contraction.

I gotta move my dang box and sweep the rocks out from under it.

Slowly, Timmy rolled onto his back and shimmied out of his protective cardboard cover. He made another note to self: *put more shellac on my box*. Once it got cold, he had to spray the cardboard at least twice to enhance its durability. Max had taught him that from the very beginning – the important aspects of education, no division mumbo-jumbo. The biggest stressor was swiping the shellac.

He crawled to the opposite alley wall and sat against the brick building. Spurts of tingly pain pulsated down his arm, and an annoying all-day cramp began throbbing at the base of his neck.

Welcome to my world. Timmy stared at the alley filled with boxes, his "neighborhood." He heard Vernon cough, a nasty, fluid-filled sound. Behind him, Billy snored loud enough to occasionally wake Skippy. Their U-Haul box sat in a primo spot, and he knew Cooter and Billy resented him like hell for it. *Screw them – they've used me for food for months.*

Somewhere down the row, a grumbling sleep-talker moaned about Rhonda and how she should take it all off.

"No, give me more. Yeah, that's it," the slurring voice purred.

Timmy wondered for the millionth time what sweet nothings he muttered in his sleep. He shut the door on that thought and stared straight up at the starry sky. The night and all its wonders made his problems seem small. The buildings limited his view, but he could cup his hands around his face and pretend he was camping in some remote forest. He gazed longingly at the faraway wonders of space. Orion's Belt twinkled innocently at him.

He had seen the constellation for the first time when he was eight. The fleeting memory of his mom winking at him merged with it. The lost time wafted through him like a whiff of pancakes cooking, a smell so delicious that yearning for them made him ache. A rare smile slipped across his mouth before he could discourage it. Skippy nosed at his boy's hand, trying to coax him to come back to their box, but he needed air.

"Go ahead, Skip – it's okay. Go to bed."

Skippy hesitated, but barely able to keep his eyes open, he pushed through the plastic wind-blocking strips, and crawled into their box bedroom.

Timmy leaned against the brick of the east building and admired their U-Haul condo – he had walked over an hour to bring it home, his arms so tired he had to rest it on his head. The Gerries had drooled, and at one point, Max demanded they share it. No one had an intact refrigerator box, and how could the old man allow his boy to have a better box than anyone, even him? But Timmy argued that his already growing bottle cap collection needed a box that big to display it.

I had just turned eleven and a half... With sleep overtaking him, he remembered that day two months earlier. In mid-October, he wandered every day in search of food with heavy doses of adventure. He ended up miles away from the warehouse where they were squatting, in a small housing development off Slater Road. That's when he saw it. An enormous U-Haul box perched pretty as you please on a curb next to a jillion other smaller ones. The moving truck was backed into a steep driveway, and a young couple traipsed in and out of it, pulling box after box out. They danced into the house like they thought it was heaven or something. Timmy didn't get it. The house was tiny and needed a paint job, but the young couple and their small son acted like it was a castle.

I'd take it now, wouldn't I?

It was two weeks before Halloween, and Max had surprised him with a beat-up Swiss Army knife. It made him feel like a man, and he would manage to keep it for over a month. The switchblade, though important enough to keep close, didn't get used for day-to-day activities. It was a weapon, not a tool.

Timmy wasn't too scraggly yet. Most of his injuries from Baldy and That Night had healed, and his hair still got shiny when he cleaned up. The gaunt face and sunken eyes came some time in late November. A volunteer at a shelter said it was malnourishment, and chastised Max for not bringing his grandson around more.

That Fall afternoon before Halloween, he and Skippy had been out for a hike, enjoying the Indian Summer. Timmy kicked a can, with Skippy yapping at his heels. When he whiffed, he turned to look down a street he was about to pass. That's when he saw it – a box so perfect, it must have held a double-wide refrigerator. Timmy pictured it serving as a fort, a playhouse, or even a racecar. But he also knew they were days from ending up back in the alley.

So, he scouted the people, coming in and out of the house, in and out of the truck. It would be the envy of everyone in a cardboard condo complex. He'd never had to sleep under a burlap sack with no box, no protection, no anything. Max had always shared, but now, Timmy would be taking care of himself. He studied the family coming and going, like a shifting tide, each time carrying boxes, lamps, and small pieces of furniture.

Eight or ten empties sat by the curb. He couldn't read the scrawled words from where he stood, but he guessed each was labeled with former contents. Most of them were wardrobe-sized or smaller, but Timmy eyed the one he wanted, speculating that even on its side he could stand on his knees and not hit his head. He got so excited just thinking about it that he practically danced down the street. He considered just prancing right up and asking for it but didn't want to frighten the family into calling the cops.

So instead he stood like a zombie watching the new homeowners when suddenly a shrimp of a boy, five or six years old, came be-bopping out the front door yanking an Orioles cap onto his head.

Better get with the program and switch birds, kid.

Both shoelaces flew behind his feet like loose threads, but Timmy couldn't concentrate on that. What held his gaze was the boy's face. The little twerp had some kind of chocolate mess smeared from ear-to-ear and forehead to chin. The rug rat proceeded to march straight down to the road's edge and push over the box like it was nobody's business.

"Shit," he muttered. "Get outta my box, butthead."

Chocolate Boy started batting around inside the cardboard walls like he owned it or something. He could walk into it as it lay on its side. Timmy frothed at the mouth for that box, but he wanted it in tip-top shape.

"Man, kid, cut that out." His clenched his fists in apprehension.

His calculations figured at least three of him could lay side-by-side and could kneel and have a foot to spare. With as deep as it was, he would also be able to block out much of the cold with the burlap sack he used for can collecting.

"C'mon, Timmy. Life is short." Before he could lose his nerve, he marched toward the house like he was a soldier ready to storm into battle. He timed his pauses, hesitating strategically until the mom and dad disappeared into the house. The little chocolate shit kept jumping up and down and was now rolling around inside of it causing creases that would never stiffen again.

"Jesus, kid, go take your Ritalin." The Three Musketeers had a classmate at Woerther who took Ritalin twice a day and bragged continually about it. Timmy had never seen a kid with so much uncontrolled energy – until today.

The midget launched himself to and fro, and Timmy suspected Mom and Dad sent their son out to play just to have him out of the way.

"Timing is everything." He stopped two houses shy of his target. Shorty emerged, smiling like a dope, and ran around the yard like he was tethered to a pole. "Get dizzy and pass out, runtface."

Just as the parents carried a cedar chest in the door, Timmy made his move. With a quick dash while Midget Man spun his circles, Timmy raced for that box with the dexterity of a cat. Sleeping on benches and hard floors hadn't taken a toll on his joints yet, so he was still as spry as a jack-rabbit. The distance narrowed and just as he grabbed the flap, Midget Man shouted at him, scared the dickens out of him just from sheer surprise. Timmy froze, a thief caught with his hand in the till.

"Hey, that's my box," the little boy yelled, and stomped a foot in objection.

Timmy glanced at the front door and saw the coast was still clear from the parents.

"Not anymore, shithead." He grunted, pivoted, and raced back down Kennett Street with the finest box ever to grace the planet.

"I'm tellin' my mommy and daddy on you!" The kid screamed but was playing with another one by the time Timmy turned the corner. Timmy suspected when Chocolate Boy's parents emerged, he would share how some big kid stole their box. He might even tell them about the bad name.

Mr. and Mrs. We-Just-Moved-Into-Our-First-House would wonder for a few fleeting moments if they had chosen a rough neighborhood in a city already known for its crime. They would coddle their spoiled brat, take him back inside, and smother him for a few weeks before figuring out the incident wasn't the norm.

Who was Timmy to blame them for such thoughts?

I was scared of people like me when I was him, too.

Chapter Seventeen

Déjà vu swept over Timmy like a scratchy camping blanket. Hadn't someone just winked at him? But then a memory of box-hunting overlapped it.

Sam's voice echoed from somewhere in the distance. He sounded wounded, like a rabbit howling from the jowls of a hungry dog.

"Sam?" Timmy called uncertainly down Catalina Avenue.

"Hey, kid, wanna know what I done to him? You seen it before, 'member?" The grimacing smile of Muscle Man sent Timmy's groin coiling into his stomach.

"What did you do to my brother? You better not hurt Sam!" The same trembling tone brought back a dream he'd had about a bike, but it drifted past his fingertips like a long ball he couldn't quite bring in.

"That his name? Cute kid. Shame he ain't no more. But I reckon beauty's in the eye of the beholder, huh?" A squealing cackle sent goose pimples racing up and down Timmy's arms and legs.

The muscle-bound goon stood on the front porch of a strangely familiar house, though Timmy seemed to know that it didn't belong to the giant. But who was he to point out such a detail?

"Please, mister, I – I –" He what? Timmy didn't know what he wanted to ask the WWF wannabe. Directions to Taco Bell? A buck to buy a Heath Blizzard? And who could think with all the rippling tattoos wiggling all over his body? The woman across the right side of his chest clad in a skimpy red dress danced as the man flexed and released for intimidation.

Timmy's eyes locked on one that covered the entire left upper arm – an expertly detailed heart pierced by a fancy dagger. Greenery laced around the handle and snaked across the heart itself. Its beauty was challenged only by its eeriness. It brought fleeting images of shouting, gunfire, and funny smells he couldn't quite place. Hadn't he seen that before?

"I'm lost." But he understood that he and Sam had been here before. His brain shut out that thought quickly, like a protective shield blocking laser beams from a Klingon warrior.

As the leaning tower of muscle stood upright and ambled down the steps, Timmy stood his ground thinking if Sam withstood whatever this dickhead dealt, so could he.

"Brave little shit, ain'tcha?"

Timmy knew that wasn't really a question. He remembered his mom telling him some word that meant when you asked a question, you didn't really want an answer. He didn't have the time or energy to retrieve that little tidbit. Why did he remember that shit anyway?

Hands the size of Texas reached for him. It all seemed strangely repetitive.

"Make like cloth and bolt," he could hear Sam's voice tell him clear as day—all the Samisms of Before.

"C'mon, Timmy, come see what I done—"

The space between them grew smaller and smaller.

"I don't wanna," he admitted in a voice so small he wasn't sure he'd said it. How did Muscle Man know his name?

"Cuz you told me, 'member? I seen ya lots of times when your eyes closed. Ain't no hotshit richie no more, is ya?"

Had Muscle Man just read his mind? Timmy hadn't said anything out loud about his name. Had he? Suddenly nothing seemed to make sense, except the certainty that this thing wanted to kill him. And somewhere in the back of his mind, he knew why.

"C'mere, Timmy. Let me take back whatcha took. 'Member that, you little pissant? See this?" The thug pointed to his face, a bloody mess of shattered bone and tissue.

Timmy gasped. He did remember, sort of.

"I did that."

"You got it, you little shit." The smell from the pores closing in on him finally freed his frozen feet. Sulfur burned his nostrils. Just as the massive palms closed on the last twenty inches, Timmy's panic spurred him into flight. The hands, once again, hovered in midair with nothing to grasp but lost opportunities.

The beast wouldn't let Timmy get off so easily next time. Shivering in his sleep, a voice reached for him.

***

"What're you doin', kid?" A gravelly voice yanked him awake. A hand touched his shoulder and Timmy nearly jumped out of his skin. He couldn't remember why he was outside his box, sitting against the building.

"Huh?" Timmy stared blurry-eyed at Max, wondering how the heck he had confused some hulking monster with this decrepit, wind-burned man. The calloused hands, pale and gnarled with arthritis, patted his face. Max stared down at him, confused but worried. His grandpa loved telling Timmy stories, a few about his mom, and as vague as they were, it somehow helped to talk about her. But the stories he loved most were about Max's ex-wife, Taneisha, and their son Drey. These felt like old movies, detailed and real. It made him sad to know Max had a family out there somewhere who didn't want him anymore. *Me, too, Max, me too.*

"Wake up, Timmy, you're havin' another goddamned nightmare. You're gonna wake the dead if you don't shut yer trap." Max knelt beside the boy who had fallen asleep sitting against the east wall staring at the stars.

Gee thanks, Max.... But at least the nightmare had evaporated with the rude interruption. Dawn breaking made it all seem stupid and silly.

"You was holdin' your arms out like someone was tryin' to

getcha." Max belched. "Did he?"

Timmy shrunk from the old man's breath, rancid enough to wake the dead. "Did he what?" He leaned forward, and Max draped a camping blanket around his shoulders.

"Getcha. You know, they say in your dreams that if somethin' bad happens, like you fall and hit the floor, you die. So if the bad guy gets ya, then do you wake up?"

Good ol' Max. Always blunt, seldom sensitive. He didn't console as much as inform. If his grandpa told Timmy not to be sick, scared, or a nuisance, he did his damnedest to oblige. He knew Max didn't want to be bothered with a stupid kid, no matter what benefits having him around offered. And there were a lot of them, Timmy had discovered over the past three and a half months.

"Get dressed, Timmy," Max ordered. "Better yet, why don'tcha catch a little more sleep so you don't look like hell today. I want somethin' to eat for lunch and you need to look a tad fresher if yer gonna score. You're losin' yer baby fat or yer losin' yer touch. It better not be that."

Timmy stared at the old man like he had an alien on his shoulder. But Timmy obeyed, not so much out of respect but the desire to shake the creepy feeling he had woken with.

"Fine." He crawled into his box and pulled the scratchy blanket all the way over his head. *I hate you sometimes, Max – I wish you'd find a new servant.*

He closed his eyes and concentrated on brighter days, more glorious mornings. His mind wandered to a golden afternoon in the last June worth remembering, and he drifted to sleep. Once there, he rediscovered the first day of his last summer break when his deepest thoughts were of the coolest ways to launch Brent out of bed every day.

***

June—Six Months Earlier

The first acts of summer always meant role-playing, because we were, after all, the Three Musketeers. And we were eleven.

When many of our friends talked big about the three-month break, they seldom walked the walk. But not the three of us. Our imaginations ran rampant and spawned creative days filled with baseball, swimming pools, and awe-inspiring antics. Sword fights, bull-fighting, and all-out battles to save the throne.

"Wanna soda?" I suggested, cocking an eyebrow mischievously. Wicked grins of understanding spread across the faces of my two best friends.

"I, Athos, agree that a beverage would be quite refreshing." Brent's accent wouldn't win him any Broadway roles, but it kicked ass as far as we were concerned.

"Ah, but young Athos, where would you be without your matey Aramis? Might I join you in this thirst-quenching quest?" Scott held his arm across his chest as if clutching the corner of a cape in front of him.

Both studied me for my own proclamation. Brent fidgeted, hoping I would conform. But in light of my choices, how could I be a follower when offered the opportunity to lead?

"But what would an adventure be—" I spoke in my finest accent, an Italian-English drawl that would have made Alexander Dumas cringe, "without the accompaniment of young D'Artagnan?"

Brent groaned. He hated when I chose the fourth musketeer rather than Porthos. I thought the name sounded like a Johnny-on-the-Spot and lacked style. With a character like D'Artagnan, who wouldn't want to be him? Dumas had far surpassed himself with that name – even though I was shocked when I saw how it was spelled.

The moment Mrs. Evans read of their wild adventures, our

classmates agreed that Dumas must have been psychic. He must have known Brent, Scott, and me in a former life. We had subsequently rented every version of the movie we could get our hands on and acted out all the scenes, much to our parents' chagrin. At first, they all thought *How cute. Oh, honey, look at the boys, aren't they adorable*? It progressed quickly to *Oh, God, not again.*

All three of us raised our imaginary swords to the sky in salute.

"All for one and one for all!" we cried in unison.

By the time we reached Casey's, we had each found a stick to rival the finest swords in Europe. We entered the store like royalty shunning peasants. We peered through the cooler doors for our sodas of choice. I grabbed a Dr Pepper, Brent nabbed an RC, and Scott pulled out his trusty Orange Crush. It might have been all for one in some regards, but we each had our own tastes when it came to drinks.

"I say, young D'Artagnan, might you spare a few lire for a friend and his RC?"

I suppressed a giggle. "I think, Aramis, I could spare one or two." I rummaged through my pocket for a spare fifty cents. I dropped the quarters one at a time into Scott's upturned palm.

"It would be my privilege if you'd allow me to contribute to our good friend's cause," Athos piped in.

"Why, Athos, I would be honored." Aramis put his hand to his chest as if the generous gesture took his breath away. I carefully plucked one of my quarters from Scott's hand, while Brent replaced it with one of his own. The Casey's clerk watched the entire exchange with amusement. She exceeded our mothers' collective ages by approximately eighty years.

I, D'Artagnan, speculated she might have known the three, rather four, musketeers in real life. The thought made me snicker, and she raised an eyebrow in disapproval. I hadn't realized I was staring at her. The wrinkles folded over one another so much, I wanted to see if I could stretch them out, like straightening the comforter on my bed. All four of my grandparents had died before I was born. Even old lady Hansen from down the street didn't have that many. They looked soft.

"You boys use those imaginations well, and they'll serve you a lot of years. Use them for mischief, and you might serve a lot of years instead." She smiled through her scowl.

I stared at her, trying to decipher the statement. I finally chuckled to imply to the guys that I had gotten it. By the looks on their faces, I didn't feel so bad for my own confusion. Athos and Aramis were equally befuddled.

Once outside, all three of us gulped massive swigs of soda around our laughter, certain our performance would have won us accolades. We never minded that our rehearsals entertained ourselves far more than any audience we could find. I suspected we weren't even that funny. But somehow, we kept ourselves in stitches. At eleven, it wasn't too hard.

"Hey, I have an idea!" Scott's eyes beamed with orneriness.

I felt a queasy anticipation at the gleam in his eyes. He had a tendency to be over-the-top. Brent and I spent countless hours keeping Scott out of trouble. During the school year, it was a full-time job. In the summer, at least we could lead him to calmer waters.

Scott was the Tasmanian Devil of our trio. Or Eddie Haskell, my mom said. We watched endless reruns on TV, and we agreed. Scott and Eddie had a lot in common. Brent had been equated with Daffy Duck, maybe even Sylvester, and on occasion Wylie Coyote. Kind of a screw-up but lovable as all get out.

I could have been the Beave's older brother Wally, or maybe Kevin Arnold from *The Wonder Years*. I wasn't necessarily a goody-goody, but my straight A's and genuine likeability made me as popular with the teachers as well as my classmates.

"Nah, no you don't," I said, and Brent and I both hit Scott hard on each arm and walked off into the proverbial sunset. So much to do, so little time. And no time for any nonsense that could get us into trouble.

All for one and one for all.

Chapter Eighteen

"Goddammit, kid, snap out of it!" Max's impatience brought Timmy forward fast. "And who the hell is Athos?" He loomed in the box's doorway and yanked at Timmy's feet.

Oh, God, Brent, Scott. He felt dizzy, trying to acclimate to the here and now, and being ripped from Before. *I gotta stop talkin' in my sleep.*

"I'm gonna slap you into next week if you don't get the hell up." Max grabbed Timmy's scrawny calf hard enough to hurt. "You don't find me somethin' to eat today, shrimp, I don't wanna see your ugly mug. You got it? When I told ya to go back to sleep, I didn't mean to sleep all goddamned mornin'. It's damn near eight o'clock. Christ, you'd even be late for school if you was able to go." Max scowled at the Gerries hunkered around the barrel. They snickered and watched Timmy slam around inside his box getting dressed and then cheered when he kicked a can clear across the street as he left. None of them said a word. No one dared when Max was in a mood.

Timmy smacked a cup off a window sill and whistled sharply for Skippy. Once out of earshot, he growled, "No wonder she divorced your ass, old man. I can't believe she ever had your baby."

Of course, Timmy would never say anything so brazen *to* Max, but it felt good to vent anyway. When he came to the end of Brookline, he whistled sharply. "Skippy!"

Trevor—catch the Frisbee! Sam squealed with excitement as the lab launched his sleek body into the air and nabbed the white disk before it got past him. "Great catch, Trev!" I yelled, and both of us rolled around the grass getting a Trevor bath with a tongue big enough to clean the left side of my face with one swipe.

"Trevor," Timmy whispered. A yellow Labrador, his and Sam's. Time was orienting itself and memories settling where they belonged. And every one of them churned his gut.

He knew he had to find a way to coexist with his Before life. Max tried to explain the dangers of living in the past, and Max knew, he said, because it had sucked him into the bottle.

"Been there, done that," he'd say, and take a hard slug from a stinking fifth of Scotch or whatever the taste of the day was. Timmy would grimace, remembering the burn after the old man let him sample the nasty liquid fire.

"Why'd you leave then? I mean, I know about your wife spendin' too much money and your killer job. But why *really*?" Timmy studied Max's face, twisted in an expression of trying to remember – either that or avoiding it.

"Ah, shit, kid. Before we divorced, I thought the three of us could make it. I had a great job with Bentley, Chase, and Reese. But once Taneisha took my boy and headed for the hills, it wasn't long before I started drinkin' hard. I started gettin' too drunk to work, so I didn't have as much money. But I needed money to buy booze. And I needed booze in order to live with what shit my life had become. Then to add a twist to the cycle, I started popping speed to deal with my hangovers. And the nasty little pills made it damn hard to work. Damn vicious cycle. And then I got fired." Max dropped his head.

"Yep, at least you ain't a druggie no more." Billy had smacked his friend on the back then let out a long, liquid-filled belch. "Two years you put up with that bitch haulin' you through court, didn'tcha?"

"Yeah. Broke my heart. She got full custody of Drey, cuz I was boozin' so bad. So one day I decided I wuddn't payin' another goddamn dime of alimony. She was takin' a thousand bucks a month—nearly a fourth of what I was takin' home. I thought, *screw this*. After a *Gilligan's Island* rerun, I packed a pair of sweats, some underwear, socks, my toothbrush, and a picture of Drey, and walked out that front door for the last time. I even left the TV on."

"Have you seen Drey since then?" Timmy's mind swirled

with the idea of not having seen his son, plus he still had difficulty wrapping around the idea of a thousand dollars a month being a fourth of Max's take home pay. That sounded like an incredible amount of money to him now. In his Before life, he had no idea how much money his parents made.

"Yeah," Max mumbled. "A coupla times. Once I went to his middle school and watched him at recess. I was too drunk to say anything to him. Then a few years later, I kind of run in to him on purpose at Zumwalt High. We talked a little, but he seemed sorta embarrassed to be seen with me. Damn near broke my heart. I raised that boy for eight years, but by then he barely remembered me. I ain't seen him since." Max bowed his head and Timmy thought he saw a tear run down the old guy's cheek.

"So you drink 'cause you're homeless or you're homeless 'cause you drink." Billy's statement wasn't really a question, but he glanced at each of the men for some kind of response.

"Chicken or the egg," Ralph responded. Timmy's brow furrowed. He thought about that one for hours.

I don't wanna end up like any of you. I don't wanna stink – I don't wanna embarrass people – I don't wanna hide from the world.

Rounding the corner onto Balinger Avenue, Timmy the Homeless thought it was time to do something about it.

Chapter Nineteen

Timmy jogged to one of his hiding places and pulled out the last half of two stale sandwiches he had gotten from Ernie's three mornings earlier.

"Asshole thinks I'm spendin' my day gettin' him food, he's whacked." Anger welled in his chest. "After this, no more errand boy." This time it was more than a gripe – he felt a shift inside. He had known for months he was Max's meal ticket and wondered for the millionth time if that's why his grandpa had taken him in. But when it all boiled down to it, he didn't care.

"No more. I'm. Not. Kidding!" he shouted. "No more!" Hustling to an alley eight blocks away, he found his loose brick and tugged out the last of the stash. With a quick sniff, he was fairly sure it passed inspection. "Won't kill him," he decided and headed back.

"Well that was quick." Max motioned for him to hurry and cover the paper plate.

He's so freakin' paranoid, he thinks one of these bozos is gonna yank it right outta his hands. Max tucked the plate under his jacket and made Timmy stand guard. Vernon had swiped a plate of cookies right before Halloween, and Max exiled the broken-down bum for nearly a month. When Vernon finally came back around Thanksgiving, he had two more broken teeth, a whiter beard than Santa Claus, and a limp.

"We can't afford to share with these idiots. Not today." Max inspected the plate's contents and took a nibble.

Timmy didn't give a rat's ass about the others. But the orders had worn him slick. *No more,* he asserted, repeating his new mantra. He didn't like his grandpa using him. The old man had him hustling T-shirts at ballgames, hats during Halloween on the street corner, and once during an unseasonably warm November day, the old man plopped a box on the lawn by the Arch and made him sell lemonade like some five-year-old. "If we share, we starve," Max lectured. The old man took a chomp from the sandwich, picking the moldy spots off and tossing them to the squawking birds.

Timmy smirked. Max confirmed the hardest lesson the boy had learned on the street – it was a shitty world and the weak either toughened up or got taken out. Only Timmy could take care of Timmy. He touched the jagged scar on his left cheek as a reminder.

Max crammed a bite into his mouth and chewed without closing it. Timmy's disgust neared the boiling point – the manipulation, the dishonesty.

Had Max lied to him back from the beginning? Timmy had begun to second-guess his decision to return to Brookline that night after Cameron and his gang kidnapped him. Maybe Family Services wouldn't have been so bad, and maybe the cops would just send him to juvie for a few years. What could be wrong with anything that provided a roof and three squares?

"Don't forget I'm just eleven, Max. Just...don't forget."

Max didn't respond, just kept chewing with his mouth open. Timmy wanted to smack it closed. What he didn't admit to his geriatric grandpa clamored around in his jumbled brain. *Even if Baldy died Labor Day weekend. And no matter what happened in the storm drain, nothing can be worse than this. At least they feed you in prison.*

Anything would be better than this shitty life.

He crawled into his box, rummaged around for an extra sweatshirt, and grabbed his boots. When he sat down on a bucket at the edge of the alley, he remembered when he had nabbed them. They had been the catch of the century. The blessing proved in them being two sizes too large last September when he ventured down Olive Street and spied them on an apartment's back stoop. His sticky fingers had snatched them and no one had been the wiser. He had gotten good at it because Timmy the Homeless was invisible.

Shoot, people don't see me sometimes when they look

straight at me.

A flash of memory forced him to brace himself on the bucket, woozy enough to pass out.

"Good lord, Timmy, if I buy you those, you'll outgrow them in six months. Buy shoes that have a little room left in them. Especially at these prices."

"Momma?"

Her voice in his head knocked the air out of him. *Tennis shoes – she was buying me shoes for school.*

Sam laughed, so I threw a shoe right at his head. He ducked and the tennis shoe slammed into a display of Birkenstock's that went flying everywhere. Mom glowered at the two of us and through pursed lips said, "March."

"Ah, God," Timmy moaned. "Why did you leave me?" But deep down, he knew better. *He* left *them.* He was the one who ran.

That much he did remember.

But they couldn't run. They couldn't escape.

"Hey, kid. Ain't nobody leavin' you." Cooter squeezed Timmy's shoulder, but the boy heard Max snarl something hateful.

"Screw you, Max." The words surprised Timmy – speaking his mind without vetting first.

"Get outta here, you little shit!" Max shouted, throwing a can that barely missed Timmy's arm.

My throw at Sam was better.

But before risking the wrath of Max, Timmy darted out of the alley. He sprinted down Brookline, then raced through block after block of filthy buildings. When a stitch stabbed his ribcage, he slowed and called out for Skippy again. He sucked air between whistles, but no dice. He stood near an intersection with his hands on his knees waiting for the pain to pass. But the exhilaration felt good.

Could foster care be worse than this? Could death? He'd wondered that more than a few times.

Timmy shoved the thoughts away. Too hungry to hypothesize or beg for food, he set off to do a little dumpster diving. The café owners' rejections or attempts to save him could be exhausting and depressing. And sometimes doing the dive paid off better. One day, he found an entire grocery sack of half-eaten bags of chips. Someone had opened pretzels, cheese puffs, barbecue chips, and Chex Mix but hadn't eaten them all. They had been a little stale but still tasted heavenly. Max raved up and down the street to all the area bums that his kid had landed the score of the week.

Timmy grinned in spite of his resentment. When he hit Allenton Street, he went to the biggest alley that led behind several apartment buildings and a few small restaurants. The dumpsters were always full on Mondays. Tuesday was trash day.

Just as he heaved himself over the top lip of the first dumpster, he heard the pitter-patter of feet that caused a similar reaction in his heart.

"Hey, Skip!" He dropped to his feet just as the terrier vaulted into his arms. "How's it hangin', my man?"

Skippy's tail wagged as wildly as Timmy's would have if he'd had one.

"Yo, you mangy mutt, you stink! You been rollin' in your own dooky?" Timmy laughed through his grimace as Skippy sprang free from the boy's grasp. He immediately sat at the base of the large metal dumpster and let out a high-pitched yip.

"Gotcha. Let's find some grub, buddy."

Skippy yapped a quick *Duh, whaddya think I'm here for* and scampered around the base of the garbage bin as if circling for a nap. Timmy knew the hunt would be far more productive now that his best friend's higher-powered sniffer was involved.

"Where you been all mornin'? Wait, never mind, I don't wanna know. It's okay, Skip, I understand. You got a girl and who's to blame ya? You're one hot pup."

With his nose in high gear, he yapped at Timmy to get the

lead out. They trotted halfway down the alley to a dumpster behind Vinnie's Italian Deli. Anthony Vincent fed them occasionally and had the boy dreaming about hoagies. But the two were hours ahead of schedule for Anthony. Skippy's feverish scratching spurred Timmy to climb up the rusted green trash bin and lean over the edge, the metal pushing hard into his empty stomach.

"Don't see nothin', Skip. Wanna come look?"

Skippy let out a sharp bark, so Timmy jumped down and tossed the small mutt over the rim.

Timmy jerked himself back up and watched Skippy rummage. He cringed knowing this adventure would require a bath in a restroom somewhere for both of them. After several minutes of a few nibbles and false leads, Skippy looked up in defeat.

"It's okay, boy. Let's go." At the mention of the "g" word, Skippy perked his ears and bounded into Timmy's arms. He scratched his boy a little on the neck as he clung for dear life, and the two dropped to the ground. Even though they had done this a billion times, Timmy could never figure an easier way to get his buddy out. He kept thinking eventually he would clip Skippy's claws but never found the time or the tools.

Back farther in the same alley, the canine went nuts clawing at a Roughman trashcan parked outside another sandwich shop. They didn't haunt this one much, because it had changed hands more than a couch potato switched channels. Samisms came less and less often, but sometimes a good one resurfaced when it fit.

After popping the lid off, he tipped the can on its side and let Skippy do the honors. The crazed terrier dove in like a kid in a swimming hole. Before Timmy could ask him how it was going, Skippy backed out and yapped at his partner that they had scored. Timmy got down on his hands and knees and started pulling stuff out. Skippy clawed past the rubbish until his boy pulled out a foil container the size of a casserole dish with a labeled cardboard lid on it. It didn't look like it had ever been opened. Onofrio's Delicatessen was etched in fancy lettering. Timmy quickly tossed the lid aside.

"Holy cow, Skippy, you are one great detective!" But Skippy's nose was right back in the trashcan tugging on a small Styrofoam container with his teeth. There were several more where those came from, so Timmy rummaged until he found them all.

When all was said and done, Skippy and Timmy sat on the filthy concrete staring at a pan full of meatballs and small containers of varying sauces. The boy stirred the meat, mixing them with the angel hair pasta underneath. With a grin of celebration, he drizzled sauce number one over a portion of the pasta.

"Boy, Skippy, you're the man." He rubbed the dog's head, ears, and scruff. Skippy nuzzled Timmy's neck and licked his boy on the nose. A container of pepperoni sauce, one Italian sausage, and another plain red sauce sat next to the pan of pasta.

They had died and gone to heaven. The greenish tint to the meat didn't stop them because it tasted delicious. Timmy spread some pasta and a few meatballs on the foil for Skippy. The terrier waited patiently as his boy cut them up, then Skippy methodically ate a bite of meatball and then ate a few strands of noodles. Timmy watched his mutt with a sauce-smeared smile.

"I never saw a dog savor a meal like you do, Skip. You are a big goof." He giggled around a mouthful of his own noodles and wondered if Skippy ate slow because he understood the perils of stomach cramps. Food hitting an empty stomach could be just as nauseating and cruel as not eating at all.

"You're smart, Skipmeister." *Smarter than most bums.*

They both sat and ate in silence, licking their respective chops, wondering when they had ever scored so big. Timmy suspected never.

When they finished second helpings, he cut them off and

wrapped it all up. He had learned the hard way – certain Labor Day buffets came to mind.

Skippy turned a million circles asking for more, but Timmy stayed firm.

"No, Boy. We gotta save 'em. We'll have three squares today thanks to you. Whaddya say we give some to Max?"

At the mention of Max's name, Skippy twirled several circles and jumped in the air as the boy rose creakily to his feet. He rubbed at a cramp still lingering in his back.

The two of them bounced back to Brookline, a spring brought about by meatballs and quality time with a best buddy. The terrier's tail may have wagged more noticeably, but Timmy's was keeping time.

Chapter Twenty

Timmy shared his meatballs with Max the next morning. After the old man devoured ten or twelve with more than his fair share of sauce, he sent Timmy and Skippy away. Timmy knew better than anyone that Max's blistering hangovers wreaked havoc on anyone in his path, so they steered clear when Max was hanging. And today could reach a category five.

"Let's go be tourists, Skip. What'll it be? Forest Park, the zoo, or you wanna hang out by the stadium?" Timmy had learned that the farther away he wandered, the more in control he felt.

Skippy waffled, never the decisive one, so the two took off without a destination in mind. They ended up at the Arch three hours later. It drew them like a giant magnet. Timmy plopped onto the soft manicured lawn of the Riverfront. Even in the winter, the grass was plush and green. They could almost pass for a healthy kid and his dog, if the person looking didn't see the grimy shirt, take too close a glance at the oily blond hair, or stand near enough to catch a whiff. Puberty had started to magnify his sweaty smell.

"Look, Skip, look all the way up." Timmy pointed to the top of the Arch, always mesmerized by it. But Skippy was having none of it and took off after a squirrel. Timmy tucked his hands inside the sleeves of his coat and pulled the collar over his mouth. He remembered being awed by the landmark as a kid, then terrified as his mom and dad coaxed him into the elevator that would wheel him to the top. His head literally swooned as he peered out the tiny window at the ant-people below. He felt like a giant, a superhero who could fly. A woman would cry to him, and he would have to jet off into the clouds to save her.

"I'm here!" he would bellow, and a grateful lady would thank him with kisses and treasure.

He lay back with his arms crossed for a pillow behind his

head and ogled the amazing sculpture. Skippy had returned and was rolling in the grass next to him. The terrier wiggled around, licked Timmy's ear, and left his nose resting against his boy's neck. A small clog jammed in his throat. If he could bottle this moment, snap a Polaroid and make this feeling eternal, then the emptiness inside him might go away.

The barrier between Before and this moment of brief happiness blurred, and as he lay in the cold Missouri grass, he decided that aside from Skippy, the past appealed too damn much to keep pushing it away. Dangerous or not, Sam's laugh pulled him back to the last summer Before, the one he and the other musketeers had slashed and dashed their way through.

The turning point of his life.

***

July—Five Months Earlier

"I rock, yeah, I rock!" Sam danced around the kitchen. His jig made me giggle.

"Just spill it, Sam, we all already know you rock. You're the man and all that good junk." Mom's delivery was so straight-faced, it made me want to tease her, but I held my tongue. They couldn't appreciate his humor like I could. Adults were just too darn serious.

"Okay, family, all of you need to have a seat. Life is just sooooo good. Sit, sit, sit." He motioned each of us to our natural positions at the kitchen table. Mom and Dad stared at him like they expected him to bust into some stupid joke. Or maybe to ask for something so big he needed to put on a show for it. One thing was certain, he held the strings to each of us like puppets.

Mom and Dad crossed their arms, smiling in spite of themselves. Mom cocked her skeptical eyebrow and told Sam to spill it or he was cooking dinner.

"Remember that application I put in, oh, about twenty-thousand years ago? The one I stayed up all night to get *juuust* right? C'mon, don't tell me you forgot that one?" His face screwed up in an expression that made Dad chuckle. Sam could do that to us. His blond hair framed a dimpled face, one that spread joy like flipping on the sun after a thunderstorm. He wiggled his nose like some crazed human rabbit.

"Sam, what are you talking about? You've filled out a million applications – summer jobs, college prep courses for next year. You even filled out that foreign exchange student program. Which, by the way, I wouldn't be too thrilled about, so just spill it." Mom waved her hands in a hurry-up motion.

"Geez, Mom, thanks for the vote of confidence." Sam's face went stoic for an instant then broke into an enormous smile. He threw his hands in the air like a referee signaling a touchdown and exclaimed, "I'm going to the Foreign Exchange Institute at Northwestern in Chicago! I got accepted!"

"Oh, Sammy, I'm so proud of you." Mom jumped out of her chair and hugged my brother like he had just won the lottery. But hadn't she just said she wouldn't be too thrilled with that?

"Son, congratulations." Dad embraced Sam in a bear hug, envy rippling through me at the pride in his voice.

"So, how long're you gone, Butthead?"

"Wow, Timmy. Already makin' dibs on my TV while I'm gone? Don't even think about it," he mimicked in his best Mafioso voice.

Mom blurted, "Oh my god, Sam, it says you leave the tenth of August! That's in just a few weeks. You'll be gone for three weeks." She kept reading, oblivious to the questions we were bombarding Sam with. "You realize we'll have to get you all set for school, because you'll miss the first three days? We have so much to do!" She beamed, and I couldn't help but wonder if I would ever do anything this exciting.

"What about football, Sam?" Dad then launched into the conversation he needed to have with Coach.

I could see a miniature me mushrooming in Sam's shadow. Then again, the idea of his TV, Game Boy, and Nintendo 64 vacationing in my room – the Musketeers and I could have a wicked marathon. I would have to play it cool—no point in making him feel like I *wanted* him to go. Finally getting a peek at the magazines under his mattress would be worth it.

The celebration dinner that night at Red Lobster created a fever in our family. Things to do, places to go, people to see, Mom declared, and all the while, Sam busting at the seams. He was already planning the study abroad opportunity the institute was preparing the students for. If he chose the more popular places, he might have to wait until his senior year. But if he was willing to be reasonable, he could go junior year. There were lots of *ifs* that worried me. A few weeks to mess with his stuff was one thing, but an entire school year? People forget one another in less time.

***

God, I miss him. How could Timmy have known that once his brother left, he would set in motion a chain of events that would change his life forever?

I still miss him.

Or at least the idea of him. Timmy could no longer conjure Sam's face on demand – it was the major appeal of the dreams. The details, like the flecks of gray in his blue eyes, the cowlick a little off center of his forehead, and the dark brown hairs that stuck straight up from his right eyebrow that he would spit-slick down.

Fighting off the panic, Timmy tried to picture his brother's mouth – the smile that spread through the Weaver family like bad gossip. A Samism well-applied, but he couldn't quite grasp the details. What did his teeth look like? Were his lips full or thin? A football-sized lump lodged in his throat.

Why can I see him in my dreams but not now? Is that

even my life at all? Max had explained to Timmy that people saw the past through rose-colored glasses, and when the old man explained what he meant, Timmy thought hard about it. *Do I do that? Have I made them greater than they were?*

Skippy let out a long sigh that tugged Timmy back to the lawn on the Riverfront – at peace under the Arch but still in battle with his own demons. The mutt didn't know how good life could really be, but God, wouldn't his daddy love to give it to him. Then again, the peace of lying in the arms of a boy who loved him might be the perfect slice of heaven for a stray pup. *You don't miss what you never had.*

Timmy wished he couldn't remember the other life at all. Maybe it wouldn't hurt so bad being without it now.

Before he knew it, he dozed off. His nap, nearly two hours of deep, uninterrupted sleep, offered no monsters, no Sam, Mom or Dad, and no alarm clocks. When a little girl with a whistle gave it a shrill blow, Timmy sat up as if he had been clubbed over the head.

"Shit, Skippy, get jiggy with it, boy. We gotta snap!" The sun had slipped from three o'clock to the horizon in what seemed like minutes.

Skippy yipped excitedly, unsure why they were in such a hurry but pleased as peanut butter to be on the move. He was well rested and up for action. Despite his panic, Timmy giggled as the goofy mutt raced ahead, then sprinted back and whipped circles around his boy.

"Go on, boy, let him know I'm comin'!"

But Skippy wagged his butt so hard, he was vibrating. *Huh-uh, I ain't facin' drunk grandpa without you!* Skippy might not be able to talk, but his wags said plenty.

And right as rain he was to think that. If Max had gotten hungry and Timmy wasn't there to serve, the old man's wrath could curl toenails. Then again, those meatballs should hold the old man over all week. Max didn't eat much – his was a liquid diet. But he never failed to gripe about what little he got.

Skippy raced ahead but kept looping back. A stitch jabbed Timmy's side after fifteen or sixteen blocks, forcing him to put his hands on his knees to suck air. The few miles were part of the adventure early in the day, but in a hurry, it felt like a marathon. When he could, he took off jogging again and made the turn onto Clairmont, less than a mile from Brookline. Some old fogey Timmy barely knew shouted, "Boy, Max been lookin' everywhere for you!" Huddled in a doorway with a brown bag bottle, the bum cackled and took a swig.

Give me a break.

He stopped one street away for another hands-on-knees rest, gulping air into his freezing lungs. He coughed, the brisk air burning his chest now that the sun was long gone. A draft slipped through a fresh rip in the knee of his jeans.

It's gotta be after eight. Shit.

He hollered for Skippy, but the mutt was too far ahead to hear. When the ache in his side subsided, he turned onto Brookline at a slow jog.

"Hey, kid, old man's barkin' up everyone's tree." Cooter rifled through a fresh batch of papers, always on the lookout for something. Bums up and down the street shouted words of warning as he entered the cardboard jungle. It amazed him how he could be walking down sidewalks among regular people only streets away, but then Brookline was like entering into a time warp. The stench of sweat, alcohol and nasty cigars wrapped around him as he re-entered the world of invisible people.

"What the hell you do with them meatballs? Don't you know it's dinner time? You been gone all goddamned day again, and from now on, you will mind me and be home before dark. You got me?" Max kicked a Budweiser can that splatted against an alley wall with a liquid *thunk*. Vernon reached down, shook it, and drained the last swallow.

Timmy grimaced in disgust. Still sucking air, he held his tongue. When Max had a jumpstart on the bottle and his anger already charted on the Richter, sometimes it was best to lay like broccoli. When the gnarled, arthritic hand hit the back of his head and sent him to the asphalt, Timmy's knees exploded in pain when he hit the ground.

"Max –" Cooter grabbed for the old man's arm, stopping the second pop.

Timmy scrambled out of arm's reach, pulled himself to his feet, and touched the spot where Max hit him – tender and already swelling. He rubbed his knees and swallowed the tears threatening to defy his *I'm no crybaby* motto.

The old man rarely struck anyone, much less Timmy. He was usually all bluster. But the booze had been flowing heavier and faster, a symptom of the silly season, Cooter said. When the Gerries explained what that meant, it made sense but it didn't make it easier. Timmy wanted to blurt that it was his first silly season homeless, so have some sympathy. But that ran in short supply with the Gerries, especially Max.

"That's enough, Max." Cooter stepped in front of Max, his grandpa still squaring off like he meant to smack Timmy again. Billy laughed, clearly pleased the two were at odds again. Everyone in the alley held their collective breath waiting for Timmy to find his voice or for Max to be upgraded to Def Con 5.

"Stop orderin' me around...you're not my father." Timmy braced himself, a defiant scowl adding venom to the statement. He tried not to gag on Cooter's stench – the guy's sour sweat burned his nostrils. Timmy's filthy T-shirt reeked, but at least it was his own. He vowed to wash his entire eight-piece wardrobe the next day, no matter how he had to do it.

"What'd you say to me, you worthless piece of shit?" Max whirled on his drunken friend. At first Timmy thought the old man was talking to him, but before Cooter knew what hit him, Max's fist connected with the younger bum's nose. The crunch and spray of blood made everyone groan. Timmy ducked, certain the next blow would be up close and personal.

"Get up, kid, or you may never get up," the old man growled. By the swagger, Timmy knew Max meant it. He didn't have many bruises from his grandpa's rage, but the few had been enough to warrant respect. It was the booze, he knew, but that didn't help him now.

"I've had people lookin' for you for over two hours. And this spiteful shit is the thanks I get?"

Screw you. He caught a brief memory of his mother having to call around to neighbors when he had forgotten about a dentist appointment one summer day. A lady he barely knew saw Scott, Brent, and him playing stick ball on a side street and told him he better get his bottom home in a jiffy.

"Where're them meatballs, boy? I need some of our meatballs. And better damn well be close by. I'm sick of waitin' on you." Max snarled, and Timmy shuffled backward out of his line of fire.

My meatballs, Max, MY meatballs. But aside from not having the guts, he knew better. The old man was still within kicking distance.

"You never eat twice in a day." Timmy backed up as he spoke. Skippy chose that moment to come bounding into the alley and leaped onto Max like he didn't notice the storm brewing. The unconditional love seemed to suck the fight out of the old man.

"I gotta have some of 'em, boy. And don't you worry why, you hear me? Where would you be without me? Now get those damn meatballs, *now.*" He gestured for Timmy to skedaddle. Max had that mean drunken look in his eyes. Blood-shot and milky, and in the firelight of the burn barrel, they were devil red.

Edging toward the sidewalk, Timmy snapped, "Fine. But it'll take me at least ten minutes."

"Just hurry," Max barked, as the boy headed off into the dark without another word. He didn't want Max to discover his closest hiding place, so he turned left at the end of Brookline and circled back. The old man could never be trusted when scotch out-ratioed the blood in his veins two to one.

When Timmy finally got to the underpass on Hanley Road, he crawled up the concrete slab to the small space where the road met the ground. He remembered his dad telling him once in a tornado warning that they might have to pull over and take cover in a similar place. Now Timmy had to fight squatters who sometimes came to escape cops or rain, but mostly this just served as a kickbutt hiding place. He reached his small chafed hands past a cinder block, shoved a stone sideways and then pulled one of the foil trays free. It was too dark to see, but he knew exactly where it was. He nearly flipped it over, his heart ramming in his chest at the idea of telling Max to ignore the gritty new seasoning.

He squinted to see as he drizzled red sauce over a section, used two fingers to scoop it into a Styrofoam carton, and then placed the lid back on the container. Thankful he had scrounged an empty take-out box from the deli trash, he divided the pasta into equal portions. He had no intention of giving Max more than he deserved. After he licked his fingers clean, he replaced the stone, the block, and then brushed some stray rocks in front of it to make it look natural. A whiff of on-the-verge pungency let Timmy know they needed to eat them sooner rather than later.

"I know, I know. It's all right, boy." Timmy shooed Skippy who had tummy crawled up next to him, wanting to know what the heck he was doing with their dinner. He let Skippy lick his fingers. "We'll eat some later, okay? I promise." He kissed Skippy on the nose before they shimmied out of the small space and hurried back.

"Jesus, boy, where you hidin' this stuff, in Illinois?" Max's eyes were all liquid now and the scowl told him they'd better deliver and then scoot. Hurricane Max had upgraded to category four.

"Maybe." He handed Max the tattered foil container. Max yanked it from him and hobbled deeper into the alley, past the car seat, to a few stray boxes that served as guesthouses. Timmy watched the old man get down on all fours and hand the food to someone inside. A trembling hand came out of nowhere with a bottle. After the exchange, Max jumped up as if his arthritis never existed.

Well ain't that a pisser. Timmy glared at Max, but the drunken bum didn't bother to glance his way. Instead, he plopped onto the car seat and unscrewed the cap. The tattered upholstery spit stuffing every time someone sat down, but Max wedged his scrawny butt onto the makeshift couch, propped his feet on the giant wooden spool that served as a table, and proceeded to drink. Not sips but long pulls that contorted his face in a grimace, then in mere seconds, a smile spread across the old man's face.

Fuming, Timmy tried to quell the emotion bubbling inside him, but he couldn't. "I'm givin' *my* food so you can juice yourself?"

"Shut the fuck up, boy. You better mind your p's and q's, you got me?" Max didn't even look at him, but took another slug off his bottle instead.

"You make me wanna puke. All of you!" Timmy turned and faced the rest of the Gerries whose eyes were wide with shock. He knew what they were thinking. *Kid, you're gonna get slapped into next week.* But the rage building inside of him refused to simmer. Skippy, tail tucked and shivering, cowered between his two favorite people, clearly torn by what to do.

"Let's go, Skippy." Timmy snapped his fingers and stomped out of the alley. The terrier took a hesitant step toward his boy, then turned back at Max. The old man waved him off, so Skippy scampered toward the sidewalk. "Pretty soon I'll be big enough to stand up to you," Timmy whispered. No one heard him, but it made him feel better to say it. An unfamiliar pang registered at the same time. Timmy didn't understand pity, but it didn't stop him from feeling it.

The boy and his dog wandered down Brookline, turned onto Stockton, and ventured into the world of honking horns and blaring music only a few blocks away. At this time of night, he had to lurk in shadows and stay alert. Scary people roamed northern St. Louis at night. But anger still festered inside him, and walking always tempered it.

"GO RAMS!" a distant voice shouted.

"Warner rules!" another answered.

"Oh, that's right, Skip. Rams play tomorrow! Only two more home games, and we've just lost two all season. We need somethin' fun to do around here." He kicked at a Styrofoam cup. When it fluttered in the air and fell only a foot ahead of them, he stomped it with a muffled crunch. "Let's spend the whole day down there tomorrow, you wanna?" He gazed up into the sky, stars beginning to blink in the dark night, and felt the chilly breeze wash the last of the bad feelings away. He refused to allow the anger to take root, or he knew it would consume him.

He found an abandoned printing store, huddled in the doorway, and patted his lap for Skippy to hop on. "We're already a cinch to be in the playoffs, Skip. If we win tomorrow, we're sure to get home field. Last two games against the Bears and the Eagles—man they ain't stoppin' us." He smiled, relishing the idea of a game to look forward to. There were no shirts to scalp or the game would have been a bigger deal to the rest of the Gerries. Max knew a guy who knew a guy who scored T-shirts every once in a while.

Max'd tell me to bug off anyway, since I pissed him off. Better get back on his good side for the playoffs.

Timmy had set up shop three or four times this season, selling shirts in parking lots surrounding the respective stadiums. For Ram's games, sometimes they got sweatshirts, T-shirts, even giant foam fingers with *Go Rams!* on them. Timmy would plant himself right outside one of the main entrances, and with the hubbub at the Dome, security never hassled him. He loved the buzz of all sports, but football ruled. Short enough seasons that every single game mattered, and Kurt Warner kicked butt. The play-offs meant big bucks for them if Max got the goods.

Slipping into Busch Stadium for Cardinal games was the easiest simply because he had more practice at it. But seeing linebackers bathed in sweat colliding with men as strong as small locomotives gave him such a rush. The last time – Cleveland in October – he'd sold shirts an hour before kick-off until the end of the night when cars wound their way onto the web of highways surrounding the Riverfront. He listened to the whole thing on a transistor but itched like mad to watch – to see tackles, touchdowns, and trick plays.

"Remember that game against the 49ers, Skip? That was a rush!" After clearing nearly thirty shirts in just two quarters, a scalper slipped him a ticket. That had re-ignited the fever. He retold the game later in an animated play-by-play to the whole gang of Gerries at the abandoned warehouse they were squatting in at the time. By the light of a Coleman lantern, he relived the game to everyone who would listen. The next day he celebrated by buying himself a Whopper and a pair of jeans from a consignment shop. No Salvation Army freebies this time. He paid a full four bucks for Levis with only a slight tear at the edge of a back pocket. Max had even gone with him that day, treating Timmy for a job well done.

The warm memory evaporated as the wind whistled through the shattered store window. The brisk air swirled trash into the doorway, forcing him to burrow deeper into his jacket and pull Skippy closer to him. "Skippy, at my house – my *real* house – football was a religion."

Skippy wagged at the happiness in his boy's voice, not caring about football but the warm house would have tripped his trigger.

"Our TV cranked loud enough to reach into the bathroom when nature hit, Mom would bring us cheese and crackers, *and she even watched with us!* She *loved* football." Timmy smiled with the memory, all the times he dashed into the kitchen for individual beverages of choice – Bud Light times two, Pepsi for Sam, and his tried and true Dr Pepper.

A lot sure had changed since then, but fifty cents did still buy a Dr Pepper, as long as it was in a can. But in his world, little else ever changed.

"Skippy, you know what?" He glanced down at his scraggly friend and kissed his cold nose. His mutt wagged so hard his whole back end wiggled.

"Tomorrow at the game, I'm gonna buy me a Dr Pepper. Still got a little cash in my Altoid tin." The idea of an ice-cold soda made his glands water. It was a luxury he seldom afforded himself. He kept loose change in his one un-holey pocket for emergency bus fare. "Let's get back, Skip. Get rested up for game day. The Gerries'll be sloshed by now...I hope." He set Skippy on the cool concrete and hopped to his feet, trying to get his blood circulating. His fingertips and toes were numb, the bitter December night cutting through the layers of flimsy clothes.

The two of them hustled back to the alley, no one even noticing as they slipped past the Gerries gabbing around the burn barrel, conversation more of a slur. Skippy burrowed into their sleeping bag before Timmy could even sat down.

"That's right, buddy, warm it up for me." He tugged a large hoodie over his Nike pullover and peeled off his boots and sweaty socks. Sitting down, he could make out the bottle caps in the dark, the burn barrel casting a glow down the alley. Skippy nosed the Salvation army issued blanket to let his boy know he wanted under the cover.

"Fine, you bossy thing." Timmy lifted a corner, and Skippy weaseled deeper into the sleeping bag. Timmy finagled his way inside, nestled beside his warm terrier. He loved being rolled up like an enchilada with his mutt for added heat. He tuned out the sounds of the alley, the drunks bantering about football and glories of their past.

Whatever. You kill too many damn brain cells to

remember your name much less the glory days. He couldn't imagine Max as a teenager, or Vernon, Billy, or Ralph. Cooter, yes, but not the rest of the geriatric bums.

"We're gonna bust outta here, Skippy." Timmy stared at the caps on the roof of his box, too dark to see, but he was comforted knowing they were there. "It's time." He stroked Skippy sidled up next to him – peanut butter and jelly style.

He could feel the tides rolling out to sea, the tectonic plates shifting. Max raised his hand to Timmy more and more and offered less and less. Subtle changes were taking place in Timmy's attitude toward life, and he sensed that winter would be too long to tolerate in the alley. Change didn't happen to people, people made it happen – and he knew it was time to put the ball in play. The longer he waited, the heavier it would get.

"I got a little Kurt Warner in me, Skip." Timmy closed his eyes, rubbed his terrier's head, and started to plan his big play. "Even some Isaac Bruce." He could almost hear the crowd chanting *Bruuuuuuuce.*

Grinning as his eyes grew heavy, he considered variations of the plan. *Balance the running and throwing game.* He might not have a Rams' uniform, but he had the touchdown mentality.

Chapter Twenty-One

What did the ancient geezer want now? Need some grub after binging all night?

Timmy thought he had been jerked awake by Max who had returned from some late-night rendezvous, another midnight drinking tangent. But the shuffling behind him jumpstarted his heart.

"Where are you, you little shit? I can smell you. Got a certain scent aboutcha, boy." Hesitation, then the voice continued. "Can'tcha smell me, dog?"

Gruff, hateful laughter made Timmy tremble in his box. He would know that voice anywhere. And yes, he could smell the foul stench of sweat, filth, and nasty cologne. Too much of it, and he had gotten a taste of it when he bit his....

"Boy, where are you?" Someone sniffed loudly – to intimidate.

Timmy stared at the box's opening, waiting. He lay inside thinking at any moment, a boogeyman was going to rip the top off or burst in VERY uninvited. He tuned in to all the sounds he didn't really want to hear. Feet scooted on nearby gravel, he thought maybe someone touched his box, then came an oppressive silence that made him want to scream. He clutched his privates to prevent leakage. Suddenly a head poked down from above and glared in. The mug of a muscle man, even upside down, looked familiar, but then again Timmy was no master of faces or names.

He studied the eyes, gapped-teeth, gold-capped smile, and kept watching as the enormous thug who had squatted to have a better right-side-up looksee.

"Big box for such a pipsqueak," Muscle Man hissed.

"All the better to eat you with, my dear," *Timmy could imagine him saying. And then Timmy could see it – what he had been looking for.*

The upper arm, the right arm. Hadn't it been on the left arm before? He couldn't remember. The greenery, expertly detailed, laced around a pearl-handled knife. The artist had added a glint of white to make the blade appear menacingly sharp. Only the beginning of the shimmering metal showed, because it was immersed three-quarters deep into a crimson heart. Inked fancily through the red was a name Timmy could not quite read.

Because it changes. *Depended on the individual Muscle Man and what a bad-ass he was.* How do I know that?

"C'mon on out and play, Timmy. Or D'Artagnan. Whatever the hell your name is. We can go wake Brent up in the most boss way ever. Or better yet, let's get yer pretty boy brother to come out 'n play." Monster Man tried to lure him with a sinister smile – he even waved for the boy to join him. Was he crazy?

But – but...

Timmy's confusion swirled through his gut and made him want to vomit. Emotions cascaded through him like a Current River waterfall.

How did this man know Brent? Or Sam? This was now, that was then. S.E. Hinton had done it the other way around, but Timmy knew better. Brent and Sam were part of the back-then stuff. So was D'Artagnan. Not Dumas' version, but theirs – his trio. When he was somebody.

"You ain't nobody no more, dog. We even done 'em in front of you. I earned my gold, woulda gotten my tag, too, remember? You should remember cuz you was there." He snickered. "You didn't like it so much then, didja?"

And Timmy caught a flash of memory. He knew what that meant, didn't he? His mom screamed, and he squeezed his eyes shut to make it go away.

"I can make you go away," Timmy snapped with more conviction than he felt. But he knew it was true. He stared at the looming figure facing him from the box's opening.

With his mind, Timmy pushed his thoughts forward. Past

getting up and scrounging for lunch and imagined himself along the shore with Skippy, the casino boats bursting with life.

He opened his eyes and Muscle Man was gone.

There! I can make you go away when I want to.

But somewhere deep in his sleep, Timmy watched carefully for the hands, those dish-plate sized paws, and that ominous tattoo. Because even though he could make it disappear, he could never really make it go away. Because *it* was always with him, *it* made him who he was, didn't it? And Muscle Man blamed Timmy for something he had done. And it had been brutal, hadn't it?

Murderer, murderer, murderer, repeated menacingly in his head.

Timmy shivered in his sleep.

Chapter Twenty-Two

Timmy jerked awake, scooting his box nearly an inch in the process. And that was no easy feat. His primo box, complete with bottle cap collection, had suffered minimal wear and tear over the months, made more durable by the cap-covered walls and constant shellacking.

He sat trembling for a moment, trying to shake the nightmare images of the flexing biceps, bigger than Schwarzenegger.

Bigger than in reality, I think. He's why I was in the storm drain That Night.

He felt for the baseball cards in the pouch of the pullover among his many layers. The calming habit included trying to recall the order of the cards. Anything to refocus his brain, because the memories came clearer and more often. The smells, the sheer terror, the shouting. He sucked air deep into his lungs, the biting cold penetrating the plastic strip door. Within seconds, he was wide awake. Skippy squirmed beside him, but Timmy rubbed the terrier's head and soothed him back to sleep.

It took his eyes time to adjust. He touched the caps even though he couldn't see them. Hundreds of them wallpapering his box – soda, beer, even a few bottled water tops. He wished he had batteries for his flashlight so he could count them, but falling asleep too many times while counting warranted more double A's than he could scrounge.

Lying in his box, imagining the bottle caps in the pitch darkness to ward off the plate-sized hands, urged Timmy to contemplate his plan in more detail.

"For starters, Skip," he whispered to his boxmate, "I'm gonna clean up today. I might even wash your head, if you let me. Then we're going to splurge on a bite to eat... I know, I know, we got meatballs, but let's save those for leverage. It's time for stage one, buddy. It's time." Saying it out loud somehow made him feel better.

Skippy let out a sigh of agreement. Timmy felt under the sleeping bag and small couch cushion that doubled as his pillow for the Altoid container. As he pulled the rusted lid open, he fingered the bills. Six – the last of his stash from game-day sales. Max needed to get more shirts, or he would be completely broke. Not that it would be the first time.

Maybe I won't be here that long.

He didn't usually dip into his emergency fund unless five or six days passed without solid prospects for food. Splurging on McDonald's or Burger King somehow made him feel normal. His go-to treat was a Quarter Pounder with cheese or a flame-broiled Whopper with an ice-cold Dr Pepper.

Funds were coming, because the Rams were a cinch for the playoffs. Goods to sell and profits to gain, Max said, and fans dug deeper around the holidays.

All week, he had been predicting a Super Bowl victory. He had held up a bottle a day to toast. "Mark my words, fellas, we're Super Bowl bound. Warner's got the arm and Martz's offense can't be stopped. Have I ever been wrong?" Max belched laughter.

That morning, Ralph had coughed, "1996," and everyone laughed.

Cooter whispered to Timmy, "That's the only year Cards made the playoffs this decade...ol' Max says every year they're goin'. He's not the most reliable prognosticator."

Not privy to the word, Timmy got the sentiment. Gerries didn't challenge Max, mostly because they didn't want to hear him bitch. They didn't want to hear him gloat either. Most of the Gerries hated the Rams, griping that there weren't any damn rams in Missouri.

"Bring back the football Cardinals!" they would shout. "At least we got redbirds here."

Timmy shook his head in the dark, never half as entertained by the Gerries as they were to themselves. Waiting for sunrise, he played out scenarios in his head, wondering which of his options made the most sense. Rams in the NFC Championship could bring in serious cash if Max's shipment came through. Timmy wondered what the old fart had to do for that shipment but knew better than to ask.

As the first glow of dawn slipped into his box, he could make out a few bottle caps. At last count, he had one thousand, two hundred and fifty-three – including the new Diet Barq's he'd added earlier. The Guinness Book of World Records Max had found claimed he was still thousands from the record. Some rich yuppy in New York City probably had the money to buy any and every drink he wanted. A few were sold exclusively in Japan and other impossible places.

Better renew my passport. Timmy smirked. *There should be a prize for display style.*

His box had garnered impressed views from folks all over northern St. Louis. Even workers at the soup kitchen would save caps for him. It was the one honest hobby he had, since life in shelters, condemned buildings, and alleys lent itself to clever means of acquisition. The first time he swiped something, he confessed to Cooter what he'd done. The guilt had piled on top of the crimes he kept close to his heart.

"Nah, man. You gotta resort to clever means of acquisition in order to survive. You hear me? Don't never steal from somebody you shouldn't and don't take shit you don't need, you hear me? But you gotta take what you gotta take, Timmy. No guilt, no remorse." Cooter, still young enough to slip in and out of the homeless world, taught Timmy the ins and outs of how to cling to humanity, as he described it. Filing it away every time he learned something, Timmy intended to get out and stay out, not succumb to the demons Cooter fell prey to. He understood why the geriatric old bums stuck together, but not Cooter. Anytime the young guy disappeared for a few days, Timmy missed him but hoped he would take whatever opportunity he'd found and escape permanently. Every time he returned, it scared Timmy that escape, true escape, might be impossible.

But he learned from Cooter that clever means of acquisition had its merits. He'd found a place mat with cartoon characters he didn't recognize at Goodwill. It said seventy-five cents, but he got the five-finger discount. It now served as a tablecloth on a boot box inside his makeshift home. Sitting on it was his Tigger watch he saw on a sink in a gas station. A mother had helped wash her seven or eight-year-old's face and hands then walked out without it. Timmy considered leaving it but knowing the time and date could be of value for food and trash routes. A gold cuff link he'd palmed at Salvation Army he kept for bartering. Two pencils with erasers he'd swiped at Mickey D's to draw on the remaining space on the back wall of his box. A visor mirror from an unlocked car that had been left for days sat propped up so he could see himself, even though he seldom wanted to. And a few marbles rolled around the tabletop just in case another kid came along who wanted to play – not that it had happened in three months, two weeks, and four days. He kept track of that mark with the pencils.

My sentence....

All of that left just enough space for the flimsy green sleeping bag he'd gotten from the Salvation Army in October. He had to fold about a foot of the end in order for it to fit inside the box.

At one time, Timmy even had a battery-powered lamp, but it had gotten stolen in less than twenty-four hours. Some things he found had kid appeal, but others were hot items to everybody. So, he discovered it was best to keep his trap shut, otherwise goods were known to grow feet and walk away.

Everyone had mirrors, but certain items ranked higher. Lights, fans, and any form of protection. Knives, whether homemade shanks or lethal switchblades, topped the list – whether for barter or need. Timmy had the Swiss army knife

Max had given him stuffed into his jeans pocket and only used it when no one could see. But the blade he'd used on Baldy currently resided in Billy's back pocket. The asshole had snatched it right out of Timmy's hand when he was using it to cut open a can of baked beans. At first, Billy claimed to be helping, but when he handed the open can to Timmy, he pocketed the knife and hissed that little shits only needed little knives.

Max might've forced Billy to return it if he'd known, but Timmy decided he would steal it back when the time was right.

A memory of Baldy clutching his midsection made Timmy shiver. He shook away the memory as he heard the clank of Gerries rising. Skippy wiggled out of the sleeping bag and dashed out to greet the men stoking the fire.

Today's the day, Timmy. Make something happen.

With an uncertain conviction, he sat up on his knees and shoved the Altoid tin into his back pocket. He peeled away layers, leaving a t-shirt, the pullover with the baseball cards in the pouch next, topped with the hoodie, and tugged the Salvation Army jacket on last. Fastening his watch, he then pocketed the rest of his things, just in case.

"Yip-yip, yap-yip!" Skippy turned circles around Timmy as the boy emerged from the box and stretched. Flurries drifted lazily, sticking to everything they touched.

"Geez, Skip, fleas got you in a tizzy?" He reached out and tried to pat his best friend's head, but the terrier would have none of it. Skippy raced to the end of the alley and turned back to look at his boy. *C'mon,* the gesture signaled. Timmy knew it well.

"Give me time to match your energy, Skippy. Dang. Are you hungry?"

The H-word sent the mutt into a frenzy. He dashed circles around the Gerries surrounding the burn barrel, to the back of the alley, hopping off the bucket seats, and yipping shrilly with every twist.

"Wish I had that kinda energy," Ralph mumbled, scratching his beard before tugging the knit cap lower over his ears.

A couple of other guys Timmy didn't recognize laughed, holding their hands over the heat. No sign of Billy, Max, Vernon, or Cooter.

"I'm comin', I'm comin'." He did a double check in various pockets for the important things – the Altoid tin with the few dollars, the Swiss Army knife, and his baseball cards.

Never leave home without 'em.

Timmy paused at the burn barrel. "Where is everybody?" Not that he cared, but it wasn't the norm. A nervous excitement stirred in him – from his plan and the prospect of the upcoming game. Both played a role in his future.

"Dunno...nobody tells me shit." Ralph shoved a stick down into the barrel, shifting the glowing embers, and dropped leaflets in to ignite it. The rising sun should draw the whole crew around the barrel. The fire igniting was like a signal for the Gerries. He cocked his head and listened for snores, but other than Skippy's yips, the only sound was something dripping in the back past the car seats.

"Gotta be a good sign, unless one of 'em got arrested. I'm holdin' out for the first." Waving as he headed up the street, he whistled. "Let's go, Skippy Doodle. Channel that energy and score us some breakfast!" A memory tugged at the use of the nickname.

The two rounded the corner onto Stockton with Skippy spurting ahead and circling back to spur Timmy to get the lead out. Not sure how the scraggly mutt always managed to wake up so energized, his boy mapped out their route. By ten a.m., they scored a six-inch hoagie from a sub shop and hunkered in a condemned warehouse doorway to split it. The nickname kept niggling at his brain, but the memory wouldn't come. As he tore apart the sandwich, giving Skippy bites between his own, he knew with food came comfort, and with comfort came peace. It was in that peace that he could slip back. Cooter had warned him about living for the dreams, but forgetting them, Timmy knew, would be far worse.

Without them, there's nothing of me left.

When they finished the sandwich, Timmy leaned his head against the cold brick and waited for the past to wash over him. He didn't even care that he was cold. Instead, he let the memories sweep him away.

***

August—Four Months Earlier

"Today's the big day, Sammy doodle!" Mom turned the bacon and poured herself another cup of coffee. When she cooked breakfast, it was like she had three hands – a thing of magic.

We all had our fair share of nicknames, though Sam's all made him sound like a Cocker Spaniel. Names changed with the fads. Current movies, various hip commercials, or flash-in-the-pan TV shows.

"Moooom," he groaned. But he grinned, not too bothered in the wake of his excitement.

"Yeah, Sammy doodle, you gonna write me?" I giggled, knowing how he hated the name. A commercial for a little kid's drawing toy had a jingle that inspired the name, though we didn't need much inspiration for most of them.

"Every other day, Timmaroo." He nodded decisively. It was my turn to grin. That was a nickname Sam had made up when I was a baby, but he hadn't used it in ages. Tit for tat, Mom would say.

"So tell me again how long you're gonna be gone." A jillion weeks was all I could remember. The thought made me queasy, excited, and nervous, because it would be the beginning of a new school year for me – *middle school.*

I shoved the thought away, not ready to wish away my summer and definitely not ready to think about the hurdles of middle school. In the meantime, I had a normally off-limits bedroom to explore. Every time I thought past it, butterflies took flight in my belly. Selvidge Middle School wouldn't know what hit them. The Three Musketeers would conquer the halls.

"Be back right before Labor Day weekend. Think that's about the tenth time I said so, too." Sam's smile almost touched both ears. He floated on cloud nine, and I doubted we'd be able to tether him for dinner.

"But you'll miss school. Missin' football practice could blow your chance to start. The coach may say it won't hurt you, but you gotta get your practices in," I offered, as if no one had thought of this little bit of information. I had heard them discuss it but still couldn't get over that he was willing to miss a few games while he caught up on practices.

"I know. But this is too awesome an opportunity for me, Timster. No two-a-days or all the beginning of the year mumbo-jumbo. I'm makin' like a groupie and skippin' town!" The Samisms never stopped.

Mom ruffled my hair, even though she knew I hated it. "Timmy, don't fret. We've talked to his coach and his teachers, it's okay."

We usually had to be next to dead to stay home from school. Mom believed real illnesses produced a by-product, and she never bought the stomach routine unless we could produce liquid from an orifice – her exact words – or a fever.

Mom and Dad gave Sam all sorts of instructions. Phone numbers for emergencies from Dad's pager at work to his secretary's personal pager in case Dad couldn't be reached. They had jotted down everyone's cell phone from all sides of the Mississippi. Mom straightened the collar of his dark green polo. Dad brought his duffle bag out from the hall and dropped it by the front door. The plop made me jump.

"C'mon, guys, let him breathe, geez." I wasn't going to hug

him or anything, but if he made the move like he wanted me to I would – just to make him feel okay about leaving.

"Hey, runtface, make like a garter belt and keep it together, got it?"

"Got it!" I saluted, and we stood stiff for a second or two. Then we burst out laughing, and he hugged me. A tough brother-to-brother embrace that made me feel grown up.

"For real, Timmy, have a great summer. Take good care of Trevor. You gotta feed him every day now, morning and night. Give him lots of treats. I won't be here to take him swimmin' and stuff, so you guys be good and include him. And don't let Scott get you and Brent in any trouble. He's a loose cannon." Sam tousled my blond hair, already so bleached from the summer sun that the yellow had nearly faded to white. I didn't mind the gesture quite as bad coming from him. Not on this day.

"Okay," I managed around the swelling in my throat. I vowed not to cry since I turned ten last year and developed the adage that Timothy Ryan Weaver was no crybaby. I had to bite my lip to make good on that.

"Timmy, you wanna go with us to drop him off, or do you want to go over to Scott's? We'll probably stop for Chinese. You can come, or I can bring you some back. You decide."

I knew Mom was making sure I was okay with all the attention Sam was getting. Did I want to go and spend two hours dealing with Lambert Field brouhaha and have Chinese with chopsticks, or did I want to be free to run with my friends and then get Chinese later?

"I – um –" I waffled. I wanted to go, but I didn't want to hear them dote on Sam and get all gooey.

"Well, make up your mind. We're leaving in about twenty minutes, and we'll need to call Scott's mom to let her know you're coming over."

"C'mon, Timster, come eat with us. The Great Wall won't be the same withoutcha." Sam play slapped my face.

"Okay," I agreed with mock indecision, but the instant Sam asked me to come, I was as good as seat-belted in the SUV.

Dad hauled Sam's suitcases to the Escalade, while Mom fussed with snacks and organized toiletries with the systematic order of an Army sergeant. By the time we all loaded into the Cadillac, we were famished. We enjoyed dinner, laughing at Sam's antics as he spilled noodles on his polo, all of us going back for seconds and thirds, then sending him off for the trip of a lifetime. Mom and Dad both expressed concern for how we'd come unglued when Sam went on the subsequent foreign exchange trip. Three weeks was nothing in comparison to a whole school year.

I didn't even respond to that comment. I hadn't considered what this three-week venture meant for the long run.

Those three weeks, while fun, exposed what we knew about our family. Meals were quiet without Sam's silly euphemisms and quick wit. The Weaver household, we discovered, was ordinary without him. Sam was the crazy string that held us all together.

***

Skippy's barking jerked Timmy to the warehouse doorway, freezing rain drizzling lightly on his face.

But Skippy had a better agenda. Timmy took a deep breath, trying to shake the memory. The dark green polo haunted his sleep more and more lately, and it dawned on him that Sam wore it leaving that day. But did he have it on when they picked him up, too? He couldn't remember, because picking him up blurred into where he was now. Pieces were coming back to him, details to stitch together That Night, but so much of it was like vapor he couldn't grasp. Because of that, he had given up resisting the dream-memories.

"Hey, Skip, whatcha got?" Timmy hustled over to a restaurant's dumpster, deciding the search for dinner would be entertaining and a heck of a lot better than semi-spoiled meatballs. It didn't mean he would offer them to Max. *Let him find his own meals for a change*. Then again, a little diarrhea might serve the old man right. He tossed the terrier up and over and hoisted himself onto the metal bin's edge.

Skippy rummaged through the papers, trash bags, and miscellaneous garbage. He nibbled at a few scraps, but after a few minutes looked up and whined.

"Sorry, boy, no dice, huh?" Timmy clapped his hands and held them out for Skippy to jump. The terrier, as always, leapt and clawed the heck out of Timmy's neck, but the two managed to hop down and continue exploring.

"We've kind of made our way to tourist central, Skipmeister. God, look at all the Christmas decorations." Timmy was sure they'd been there all week, but why hadn't he noticed them? *Because I didn't want to.* "We're still hungry, aren't we, boy? I guess we could go ahead and have my celebration meal. Are you hungry for McDonald's or Burger King?" Timmy laughed as Skippy cocked his ratty-haired head, confused why his daddy kept using that word and didn't do anything about it.

The giant clock at Union Station confirmed the snail's pace of the day. It was just shy of noon. Couldn't Christmas just hurry up and melt into another miserable day? He doubted it since what felt like five o'clock was a measly eleven forty-nine. He made a note-to-self: *stay awake as late as possible tonight just so I can sleep 'til sunrise.*

The predawn hours were the worst. Lonely, depressing, and too dark to count caps or draw. The holiday season blanketed this part of the city – lights, music, the hustle-and-bustle of shoppers. Less than a week before Christmas, all Timmy could do was will it to pass quicker.

Skippy bounded ahead, always leery of traffic and even strangers. He was smarter than most kids, Timmy decided. Max's crew often depicted Skippy as a rocket scientist and the terrier mixed mutt would sit and revel in the praise. He might not have known what the Gerries were saying, but he was perfectly aware they were saying it about *him*.

As they got closer to Union Station, he heard voices like angels in the gray afternoon. The music floated through the air like the sounds of a faraway carnival. A car honked and other city sounds accompanied it, but a man stood in the doorway, holding it open for someone, allowing the carol to filter across the street.

"...all is calm, all is bright. Round yon virgin mother and child...."

His mind reeled with déjà vu or just pure memory. How long had it been since he had taken the school trip downtown? Every year a different class crammed onto big yellow buses to file into Union Station to go caroling. It was an annual field trip his elementary school and a bajillion others had done as far back as he knew. Sam claimed to hate going, but his family all doubted it – a chance to be on stage?

Timmy scanned the surrounding streets and saw what he knew would be there. A school bus parked in a lot with Woerther Elementary printed in block letters on the side.

His very own former elementary school had kids at Union Station singing for the customers and employees. Timmy's heart raced, feet itching for their usual response to stressful situations. His past life coming so close to his current world made Timmy's heart pound hard enough in his chest to rattle even the slimiest teeth. He slowed, confronted with his Before life. Skippy barked for him to get moving. How could he tell his new best friend about the old ones? Timmy thought the Skipmeister might just be jealous if the two worlds met. The terrier and Trevor would have to duke it out. What Timmy wouldn't give for the opportunity to find out.

Trevor. God, where was Trevor? Who had taken him in or had his parents gone back for him?

Timmy jogged to join Skippy, took a deep breath, and

approached Union Station's massive doors. The man had left, allowing the doors to close. A woman bogged down with bags leaned against one door to open it. Another customer slipped out as she went in. For that brief instant, Timmy could hear the familiar beginning of another carol. The music was cut off again when the door closed, barely audible. He knew going in meant adding lead to the weight in his heart. But there was a pull, like a magnet to a refrigerator.

With trembling hands, he tugged the handle, but the huge door resisted his scrawny effort. He heaved again and entered the ornate lobby. He immediately blended into the background. It was easy for him to be invisible – people tried desperately not to look at him. Today, he was thankful for the growing crowd to hide behind. The sounds of elementary school voices soothed and terrified him.

"...then one foggy Christmas Eve, Santa came to say...."

His head swam, but he finally found the courage to look at them. He studied the clean, privileged faces of what appeared to be third and fourth graders. Brushed teeth, combed hair, healthy eyes. Who cared that they were dressed in the trendiest clothes and most stylish shoes?

I used to be one of them.

"...and how the reindeer loved him as they shouted out with glee...."

He searched for part of himself in each of them. That golden glow of opportunity surrounded them like an aura. Then his heart lurched, caught on a lump that jumped into his throat. One girl stared over the heads of everyone in the audience. The all too familiar eyes, snotty grin, and brown ponytail that had been such a staple of her image. She had flipped him off with it more than once, hadn't she?

It can't be. No...

He stared hard at her. Anger swelled inside of him. Hadn't he wanted to call them, tell them he was okay? Hadn't it crossed his mind more than ten million times to just suck it up and dial the number he knew by heart? That maybe they could help him?

But Max said no. *You'll put them in the same danger your parents are in.*

"If you done something so awful that the cops is lookin' for you, you'd be puttin' them in just as tough a spot, Tim. They'd be accessories to your crimes. You don't wanna do that, do you?" He continued to explain the ramifications of doing something so stupid and selfish. Timmy always nodded and pretended he understood.

It sounded so logical, like many of the detective shows his mom and dad obsessed over. The weird world he lived in mirrored eight or nine episodes he had seen Before. Flashes of memory no longer waited for sleep to emerge.

A hand on my throat...squeezing, someone screaming, guys laughing. No, not just guys. The tattooed man. And the sound of Sam, my tough-as-nails brother, crying. Why was he crying? Had I ever seen him cry...ever? Please...oh, God, please help me remember.

Timmy's eyes hazed, his mind crippled by the cruel vision. A massive tattooed man's biceps rippling, yanking his mind between the present and the past. Just as he shivered from the chill of the recollection, her eyes drifted to his, but she looked right on past. The invisibility cloak did its job, shielded the human race from its Achilles Heel – Max had explained that one to him, and Timmy liked the comparison. Then her gaze trailed back and peered into his baby blues. She held onto his gaze with the slightest hint of recognition. She studied him hard enough to create a crease between her eyes – a moment passed, fifteen seconds of pure clarity.

She knows me but can't place me. Watch any good slasher shows lately, Miss Snotty Pants?

Timmy doubted it. Stephie's holier-than-thou attitude appeared unchanged simply by the way she carried herself. It was in her demeanor, her clothes, the snide curl of her lip as she sang.

It was Timmy who finally pulled his gaze away, sucker-punched by his past. Quietly, while she was looking at someone else, he slipped out the enormous doors and joined Skippy in the frigid December afternoon. Out on the sidewalk, he bent over and placed his hands on his knees feeling like he might vomit. He sucked air hoping the nausea would pass.

That life. This existence.

The two were never meant to clash. In Timmy's mind, his world had frozen in place. No one aged, no one moved on, no one forgot him.

But he knew better. They had to know something, because his house was for sale. Did they think he was dead, *assume* he was dead? Why not? It was stupid to think anything else. Of course they moved on. It had only been six months, so hopefully they hadn't forgotten him. But maybe thinking of him embarrassed them. He could hear Stephie judging him, speculating that he'd probably done something terrible or had been a coward and run away. Or got abducted by aliens. He didn't know. But no matter how much he hated himself for the thought, he wished all of them had died. Because deep down, he felt like *they* had left him. A bitter anger furrowed his brow, spurred him to kick a Bud Light can with enough fury to hit a car and set off its alarm. Skippy tucked a nervous tail at his boy's sudden anger. But the rage died the instant he saw the terrier slink from him.

"Ah, Skip," he muttered, his voice hitching. He swallowed hard to dislodge the lump, but it wouldn't go away. He reached down and pulled Skippy into his arms and buried his face in the fox terrier's scraggly fur. If any tears fell, his best friend absorbed them before anyone could see. Not that anyone would look.

Chapter Twenty-Three

"Hey, kid, I thought you'd be down at the Riverfront." Cooter grabbed his knit cap and tugged it on. The burn barrel was surrounded by guys jabbering about the game, most of them newbies, and all of them guzzling beer like water. "Max and Billy are setting up just north of Busch. Get your hiney over there, 'cause they got *shirts* for Sunday's game." Cooter beamed, anxious for the excitement, motivated by the possibility of some cash. "And I'm talking LOTS of shirts."

Timmy had wandered back to Brookline, still heavy-hearted from his encounter with Stephie Kruschaven. But he and Skippy wanted to be part of the scene, even if the brush with Before sucked the get-up-and-go out of him. "Oh, man, I was right there. Okay, let me get my gloves. We bringin' 'em back here or hidin' 'em somewhere?"

"Dunno. Max has a plan though. You know it." Cooter slapped some guy on the back Timmy had never seen before, gabbing with another guy around the burn barrel.

He and Skippy didn't need any more motivation than the potential for profit. With the plan ready to be executed, they made like a leaf and blew out of the alley faster than an open bottle of booze. *Sam would like that one.* Cooter shouted that he'd be down there as soon as he could.

When they found Max nearly an hour later, the old man clapped his hands and shouted that it was a *good* day. He babbled about how tomorrow would be prep and placement day, so they'd be ready and in a primo spot for Sunday's game. He was lucid for the first time in weeks. "Kid, we're gonna have a shipment for the Bears next week, too, and hopefully for the first round of the play-offs. Get your game face on. It's gonna be a profitable week." He rubbed his hands together like he was ready to wheel and deal.

The excitement spread like a virus. Billy, Vernon, and

Ralph helped unpack boxes, while Max scouted for a hiding place. "Kid, you and Skip help me find a spot in all this construction to stash these for tomorrow. This game is less than 48 hours away. We don't want to tote them back to the alley. Too many of 'em and too many money grubbers back there."

The construction workers had all left for the weekend, so Friday night offered plenty of hiding potential.

"Where we sellin', Max?" Timmy scoped out a few pieces of machinery that might serve as a barricade.

"Bout three blocks from here...near Stan the Man. It'll be a few blocks from the Dome, which will keep security from buggin' us." Max and Billy had divided the shirts. Timmy wasn't sure why, but he knew better than to ask.

Vernon oohed and ahhed over the blue and gold tees. "These are sweet, Max. And boy, we win this bad boy, we got home field throughout. Can you *conceive* of the profit if we make it to the big show?" He let out a whistle.

Max shook his head, the massive smile never wavering. "You find a spot, kid?"

"I think so!" He couldn't help but laugh and enjoy the surge of optimism coursing through him. Skippy felt it too and raced around them yipping. Max threw a tied-up sock, and Skippy bolted across the fresh concrete enclosure to nab it and had it back while they all cheered him on.

"Go get it, boy!" Max threw it again, all the way to the street, and Skippy tucked his ratty tail between his legs and darted after it. "Tim?" Max studied the boy, but Timmy couldn't meet his eyes. With a plan in place that meant a life for himself and not his grandpa, a wave of shame passed over him and he knew his smile had faded. He still couldn't shake the encounter with Stephie.

"I'm good. Just really hungry. But I'm good." He put on a façade and grabbed the sock to throw.

"Hey, kid, here you go. Go get us a couple of slices from that vendor on Market." Max tousled Timmy's hair and handed him a crisp twenty-dollar bill.

Unable to keep his mouth from falling open, he recovered before he spoiled the old man's mood. "Wow, thanks, Max. Be right back!" He took off jogging, with Skippy nipping at his heels. As soon as he got around Busch Stadium, he slowed and tried to take it all in. The shirts, the brush with Stephie, the prospect of real money to fuel his escape plan.

His brush with Before still hung around him like a heavy fog. Stephie Kruschaven had always been a snot, and Timmy never liked the little cucumber. Going to Scott's house every morning in the summer only widened the chasm between them. He, Brent, and Scott contemplated her coolness on many occasions, wondering if perhaps she had been adopted or alien born.

Stephie Kruschaven. Timmy mulled it over in his mind. She would be in third grade now. When he first got to know her, his goal was to do anything he could to piss her off. And it usually worked.

When he found the pizza street vendor, he bought six slices, knowing he needed to keep Billy and the others just as happy. Skippy led the way back after they shared one slice and wrapped one up for later. By the time everyone inhaled theirs, he told them he was going to tour the half-finished concrete structure to scope out the best hiding places. He and Skippy explored and found a massive concrete tube and crawled inside to take a rest. They'd found a perfect hiding place and now, Timmy needed to process the day, the encounter.

Before and After had collided, and it set his brain in motion about what it meant and how it thwarted his motivation to escape.

***

July—Six Months Earlier

"Just take the damn picture, Stephanie." Mrs. Kruschaven stood with her hands on her hips.

Click! Our faces frozen in eternal goofiness. Brent's peace sign loomed forever over Scott's cocked head, while I grinned like a dork at the stupid gesture. Why was that always so funny?

"Let's hit the Batman. Then we'll ride The Screamin' Eagle." I nodded, waiting for the Musketeers to agree. Stephie and Mrs. K conspired about where to eat.

Food was a sidebar, an afterthought as far as we were concerned. When we hit the entrance, Six Flags meant roller coasters, bumper cars, and free throws for cool miniature basketballs.

"Hey, Mom, we're going, okay? Stephie, if you want, we'll meet you back here and ride the Tidal Wave later." Scott tolerated his kid sister well enough, though Brent and I never understood why. She spewed negativity and sarcasm like lava from Mount St. Helen's. Most of Scott's friends steered as clear of her as possible, like from the next block. Brent liked to crack that joke around everyone *except* our third Musketeer, but Scott never blamed his friends for making fun of her. We knew he did it more for his mom.

"Sure, but I really want to ride the Batman, too. C'mon, Mom, I'm tall enough now, and they don't make me sick like the turny things do. Please?"

"Steph, you said you were hungry." Mrs. Kruschaven shook her head. "Well, make up your mind."

Most seven-year-olds had long since mastered that *I want something* tone. And Stephie was no exception. But a weird thing had happened to her since she'd started second grade. Before that, she was just a kid, a measly first grader and whiny as all get out. But since going into second grade and conquering it like a gorilla on an ant farm, Stephie and her friends had gotten all hoity-toity and high-falutin. With third grade on the horizon, she was beyond intolerable. She mastered high and mighty but got clingy when it suited her wants and desires.

Before anything drastic could happen, I made eye contact with Brent and Scott, and we mentally plotted to make like cloth and bolt. Time was wasting and the Batman line was multiplying by the minute.

"I want to ride the Batman." Stephie folded her arms across her chest.

"Boys, do you mind if we join you?" Mrs. Kruschaven studied each of us closely for reservations. But we couldn't whine too much. With season passes, the park served as our summer playground four or five times a month.

"Sure, Mrs. K, we don't care." I could suck up with the best of them.

"No problemo, Slimmo. Come run with the big dogs." Brent always referred to us as big dogs, and I knew Stephie thought that was dumb. Then again, she thought *everything* we said was dumb.

"All right then. Let's do the Batman!" Mrs. K led the charge.

Brent did the Batman theme, the *dunanunanuna Batman* thing all the way there. I whopped him on the arm, but it only made him start over. The line for the ride only spooled around half the rows, but the arguing started at the get-go.

"Stop it, Scott, I mean it. Mom? Make him quit." Stephie pushed at him, more to bait than to ward him off.

We wound around listening to the piped in penguin sounds, accented by Stephie and Scott's bickering.

"Bite me, Stephie."

"Shut up, Butthead," Stephie barked. "You're so immature."

"Me immature? Please. C'mere, Runtface, I'll show you who's boss." Scott proceeded to give his little sister a noogie. Her hair teased under his knuckle, and she screamed in exaggerated pain until Mrs. K told them to knock it off.

Brent and I tried to ignore them. But other people stared when Scott started kicking the back of Stephie's heels as they inched forward a few paces and then stopped each time the line stalled. Scott couldn't be normal and hop on the bar railings like Brent and me. No, he had to make a scene. The Tasmanian Devil swirled with pent-up energy. Brent and I teased him that he needed some Ritalin.

When we got to the top, we chose lines. "We're ridin' up front. We'll see you losers on the other side!" The three of us jetted toward the first slot even though it was longer than the rest.

Mrs. K called out for us to hang on and started to count how many were in each line.

"I want to ride up front, too." Stephie ran after us, but with four to a row and five of us, it wasn't going to work, unless Mrs. Kruschaven rode alone. Mrs. K scowled at the front line – fifteen deep – while the rest had five or six.

"You boys ride this all the time. Ride in the second one. You can ride it again later." Miss Bossy Britches spoke as if she were the mother.

"You two are hungrier than us. We'll wait and ride in the front, you and Mom ride wherever, then we'll meet you at the diner for a bite. You can order for us."

"Sounds fine to me. Here, Steph, you and I will get in the second row." Mrs. K pulled on Stephie's pink tank top, but the spoiled brat didn't budge.

"Or we could ride in the very back and prob'ly end at the same time. That'd be better," Scott decided. And he was right. There were even numbers all the way to the back car, and people generally helped out by maneuvering lines if you asked them.

"Then I want to ride in back," Stephie challenged.

God, I'm gonna smack you. Scott, get control of your sister. But I didn't say a word.

"Don't stare at me like that. If you guys are going back there, then I want to be back there."

Since when?

If Scott told her the sky was blue, she would have argued that it was actually periwinkle. Now all of the sudden she was trying to join us at the hip.

"God, Stephie, you always have to have your way. Fine, let's all ride right smack dab in the middle. Happy?" Scott stomped to line five and stood there like a dope. People frowned at him.

"No, I want to ride in back now, and there's no reason one of us shouldn't."

Mrs. K told Stephie to just get in a damn line. The girl didn't move, so Scott stalked over and smacked his kid sister on the back. *Whop!* We could all hear it. Her ponytail even bounced with the impact.

"MOM!" She shouted, initially a reaction of shock, but what the word meant was *Do something about this child*!

"Scott, you know better than that. If you two can't get along—"

"We can if he'll just let me ride in back. Or maybe up front."

"And you get your way?" Scott lifted his palm to hit her again, and Mrs. K glared at him, ordering him to put that hand down.

"Oh, like you never get your way, puh-lease." Stephie rolled her eyes. "Just ride in the back and I'll ride with you three. Mom can ride the next one up." She then mumbled about boys and something else we couldn't decipher.

That's when I snapped.

"AHHH! What'll make you and us happy, Stephie? Can't you compromise at all? Or are you too good to just *give* a little? Is there anything that'll make you smile and go along with anything ever in your life?" My blood boiled – and she referred to *us* as childish. "Jesus, you're so freakin' *bossy*."

I hate you, I wanted to add, but then I saw Scott's face – eyebrows up as if to say, *What the hell are you doing?* The glare humiliated me but also made me a little mad. Didn't he realize what a scene they were making?

Stephie's mouth fell open, so did Mrs. K's, and I suddenly felt like a complete butthead.

"I'm sorry, but man, it's tough to listen to the two of you argue. It's embarrassing. Look around you." I caught Brent's eye, and he smiled in agreement. The support helped. "You guys don't ever say anything nice to each other–ever. And you'd argue about the time of day. I mean, *look.* People are *staring.*"

She and Mrs. K. both turned to see people quickly look away.

Tears made a quick appearance, but Stephie blinked, and the precociousness returned like a pulled blind.

"Bite me, Timmy," she hissed, enunciating my name like I was a child being scolded. "Mom, let's go over here." And with that, Mrs. K and Stephie moved to line two, and the boys and I headed to the back. Scott's mom cast us a look that said *Sorry, boys*, but it didn't help my cause with the little brat or the guilt pulsing through me.

Later, we stood in line for food at the diner outside Batman. Stephie stood directly behind me and whispered huffily, "I hope someday you need me, really need me, so I can spit in your face." Spittle flew from her mouth in her fit of anger, and it was all I could do not to laugh. She knew her mother couldn't hear, or it would ruin her perfect persona with her mom.

But something inside me twinged. As much as I wanted to deny it, it hurt my feelings. Like I'd ever tell her. When pigeons don't poop, Sam would say.

"Ooooooh, I'm so hurt," I retorted, though not with much conviction. "Who pissed in your Cheerios, Stephie? And not just this morning. Your life is a bowl of piss-filled Cheerios, and I think you like eating them."

There. I felt better. It was a comment I had heard on a TV show, and it carried the bite I wanted. I pulled a Stephie and turned my back on her and huffed away. I would have flipped my ponytail at her if I'd had one. I went to the bathroom and came back just as they were ordering. I told Brent just to double whatever he was getting to avoid making anyone behind us mad.

After that day, Stephanie Kruschaven terminated all verbal communication with me. Not even to shun me, condescend, or ridicule. I got eye rolls and ponytail flips, but that was it. When I entered their home, which I did at least five times daily, Stephie didn't so much as make glance my way.

Out of sight, out of mind.

***

Sitting in the concrete tube, Timmy regretted not waiting around to speak to Stephie. Wouldn't that be the perfect launching pad to re-enter the world, regardless of the consequences?

But I ceased to exist for Stephie that day, so why should she notice me now? He realized with a sick horror that her dream for him had come true, and he suddenly wanted to apologize to her more than he wanted to breathe.

But he wouldn't. As much as he wanted to go back, to resume being Timothy Ryan Weaver again, to sit at a breakfast table and read the comics, he couldn't. The day and the opportunity had passed. *That Granville sign in my yard on Catalina saw to that, didn't it?*

What could Stephie do for him anyway? There was still the small problem of the police and the possibility of putting them in danger. Even Stephie Know-It-All couldn't make That Night go away. *Or all the bad things I've done.*

A brief trickle of memory, a flash of muzzle fire, the smell of gunpowder so strong it burned his nostrils. Who had the gun? He couldn't remember, but he wondered if he concentrated hard enough, he might be able to. Then the brief ribbon of memory slipped through his fingers and the image was gone.

Timmy let out a ragged sigh, relief and exhaustion sweeping over him. Remembering held the key to his future, he knew, but moving forward was more important. Even if at negative Mach speed.

Dance with the one that brung ya, his dad once said. He didn't get it then, but he did now.

The riddle now was to figure out who brung me.

Chapter Twenty-Four

By Sunday morning, the energy along the St. Louis Riverfront was intoxicating. It even reached the alley on Brookline. The Gerries tried to keep up with Timmy and Skippy as they hustled to get set up. Tailgaters already sat in chairs, popped open beers, lingered in parking lots and along the street blocks from the Dome.

When the guys got the makeshift table set up, Max pulled out a T-shirt and handed it to Timmy.

"Oh, Max, that's so cool!" The smell of the brand-new shirt almost matched the softeness.

Skippy sniffed it, burying his nose in the new fabric. The navy T-shirt was embossed with the gold Rams' logo, crisp and already inscribed with *NFC West Champions*. The last three games were as good as played, since the team was 11-2 and no one else in the West even had a winning record. A magic season, the Gerries called it.

"Do we get one, too, Max?" Billy fingered the material like it was silk.

"If sales are good. It is going to be a *good* day, boys. And we have shirts for the Bears next week, last home game of the regular season. I got some for the playoffs too. Dig this." Max rummaged to the bottom of one box and pulled out a hoodie with a Ram in various displays dominating Vikings.

"Oh, wow. That's awesome." Timmy grabbed it and in his excitement, dropped it. He brushed it off, then admired the Ram butting a Viking through the St. Louis Arch.

"Put that one on, Timmy. It'll sell our product better. But clean up your face, first. I'll cut your hair before we set up. You got your blade?"

Timmy grinned. "Sure do!" He tugged the Swiss Army knife out of his pocket.

"No, we need the sharper blade. The switch. You got it on

you?" Max saw the exchange between Billy and Timmy, and the kid had to credit the old man. He wasn't dumb. "Billy, you swiped *my* knife from him?"

The cloud of anger that washed over Billy's face made everyone step back. "I didn't swipe *your* knife. I took the knife this little shit used to gut a man. He's too young for a man's blade, and you know it. Here." Billy took it out of his own front pocket and handed it to Max.

For a second, no one breathed. No one spoke. No one moved, not even Max. Then he shook his head, told Billy to get the crap set up, and steered Timmy past the fountain west of Busch Stadium. They slipped into a pizza shop and ignored the stares as they headed into the men's room. It took twenty minutes, but both smelled better and could pass as human. Studying his reflection, Timmy had to admit he could pass for *normal.* Max had even scraped away much of his scraggly beard.

"All right, squirt, let's do it." Max smiled at him in the mirror. For a moment, Timmy could almost get a sense of what life with the old man as a real grandpa could have been like. He did look a little like his mom, didn't he?

"Don't get sentimental on me. We got shirts to sell and a game to win!" Max marched right back through the sandwich shop. Timmy continued to run his hand over the sweatshirt's logo, the intoxicating smell of new material making him as warm on the inside as out. The fleece lining was softer than anything he'd ever felt.

Do I get to keep it? Timmy was afraid to ask. Knowing how stingy Max could be, it was a crapshoot.

Heavy cloud cover blanketed the sun as it tried to clear the buildings. He glanced at his Tigger watch. 8:19 a.m. Pretty early to start selling shirts, but fans filled the streets, already drinking and laughing.

When they had their spot on the sidewalk in front of Busch Stadium set-up, Max stood center stage and announced, "You know what, guys? Let's up the price a smidge so each of us can keep one." Max took in the cheers with pleasure, then tossed a shirt to each of them hovering like hungry wolves.

Timmy beamed. *It's mine!* It was one of the first brand-new shirts he had owned in over three months. Max had never let them keep the merchandise. The old man's generosity filled Timmy with guilt, but he squelched it from ruining the mood. He knew once the bottle tipped, things would lapse, just like they always did.

"Here ya go, Billy. Cooter. Ralph. Vernon. Hey, Sweenie! Come grab one!" He hollered at a guy sitting on a bench across the street. Timmy cringed at the old man's unnecessary charity, knowing it meant less profit if he chose to give them away to every freeloader in the city. *But they're not my shirts.*

After the old cronies pulled on T-shirts, they swapped shots of their various bottles and chattered about the game. Skippy raced from one to the other, excited by the buzz.

Timmy sorted the shirts by size on the tiny piece of wood that served as a table. Set on top of empty boxes, it worked fine, and he wouldn't have to worry about leaving it when all the shirts were gone or low enough to sell closer to the Dome.

"Hey, kid, don't sweat us givin' a few away." Max peered to his left and right, varying Gerries chugging hard on their bottles now. He covered his mouth and whispered, "I got these totally free – *one hundred percent profit*. They, um, fell off a delivery truck." Max coughed a couple of times, and Timmy chuckled, getting the five-finger-discount joke he'd learned during the first game of sales.

"So after the game, I'll take some close to the gates, right? Or should I steer clear, maybe hang out in a parking lot?" Timmy understood the protocol when Max had scored a shipment. The old man had a connection – Jose, an old friend of Max's. But those knock-offs came on the up and up, and the only reason Jose had Max and the crew sell shirts was to save on paying real employees. But Max was loyal to those close to him, so he would never steal them. He'd said a hundred percent profit. *So how the heck did he get 'em?* There was no point asking. Timmy wouldn't get a straight answer anyway.

"Parking lot is good. You can lurk around the gates if you wanna for a little bit. Might sell all of these and be able to take a few up there before the game. Just take care of the cash. I promise I'll give you a good cut, 'kay?" Max ruffled his hair and touched the inch-long scar on his cheek. Timmy felt an unexpected surge of emotion and hugged Max without even thinking.

"Glad you like it, Timster. And don't worry, the shirts ain't hot. But be on the lookout. Might be some, um, pissed off boys who wanted this score."

Hey, Timster, you and the Mouseketeers come swimmin' with us this weekend. Sam's voice rang as clear as the shouts nearby. His two worlds were headed for a sure collision. Preparing for the crash was taking a toll.

Shaking off the memory, he nodded. "Got it. I'll just hang in the back parking lots. Skippy, you gotta be my watchdog, okay?" Timmy scratched the terrier's ears making his hind leg thump.

"Man, we are going to *clean UP!*" Max slapped his leg, getting the other Gerries riled again. Everyone toasted and started whooping and hollering. "Oh, and, Timmy, there's a present for you in the open box. Check it out once you're set up." Max winked at him. "We'll check on you in a bit!"

"GO RAMS!" Billy smashed his bottled against Ralph's, one of them cracking but they didn't care. There seemed to be plenty of back-ups, all packed in brown paper bags in a Radio Flyer red wagon.

Where'd you get all this stuff, Max? Timmy felt a sliver of unease slip down his spine, then dismissed it. He was more interested in finding out what the surprise was.

The Gerries headed toward the corner, Max pulling the wagon while each predicted the score. Laughter followed them, still audible when Timmy dug into the box looking for the surprise he hoped would be edible.

All around him, hundreds of Rams' fans laughed, threw footballs, and somewhere he caught a whiff of something grilling, filling the air with maddening smells. Random cheers, clanking bottles being toasted, music blaring somewhere close by. He liked the madness, the crazy enthusiasm of the pre-game celebrations. A kid about his age launched a football that flew over their heads, and a grown man – probably his dad – made a leaping grab.

"YEEEEEE-HAW!" someone screeched, making Timmy laugh. Skippy raced around like a terrier possessed.

"Look what we got, Skip, McDonald's!" He tore into the sack. Quarter pounder with cheese, French Fries, and a baby burger for Skippy. Underneath was a bottle of Dr Pepper. Cold or not, his stomach growled in anticipation.

He laid out their mid-morning brunch, tearing up Skippy's burger for him. He turned up the little transistor radio to listen to pre-game, and took his first glorious sip of Dr Pepper. It was ice cold since it hovered just shy of thirty degrees outside, but so was the Quarter Pounder. Taking his first bite, he didn't care if it was cold. He swirled the delicious hamburger around in his mouth, chewed it to a pulp, and finally swallowed. After only his third bite, hopped up halfway through his meal to sell his first shirt.

"Thanks, Mister!" He pocketed the five-dollar bill and didn't get to sit back down for another thirty minutes. By 11:00, he had sold most of his shirts, finally finished his fries, and got tickled at his furry best friend for sacking out in one of the t-shirt boxes.

"Skip, you're not the *best* assistant." The mutt lifted his head, thumped his tail against the cardboard, as if to say, *Yeah, but I'm cute.*

"We're gonna kick the Giants BUTT!" someone screamed.

Timmy gathered the remaining shirts, threw their trash

away, and took apart the makeshift table. Skippy bounded around Timmy as his boy set the boxes against Stan's statue.

The area buzzed with energy – ticket scalpers, people heading toward the Dome, with laughter and music serenading them. Unlike teams with one massive parking lot, Rams' fans had to be resourceful. They tailgated on upper levels of parking garages, in little lots on side streets, and hung out wherever they could find a place to chill. But everyone was wrapping up, getting pumped by the countdown to kickoff.

Football mania filled the late morning air. Timmy found it almost intoxicating. He and Skippy wandered closer to the Dome, the last of his t-shirts in one arm and the transistor dangling from the other wrist. He watched people barter for scalped tickets, listened to the dealers make offers too good to refuse. One even tried to wheel and deal Timmy, a ticket for ten shirts. The boy considered that one for about ten seconds and then could hear Max screaming at him about the lost fifty bucks.

Man, I could make a mint with those tickets. And he knew it was true. But he knew better.

"Sold-out show, folks! Getcher tickets here!" one guy called, accosting people as soon as they got out of cars. Many steered wide of the seller, bringing them right by Timmy. He didn't even have to make his pitch.

Skippy darted at people and dashed back toward his boy. *C'mon, lady, come look!*

"Ah, look, Bobby, awesome shirts. Isn't he adorable?" A tall woman reached down to pet Skippy then glanced at Timmy. She furrowed her brow.

Timmy smiled and held up a shirt. "Um, T-shirts are five dollars, ma'am."

"You got it, son. Give us two." The perfectly groomed guy, way older than Sam but younger than his dad, pulled a twenty from his wallet and slapped it into Timmy's palm.

"Keep the change, kid. Enjoy the game!"

Easy come, easy go.

The woman and her boyfriend or husband dashed off without looking back at him, taking off their coats and pulling the shirts over their turtlenecks.

"How 'bout them apples, Skip?" Timmy slid the bill into his pocket, mentally banking the extra. "Biggest tip yet!"

The atmosphere was electric. Only a block from the stadium, he and Skippy soaked it up. "This is so cool, Skip, so cool."

Radios blared pre-game stats, kids shouted and tossed Nerf footballs, and voices overlapped in a bizarre conversation. As people flowed by, it didn't take long to sell all but four shirts. Skippy reveled in the constant pats and compliments – he hadn't even objected when Timmy put a Rams bandana on him. The mutt was gobbling it up like a sweet-freak with a Twinkie.

Fifteen minutes before kickoff, Timmy was trying to decide where he was going to go to listen to the game, still holding up the shirts to possible buyers. He wanted to be close enough to soak up the energy of the Dome, even though little could be heard standing outside of it.

"Hey, can I get that one you got on?" a man asked, motioning that it would be for his teenaged son standing next to him.

Timmy stared at the boy and he froze. *Oh, my god.*

Their eyes met, and Timmy searched them for some sign of recognition.

So much for *All for one and one for all.*

"C'mon, Devin. I don't think the kid wants to sell it." The father backed away, a little spooked by Timmy's glare.

But Timmy couldn't shake it. The resemblance was uncanny. He would've sworn on a stack of Bibles that the guy standing before him was Brent Matthews, aka Athos. Relief and sadness mixed with a blend of confusion. That head-on collision still had his brain reeling.

What would he have said? Nothing he could say would

explain why he disappeared for four months. What would he tell them about That Night and how he ended up wearing a bloody pullover? How could he explain hiding for this long, missing the beginning of middle school. Or the gut-wrenching fear that early morning under the deck spying on his house that was no longer his house?

It's not like he could go back to Catalina Avenue and play musketeers with his best buddies.

"Kid, you okay?" A man's soft voice reached him from the end of a tunnel.

"Yeah –" Timmy tried to focus on the stubbled face. "I – I just saw – oh, never mind. Wanna shirt? I got four left."

"How much for the rest of them?" The man stood several inches shorter than Max – *or my dad.* But he had the same laugh lines and wisps of gray around the temples.

"Seriously?" His heart fluttered. He had worried he might not sell the last few. "Twenty dollars for the four!"

"Sure. My wife and youngest will love 'em." He took out two tens from his wallet and hesitated before handing them to Timmy.

Uh-oh, a hustler.

"Tell you what, kid, what if I gave you ten bucks and this extra ticket? Only two of my kids ended up comin'. My youngest caught a heck of a cold, and he had to stay home with his mom. She prefers watching it on TV, cuz she doesn't like watching football on carpet. Truth be told, she likes commercial breaks to go to the bathroom or the kitchen. Anyway, it crushed Alex, but even a game isn't worth pneumonia. Ben and Seth will love 'em. So how about ten bucks for a thousand-dollar ticket?" The man's smile made Timmy's heart hammer with excitement. His tip would cover the break.

"Well?" The man raised his eyebrows wrinkling his forehead.

"Are you sure? I mean..." Timmy's head was swimming. Good luck always came in threes, Max constantly preached –

selling all his merchandise before game time, a brand-new Rams sweatshirt, and now a ticket to the game?

Wow.

Timmy's smile was so big he couldn't talk. His excitement built as he handed the man the shirts. Skippy yipped at his feet, not knowing why his boy was so happy but wanting to be part of it.

I'm glad I washed up. Would the man have offered it to me if I hadn't?

"Bad news is," the guy added dramatically, and Timmy's heart plummeted to Arkansas. "You gotta sit with me and the guys."

He thought for a fleeting moment the guy was going to say he was a cop. Timmy cased the two boys, the oldest maybe ten or eleven. The youngest looked about nine. A kid.

"Sure, Mister, that's no problem at all. Let me go tell my boss real quick, okay?" He had already spied Cooter bantering with some guys on the corner across from the entrance.

"Give me a sec." Timmy felt the bulge of cash in his pocket and sprinted down the sidewalk, across the street, and through the swarm of people. Skippy, right on his heels, yapped the whole way.

"Cooter! 'Scuse me, ma'am." He weaseled past the bum's customers. "Cooter, I – I got a ticket. The guys dropped off the radio flyer but I don't wanna lose it. Can you hide it somewhere?"

"Well, holy shit, kid. How the hell did you manage that? Well, you do me a favor then—so I can go enjoy my own recreation, huh?" Cooter nuzzled the bleach blonde hair of a woman so painted, Timmy thought she might be a mannequin until she giggled and nibbled Cooter's ear.

"Sure...what is it?" Timmy glanced across the street at the man holding the bag of T-shirts—*boy, that was stupid of me...not taking the ticket first.*

"Just sold all my goods and don't think I should be packin'

all this. Aren't you s'posed to see Billy after the game?" Cooter whispered something in the woman's ear that made her giggle. He then cast a glance across the street, over Timmy's shoulder, and head nodded to someone.

"Uh, yeah, I guess." Timmy tried to see what Cooter was staring at. As for Billy, he didn't have a plan to see any of them until after the game, did he? Billy and Max had been swallowed by the masses after returning the wagon and said they'd see him back in the alley. Timmy knew that meant they'd be swimming in a bottle or two long

all that cash—*if someone robs me, Max'll tan my hide.* He before then.

"Do me a favor, okay? Me and, uh, what'd you say yer name was again?" Cooter leaned closer to Miss Painted Face, and she murmured something that made his cheeks flush. "Whewee! Anyways, Billy said he was gonna check on you, and I don't wanna have all this cash on me. Give this to him when he comes over, okay? Now don't you forget, or he'll have my ass. Plus, I want my cut. Tell him I made good, sold every damn one of 'em!" Cooter shoved a folded wad of bills into Timmy's hand.

Jesus. His heart slammed in his chest, the idea of stuffed it into his other front pocket, both now bulging.

"No problem. I got a ticket and...and as soon as Billy comes by, I'm goin' to the game. He with Max?" Timmy was about to come out of his shoes, and he knew the man and his boys could disappear any minute.

"Uh, yeah, um, I think so." Cooter cast a nervous glance toward the Dome. Timmy watched him study his shoes.

What's up with you, Cooter?

"Hope you have as much fun as I do, kid." Cooter whispered something in Miss Painted Face's ear, and she giggled.

"You don't have a prayer, Cooter. She ain't gonna throw any touchdowns." Timmy grinned. "Don't forget about my wagon."

Timmy didn't wait for a cheesy Cooter answer. He bolted back across the street. "Thank you so much, sir!"

"Glad you can join us." The man held out the ticket to Timmy. "By the way, I'm Mr. Knight and this is Ben and that's Seth. You are?"

"Timmy...I'm Timmy. And thank you so much. This is...this is awesome." As he held the ticket, he wanted to run a circle around the Dome and cheer like a maniac. "This is Skippy. You hold down the fort, okay?" He hugged his terrier, then floated with Mr. Knight and his sons toward the entrance. They became part of the swarm, elbow to elbow with regular people – Timmy could even feel their breath on the back of his neck.

I can't believe I'm here....

The ticket-taker took his and tore it in a fluid, practiced motion.

"Enjoy the game," she said, and Timmy wanted to let out a loud *yahoo!* He was beyond words. He tucked the stub into his back pocket thinking it could be a fine bottle-cap accent on the inside of his box. *Or on a wall in a real bedroom.*

The thumping sound of kick-off music made Timmy antsy, eager to get to his seat and take in the whole scene. But Mr. Knight headed straight to concessions to buy four hot dogs, sodas, and a beer before they hustled to their upper level seats. They were getting to their seats as the Giants kicked-off, but to Timmy it didn't matter. Being inside, about to watch the big game, was icing on a giant cupcake. Ben and Seth both mumbled that it was a good thing no one had run it back for a touchdown. Mr. Knight scowled at his boys, but within minutes all four were screaming at the top of their lungs as Isaac Bruce caught a thirty-yard pass from Kurt Warner.

"BRUUUUUUUCE!" everyone chanted, sounding like a thunderous boo.

He beamed, gloating that Clint and Billy had to sit their

sorry asses outside and listen like the losers they were. Max had said they would listen to the play-by-play on the radio outside the Dome and being near it all was just as good as being there, the exclamation point, he proclaimed.

Timmy knew *this* was the exclamation point.

Mr. Knight jumped up and down beside his boys and it reminded him of his own father. His dad would have eaten this up with a spoon.

Marshall Faulk broke loose for a first down, and Timmy whooped at the top of his lungs. When the Rams scored their first touchdown all three of them high-fived each other and turned and slapped his hands just like he was part of their family. The gesture suddenly made him feel like he belonged to something, that the months of hiding could be over. These people didn't know he was a criminal – they didn't know he'd done bad things That Night or any other time, because he hadn't told them. So what was to stop him from continuing that lie of omission?

"Ah, Dad, look at that guy run!" Sam jumped up and high-fived their father, knocking over a lamp. Nothing broke, but Mom panicked and didn't relax until she had inspected every inch. Then she cheered louder than they had.

Timmy tried to shake the ghosts, but being around Mr. Knight and his boys felt so real, so *right*. A quarterback sack erupted the crowd again and Timmy joined them, screaming his head off.

At halftime, Mr. Knight took them to the concession stands. Timmy felt awkward standing with them, like a tag-along. Ben and Seth each got a bag of peanuts and an order of nachos to split.

How could they be hungry after that delicious hot dog? Timmy had eaten more today than his stomach was used to. Cold Mickey D's seemed like a lifetime ago.

"Okay, Timmy, what's it gonna be?" Mr. Knight turned, pulled some bills from his pocket, and waited. Timmy had his own hands stuffed into his front jeans pockets to hide the wad of bills he had.

He was too taken aback to accept anything. When the father had ordered hot dogs before, he had just handed them out to everyone.

"Uh, no thanks. I'm good."

The two boys gawked at him as if aliens danced on top of his head.

"Dad always buys for anyone he takes to the games. It goes with the territory," Ben explained.

"He's an ar-chi-tect," Seth sounded out carefully. "He likes to buy stuff for people. Makes him feel good."

"So?" Mr. Knight's raised eyebrows created the row of wrinkles on his forehead again. Timmy would've laughed if he hadn't been so nervous about how to respond.

"Well, sir, I...I would love a bag of peanuts and a soda." This was all so foreign – part of Before.

"God, Sam, if you eat another peanut, you're gonna turn into an elephant." A Cardinal base hit distracted them all as the crowd burst into cheers for the RBI that put the Redbirds ahead.

"Okay, we'll have three bags of peanuts, three Cokes, and I'll have a Budweiser. Anyone want nachos?" Mr. Knight turned to them to see if there were any takers.

"Wait. Could you make that a Dr Pepper?" Timmy caught the lady shoving cups under spouts.

"Sure," she answered, and moved one cup under the familiar brown symbol. The afterimage of his dad made it hard to look at Mr. Knight.

Two in one day...this is like Before.

When the guy behind the counter handed him a gigantic cup and his own bag of peanuts, Timmy thanked Mr. Knight again. He felt awkward taking handouts from anyone. Especially with wads of money in his pockets—no idea how much exactly, but a *lot*. It made him giddy just to think about it.

"Want nachos? I'll split 'em with somebody." Mr. Knight glanced at his boys who shook their heads, then to Timmy.

"No, thank you, Mr. Knight. These peanuts are what ball games are all about." He and his father had always bought peanuts for baseball games. Sam was the hot dog and nachos fiend.

After he paid and they made their way back to their seats, Timmy couldn't dispel the dream-like feel of the day.

Cameras flashed, music vibrated their seats, and a hum pulsed through the crowd. And here he sat with his temporary friends, a grin the size of the Mississippi plastered on his face.

Even if for only three hours, life was normal again. Beyond normal. It was *good.*

I want this life back. What I did in August, That Night, can I undo it? And Baldy – I bet he wasn't hurt that bad. I could change my name, tell people I'm someone else. I look different enough and –

"RUN! RUN! RUN!"

The crowd went crazy as Torry Holt made a leaping grab for a fifteen-yard gain.

"That rookie is gonna be somethin' else!" Mr. Knight shouted and high-fived Seth.

Man, a speedster rookie, Trent Green in primo shape, and picking up Faulk from the Colts? Rams might be worth a watch, Dad. Your Chiefs can't do squat in the post-season. You might hafta split time! Sam's face swam in and out of focus, making the dream-effect more surreal.

"Holy cow!" Ben screamed, as Hakim caught another laser throw from Warner, no one with a prayer of catching him. They all shouted, "RUN RUN RUN," as he bolted downfield for a 65-yard score.

"TOUCHDOWN!" They all yelled in unison, the double high-fives all around, even with fans in front and behind them. The music boomed, the TD celebration deafening in the Dome. Timmy relished it all—the energy pulsing through the crowd, the wild outfits, beer bellies with words painted on them, and huge signs people had colored hoping the TV cameras would zoom in on them.

He was dizzy with excitement, topped off with a sugar buzz, and he ached to freeze this moment.

In almost four months on the streets, he had managed to become anonymous, invisible...disposable. And days rolled together with nothing to differentiate one from the other. Now, in less than a week, he had seen a musketeer's sister and was deeply immersed in an encounter with family life so much like his own, it was easy to pretend. Timmy stared at Mr. Knight and squinted. With a little imagination, the man could pass for his father.

"C'mon, Timmy, rub harder. Use those muscles." Timmy was distracted during the nightly massage. The scrolling school names at the bottom of the screen determined whether he had a brutal spelling test or a snowball fight with fellow musketeers. "Sorry, Dad." He resumed kneading his dad's deltoids, then gave a YAHOO! when his school's name showed up.

Suddenly everyone jumped up and roared as a Rams' defender, Mike Jones, intercepted a Collins pass. He hollered as loud as he could, making Ben and Seth laugh.

Something inside Timmy had been shifting for days, but this moment, this dose of untethered joy, cemented his determination. Seize the opportunities or let life pass him by. *Not today, not now, not again.*

Flashes of his dad booing bad calls or whooping maniacally when a Chief ran for a touchdown – the crazy days of Marcus Allen and Tony Gonzalez, so contagious even Mom lost control a time or two. Sam had bit his lip, jumped up, and slammed the Nerf ball in his hands with the others but remained silent as a mouse. He dealt with excitement much differently than Timmy and their dad.

Not if you were here, Sam. You'd jump out of your skin

and scream your crazy head off.

By the end of the game, Timmy's voice had been zapped. The screaming- cheering combination was brutal on his vocal chords, and Ben got tickled at him. The privileged boy had no concept of Timmy's world, figuring out how to slip into heated stores to allow frozen toes and pulsating ears to thaw. Or the sensation of a throat so cold it burned. But when Ben started snickering at him, Timmy couldn't help but join in.

"YOU NEED TO TAKE A REST!" Ben shouted over the crowd.

"I KNOW!" he hollered back.

They both giggled but continued to scream. The place nearly came apart when the Rams won, driving a stake into the Giants' season. Everyone around them mocked the hated rival – *why do they call them the football Giants, Dad – there aren't any baseball Giants in New York. I don't get it.*

"Whoa, watch where you're goin', runt!" A massive shoulder slammed into Timmy.

"Sorry." But he was flying too high to worry about people around him. He wasn't even sure his feet touched the ground. He checked his pockets, just to be sure the bulges of cash were still there.

Mr. Knight created a barrier around the three boys as they fought the crowd and streamed out in single-file, being smooshed by the hundreds of people crammed into the same space. The sweatshirt covered his front pockets but he had to be extra careful. These rolls of cash held the key to his future.

"Great game, huh?" Mr. Knight's face was flushed as they fought their way to a clearing beside the escalator.

Timmy jabbered to Ben about Faulk, Bruce, and Holt but admitted he wanted to be Warner, to throw the long ball.

"Can you believe that guy was a back-up? Played Arena League?" Ben shook his head, with an incredulous gleam in his eyes.

"I know! Trent Green woulda been awesome, but man.

Warner's got the grease. Mr. Knight, this was the best." Timmy pressed his heels to the concrete, just to make sure they were touching.

"I'm sure glad you enjoyed it, Timmy. You were fun to have along...you know your football! Wanna join us for ice cream at Ted Drewes?" Mr. Knight pulled keys from his front pocket. The Cadillac symbol on the key jangled a memory in Timmy's brain.

"Oh, man, I couldn't eat anymore or I'd pop. But I just can't thank you enough. Today was totally cool." He couldn't stop smiling. Mr. Knight and his two sons all held out their hands and shook his – like a grown-up.

"You take care of yourself, Timmy," Mr. Knight said, as his boys waved bye and dashed into a fan store. "Uh-oh, I think I'm in trouble. They're gonna break me in there."

Timmy grinned and thanked him again, then watched the father waltz into the store to buy the world for his sons.

The Brent lookalike came out of the store laughing, babbling about the game to his dad. He glanced at Timmy but the invisibility cloak worked its magic. No matter how much he cleaned up, he still had the stamp of poverty on him..

But the plan that kept lingering in the back of his head resurfaced. He caressed the bulges in his pockets – a real ticket to freedom. His fellow Musketeers had to have dealt with his disappearance, Timmy accepted that, had wondered time and again about how they must've responded to what happened to him.

What did they know? What had the papers said? Everyone had to know he had survived, hadn't they?

With the plan came knowledge, truth, and Timmy knew it was time. If he wanted a future, he had to find out what happened That Night. He had to know what he had done.

Time to put up, because he'd shut up far too long.

Chapter Twenty-Five

When Timmy exited the Dome, everything felt different. The afternoon breeze was just as cold, the film on his teeth just as sticky, the walk back to Brookline just as long. But he had a plan – he meant to find out what Max knew about That Night, and if the old man couldn't help, Timmy was going to the library. *Time to put up.*

"RAMS ROCK!" Music blared from everywhere – a stadium anthem to his left, a country sing-along somewhere behind him, a classic Seger song his mom and dad used to dance to blended with it. The echo made it impossible to tell the origin of any of it. People laughed, cheered, high-fived each other. Cigarette smoke plumed from tents of people partying – after-game gatherings as festive as the pre-game parties.

It excited Timmy so much, he wasn't even cold. The fleece-lined sweatshirt helped, but he covered the blocks to find the boxes by Stan the Man. Flipping a box open, he pulled out his ratty Salvation Army coat that no one bothered to steal, and tugged it on for ease of carrying. He patted the inner pocket and found Billy's transistor radio safe and sound. No Skippy but the terrier knew his way around the city and the trek back home better than Timmy.

"Hey, kid, where'd you get that sweatshirt? That's *sweet!*" A guy in his mid-twenties or thirties was so bold, he parted Timmy's coat to inspect it.

"Got it before the game." He stepped back a step, out of habit. "

"Oh, where at?" The guy – a richie, Max would've called him – said something else, but Timmy caught a glimpse of a group of gang bangers less than ten yards away barking at people. One of them aimed his finger like a gun at them and mouthed *Pop!* The thugs swaggered toward one of the party tents. An enormous man's bicep flexed, making the tattoo he couldn't quite see expand. The dude and his cronies circled two women holding red cups, like wolves prowling around deer.

"Kid?" The nosey sweatshirt admirer said something else, but all Timmy could focus on were the guys goading the women until one of them spilled her drink. They didn't belong, like sharks out of water, a palm tree in downtown New York, a bikini-clad model on a ski slope – all perfect Samisms for the situation. The tent was filled with a steady flow of yuppies in dress coats and scarves, a row of limousines waiting to escort patrons of the party home. But the thugs waltzed right up like they owned the place.

One WWF wannabe struck a weird chord of familiarity. He side-glanced Timmy, saw the kid staring at him, and feigned a snapping motion. Timmy jumped and did all he could to swallow the scream. The banger turned around to laugh a little too loud with one of his buddies behind him. That's when Timmy saw it.

Oh, god...

He felt the blood drain from his face as he caught sight of the dagger-in-heart tattoo dancing on the guy's left deltoid. The waning sun peeked out from behind clouds, enhancing the intricate greenery and the red heart shining brightly below it. The pearl handle glistened with such detail and artistry, Timmy suspected the creator had practiced his craft often. *M1Gram* was tattooed in the dead center of the heart.

I know what that means, don't I? But yet he didn't. Something tugged at Timmy's insides. *He looks like – like....*

Timmy fell backwards and by pure luck, hit the base of the statue and sat on the ledge. He couldn't catch his breath, couldn't seem to get oxygen deep enough to satisfy his heaving chest. Aware of Mr. Nosey asking him if he was okay and telling him to breathe deep, Timmy nodded, as if to agree with something the guy said about hyperventilating. A hand on his shoulder brought on a touch of panic, knowing anyone could steal him blind right now if he didn't get himself together. But the after-image wouldn't go away.

You know whatcha took o' mine, dog....

"Slow down, son, you're gonna pass out." The voice, so much like his father's, cut through the fog. He opened his eyes and for split second, it *was* his dad. Oh how he ached for the protective halo his dad always provided when he was scared or hurt or in need of anything short of a miracle. Even then, his dad would try.

The dream, the muscle-bound thug from his nightmare had just walked past him, hadn't he? Except it wasn't exactly the same thug. Timmy somehow understood that. But now the pieces were starting to fall into place. Certain details made sense now. That Night swam into focus for a brief moment, noodling Timmy's legs.

Oh, God.

"Yo, kid! Can you hear me?"

This time he was finally able to open his eyes and look up. Mr. Nosey seemed genuinely concerned.

"Uh, I think I just saw a ghost," was all he could mumble.

"You look like it. You turned completely white, boy. You got folks with you?" Mr. Nosey's eyes narrowed. "You're not hustlin' out here, are you, kid?" The man pulled his own jacket open, revealing a police officer's badge clipped to his belt.

Timmy's heart, already slamming from seeing the Tattooed Goon, lurched. A confrontation with a cop trumped all other emotion. The plain clothes hadn't set off alarms. But he'd let his guard down and probably wouldn't have noticed twenty uniformed officers holding handcuffs in his current state.

Instinctively, he felt his front jeans pockets, tried to resurrect the rush of seeing Hakim tearing down the sideline, and revealed the ticket he'd slipped into his back pocket. In the other back pocket, he knew, was the Swiss army knife – metal insurance, Max called it. Trouble, if the officer did.

"Just left the game with some friends. I think I had too much to eat. Got real nauseous there for a minute." Timmy held up his hand like he might puke. "But Uncle Max, he's over there somewhere." He head-nodded toward the upscale tent.

"All right, kid. You get on along, okay? And watch out for those bangers. They're bad news." Mr. Nosey patted him on the shoulder and walked away without looking back.

Don't I know it, he wanted to respond. Instead, he waited for the world to right itself, sucking air and shaking his head to rid it of unwelcome images. The thugs were gone, but still lingered in his mind like an after-image. Knowing he'd never find any of the Gerries in the mass of people, Timmy weaved his way back toward the Riverfront, through hundreds of fans still milling about, drinking beer, reliving the touchdowns, turnovers, and playoffs. The electricity rejuvenated him. As renewed energy spurred him along, he hustled north, back toward no-man's land and the concrete world of burn barrels and bums.

He gave an occasional sharp whistle for Skippy, just in case. As he left the protective cover of buildings and shared heat of all those bodies, the chill forced him to button his coat and pull up the collar.

With the overlapping of worlds, he remembered a time he and Sam be-bopped back to the car after a Cards game, humming tunes and seeing who could guess the other's the quickest. He hummed one Sam could never get, a boy band song he hated. Timmy couldn't remember the name but didn't think it would keep him from being able to recite every word or hum every note. The mind, he knew, was a strange thing.

As he passed a group of men huddled around a tiny burn barrel, miniature compared to the one in their alley, he called out, "Go Rams!"

The guys held up their bottles and cheered.

"Hey, you guys seen Max?" Their fire popped and crackled. He didn't see what street he was on, but the area had the same broken down feel to it, close enough to home. And one of the bums had been around Brookline a time or two.

"Not for a while, kid. Think he went in search of Jim Beam."

"Or Johnny Walker."

"Or Jack, hell he don't care which of those boys he finds. Any of the wise men do him just hunky-dory," another drunk snorted. All of them cackled and took swigs of their own wise men.

Stupid hypocrites – drink while they judge an old man about his drinkin'. Max had taught him the word sometime in late September, when they had lessons, and boy, his grandpa was right. Drunks were the worst kind.

Even after his thug-encounter, his excitement was palpable. He speed-walked down side streets and past various late-night eateries. St. Louis was abuzz with Rams' fever, no matter the part of the city. He hummed as he be-bopped down street after street. He had stopped in the alley behind Vinnie's Deli to count the cash. He slipped a couple of twenties into his sock, just in case Max was too drunk to remember Timmy's cut. The old man didn't exactly balance books, and now that he had Cooter's cash, too, he considered heading for the hills with all of it. It made him feel like a thief, but weren't they all? He scribbled the adjusted total on the back of his ticket, partly so he wouldn't forget but mostly to show Max and see the old man's eyes go wide.

Two-thousand one hundred eighty-five dollars.

Timmy's head swam. It had to affect Max the same, didn't it? And then they would talk, *really* talk.

"Yo, Skippy, where are you, boy?" Timmy gave a shrill whistle, but no pitter-patter, no sharp barks of response. He did an about-face on Brookline, pretended to be a soldier marching in a parade, humming some old song from music class about a bunch of trombones until he reached the alley.

None of the regulars hovered over the barrel or sat on buckets shooting the breeze. A few bums who'd been freeloading that morning gave him a glassy-eyed glance. A little deflated not to be able to gloat about his ticket or even his sales, he gave them a wide berth and slipped into his box.

A few more fringe bums shouted as they joined the heat moochers. They squawked laughter loud enough to raise the dead. Timmy tugged the cash out of his pocket, spread it out on his sleeping bag, and ogled it for a few minutes. Then he sorted the bills, remembering his days as banker in Monopoly. But this...these bills were real. And they could change his life, couldn't they? When he finished, he had neat piles of ones, fives, tens, twenties, and even a single fifty.

"Wow." Combining the stacks, highest bills on bottom and ones on top, he wound a rubber band around it, and stuffed it deep into an inside pocket of his coat. He folded the jacket in half and laid it under his pillow. It was hours before bedtime, barely eight o'clock. But he couldn't leave his stuff and didn't dare wander around with all that cash on him. Caution was the mission, the word of the day, and the top priority.

Deciding to just lay low the rest of the evening, he lay on top of the sleeping bag, rested his head firmly on the thicker-than-usual pillow, and stared along the top of his box. There wasn't enough light to make them out inside the box, but he visualized them.

Corona, Corona Light, Sam Adams, Stewart's Orange Soda, Diet Dr Pepper, Diet Sprite.... A smile crept across his face. He loved his bottle caps, but tonight he didn't feel like picturing them or counting them. If sleep didn't come, he decided he would just lie there and think about the game, about selling shirts, about Bruce and Warner and Faulk and Hakim's catch. Too many days were carbon copies of the ones before, so a football game and a visit from a past demon gave him a lot to think about.

I wonder how much Max'll let me keep.

Timmy twisted so he could see out his box at the men standing around the fire barrel. The burlap door, still pinned to the top, allowed him a perfect view of the entryway. When Max got back, Timmy would share their massive take and blow the old man's mind. Lying with his hands behind his head, he gave his fifteenth sharp whistle, hoping Skippy might have wandered within hearing distance in the last ten minutes. His heart surged when he heard scampering feet, and his best buddy launched into his box.

"Hey, Skipmeister, how's my boy?" Skippy licked Timmy's entire face, the smell of hot dog, peanuts, and sweat sending him into a tizzy.

"Slow down, Skip, I missed you too!" He giggled, letting Skippy bathe him with kisses.

Exclamation point to a glorious day, minus a brief run-in with That Night. Skippy sniffed the hoodie, then scratched at it until Timmy lifted the waist band so the mutt could crawl under and smash into Timmy's chest.

"Sheesh, Skip, good thing I got layers between us. You stink!" Timmy giggled, realizing he was far cleaner than his furry buddy for the first time in a while. Even working up a sweat at the game couldn't compete with his previous weeks of grime. Or Skippy's dumpster-diving filthy fur. But he didn't care. Despite the brief scare from a Muscle Man lookalike, Timmy felt good.

He might even wait a few days, until after Christmas, to interrogate Max. Enjoy the holidays, even buy each other a real present, get a small tree. A few days of celebration could cheer the place up, and maybe it would ease the guilt of leaving Max when he set his plan in motion.

Before he could begin his to-do list for the week, he fell asleep.

Chapter Twenty-Six

Swirls of color swam before the boy, though he missed most of it. The massive deltoid of a thug sitting on Scott's front porch consumed him. Except it wasn't really Scott's house – it was small, with bars on the windows. A rough neighborhood that tugged at Timmy's memory, to an After time.

"Get outta my life," Timmy shouted, trying to make good on his claim not be a cry-baby. But for some reason, every time he saw Muscle Man, he just wanted to burst into tears.

"Can't, dog, this ain't my dream."

*Timmy stared, confused and angry that he kept having to contend with this guy, this memory, the stupid repetition. But the new version of Muscle Man's face differed, didn't it? Eyes closer together, corn rows, only two gold-covered teeth. The tattoos though...*those *were the same.*

"So, dog, whatcha gonna do when they come for you?" The thug gave one sharp laugh at his personal chanting rendition of the Cops *theme song. No, not quite a laugh but a bark – mean and sinister.*

Timmy despised this guy more than the snakes he used to imagine crawling on him after seeing a movie when he was eight. Because he understood on some deeper level that this hood –wasn't that what his mom had called them? – had done something horrible to him. Or was it the other way around? Either way, Timmy was certain this loser played a part in ruining his life That Night.

"Who's comin' for me?" he snapped. But dang it if he didn't wish he could snatch that question back. Timmy didn't want to give the jerk the satisfaction of scaring him.

"My boys, Tim, my boys. You remember whatcha done, don'tcha? Now they wanna bite o' some fresh meat. Yer cute brother left a great taste in my mouth."

For one fleeting second, Timmy did remember –

"Shit, Drey, do 'em!" The muzzle flash made Timmy yelp. Shouts, someone pounding the hood of a car – he had clapped his hands over his ears, hadn't he?

That Night swam out of focus – his mind had completely erased it like his old Etch-A-Sketch. Just a swish of the knob or a hard shake, and presto, it disappeared.

Timmy squinted, tried to bring back the memory, but it evaporated like the lost lyrics of some song the radio never played often enough.

"See? I knew you'd remember, you little thief. So it's payback time. You understand about paybacks now, don'tcha, boy? No little richie no more, are ya? Ain't ridin' around in a Cadillac neither, huh? Guess you ain't doin' much ridin' around like that these days."

Muscle Man stood and swaggered toward him. Timmy stared up and down Catalina Avenue to see if anybody was out mowing, walking a dog, painting a house, getting their mail, or inspecting for boogeymen.

Nada. Not one single, solitary person in the entire neighborhood was outside on a bright, sunny August afternoon. Where the heck was everybody?

Wait. But it's not August, *his mind pieced together. But it had been then, hadn't it?*

Muscle Man closed the gap. Fifteen feet, fourteen, thirteen, twelve. In a matter of minutes, the massive hands would grab his scrawny neck. Timmy was as certain of that fact as anything he had ever known – even D'Artagnan's role as a musketeer.

"Please, Mister, I don't know you. Why're you tryin' to hurt me?" The words limped out, like a whiny crybaby, and Timmy hated himself for it. He remembered someone mocking him for acting that way.

"Stop it," the voice mocked. "You hurt me, remember? You ain't no Momma's boy no more, huh? No minutes gonna help you no mo'. Naw, guess we showed her, dog. And how's that

pretty boy brother of yours? Ooooh, I 'member him." Hands reached for Timmy, while the thug chuckled, and when he got within breathing distance, Muscle Man winked.

Chapter Twenty-Seven

"No!" Timmy croaked and sat up so abruptly, he nearly tossed Skippy out of the box. The terrier whimpered, sensed the boy's anxiety and immediately nuzzled his furry head into Timmy's neck. He hugged Skippy fiercely, letting his best friend help push the bad man from his dreams. Skippy licked frantically, hoping kisses would ward off the demons.

Scraps of memory remained from the dream. Fragments, disjointed bits of true memory, like disjointed facts that drove investigators mad on a murder case.

"He has something to do with my family, Skip. That man, he did something with them. Why can't I remember?" Timmy shook his head, ran his fingers through his hair, still too clean to stay in place with the gesture.

Skippy took care of Timmy by licking his face at least thirty-five times.

"Okay, Skip, it's good, I'm better." *Thank God for small favors like little terrier mutts.* "I just wish I could remember. Not just the flashes, but all at one time." And with a sudden revelation, Timmy decided he needed to start a journal. The memories, the nightmares, and the flashes of déjà vu all led back to that turning point, the summer that seemed eons ago. That Night. He knew if he recorded the small details, maybe he could piece together the frustrating puzzle that lay in a thousand pieces in his brain.

He didn't know, but it was time to sort the jigsaw, pull out the edge pieces, and begin the process of making them fit. If he didn't, he was going to go crazy. After he talked with Max, he was going to the library. *Or was I waiting till after Christmas?* After so many consecutive days of the same nightmare, he didn't know if he could wait.

He scrambled around his tiny shoebox desk for the little

notepad he had found several weeks ago. His Tigger watch blinked 9:45 p.m. His heart sank.

I slept less than a measly hour.

Crawling outside the box for more light and room, he wrapped his sleeping bag around him, and tried to make the first pencil entry by the glow of the burn barrel. The fire had diminished to glowing embers, so he tossed in a few sheets of newspaper. Everyone had made like cloth and bolted, probably to soak up the fever around the Dome. The Gerries didn't like to miss a chance to party. Timmy had grown accustomed to the silence, and in a weird way, preferred it.

With tedious precision, he jotted notes, tallied facts as clearly as he could remember, and before he lost the images, he heaved a chest-clearing sigh. Then he began to draw.

After ten minutes of decisive strokes, erasing madly, and sweeping away the eraser bits, he stared at the tattoo that seemed to have so much to do with his past. Though his sketch was far more crude than the elaborate drawings on the deltoids he had seen, it still filled him an eerie foreboding. Satisfied, he lay his head back against the brick building and closed his eyes, trying to picture That Night – to put to rest the demons that had haunted him for nearly four months.

"Holy shit! Christmas came early didn't it! We usually hate it, but hot *damn!*" Billy barged into the alley clanking two bottles together, bellowing Rams cheers. Ralph and another ancient geezer shouted the words to "Celebration," but made no attempt to sing on key.

"Hey, kid, howthahell are ya? We heard you got to go to the *goddamned* game. That true?" Vernon slurred, marching up to Timmy and slapped a high-five that almost knocked the boy over. Catching his tiny notepad, he couldn't help but bust into a grin. The rush returned like a freight train, derailing the melancholy.

"Well?" Billy walked toward him, taking a huge slug of whiskey. He raised his eyebrows, like he wanted something.

"Well *what?*" Timmy shoved the notepad into his jeans pocket, concealing his drawing. He couldn't imagine how he'd explain that tidbit of memory.

"Details, kid. Tell us about the game!" Billy, normally crotchety and anti-social once he tipped the bottle, teetered, well on his way to morning hangover.

"Oh, man, it was awesome! You guys shoulda seen it. Warner's arm is a rocket," Timmy started, then caught himself. It was hard not to gloat, but he could tell by their expressions that despite their envy, they were eating it up. He told them about the touchdowns, the interception, and thunderous crowd.

"So you had fun? That's the important thing. Now –" Billy wiped the back of his hand across his slobbery mouth. "Fork over the dough. Ain't had hardly a damn thing to eat all night. Swiped a few chicken fingers during the game, but man, it was a madhouse in there. But I'm hungrier than a bear in heat. Max wouldn't give me a single damn dime." Holding his hand out, he motioned with his fingers to give it up. "Jesus, this place reeks. And why didn't nobody get us somethin' to eat. You guys ain't good fer shit," Billy griped, his hand still extended.

Timmy could hear Max knocking Billy for all his complaining. "Bitchin's like a damn rocking chair. Expend a helluva lot of energy but sure don't getcha nowhere." He spent quite a bit of time thinking about that one.

"I gave it to Cooter. He took it for me so I wouldn't have that kind of cash in the game. I'm sure he already gave it to Max. I thought he woulda' told you," Timmy lied, the words spilling out so smoothly he surprised himself.

"Shit. He had himself a girl. With all that money, we may never see that idiot again. If he gambles that cash away, I swear to God, I'll kill him. And you, you stupid little shit." Billy took a menacing step toward Timmy. "Did you keep some? Skim a little of my money after all those sales?"

"It ain't your money, Billy. And I told the other guys sellin' for Max that Cooter had the profits. So they all know." Timmy swallowed the quelling anger but a strange fear crept into his stomach at the grin spreading across Billy's face. Ralph covered a smirk, launching more butterflies in Timmy's stomach.

These men had taken advantage of him for so long, he didn't know what to believe or who to trust. Cooter was the only one who seemed to genuinely care about him, and Timmy had just thrown him under the bus. He fought the urge to feel his back pocket for the army knife or to glance toward his box where he'd hidden over two thousand dollars in his jacket.

But the sneer on Billy's lip kept him still.

"Yep, kid, you done good for us." Ralph snickered and winked at Billy. "But you shoulda brought it back here."

Ralph *never* spoke to Timmy. Demands for food and a few mumblings around the burn barrel, but little else. Timmy appreciated the absence of Ralph-speech, because he couldn't stand seeing the old dude's rotting teeth. Or the bright white sprigs of hair shooting out of the dark eyebrows so bushy they could've doubled for mustaches. And all that kept his attention from the old man's nose hairs.

"Whatcha starin' at, boy?" Ralph squinted, forcing the two thick eyebrows into a near unibrow. Timmy suppressed a shiver. The ancient geezer's change in attitude meant something, didn't it?

"Nothin'," Timmy muttered.

You got a bug up your ass, Ralph? It was an expression Max used often. It seemed fitting now.

"Then quit starin' at me, punk," Ralph bit harshly and took a long swallow of scotch.

Timmy couldn't help but gawk. "Bite me, Ralph," he snipped. "You guys're losers. Don't you ever think about anything other than booze? You make me sick." With trembling hands, he jumped to his feet, brushed the grit from his butt, and crawled in his box for the necessities.

His emotional outburst might not have been the wisest move, but his disgust and new proclamation to *put-up or shut-*

up added serious calcium to his backbone. He felt their eyes on him as he tugged on his heavier-than-usual coat and marched out of the alley. When he got fifteen to twenty feet away, he pulled the Army knife from his back pocket and waited – just in case. He didn't want to turn his back, his paranoia peaking. He couldn't see them, but he could still hear them. Cackling, someone sang out the chorus to Tom Petty, but improvised, "You be free fallin', kid, free fallin'." They all laughed.

What the heck? Oh, Cooter, stay away tonight. Please, God, stay away. Timmy could just imagine it...*Give me the money? No way, I gave the little twerp mine!*

But Cooter seldom crashed in the alley with them, unless he had started partying there. The young bum had women, like the painted one at the ball game, and they usually kept him from having to sleep out in the cold. He could disappear for days at a time, and with the look in his eyes staring at her earlier, no way he was coming to Brookline tonight. But he would be back eventually.

Before that happened, Timmy needed answers. He needed Max. He wouldn't give the money to anyone except Max. Or at least half of it. And in return, Timmy expected some answers. No waiting till after Christmas now. Without realizing it, his plan had set itself into motion.

"You'll want somethin' from us, boy, so you best watch your shit!" one of them shouted. It wasn't Ralph or Billy. Most of them liked Timmy well enough – all except Billy, and Ralph now seemed to have realigned his loyalties. Vernon always backed Timmy but didn't have the balls to stand up to anyone.

"Little pussy!" Ralph snapped, plenty loud for Timmy to still hear. "Gets to sell the goods and lands a damn ticket to the game. I'm glad he won't be – *Ow!* What'd you do that for?"

Billy hissed something to Ralph to get him to shut up. *Never had to worry about that before.*

Timmy couldn't stand it. His new determination and uncertainty where Max was ignited a fire inside him.

"What the hell would I want from you?" he demanded, as he stalked back into the alley. "I feed your asses all the damn time, without a thank you from any of you...not once, *Ralph,* have you ever said thank you. And without me, you'd starve. So...so...YOU'RE WELCOME!" He tried to ease the tremble in his voice, but he couldn't stop. "When you sober up, you'll wanna eat, then you'll want somethin' from *me.*" He kicked at an empty bottle, sent it crashing into the west wall of the alley. He stormed back out into the street, Skippy standing near the corner with his tail tucked. Timmy turned and glared at the bums who stared open-mouthed at him.

Yeah, wallow with your three wise men. But Jim, Jack, and Johnny ain't gonna feed you. And what's wise about drinking yourself into a hangover every stupid day?

"Yeah, I want somethin' from you, kid," one of the freeloaders around the barrel shouted. "A fifth of Hill & Hill!"

They all snickered. More stragglers had gathered around the barrel, probably to get first-hand accounts of the ruckus. He couldn't make out any of the faces except those in the glow of the fire.

"Don't reckon I could find one of them in that pretty little box of yours, could I?" the same voice called out. *Was that Vernon?*

Before he could lose his nerve, Timmy blurted, "Yeah, go ahead, get plastered. It's all you drunks do. You make me sick." He stood his ground in the middle of the street, not getting closer but not exiting either, unsure whether to run or wait. He didn't want to lose his box, the treasures inside. He'd grabbed the cash, but there was a lot more of value in that box to him than just money. *Screw you!* he wanted to add, but the fight in him had fizzled, tears nipping at its heels.

I'll never be one of you, he wanted to scream in Billy's face. No matter his failures, he would never chase them with a bottle. He'd learned that lesson living in the alley.

"Little punk, we'll see how well you get along with Max

gone!" Ralph snapped.

"Shut the fuck *up,* you idiot," Billy hissed.

Timmy's heart plummeted like a broken elevator.

Shit, why hadn't Max come back with Billy. They'd been together when he saw them last.

A bubble of panic welled in his chest.

"The little shit's gonna find out, Billy, not sure why yer not just sendin' him packin'." The voice he'd thought was Vernon's was a younger guy around the barrel.

Timmy didn't realize he was moving until he stood a foot from the guys holding their hands over the fire, *Max's* fire.

"What did you just say?" His tone contained little of the machismo he wanted it to. It was on the verge of cracking.

"Nothin', you little pissant," the loser slurred. The broken-down bum stood sandwiched between Vernon and some guy who had squatted with them in a warehouse for a while. Timmy couldn't think of his name. Big Mouth couldn't even look Timmy in the face, because the freeloader had butted in, and he knew it.

"Who are you anyway?" He tried to deliver one of his blistering glares.

"Mind your own Ps and Qs, boy," Billy snipped, just as Big Mouth, facial hair all the way to his eyes, mumbled *Carl.*

"Well, *Carl,*" Timmy snapped with as much venom as he could muster, "you don't live here, so mind your own damn business. Max'll kick your ass out when he gets back."

"Fuck you, kid," Carl shouted, edging closer to Vernon after he said it. He fit the bill parasite description Max had warned him about, the ones who roamed from skid to skid mooching. *Mooch and migrate,* Max had taught him, talking about the vagrants who begged from other homeless – lowest of the low.

"Jesus, you guys just couldn't quit, couldja?" Billy groaned and shook his head. "C'mere, kid. It's time to chat." Billy patted the bottom side of a flipped over paint bucket.

"Yep, tell him the ways of the world, Billy," Carl snipped, then grumbled something else to those close to him. The nasty men laughed, but Billy shot them a glance to shut them up. He didn't have Max's clout, that was obvious, because it didn't work.

"Kid needs to learn some respect," Ralph added.

"What're they talkin' about, Billy?" Timmy's voice hitched, as he walked toward the bucket, not sure whether to sit or run. His feet always itched to escape. Instead, he swallowed hard to keep the lump in place.

"It's okay, kid. Sit down." Billy patted the bucket again. Timmy sat, suddenly too tired to argue. The clog was swelling, making it hard to breathe. Billy being nice to him only made it worse.

"Wh – what's goin' on, Billy?"

He stared Timmy straight in the eyes, not wavering and not nearly as drunk as he'd seemed. "I don't know any other way to say it, kid, so I'm just gonna spill it. Max is in lock-up. And I'm pretty certain this time it's for the long haul."

"Why? What'd he do?" His mind reeled with what that meant for him. Max, his grandpa, was all he had. His protection and mentor. No matter the motives, no one messed with him because they knew they answered to Max. The old man possessed an unchallenged power in the alley, and even after months of proving his own worth to everyone, they all knew Timmy belonged to Max. Being a kid didn't guarantee his place here, food provider or not.

"Well, after the game, we got some bottles – a helluva party broke out." Billy gave a weak smile. "And the more everybody drank, the wilder it got. Some jerk grabbed Max's bottle, and it got hairy fast. Someone called the cops, but before they got there, Max cut the guy pretty good with a busted bottle. Man, all hell broke loose. It freaked me out. They was both pretty stoked, but I don't think Max got hurt too bad. But shit, I'm not sure. The damage was done though, blood everywhere, the guy on the ground. Cops came, and three strikes rule is gonna screw him."

"The what?" Timmy had heard the phrase and sort of understood, but he wanted to know *exactly* what it meant now. His life depended on it.

Oh, God, Max, you promised you'd never leave me.

"Three strikes and yer out is a law thing, kid. This is Max's third major offense, meanin' once you hit your third time, you don't go home. Prison's your new address, and why not? You get three squares, a roof over your head, and free cigarettes if you play your cards right. And I don't think any sane judge is gonna show an old drunk any leniency." Billy shook his head.

Timmy tried to process it. "If it's not so bad, why're you so scare of it?" Timmy stared wide-eyed at Billy.

Billy gave a weak laugh. "That's a good question. Except there's no booze in prison."

"May – maybe they'll just see it as a fight and cut him a break?" Timmy's mind whirled. What now? His plan hinged on answers. Suspicions he needed confirmed. But not to be abandoned again, no matter how much he wanted to get out of the alley.

"No breaks, not with what he did when the cops came. The altercation took an ugly turn." Billy took a sip of his black-labeled bottle. "One cop grabbed Max and another got hold of one arm. I don't know what the hell he was thinkin', but Max pulled the officer's nightstick and plugged him over the head with it. Knocked him out cold."

Timmy inhaled sharply, shocked that Max would do something so stupid. "Oh, God."

"Yeah. So the other policeman put his lights out. Charges against him are serious. Assaulting a police officer is major time, third strike or not. He screwed up royally this time. Sorry, kid, I know he's all the family you got."

Guilt swept over Timmy. His plan hadn't been to spend eternity with his grandpa but to get answers and then set off to re-join the real world, regardless of the consequences.

Maybe I'll see him in lock-up. But deep down, he knew that would never happen.

"I don't know what to do – I mean, I –" and then Timmy stopped. He was about to ask Billy what he should do with the money.

"Well, we'll need fed just the same, kid. Your rent ain't gonna be free. And I think some things will change a bit around here." He glanced toward the entrance of the alley, at the Gerries bantering around the barrel, a slow smile spreading across his face.

He thinks he's gonna be boss, but they don't listen to him. And he really doesn't like me. For a brief instant, Timmy regretted not trying a little harder with Billy. But it was too late now.

"Can I go see him? I mean, I gotta talk to him." *I gotta know what he knows.* Max's story for four months started with protecting Timmy for his parents until they got in touch with him to hiding out. Then it was about staying away from shelters and not going to soup kitchens too often because of what he'd done, and now the focus was laying low so cops couldn't find him for the various crimes he'd committed. Max seldom talked about his mom and dad anymore, and anytime Timmy asked, Max shut him down.

"Naw, I wouldn't, kid. He's in county, and that would embarrass the hell outta the old man. Plus, he might even be in the hospital. I don't really know. I don't exactly have a good relationship with the law, so I didn't ask. Before the cops came, he told me to look after you, so you should be okay here for the time bein.' But I'm gonna level with you, Timmy. If these folks want somethin' of yers now, they're gonna take it. And you're pretty resourceful. All them bottle caps of yours look pretty fun to some of these younger boneheads, especially when they're juiced. Not to mention your mirror, your little table, hell, your box. You and Max have yourselves a nice little nest here. Can't say as I would blame any of 'em. Max's space myself. Matter a fact, I think I might as well." Billy poked his head inside the flap of burlap to inspect the box they were sitting next to.

Timmy watched Billy root around in Max's things and bristled at the drunk's nerve. But he didn't say a word. He clenched his fists so hard his jagged nails dug half-moons into his palms. If he planned to make a change, brains played a more important role than a big mouth. Hadn't he sworn not to turn out like Max? Now was his chance to prove it.

"Boy howdy, lookie here." Billy rummaged through the blankets, then started shaking things. "Old Max has a gold mine of treasure in here."

Timmy felt the anger well in his chest and course through him. Each time Billy grabbed something, chatted excitedly about a find, or tossed an item out that he meant to keep, Timmy's heart pounded harder. He stood, measuring the distance between his foot and Billy's side. *God, I could just kick you 'til you drop.* The ferocity of his rage scared Timmy until he finally spoke.

"Don't." Timmy held his clenched fists out to his side, his teeth gritted so hard his head hurt. Being smart didn't mean rolling over and playing dead.

Billy turned and saw the expression on the boy's face and did just that.

"Now, boy, I like you okay, but you better know your place." He tossed a pair of Max's sweatpants to the filthy concrete but stood without taking his eyes off the kid.

"That's Max's, my grandpa's stuff. Keep your hands off, you hear me?"

"You'll what?" Billy asked, then watched Timmy's hand stray to his grimy back jean's pocket. Max's best friend knew well what the kid kept there – Timmy saw it in his eyes. The Swiss army knife might not be as powerful as the blade, but it would do the trick, and Billy was known for sleeping hard. He seemed to be considering all those factors when he let out an uneasy laugh.

"That baby knife don't scare me, boy. Put it away before I take it away." Billy took a step toward him. "Max liked you havin' protection, but if I want it, I'll *take* it. Got it? You may've used a knife a time or two, but you ain't got the balls to stick me. I'll skin you, and you know it."

Timmy wavered. He had protected himself before, and he wasn't afraid to do it again. Billy backed away from Max's things and grumbled that some little shit kid wouldn't last long with that kind of attitude. Timmy begged to differ. He remembered the beady-eyed bald man as if it had happened yesterday. But that had only been the first incident. He pulled the blade once to keep from getting robbed, another time to scare off a bum who wouldn't leave the alley when he was by himself – the guy had creeped him out. And after Thanksgiving, he had wandered into the triple X district and found himself face-to-face with three scrawny guys hanging outside an adult video store.

The blade had served him well that day. *Why do people make me hurt them?*

"I don't want trouble, Billy. It's almost Christmas, and I...I..." Giving voice to it, to *Christmas*, deflated him.

"Hey, Sam, let's go peek, please?" I put on my best puppy dog look.

"Go back to sleep, Timmy. It's not even six. You know the rule. Seven o'clock. Breakfast at eight." With that, Sam turned his back on me and yanked the covers from beneath my butt. I tumbled to the floor and mumbled that I was going without him. He whispered something as I shuffled to the hallway, but I didn't wait around to hear.

"Shit, kid, who gives a fuck about Christmas... You better watch –"

"Nuh-uh, Sam. I'm goin'." I slipped down the stairs, careful to skip the fourth step because it creaked. I heard another set of padding feet and glanced back at Sam coming

behind me. His blond hair stuck into the air in a million different directions and his eyes were little bitty slits. Creases from his pillow had left imprints on his right cheek.

And then I saw it.

"Wow!" My brand-new bicycle sat in the middle of the living room floor with a giant green bow on it. The Huffy had teal racing stripes and knobby dirt-bike tires. Visions of the ramps I would jump danced in my head.

"You two are so bad!" Mom said behind us. I jumped halfway out of my skin. I tried to apologize, but Mom swooped me into her arms and kissed my neck before I could say a word.

"I'm sorry, Mom, I was just so excited, and I knew something so totally awesome was down here. I could feel its energy pulling me like a force beyond my power to resist!"

"HEY! Stop it, goddammit. Jesus, kid, you're freakin' me the fuck out!" Billy grabbed Timmy's shoulders, and shook him. Timmy tried to focus on him.

Mom teased that she was gonna take the bike back, but she didn't mean it. We cracked jokes all the time. And we laughed. Boy, did we love to laugh...

In that life, Earth rotated on its axis and all was right with the world.

"Leave me alone." Timmy reached blindly in front of him, tears making it hard to tell where the mouth of the alley was. Skippy whimpered somewhere to his right. "Let's go, Skip," Timmy whispered, and then followed the pitter-patter of his pup's feet.

"You better stop chasin' them ghosts, kid," Billy barked at his back. "That bad-ass attitude don't mean shit to me and you know it. Max was my friend, but he's gone. Get used to it. I'll give you some space tonight, but get over yourself. You make idle threats and yer gonna have to follow through with 'em."

Timmy shuddered. *I have and I will, Billy. Don't ever doubt it.*

As he passed the burn barrel, it dawned on him. He didn't have to answer to Billy. He could go see Max if he damned well pleased. He glanced at his cracked Tigger watch wondering how early they'd allow visitors. It was almost eleven p.m. If he could buy time to sleep and get out of the alley before any more drama broke out – like Cooter be-bopping in – he could make good on that plan.

"I've got a deal for you, Billy. You look out for me tonight, keep my stuff safe for one more day, and I'll bring you back all the stashed food I have for Max, okay?"

"Food? Like what?" Billy's whole attitude changed. He stood and became his bitter, fumbling self again. He seemed to remember what the kid had always been – a meal ticket.

"You name it. I've got some pasta, a little pizza, but I can score you some fresh hoagies, in the morning, too." Mondays were always good for sandwiches at Vinnie's. To ice the cake, he added, "Maybe even a bottle, if I find someone to do it. How's that?" Timmy knew finding a liquor store and then scoping out a buyer might be tough. If not, he would drop an extra twenty bucks in the bag for Billy. It was worth the insurance.

"I want a Big Mac. No, wait, a Whopper with cheese and a great big order of fries. And a Coke...don't forget a Coke."

"You got it." Timmy couldn't even fathom food yet. After all he'd eaten at the game, even nine hours ago, he wondered if he'd ever need to eat again.

"So get me some of that stash now, and I've got your back for a few days. I'm hungry." Billy stuck his scrawny chest out and joined his fellow Gerries at the barrel.

Timmy crawled into his box and quickly added layers, a master at navigating the small space. The brisk December cold would be brutal this late. It warranted two t-shirts, his new sweatshirt, the coat, topped off with a knit cap and gloves. He checked himself in the vanity mirror. Time had worn him to a nub of his former self. But a hint of that boy was still there. He could see it, and it made him smile.

Out on the sidewalk, he double-checked his back pocket for the knife. Then it hit him. *The blade*. As he hustled to his two closest hiding places, he added a note to self: search Max's box when the idiots pass out. *Unless he'd had it on him when he got arrested, the blade would be in there somewhere*. For now, he was using the most powerful weapon at his disposal: bribery. The key to temporary security in the alley would be his ability to provide.

The plan was in motion. *Put up or shut-up*. Billy would eventually see Cooter, and his lie would be exposed. With it hanging over his head, he had to hurry.

Skippy yipped at his heels as they neared the underpass hideout, nabbed the leftovers, gave Skippy his share, then speed-walked three blocks to Lawrence for the remaining half of a day-old hoagie. It all passed the sniff test, and why not use it? He wouldn't be needing it anymore. He hoped.

After shoving the food into Billy's lap, relishing the stunned expression, Timmy sprinted the four blocks to the bus stop, with Skippy yapping the whole way. Running until well after midnight, maybe longer because of the game, the bus would make the trek efficient.

"C'mon, Skip. We gotta get you zipped in!" He plopped onto the bench in the partially enclosed bus stop. Skippy wagged a mile a minute, always excited for bus rides. "Jails don't close, right?" He wasn't sure, but hoped some waterworks would get him a few minutes with his grandpa. If not, he'd find a place to hide out until morning.

Timmy pulled the terrier inside his coat and zipped it all the way to his neck. With hands stuffed in his pockets, the lump was barely noticeable, as long as Skip didn't move or whine. He acted nonchalant as the bus screeched to a halt in front of him and he bounded up the steps. The bus driver nodded as they boarded the near empty bus, ignoring the bulge. Timmy suspected many of them could tell, since it squirmed a time or two, but never questioned them. Smuggling his mutt onto the bus had become an art form. They would settle into the back-window seat, and Skippy could lounge beside him as long as no other passengers could see. With it this empty, he didn't dare. Instead, he gave Skippy a breathing hole and began to think about what he would say to the old man. Max held keys to his past, and Timmy ached for answers.

Three couples boarded the bus, so he let Skippy wriggle out a bit. Timmy jotted a few details in his notepad then leaned his head against the window and rehearsed questions for Max.

After the visit, he would go hangout by the library and try to catch a little sleep before it opened. There was no point in procrastinating anymore.

He had to put up now, so he wouldn't end up like the Gerries.

Chapter Twenty-Eight

The plate-sized hands didn't seem as scary to Timmy anymore. Muscle Man flexed, making the knife twitch, and the thug laughed. What terrified him now was simple: he had been abandoned and he was lost.

Timothy Ryan Weaver stood in the middle of the Cruddy District wondering where the heck he was. The intersection looked familiar, but lately, everything *was familiar.*

"Yo, kid! Come see what I done to your favorite boy," this Muscle Man called out. It might not be the same guy, but the feature Timmy could count on danced on the deltoid of each. Sometimes the right, but usually the left.

"Leave me alone!" Timmy screamed, and then suddenly found himself on the fifty-yard line of the Trans World Dome cheering as Kurt Warner threw a bomb to Isaac Bruce. The crowd chanted 'Bruuuuuuuuce,' but Timmy knew who the guy running really was. Zeke. His name was Zeke. Wasn't it? It was the thug from That Night, and the dude was looking for him.

Timmy staggered, his head buzzing with everything inside and outside. He searched for Mr. Knight to tell him what was going on. He shouted for the guy the Brent clone to follow, to answer the call to duty. The Musketeer fill-in rose and held a pretend sword to the sky.

The two scrambled around masses of people.

"Why aren't you watchin' the game?" Timmy wanted to ask them all.

"Slow down, Timmy! Man, where the hell you been?" Brent called after him. When Timmy glanced back, it was no longer a look-alike, but his former best friend.

"No time to explain now, Brent, but the guy chasin' us can tell you where I've been and why I've been there."

Brent fell in stride with him, and the two made like cheap panty hose and ran the final leg out of the stadium.

Sam would've been proud of that one.

***

Timmy jerked awake as the bus jerked to a halt a few blocks from the county jail.

"Here's your stop, kid," the driver called out. His clashing worlds and the never-ending day was taking its toll. *Zeke, who the hell was Zeke?*

A shiver ran down his spine, and a strange ache pressed inside his chest. It was a funny, strangely familiar name. He bundled Skippy into his coat and jumped off the bus. Mosquitoes buzzed in his head, nipped at every nerve he had. Would Max be happy to see him? Pissed? The only way to find out was to take steps forward, one at a time.

"Be careful, kid," the driver called out before closing the door and lurching down the road.

Careful doesn't really matter anymore. He opened the note pad, studied the directions, and marched the two blocks to the county jail.

He unzipped his coat, let his toasty buddy jump out. "Skippy, you gotta lay low, okay? I won't be long." Timmy bent down and nuzzled his best friend. "I love you, Skippy," he whispered. Had he ever loved Trevor this much? He couldn't remember.

But if Trevor, Brent, Scott, Mom, Dad, and Sam had all been rolled into one person, I would have. That's you, Skip, you're my whole family in a burrito.

Skippy scurried to the side of the building and curled up into a tight ball. Timmy mustered all his courage and turned to face the glass door. His decision to come here had seemed right, but now that he was here, those mosquitoes bounced like teenagers without their Ritalin.

He took a deep breath and heaved open the enormous

door.

"Way past visiting hours, squirt. Come back in the morning, preferably with an adult." The uniformed man behind the desk peered over tiny half-glasses.

"But I've gotta see my grandpa, um, Max," he whined, wondering if he was going to have to produce tears. He could if he had to.

"Who's yer grandpa?" Sergeant Brown, according to his nametag, flipped through papers on a clipboard. "Max Brunhill?"

"Yes, sir." Timmy's heart hammered. *Brunhill? Wow... I never knew Max's last name.* He rubbed his forehead. *But that wasn't Mom's name when she was little...* "Please, sir? I just really need to talk to him. Please." Too much mustard could sour the request, but he couldn't help himself.

The sergeant stared at Timmy, still fairly clean from his venture into the real world. "I tell you what, kid, I'm gonna let you in, but I'll have to ask if he wants to see you. Sometimes folks don't like visitor, especially their grandkids. Depresses and embarrasses them, you know? Since it's way past visiting hours, I can't give you but a few minutes."

"Yes, sir, I understand." And he did, because Max *would* be embarrassed. But Timmy also had something of high interest to Max. About two thousand *somethings*. That would definitely be weighing on the old man's mind. He knew about bail from TV, but he had no clue how much Max might need or if it even applied since he beat up a cop.

Timmy waited while Sergeant Brown disappeared. Seconds later, a metal door clanked and echoed loud enough to make him jump. But a raindrop would make him jump right now. Inspecting the tiny lobby, the walls almost as gray as the alley, his nerves danced like downed power lines.

He's refusing to see me. He blames me...he's probably telling the guy right now all the bad things I've done... Faces on wanted posters stared at him from a bulletin board, accusing. *You're one of us.*

He hovered between running and crying – he itched to see what was hidden beyond the metal door, but something kept him frozen, barely even breathing. Before he could lose his nerve and run, Sergeant Brown came clanking back into the entryway.

Don't be mad, Max, don't be mad...

"Okay, kid, follow me."

Timmy clung to the man's shirtsleeve, startled by the crashing doors. When they passed through a series of pressurized doors, at one point trapping them in a tiny area waiting for a door to open, he shivered with apprehension. When the doors closed behind him, Timmy understood what it felt like to be trapped. Not so different from the alley or the abandoned buildings. But for the first time in four months, he felt free.

Chapter Twenty-Nine

The jail was nothing like he expected. Movies and TV shows depicted rows of chairs with phones, glass between the two people, dividers separating all the visitors. Instead, he was taken into a room the size of a small cafeteria and there sat Max – at a table, in what could've passed for Timmy's elementary school lunchroom.

This was a Max he didn't know. The old man never shared his prior brushes with the law. He glorified them to the Gerries, but when Timmy asked, Max waved his hand and responded with phrases like, "I was stupid" or "Don't go down the same road."

"What're you doin' here, kid?" The weathered face had more color than Timmy had seen in a while—food, a few hours booze-free, and a reprieve from the elements made Max look younger. But the unruly eyebrows speckled with gray were as wild as ever.

Good to see you, too, Max.

"Well, I heard you got into trouble, and I wanted to see you. Is that okay?" He played the innocent card.

"This ain't visitin' hours, so I know you must have a bigger reason than that." Max heaved a sigh and blew it out in measured bursts. "What did Billy tell you?"

Timmy took his own deep breath and slowly recounted the explanation. Max grunted at a few points but admitted it was as close to the truth as he would expect from Billy.

"What he didn't tell you was how it started. The dude jumped me as soon as I came out of the liquor store. Just grabbed it right outta my hand. No generic shit, but a mouth-watering fifth of Chivas. He didn't know I was carrying cash from a few shirts I'd sold, he just wanted my damn bottle." Max rubbed his stubbled, gray-peppered beard. Timmy stared at the sobering effect – clearer eyes and a sadness that made the old man's jowls droop lower.

"So, where's all the money, kid? I know you brung it. Where's it at?" Max's questions hung in the air like a breezeless windsock.

Timmy leaned back in his chair. He knew Max would ask, but it hurt a little to know it was probably why the old man chose to see him.

"It's safe. It –"

"You mean to tell me you ain't got it on you?" Max sounded surprised and angry. His brows knitted together, deepening the lines between his eyes.

"Max, it's safe, okay? Let me finish." Timmy had to fight to keep his nerve. The old man paused when Timmy held up a hand, but he knew Max's patience wouldn't last long.

"Jesus, don't tell me you lost my money, Timmy." Skeptical eyes squinted, watching the boy closely for any signs of guilt.

Your money, Max?

"Our money, Max. Our money. Remember?" Timmy knew better than to challenge his grandpa, but then again, he didn't really know this version of the man.

"Well, kid, I'm gonna need it for a good lawyer, so don't get too fixed on it."

"You don't need money for a lawyer, Max." He stifled the quiver in his voice. "All you need is a public defender. You told Billy last month that one was as good as another. And I have a plan for the money, to help us both in the long run. Something I think you would want too."

Max cocked an eyebrow and held his tongue. "I'm listenin'."

"Well, what if I used it to find my parents? To hire somebody? Then they'd be able to help you get out."

Max's expression soured then reddened. Timmy had said something wrong.

"Out of what? I ain't gettin' outta here – *ever*. And ...and...*shit*. I want my money, boy. I'm gonna need it for leverage, for survival." Max growled, anger edged his voice like a razor.

Timmy stared, the fury in the old man's eyes foreign and scary.

"Besides, you can't go to no private detective, not with what you've done. He'll look you up and you'll be busted before you ever start. You'd be right in here with me. Remember that dude in East St. Louis, Baldy? And what about what came before, back in August? That cop told me that –" but Max clamped his mouth shut.

Timmy's head swam. *What cop?*

Max went on. "Kid, that money is mine. I owe people. And no detective is gonna find your parents." The old man's voice trailed off so low, Timmy could barely hear him.

"Why not? What do you know, Max?" Timmy voice broke. "What cop did you talk to? What did he say?" Butterflies fluttered in his stomach.

"Forget it, kid. Why don't you just scram, huh? Go get my money and bring it to me, then maybe I can answer some questions." But the expression on Max's face screwed up Timmy's insides.

He's lying.

Fire brewed in his belly – *how could he do this to me if he's my grandpa?* "You said what I did was self-defense." Timmy spoke in a flat, almost accusing tone. "The other times, I was protecting myself. I thought I was bad, and you wanted me to believe that so I would need you. And that's okay," he added quickly when he saw Max's mouth part, the square jaw clinch tight enough to chew nails. "But I'm going to the library from here, to find out what happened to me. I'm tired. A lot has gone on in the past few days. And today, well, at the Rams game. I –" His voice trembled. Timmy swallowed hard. "I felt normal. And I've gotta find my parents, if – if they're –" He couldn't bring himself to say it, though deep down, he knew. Why else would they leave him with a bum in an alley?

"You went to the game?" Max's eyes reflected the envy in his voice.

"Yeah, a guy who bought the last few shirts had an extra ticket, so he let me come in with him and his boys." He left out that he had bargained free shirts for the ticket.

"We won," Max whispered, a ghost of a smile flitted across his face. He studied a chip at the edge of the Formica and picked at it.

Timmy's shoulders dropped in relief. "We rocked. Kurt Warner kicked butt, Max. You wouldn't have believed it! Did you get to see it?" The excitement of the game returned, temporarily filling the hole in his gut.

"Oh, yeah. We even ate chicken wings at that bar like we was somebody. Drank the bottle we smuggled in then actually bought a Jack on the rocks. Damn. It was sweet...seeing it on a big screen TV." Max smiled as he remembered. Then a dark cloud passed over his eyes. "I got something I gotta tell you, kid."

"What?" A blender stewed his stomach. Somewhere deep inside, a voice whispered, *you know, Timmy...you were there...* He clamped his eyes shut, refusing to let it in. After seeing Stephie, part of Before, it proved he hadn't made up the perfect past. It was real.

"You really think you can find out what happened to you?" Max frowned, then stared hard into Timmy's eyes.

"I'm gonna go to the library and look up newspaper articles from that August. I don't remember the exact date, but you can find anything on the Internet. I want to know what all my friends were told. I mean, I don't know what they think. I want to know if the paper said I was a wanted criminal, a murderer or what. Because *I* don't know!" His voice rose – the guard, stiff as a light pole until now, took several steps toward them.

"Sit down, boy," the guard demanded.

"It's okay, Pete." Max held up a hand that shook so badly, he could've been waving. "What're you gonna do when you find out, Timmy? Go running back like nothin' ever happened? You know that ain't possible, right?"

"I know, but I can't live like this anymore. I don't know what I'm gonna do." Emotion swelled in his throat. He fiddled with his hands to avoid looking at Max.

"Think about what you're sayin', kid. If *you* don't know, it's gonna be like a knife to the gut when you find out. You really want that? I think no knowin' is better than the finality of it. I'm just sayin'. Don't, really...*don't.*"

Timmy jerked his head up, stared into Max's eyes at the pleading tone. The old man's grip on his life loosened like an unfastened belt. He hadn't ordered Timmy not to go, he had asked. Timmy felt their roles reversing – a shifting of tides.

"I will. I'm gonna go to the library and then I'll talk with Billy about –"

"No. You can't hang there anymore, kid. For real. You're not safe around Billy. They're probably sellin' your stuff right now. Go to a shelter before Billy can figure a way to really capitalize on you." Max frowned, the worry wrinkling around his eyes genuine. "He's had ideas about better ways to make money with you, kid. You can't go back there...promise me. *Promise me.*" Max reached out to grab the boy's hand, but the guard snapped for him to sit back.

"Don't worry. I told Billy there was money in it for him if he protected me for just a day or two. I told him I'd get him some real food. Even a bottle if I could."

Max grinned. "Savvy little shit, ain'tcha? Good for you. But then cut out. Go to a shelter, understand me?"

"Whaddya think of my idea?" Timmy held his breath waiting for Max's answer. For some reason, it mattered.

"Whaddya think you'll find at the library?"

"Max, you're not listening to me." He dropped his head, gathered his bearings. "I think I'm gonna find out the truth. And I also think you already know, don't you?"

Max reached across and grabbed his hands. "Yes."

"Hands off, Thornhill," the guard ordered harshly.

"*Brunhill*, asshole," he snapped, but jerked his hands back. "Timmy, I – I never meant to hurtcha'." Max hesitated, then sighed. "But I done you wrong. That cop, he – he told me what happened to yer folks. And to you. They thought maybe you had died, what with all the blood and all. They...they..." Max's voice trailed off.

A rip to his insides rocketed through Timmy. "You've known...all this time..." Timmy struggled for air, but forced the words out. "And you never told me? Why would you do that to me, to your own grandson?" He fought back the tears, the anger escalating inside him.

"I – I'm sorry, kid. They said some gangbangers had rammed your Cadillac, but they couldn't tell what had happened after your family was attacked. That maybe the gang had taken you. I figured if they was lookin' for you, you'd be better off with us. And you said yourself you didn't wanna go into foster care...everybody knows a kid is the best peddler." Max dropped his head and directed his attention to the Formica.

"Attacked, you mean *dead?*"

Through his blurring eyes, he saw Max nod.

The world swam out of focus. Timmy tried to stand, but his legs wouldn't hold him. He felt the air sucked out of his lungs, like he ducked under water with no breath first.

And then the fuse blew. Timothy Ryan Weaver found his legs and screamed at the top of his lungs, oblivious of the guard racing toward him.

"YOU LET ME SLEEP IN A BOX FOR FOUR MONTHS! YOU LET ME *KNIFE* THAT GUY! I KILLED PEOPLE BECAUSE OF YOU!"

The sergeant had shoved Timmy toward the door but hesitated when the kid talked about killing someone. The burly guard asked him to repeat what he said, and Timmy froze. "I didn't mean to, I mean, I don't think I did, did I, Max? DID I?"

"He didn't kill nobody. Just defended himself." Max dropped back onto his seat. "Let him go, Pete. C'mere, Timmy." He motioned toward the seat.

The guard released Timmy, but the boy stood frozen between the past, present, and a blurry future. His chest hitched as the dam of tears threatened to break. *That's not completely true, Timmy...you know....*

"I didn't mean to lie to you," Max whispered. "I didn't want you to end up in some shitty foster home."

"But you're okay with me sleepin' in a box?" Timmy couldn't imagine anything worse than being homeless. *Why didn't I just stay with Mrs. Chapman that day she took me to DYS?* Another light bulb snapped on. "You're not my grandpa. The whole thing is a lie."

Max wouldn't even look up. "At least with us you were free. I mean, disturbed people can do really twisted things."

Twisted? "For almost a week in September, all I ate was three cookies from a trash can." Timmy backed a few steps toward the door, tears already falling and snot dripping from his nose. Before he could lose his nerve, he mumbled, "You were like family to me."

Wiry, gray eyebrows furrowed, and Max swallowed before he spoke. "I know, kid, and no matter what you think, you *were...are* like a grandson to me." Max bowed his head.

"I – I'll come see you." He stared at the tears streaming down Max's weathered face.

"No you won't," the old man whispered.

Timmy held up a hand, a feeble wave, but it was all he could manage.

"Bye, Max." He turned and felt his way toward the door, tears blinding him. A guard led him back the way he came, but he saw none of it. Max was probably right – he'd never see the old man again, and that scared the crap out of him. He experienced finality for the second time in his life, but one thing his dad used to say made sense to him now.

Where one door closes, another opens.

Standing on the sidewalk outside the county jail, he hoped it was true – and he knew exactly where to find that door.

Part III

Answers

Chapter Thirty

Timmy slept next to the library, tucked around the corner hugging Skippy for warmth. When the sun woke him, he was on his feet before he could even consider what lay ahead. He barely remembered the midnight walk south to the central branch. He passed back by the Dome and tried to relish memories of the game. The visit with Max had more than drained him, it had changed him. But it also inspired him. His uncertain future rested with his past. Still groggy from only a few hours of zees, he knew he could sleep after, all day if he wanted. But Tigger told him it was only seven-thirty, so he plopped onto the bottom step to wait.

"I'm finally gonna know, Skip." He glanced at the terrier trying to crawl into his lap. He gave Skippy a chin rub and pulled the ball of fur into his arms. Time dragged by. He practiced what he'd say if anyone asked. And he wouldn't dilly-dally. He would march straight to a desk and ask where the computers were.

By the time the he heard the keys in the lock, there were numerous people gathered, waiting for the library to open. As soon as the doors swung open, Timmy launched full-blown into phase two of his plan.

The smell of books swept him back to Before. His mom used to razz him for lugging home more than he would ever be able to read in two weeks. He didn't care. Back then, he liked having choices. Thinking about her was getting easier, but still hurt the same.

"Can I help you, hon?" A cliché of a lady sat at a desk and raised an eyebrow. Half glasses perched on her nose, a chain dangled from the arms, parentheses framed a tight smile.

"Yes, ma'am, can you tell me where I can look up newspaper articles?" He had practiced the question at least twenty times.

"Right around the corner. Computers are first come, first serve. If you want to print, it's five cents a page." She pointed to where the printers must be. "And don't be searching for anything inappropriate." She raised the eyebrow again.

"Oh, I won't. I'm doing some research." He had practiced that answer almost as much. He thanked her and wiped his palms on his jeans. His heart thudded too loudly in his ears, and a strange anxiety wrapped around his insides.

Most of the carrels were already taken, people tapping away and staring at screens. He plopped in front of a Dell monitor and took a deep breath.

This is it.

He opened Internet Explorer and let his fingers hover over the keyboard, unsure exactly what search word to type in the Yahoo! bar. Before he could lose his nerve, he tapped out *St. Louis Post Dispatch* then keyed in possible August dates, starting with the twenty-fifth. The Post-Dispatch header reminded him of Sunday mornings eating Cocoa Puffs.

Sports page, babe? You boys fight over these... Mom tossed his dad the sports' section, and he and Sam divided the comics. The intrusive memory stirred the acid in his stomach. A speaker directly above him clicked on.

"Kid, you going to be there long?" A college-aged guy stared down at him. All the computers around him were full.

"Not sure. But I've just started. So maybe." He never looked up, tapped more keys, and within a few minutes, he was skimming news headlines that meant nothing to him. *C'mon...I just want to find something, anything.* His leg bounced with apprehension. NASA crashed a spacecraft, some guy attacked a Jewish community center, but nothing that made sense yet.

Names of leaders he'd never heard of, places he would never go. His eyes blurred as he continued to roll the mouse button. He speed-read as he scanned the days in late August, his stomach clenched in anticipation.

Maybe it's not here. Maybe nobody cared that much. The uncertainty squeezed his bladder with an invisible fist. He clicked the mouse over and over and over. Headlines started sounding alike, his eyes glazing.

Max lied to me. He wasn't my grandpa, and he kept secrets that might've helped. A blip of memory, of a slip of paper in his hands. *It was a newspaper article...* How had he fallen for that? But then a flash of the Labor Day picnic, of times the old man defended him, even saved his life.

Timmy scrolled down. August twenty-fourth gave way to the twenty-fifth, but still nothing. *God, there's gotta be* – And then it sucker punched the air out of him. A front-page headline. A lump lodged in his throat and a strange sensation crawled into his gut as he clicked on the link. His privates suddenly felt like they were on fire, burning with such intensity that he worried he might wet his pants

Officer killed, family found slain, youngest child missing, believed kidnapped.

He willed it away, quieted the monster in his head. A voice whispered to get up, walk out, and hide for the rest of his life. What could it hurt?

"You better shut the fuck up, you little pissant," Muscle Man threatened.

The broken images made him gag, bile rising in his throat. Tired, cold, and hungry would never make him feel any more or less alone. *I can't undo it, but...but...*

His brain had overloaded That Night, and he had only gotten brief glimpses over the past months. What made him think he could handle it now?

Officer killed, family found slain, youngest child missing, believed kidnapped. He couldn't drag his eyes to the article, yet he didn't have the will to tear them away. He scanned the words, a second link at the bottom, and found their names again.

Oh, god. I remember the airport, and – and...

The words blurred, a strange smell burned his nostrils. Before he could lose his nerve, he tapped keys until he was able to print the pages. He couldn't read it right now. He could barely see. *And if I read it here and remember everything, I'm going to scream. I need air, I need to be outside, I need Skippy.*

He searched until he found the printer, saw a guy pulling the pages, and peeled a single from the wad of cash in his pocket. He wished he had coins, so he could pay and get out of there. To piece together the thousand-piece puzzle of his past was taking all the energy he had.

"That'll be ninety cents." The guy never looked up. Timmy was grateful, because he was confident he had turned white as a fish's belly.

The guy handed him change and Timmy tried desperately to focus, to shove away the ghosts that filled his head.

"OPEN YOUR EYES, YOU LITTLE SHIT!" The back of a hand hit my left cheekbone hard enough to send blood and snot spraying through the air. It connected again and again. A ring on one of the fingers ripped through the skin on my left cheek.

He flinched, and his hands trembled like a fluttering leaf in a brisk wind. He pocketed the change, said he didn't need a receipt, and backed away, his fingers tracing the scar on his left cheekbone.

The guy finally glanced up, his lips parted like he was seeing a ghost. Timmy was fairly certain he was supposed to have been one. The headline repeated in his head like a never-ending chorus, while he walked toward the front door, wading through emotional quicksand.

He squinted into the sun and descended the stone steps, lucky he didn't tumble down them. He'd just shoved answers to one hundred and eighteen days' worth of questions into his back pocket. He checked his watch – 9:30. Stores would be crazy four days before Christmas. He just needed some place quiet, private, where a possible meltdown wouldn't get him thrown into a looney bin, as Sam used to call it.

Today, December 21st, was the first day of a new life. Once he knew the answers, he could alter the course of his future. His dad motivated Sam to dethrone the starting quarterback at the beginning of his brother's eighth grade year by chanting that mantra, "It's time to put up or shut up, Samarino. Do you want to sit back and settle for less or you wanna go for the gusto?" His dad had stared long and hard at Sam, the kitchen table dead silent as they all continued to eat. Timmy would never forget his brother's response.

"Might as well take the pony by the reins, huh?"

It was time to do a little rein-grabbing himself. And why not? He had been settling for damn near four months. His dad's words of wisdom could be his new motto. Going for a little gusto was right up his alley.

Put up or shut up, Tim. Put up or shut up.

Chapter Thirty-One

Timmy tried to whistle for Skippy, but he couldn't purse his lips. Everything about him ached. The fist around his heart made it too hard to think, to breathe, to care. He trudged through the greenspace near the library. Numerous bums lounged on benches throughout the park, but Timmy found an empty one and plopped down. Four months of uncertainty clamored in his brain, his insides churning in a blender and pureed. He heard Skippy's yip and patted the bench next to him. Fighting the tears and trying desperately not to be a crybaby, he couldn't see his buddy when he nearly knocked him over. But he hugged Skippy and did his best to thank his best friend. He squeezed his eyes shut to settle the gorge in his stomach and took the deepest breath he could manage.

"OPEN YOUR EYES, YOU LITTLE SHIT!"

Timmy jerked them open –he knew the voice was in his head, but Before and After were on a deadly collision course. He pulled the two pieces of paper from his back pocket, unfolding them like it was a failing grade card.

"You ready, Skippy?" But Skippy rolled in the luxurious grasses, paused when his boy said his name, and let his tongue loll out the side of his mouth. Timmy heaved an uncertain sigh. Everything inside and out trembled – his head, his heart, his hands.

ST. LOUIS (AP)— Sergeant Amos Thompson, 28, of the St. Ann Police Department was pronounced dead on arrival from injuries suffered in a crash with three other vehicles on Stanton Street in Northern St. Louis. A Ballwin family was found brutally murdered at the scene. It is unclear at this time, but witnesses throughout the area saw three cars racing down city streets minutes prior to the accident.

Officer Kevin Rodriguez, one of the first to respond to the 911 call, said the nature of the crime was still being investigated.

"Each victim was shot with a high-caliber automatic pistol. Robert Weaver, 39; Victoria Weaver, 36; and a 15-year old minor all died of gunshot wounds followed by numerous blows to the head and body, most post-mortem. The Weaver's youngest son, Timothy, 11-years old, was believed to be with the family at the time of the shootings. He has not been found, though C.S.U. has placed his blood at the scene."

No.... A snot-filled moan erupted from him. *I won't read any more – you can't make me. Oh, mama, I need minutes...any minutes.* Timmy closed his eyes, let out his breath in slow, calculated puffs, then turned his face up to the clear blue sky. He wouldn't pray, because there was no longer anything to pray for. Someone had gouged his heart with a jagged blade and twisted. The ache faded into the background of a raging anger. He knew what was next, didn't he?

Two assailants, Shaun Holmes and Ezekiel Cawdel, both known Blades gang members, were pronounced dead at University Hospital, suffering from gunshot wounds. Two other gang members, James Daniel Williams and Anthony Roles, suffered fatal injuries in the initial crash.

Two vehicles, witnesses say, pursued the family. A Chevrolet Impala and a Plymouth convertible forced the Weavers' Cadillac Escalade into an approaching police car responding to a 911 call by the Weavers."

Oh, Momma...you struggled with the cell phone, I remember. Timmy wiped tears that were about to drip on the pages. He felt like an imposter at someone else's funeral. The fury size of the arch lodged in his throat.

"Timothy Ryan Weaver, eleven years of age, has blond hair, blue eyes, and mingled with gut-wrenching agony had his insides skewered. A lump the stands approximately four feet ten inches tall. He was last seen at Lambert Airport wearing a blue Nike windbreaker pullover, jeans, and Adidas tennis shoes. He may be the victim of gang abduction and is believed to be seriously injured. If you have any information leading to the boy's whereabouts, please notify authorities immediately. The police are canvassing the area thoroughly in an effort to locate him." '

Timmy's heart pounded, his hands trembled. That Night fragmented in his head – gasoline burned his nostrils, crashing glass sprinkled his hair, people cussed at him and...and....

"OPEN YOUR EYES, YOU LITTLE SHIT!" There was a guy who wanted to kill him, but he couldn't quite remember why. Bile settled in the base of his throat. He struggled to focus on the paper.

The police are canvassing the area thoroughly in an effort to locate him.

If they canvassed the area so well, why didn't they found him in that drain?

"Hey, Timmy, I can't believe you got McGwire's signature!" Sam had smacked him on the back, real pride in his brother's voice. In the airport. Oh, God, I remember. We were picking Sam up from the airport.

Timmy skimmed the last paragraph about the dead police officer, the upcoming visitation, and where donations to his family could be sent. *What about ours?*

He turned and laid on the bench, his knees bent and hands behind his head. The fragments of memory cascaded through him, making him dizzy and nauseous. The funny smells came back – memory smells. Gas, sweat, nasty cologne. And blood – the metallic scent of blood.

"Oh, God, Skippy. My mom. M...my dad.... I remember most of it now. I...I..." Skippy jumped up on his boy, licking tears streaming down bright red cheeks. Holding his best friend, Timothy Ryan Weaver lay under the bright sunshine, not warmed by it or anything else he could muster. Letting go of what little hope he'd managed to keep, he bawled, his chest heaving hard enough to make him gag. It took forty-five minutes for four months' worth of tears to stop.

By the time they did, Timmy's head throbbed from the pressure, his nose so stopped up he couldn't breathe. He peeled off his Rams' sweatshirt then his flimsy Goodwill T-shirt. He was sweating, despite the December chill. He wiped his cheeks, his breath hitching in small hiccups as he tried to stop crying. Every third or fourth breath caught in his throat, and Timmy couldn't stop swallowing air with each uncontrollable hitch. Skippy's tongue lapped at his boy's face making it even harder to breathe.

He couldn't think. Trying to erase the burning hole in his heart, he rubbed his eyes, wiped the snot streaming onto his upper lip, and stumbled to his feet.

"We gotta g – go back, Skip. We have so – some things to get and ch – choices to muh – make. Okay?" Timmy gagged, swallowing hard to keep from throwing up. Making his way back to Brookline on foot would take at least an hour, maybe longer if he couldn't get the lead out. But the weight of his heart made his feet even heavier. So the bus was the best option to get back before Cooter came around to share the Painted Lady escapade.

Skippy led the way, turning every fifteen to twenty feet to make sure his boy was still with him. He didn't wag. He knew his boy was hurting, in a kind of pain a kiss wouldn't fix. *Let's go!* He prompted with every turnaround.

Timmy finally managed to swallow his pity and step up the pace. They needed to get to a bus stop asap. Sometimes Cooter appeared before noon, but usually after an escapade – as Cooter called them – it was later in the day or even the day after. Timmy was banking on it. Otherwise, his lie would be exposed, his ball cards and caps history, and he would have no chance to find that blade – it would insure safety in his journey forward.

After a quick stop at Burger King for Billy's insurance policy, Timmy ate a whopper junior, tore one up for Skippy, and then zipped his buddy in for one last bus ride to the alley.

Remembering the bottle sitting on the back of the bus, Timmy peeled a twenty-dollar bill from his roll of cash and dropped it into the Burger King sack. He roll-folded the bag tight, hoping to keep it warm. A happy Billy would be a protective Billy, even if Timmy's hours were numbered.

The ride back was peppered with images of the article, *his story*. He finally knew the truth, even if it was scrambled like puzzle pieces in a box. The fact that his mom, dad, and Sam were dead plagued him with such a weight, he didn't know if he could carry it. The nightmares were real. It all swam in his head like mad piranha. As the bus lumbered north, he tried to make sense of it all, to remember.

By the time he hopped off the bus and made his way back to Brookline, his heart was about to hammer out of his chest. If Cooter was there, Timmy would hightail it past and not even slow down. None of them could catch him, he was sure of that. But if he had time, he would gather supplies he wanted and felt he needed to move to phase three of his plan.

"Hustle ahead, Skip," he urged, as they turned the corner onto Brookline. But he could see from where he paused that there were only a few bums around the barrel. No Cooter. The guy was too loud – everyone would know if the guy had returned yet.

Relieved but anxious, he followed his terrier to their soon-to-be former home. A moment of uncertainty gave him pause seeing Billy perched in front of Max's nest. Timmy's eyes and face, swollen from crying, caught the bully off guard.

"Jesus, kid, where you been?" He punctuated the question with a long slug from his giant bottle of malt liquor. *He hadn't needed me to get him a bottle.* Timmy considered pulling the twenty out of the food bag. That's when he saw the baseball cards in Billy's hands. "Holy shit, you went to see Max." Billy's eyes widened.

With the barrage of emotion Timmy had experienced in the past twelve hours, Billy couldn't have known how stealing the cards would hit the boy. Timmy balled his fists, his heart hammering – he mustered the venom he'd felt just an hour ago beside the library.

"Give...me...my...baseball...cards."

Billy's head jerked up at the tone in the kid's voice.

The middle-aged drunk didn't intimidate him anymore. Not like Max. Billy's wimpy arms and hunkered posture were laughable in comparison. Even ten years younger than Max, he had none of the older man's might. The crew feared Max for a reason. Billy commanded no respect and would never be able to assume that role, and likewise wouldn't be able to protect Timmy.

"Boy, I've had about enough of you and your mouth. We may need a come-to-Jesus meetin', you and me." He held the cards in his hands, Brian Jordan being bent as he clutched it.

"Shut up, Billy. Here's the food I promised you and twenty bucks for a bottle. Now back the fuck off, or you better not even *think* about sleepin' tonight." The hissing threat brought a glimpse of fear into Billy's eyes, though the drunk never tore them from the brown bag. The kid didn't use foul language often because his mom had taught him that people who cussed lacked the vocabulary to express themselves – and the fact that on two separate occasions she had washed his mouth out with soap. He reserved the bad words for when they needed weight. "I'll cut it off. You know I will."

Billy stood and snatched the sack. "Suit yourself, you little shit." He staggered back to the bucket seats, tossed the baseball cards onto the grimy concrete as he walked away.

Right smack dab on top lay Timmy's – *and Sam's* – pride and joy. He'd had the cards in his pullover That Night, and he was thankful for that. At least then he was allowed to keep a small part of his past. He should've grabbed them yesterday, but the money was all he'd been thinking about.

He carefully picked them up, one at a time, without bending the edges. The anger melted as he remembered why he had brought the few precious cards with him That Night.

Chapter Thirty-Two

Five Months Earlier

Sam had ants in his pants to get on that plane, and I was trying to imagine all the weeks without him in the house. Free access to his stuff, his PlayStation, not to mention control of the downstairs' remote. All of that would rule for about a week. Plus, a break from getting tackled would be nice.

"C'mon, Timmy, let's toss the football before dinner."

"Sure!" I jumped up so fast I knocked over Mom's bowl of potpourri that sat on the side table. I scooped it back into the heavy crystal, but Mom took it from me.

"Go on, klutz. Dinner's in about thirty minutes, so stay close."

"Yes, mommy dearest," Sam cooed, and we both giggled.

Mom let out a maniacal squeal of laughter, pretending to be some evil mother, and then dashed off into the kitchen.

"So, when're you goin' to soccer camp, Timmy?" Sam threw the first pass.

I made an awesome catch, spiked the ball, and mimicked a roaring crowd. I raced after the Nerf ball and made a wobbly pass to Sam who caught it easily. Trevor raced between us trying desperately to intercept passes far out of his reach.

"In two weeks, first of August. When're you gonna be back?"

"I'm not even gonna answer that, butthead. You've asked me a gazillion times." He shook his head, then threw the ball so hard it nearly knocked me over.

"I can't believe you want to miss the first week of your sophomore year." It had become an obsession. I threw a perfect spiral back to him and beamed when he acknowledged it with a smile.

"It's just three days, Timmy. They'll be handin' out a

syllabus in every class, which I can get ahead of time. And anything else can be made up. But this foreign exchange program is a once in a lifetime chance. God, if I could go to Germany like Peter Bowden did last year? That would rock." Sam whooped and hollered, then launched a bomb I had to sprint to catch up with. The ball skipped off the ends of my fingers. Trevor grabbed it in his jowls and came bounding to return it me, proud as punch that he could play.

"Ah, Tim Weaver blows the catch of a lifetime!" Sam commentated to the trees. "You're a weenie, Timmy!"

I knew he was kidding, but God, I hated missing any pass he threw. I wanted to impress him every chance I got. And now he would be gone for most of August. But Brent and Scott would be totally wowed by getting free reign of Sam's room.

Mom shouted from the front porch that it was time for dinner. We could smell Dad's pork chops grilling and our stomachs growled. We sprinted down the street, me eating his dust and wondering if I would ever be as fast, as strong, or as good at anything. Trevor bolted past us, woofing for us to hurry the heck up.

Dinner revolved around Mom and Dad's questioning Sam about the specifics. Jealousy reared its ugly head again, but mostly I just felt left-out. I would count on Brent and Scott to fill that void.

By nightfall, Sam had packed his entire wardrobe and stewed like a jackrabbit about to be let loose in a carrot garden. His flight to Chicago was a short one but taking my brother to places I could only imagine. Dad was going to get Sam up well before daybreak to catch his seven o'clock flight.

The house would be Samless, and I would have to step up to the plate to be Dad's wing man. I liked the way that sounded. I told Dad that anything Samarino could do, I could do better. Dad grinned and said he didn't doubt it a bit.

I wandered upstairs around ten, and Sam's light was already off. He had to get up early. I brushed my teeth, put on my pajamas, and crawled into bed. Just when I was about to drift into a world full of Musketeer action, Sam called my name. He was sitting on the edge of my bed.

"Huh?" I could've gotten whiplash returning from the brink of a sword battle to my bedroom on Catalina Avenue.

"Hey, Timmy, I need you to do me a big favor," Sam whispered. He paused and I held my breath. Sam wanted something from me?

"What is it?"

"Well it's something nice you do for people, but that's beside the point," Sam joked, quoting *Airplane!* every chance he got since seeing it on DVD.

"Funny."

"About the favor," he added dramatically. He was killing me. "I want you to have something, you know, to take care of." Sam pulled out a Tony Lama boot box that I had admired all my life. My heart leaped in my chest, galloping like D'Artagnan's mare. I squinted in the dark and saw his tousled hair, disheveled T-shirt, and the prize he held in his hands.

Wow.

"Take care of them, Tim, and when I get back, I think it would be okay if you kept them."

I couldn't believe what he was saying. He was giving me all of them? And did he just call me *Tim*? I felt my joints throb with the sudden burst of growth.

"Sam, you're giving me all your baseball cards?" My voice caught in my throat. "All of them?"

"Yeah, I know you love the Redbirds as much as me, and you love Big Mac. You'll have a chance in two weeks to get his autograph. I have his rookie card, you know. Plus, Ankiel may get called up by then. Go to that game and get their autographs, Tim. Hang out near the dugout. You'll be just a few rows back. You guys aren't in the box for that one. And take good care of them. Don't trade them for stupid shit, or I'll smack you silly." He ruffled my hair.

"Why're you givin' them to me?" My heart was about to gallop out of my chest. His cards were the stuff of legend. Brent and Scott would pee themselves with envy.

"Ah, it's just time, that's all. But for real, don't lose the wrapped one. You know how I feel about that one. Cost me fifteen bucks, and that was at a flea market. That card's worth over a hundred in mint condition, but you could double that if you get it signed."

I tried to thank him but suddenly found that I couldn't speak. I could barely see in the dark room, but I could hear him smile. Then without another word, he shuffled off to bed. I lay in my room wide awake now, fighting the urge to rip off the lid and inspect all those cards that now belonged to me.

Willie Mayes. Bob Gibson. Lou Brock, Mark McGwire as a Cardinal and with the A's. Even a collector Babe Ruth. The autographed Mickey Mantle Dad had gotten when the former Yankee visited Busch Stadium. My head was spinning. Stan Musial, Dizzy Dean, and Little Timmy McCarver. What did I do to deserve this? Did he think he was too old for them now? That seemed the most logical answer. But I was well past double digits now. Eleven sounded way different than ten.

I fell asleep some ten minutes later with the Tony Lama box slid carefully under my bed. The three neat rows divided by strips of cardboard, all the cards alphabetized and separated by teams. Sam had some valuable cards organized in that box. Others that were worth only a little in sentimental value. Now they were mine.

***

Two Weeks Later

"Look, Scott! It's Willie!" I screamed. Brent craned his head around me, trying to see if it was or not. We were known to have false sightings. The players treated kids by coming out and waving all the time – and usually signed a few autographs before and after every game, sometimes during. We were banking on it.

Brent's favorite player was still Royce Clayton, even though he had been traded, but I thought Mark McGwire ruled the planet. And his records would put him at the top of most any list if he kept up the pace. While the three of us stared, Dad pointed straight at Willie McGee, who had just stuck his head out ready to go on deck. I thought I was going to die. This was by far the closest I had ever been. We came to a lot of games but usually sat in the outfield. Only a few games a season did we get to use Dad's box seats from work. The Musketeers preferred the outfield, because we liked to bring our gloves and try to catch home runs. But today we were hobnobbing with the box seaters, and I could get used to the perks.

"WILLIE!" I shouted. He actually turned and greeted our flailing arms with a wave. Fans everywhere swore Cardinal ball players were the best about acknowledging the crowd, and now I knew it was true.

Willie had waved at *me*.

By the top of the seventh, we hadn't had much luck getting players to come out, because Bottenfield was pitching a great game. There had been no lulls for pitching changes, so it limited our opportunities. We had a too-close-for-comfort two run lead over the much-hated Cubbies, but Bottenfield still had it under control.

"Time for the seventh inning stretch." Dad stood, motioning for us to follow suit. We knew why he was excited. This was always his cue to go to the bathroom to get a fresh beer.

The crowd joined the organist for Busch Stadium's traditional rendition of "Take Me Out to The Ballgame," but all I cared about was edging my way to get autographs. The three of us leaned against the bar beside the dugout and inspected the faces sitting, pacing, and spitting sunflower seeds. I could see two of my favorites, Fernando Tatis and J.D. Drew. Willie McGee leaned at the far end by Big Mac. My heart hammered in my chest.

"Hey, guys, would you sign my cards?" Scott called out first.

"Sure, kid." Tatis came over and signed each of our cards, followed by Drew. Scott only had Fernando's baseball card, and J.D. pretended to have a heart attack, acting all crushed. It was totally cool. We were on a first name basis now.

"You think Willie and Big Mac would sign these, too?" I dared to ask.

"We can ask him." Tatis, shorter than he seemed on TV, called over to McGwire, who sat chomping on his gum and squinting out at the ball field. Next thing we knew, Mark freaking McGwire and Willie McGee actually turned toward us and headed our way. My heart jammed into my throat.

"Hey, guys, how's it goin'?" Big Mac bantered as he walked across the dugout.

How's it goin'? Was he for real? I glanced around to make sure the future Hall of Famer was actually talking to me. Mark McGwire just asked the Three Musketeers how it was going. We all three had just died and gone to Cooperstown. *No need for CPR, folks, it's too late.*

"We're awesome, Mr. McGwire," Scott said enthusiastically. We weren't on a first-name basis with Big Mac. Not yet, anyway.

Then he took my pen, *my Bic*, and signed each of our cards and a few other kids' hanging around us. I quickly slipped mine back into its plastic cover. Scrawled across his Oakland A's uniform was Mark McGwire's autograph.

"You better keep that in there." He grinned. "That'll be worth a lot of money when I break Barry's record."

I promised I would, then we all thanked him until we sounded stupid. He actually shook our hands. I had to ask Dad who Barry was and got way more of an explanation than I wanted. I just wanted to know who Big Mac set his sights on.

We all threatened to never wash our right hands again, but when we got home, Mom won that battle when she saw the mustard smear and sticky cotton candy on the knuckles.

***

I made good, Sam – you were stoked, remember?

Timmy neatly placed the few cards he still owned, the ones Billy had the nerve to touch with his grimy, arthritic hands, back into their hiding place.

Good thing I keep my cash on me. Timmy inspected his space and noticed the visor and its attached mirror had flown the coop. His notepad lay open on top of his makeshift table. Timmy felt like someone had used his own teeth to chew with.

My things have already been picked over. And I paid you for protection, you pig.

His lease in the alley had expired. "Good thing we're on a month to month," he told Skippy. Max's stand-by joke brought a hint of a smile, but it was all his aching heart could manage. Timmy rummaged in Max's – soon to be Billy's – quarters and found a small but not-too-wimpy shoebox. Not a Tony Lama boot box by any stretch, but it would have to do. He then began the tedious task of pulling bottle caps off the walls of his precious U-Haul home. It would serve someone well, he hoped. Then a vindictive streak raced through him. It would feel good to smash the hell out of it. Billy hadn't done a damn thing to deserve it, and the thought of the drunk sleeping there made Timmy's face hot.

Instead, he paused, stared at the hundreds of caps pressed-in or glued to the cardboard, and the task suddenly overwhelmed him. But he couldn't leave them. The hobby had progressed into an obsession, and Max kept track for the Guinness record. That would be awesome no matter what world he was living in.

He sighed and continued pulling and prying them off with

his fingers or his knife, whichever worked better. *Better a tool than a weapon.* He hoped he could keep it that way. He'd had no luck finding the switchblade, but he hadn't really expected to.

He suddenly caught an image of himself hanging out the door of an airplane a thousand feet above the ground. A parachute dangling loosely on his back, straps tattered and ripcord rusted. A maniacal instructor hovered over his left shoulder screaming for him to jump. The man looked eerily like Billy but had Ralph's nasty teeth.

The wind whipped him around like a limp noodle.

"C'mon, kid, time to go!" Then the creep laughed like a lunatic and prepared to shove him out the hatch. "But watch out, kid, first step's a doozy."

That much Timmy didn't doubt at all.

Chapter Thirty-Three

Silence blanketed the alley by one-thirty almost every afternoon. Most of the drunks had battled their hangovers all morning and almost always napped after they ate, no matter how little. Today was no exception. Timmy and Skippy had hung out across the street and even ventured toward the Stockton corner, watching to make sure Cooter didn't come around.

As soon as each of the bums found places to snooze, Timmy took the opportunity to search Billy's stuff. The idiot had left his heavier coat in Max's box.

Skippy sniffed the Burger King bag, found a stray fry, and gobbled it. Timmy's treasure beat the heck out of a fry. He held up the switchblade, the one he despised after the Baldy fight, but it didn't belong with Billy. And God forbid, Timmy might need it.

"All right, Skippy, it's time. Let's go, boy," he coaxed, though the mutt seemed less than motivated, still certain another fry might be lodged in the bottom of the sack.

Timmy gathered his shoebox crammed full of bottle caps, placed about a third of his cash on top so his front pockets wouldn't be so noticeable, then secured the lid with one of Max's bungee cords. He placed his tiny pillow and tattered sleeping bag in the center of his flimsy blanket. Resting the box on top of the pillow, he pulled each corner of the cover to the center and tied them together into a makeshift knap-sack. Wedging the inch-thick stack of baseball cards on top he used another bungee to secure it all together, then twined it around his waist and over his shoulders. The homemade backpack would slip, but he could retie it as often as he needed – anything to make travel easier.

They stood at the entrance of the alley – Timmy didn't

want to, but he looked back.

Without Max there, it felt different. With his life at a crossroads, he paused for some kind of sign.

Skippy yipped, startling him.

"What is it, boy?"

His mutt scampered five or six yards back toward the box and then came and sat at his boy's feet. Skippy repeated the cycle twice, so Timmy walked back to see what the heck the terrier wanted. He had to hold his right hand tightly over his mouth to keep from laughing. He picked up the aluminum pan that had served as Skippy's water bowl for several months. At times, the Gerries had used simple items like butter dishes and Tupperware lids, but the mutt had moved up in the world.

"Sorry, boy, what was I thinking?" He untied his pack, placed the bowl on top of his box in the dead center of his pack, then retied it as securely as possible. Skippy scurried ahead, ready for new adventures.

Timmy trudged forward, vowing not to look back again. "See ya," he whispered, more to the alley itself than to the guys. He had no allegiance to any of them. Cooter would be the only one he'd truly miss, but the guy was the one he now had to fear running into. So without risking that possible debacle, Timmy and Skippy traipsed off into the afternoon, unsure where to go but eager to get there. He had the next phase of the plan ready to execute, but he needed to sort out the details. Walking would give him time to consider the options, the possible results, and whether he could be as bold as he hoped he could be.

"Okay, Skippy, it's just you and me kid...you up for it?" Turning on to Stockton, it was all Timmy could do to suppress the article-induced images.

A bark in the distance set Skippy's tail into a fervor, and the terrier dashed down the street. Then he heard a faint yip in the distance and just like that, his best friend disappeared in a jaunt toward some unknown destination.

"No, Skip, come back, boy!" He waited, listening. He made

his way down Stockton, not so close that his shouting would stir the dead.

"*Skippy*!" But the street remained silent. No sign of his mutt or the distinctive yip-yip-yip. Timmy tried not to panic, but what would he do if Skippy couldn't track him? It was early afternoon. Timmy intended to cover some serious distance. But if he kept going, Skippy would have no idea where his boy was. The mutt would return to the alley later wondering where the heck his boy had gone. *But wasn't the water bowl a sign?*

"Skippy?" he called feebly, feeling a lump rise in his throat. "Please, boy, come back. We're not just goin' for a walk. Please – I –" A sob strangled him for a split second. He sprinted in the direction he'd seen his mutt disappear. "C'mon, boy, pleeeeeeeeeeease." He pleaded with the point in the distance where he'd seen his best friend disappear.

Racing down another street, never tearing his eyes off the point on the horizon, he screamed. "SKIPPY!"

The scream pierced the quiet afternoon, clearly a work day for the lack of anyone anywhere around. Even the homeless needed days to work up to the weekend, especially in the chill of winter. With Christmas just days away, he knew that would change in a few blocks. But here, still on the edge of invisible land, Timmy imagined Billy and the Gerries – how many streets over? – jerking awake at the sound of his shouts. The next image, of Billy kicking at Skippy, tripled the panic brewing in his belly.

He didn't think he was close enough for them to hear him. But he also didn't care. At this point, if he lost his dog, especially now, he wouldn't have a clue what to do. His only friend, his last friend, his best friend.

He stood frozen in the middle of a street. He couldn't go back, not to the emptied box, not anywhere near the vultures privy to the money he had on him, not to Cooter who would out him about the money. He knew better. With his sidekick awol, he felt abandoned and just wanted to wallow in a fresh pity party. Emotion, still hovering on the edge of every thought and breath, was about to consume him. Again.

With the makeshift pack on his back, he imagined himself looking like a kid in a disaster movie. Nowhere to go, no one to go there with, and nothing else to do but walk.

But I can't. I'm ready, and now I can't. Ah, God, when does it stop? Skippy please....

For too long, change hadn't been an option or existed for him at all. But he willed it to matter again. Change, no longer fifty cents for a Dr Pepper, meant taking risks. And this one might be the hardest yet. But he had promised himself he would put up, not shut up. And regardless of the cost, he had to go – being a thief made him a wanted man. Lingering could cost him more than his best friend. He'd known the risk when he told that first lie about the money.

Timmy turned several circles in the middle of the empty street. In his screaming frenzy, chasing Skippy as he sprinted off into the afternoon, Timmy had done what he did best.

Culverton? That's off my map. Shit.

The street name, vaguely familiar, let him know he'd taken off running and gotten farther west than he ever went. He *always* migrated east, toward the arch and the river, landmarks that served his directionally-challenged brain well. But in mere minutes, he was out of his normal loop, all in an effort to find Skippy.

He gave a sharp whistle. It was all he knew to do. Emotion made his chest ache. He made his way to the sidewalk, to a building with a giant for sale sign on the inset entrance door, and plopped to the pavement. *Ah, Skippy – come back, buddy. Come back.*

The full-circle image made his head throb. Beginning his street life hunkered in a broken-down doorway. Hoping to end it by opening one. It wasn't too much to ask, was it? Did he really think he could break that cycle? Not without his best friend.

"SKIPPY!" He screamed, his throat raw and filled with emotion.

This is it, Skip. I can't wait.

But he had to. He couldn't go without his best friend. What would the mutt do without his boy? The lump in his throat made it impossible to swallow, because he worried Skippy wouldn't find him once he got out of invisible land.

He tried to make out the time on his watch through his tears. It was almost two o'clock. Only a couple of hours of daylight, but maybe resting and traveling in the shadows would be safer anyway. *I'm givin' ya two hours, Skippy. Two hours....*

Timmy knew by sunset, Billy would likely see Cooter – the odds were for it. Monday evening after a ballgame, so close to Christmas, back to the regular routine of getting ready for the next big game. And then they would talk money, because they'd be planning for the next gig.

Billy would send guys looking for him, and Cooter might lead that charge. No matter how mealy-mouthed the bum was, Billy was vindictive and multiply that by the incentive of over two thousand dollars, and the self-appointed alley cat would kick the snot out of any dog or boy who got in his way. Timmy had always steered clear of Billy for a reason.

Panic swelled in his stomach, swirling the partially digested whopper junior. Sitting with his knees to his chest and elbows propped on them, Timmy dangled his heavy head and did something for the first time in his street life.

He prayed.

***

A stream of light trickling across Timmy's face startled him awake. The jolt of panic was worsened by the realization that the setting sun meant Skippy had likely ventured back to the alley. He should've been whistling and calling out long before now, but he had to screw that up by falling asleep.

Can this day get any worse? He didn't think so. And he knew he couldn't get too close to Brookline – not unless he wanted to face Cooter and the wrath of Billy. Once the cat was out of the bag about the money, Billy would be livid. He let out a sharp whistle, then a couple more, just in case.

I could just suck it up and take it back to them...do I really need it?

There were several hitches in that idea, the first of which being that he had little clue where he was. And the second, probably most important, was he needed to get cracking with his plan. The longer he put it off, the more likely he would chicken out. He had several options, but the one he wanted most would take kahunas. Sam always told him the toughest decisions took kahunas, and when it mattered most, a Weaver needed to make those tough choices.

He staggered to his feet, stiff and chilled to the bone. Brushing off his jeans, he whistled again, over and over for a few seconds.

C'mon, Skippy, where are you, boy? But many afternoons, if they weren't dumpster diving together, Timmy would wander around and his sidekick would head off on a chase and might not see his boy until dinner. A snaking fear whispered, *He doesn't know where I am...heck I don't know where I am. And he may not trot back into the alley for another hour or two.*

He glanced at his watch. *4:05.* The Gerries wouldn't be suspicious of him being gone. He explored and scouted for food all afternoon most days. He usually didn't come back before 6:00, even 7:00. With Max gone, the expectation to supply them with food was blurry. Billy would want it and would gripe and grumble that the kid better come through. But they all knew he was bluster and bullshit. And Timmy doubted if they would notice his box emptied. Their focus would be on a bottle.

The real hitch was Cooter. If he had returned, that was a whole other story.

Timmy shivered. He went to the corner, north he could tell

by the setting sun off to the west. Fingers in his mouth, he gave his shrillest high to low back to high whistle he could produce. Waiting and listening, he tugged at the pack on his back. Maybe Skippy would come bounding into the alley, see his water bowl gone, and remember. He's smart. He knew they were leaving.

Timmy tried not to think about what Billy would do to him. Max had been the terrier's first daddy and had protected the dog from the bum's temper on many occasions. The only way Timmy could shelter his best friend now was to corral him and escape. And never look back.

C'mon, Skippy. He let out a string of sharp whistles, so desperate and emotional, he lost air and couldn't finish the string of them.

What would Skippy think when his boy wasn't there by bedtime, to rub his head and snuggle for warmth? Timmy shivered again. How long would his best friend wait, sitting on his haunches staring at the open end of the alley wondering where his boy had gone. How long before Billy chased him off to scrounge on his own?

Tears sprang to his eyes, but he willed them away. For half an hour, he forced himself to play rock solitaire, whistling every few minutes, arranging different shaped pebbles in rows – gravel aces, pea-shaped deuces, triangular shaped threes. Max's version had passed many boring afternoons for the crew, and Timmy needed the diversion. His neck throbbed from the way he had fallen asleep, but he welcomed the pain – it kept him alert.

When he lost his fourth game, whistled for the zillionth time, he scattered his rocks and sighed. He didn't want to look at his watch. He covered it with his coat so he couldn't. But Tigger was like a magnet.

No, it's not even five yet. I'm givin' him 'til six. He'll be wanting dinner by then, or at least to get warm.

Timmy rubbed the back of his throbbing neck, giving a sharp whistle, short and sweet, trying to mask his customary long calls. Anything to keep from tipping the Gerries to his location. They might already be on the hunt for him. That idea added to the chill.

Please, Skippy, I need you. I already lost one family.... But Timmy regretted resurfacing those emotions the minute he thought it.

Two vehicles, witnesses say, pursued the family. A Chevrolet Impala and a Plymouth convertible forced the Weavers' Cadillac Escalade into an approaching police car responding to a 911 call by the Weavers.

Timmy swallowed the bile in his throat. *I shoulda died, too. I'm tired, I'm hungry, and I don't wanna fight anymore. I just want to sleep.*

For ten more minutes, he wallowed, whistled, and worried. *Please, Skippy, please come to me.* But as the hands on his watch turned, as much as Timmy begged them not to, urgency churned his gut. Anxiety forced him to make a decision.

If I'm gonna put up and not shut up, it's time. I can't sit here and wait forever.

An ache the size of the Mississippi swelled in his chest. He stood, brushed the grit from the butt of his jeans, and let out a long, ragged breath. He tried to whistle but it came out lame and listless. He turned slowly and lifted feet that felt like cement blocks. His ears tuned into the sounds of the evening hour, listening for the pitter-patter of his best friend's paws. He finally gave in and looked at his watch. 5:49. At the same instant, someone screamed his name followed by gibberish he couldn't make out.

Oh, God. I gotta get outta here or Billy's gonna find me.

This time, he heard the voice loud and clear.

"I WANT MY GODDAMNED MONEY!" someone shouted from a few blocks away. "WHERE ARE YOU, YOU LITTLE SHIT!"

Oh, God! Panic spurred Timmy's lead feet into action. *Billy.* Timmy sprinted in the opposite direction, tightening his pack as he ran, and didn't look back. He whistled in short, sharp bursts as he dashed across a street, down a side street, and even risked calling Skippy's name as he covered blocks. The distance between Brookline and his uncertain future grew, almost as fast as the lump in Timmy's throat. He slowed to listen.

"TIMMY, WHAT THE HELL ARE YOU DOING!?" Cooter's voice rang out louder than Timmy could've imagined. The younger guy wasn't gaining, but he wasn't falling far enough behind either.

Timmy had sat so long, he was stiff. So he dodged west, then south, then west again. Straight down one street was too dangerous.

"I'LL FIND YOU, TIMMY! YOU HEAR ME?!" Billy's voice boomed in the distance, clearly falling behind.

He sprinted down Choteau, zigged onto a side street, then zagged across a major thoroughfare. Shouts faded. His name faint in the distance, and then silence.

He had finally left the Gerries in the dust. The crumbling sidewalk gave way to cleaner concrete, nicer stores, and then finally houses. The terror loosening its hold on Timmy's insides didn't slow his feet for long. He would jog to rest, but every so often, he'd burst into a sprint just to give him peace of mind.

For the second time in his life, Timmy ran for his life with no clue where he was headed, and no one there to help him.

Chapter Thirty-Four

When his legs gave out, Timmy collapsed under a massive oak tree in an unfamiliar, lush city park. Elaborate statues, ornate fences, fancy landscaping – all foreign but beautiful. Street lights bathed his face as he sat almost directly beneath one. He squinted to orient himself. A stitch burned in his side, and despite the cold weather, sweat beaded his forehead. He gulped air, trying to get the pain to ease.

"Ah, Skippy." With exhaustion came the realization that Timmy was friendless. The miles separating him from Brookline were insurmountable for his terrier. The most powerful sniffer in the world would never catch his scent.

When air filled his lungs and breathing stopped hurting, Timmy stood and continued south – he hoped. The sunset was long gone and he'd crisscrossed and corkscrewed so many times, he didn't have a clue which way was up. By the cleanliness of the street, the ornate doorways and building facias, he knew he was in the land of the very visible. Every hour or so, he paused for a breather, but walked until the moon had risen high in the sky. He found a major road he knew ran north and south, he turned left and considered walking all the way to Florida. The more distance he could put between him and the Gerries, the better.

Going back was out of the question. The money was his ticket out. It had dawned on him that he could get someone to help him find Skippy later, to go rescue his mutt. That could work, couldn't it?

He trudged block after block into suburbs, passed car dealerships, shopping centers, and fast food places. Business lights blinked off as they closed. Heavy legs and cramping calves forced Timmy to find a resting spot, a place to hide and nibble on the few crackers he had left from an earlier stop at a convenience store. But his water was almost out. He could find a convenience store, but all he really wanted now was a little sleep. Then he would figure out where to go. He needed to think, to clear his head. Spying another small park, he headed for it. With drooping eyes, leaden legs, and an aching back, Timmy crawled into a thicket of bushes and removed his pack. He laid his head on it, not bothering with eating or drinking. He was too tired.

Nightmares haunted Timmy's sleep – a muscle-bound thug ransacked his box, held Skippy by his scruff. He chased the thief, hopped into the backseat of his dad's SUV. A rapid *pop-pop-pop* shattered the Escalade's windshield, but instead of his dad driving, it was Billy. The SUV skidded to a stop. Billy's face was tatted on the bicep of a thug who yanked Timmy from the backseat and kicked him clear across the field into the storm drain. A yelp pierced the night as Skippy's body fell like a sack of potatoes next to his boy.

Face down, just like I had after...after....

Hours later when he woke, fleeting images of his dog, his family, and four months of hell faded with the reality facing him. In the dark, everything seemed scarier and more hopeless. He couldn't make out the time on his Tigger watch, but he could feel the dew on his jeans – it was well after midnight from the feel of it.

I need you, Skippy.

The swelling ache in his chest was as bitter as the one he had felt for his mom, dad, and Sam. Because Skippy was all he had left. The terrier was his only family now that Max was in lock-up. And he wasn't family, was he? He was a liar.

Heavy-hearted and dejected, Timmy sat up. He fumbled through his things, relieved that everything was still there. After rewrapping the knapsack, he scrambled out of the bushes and tried to make out his surroundings with the street lamp's help. Two blocks away, he could see an intersection, so he headed toward it. Skippy would never find his boy. As he squinted to read the names, it dawned on him that he was in the same boat. *Briarwood and Fernflower?* Things didn't even look familiar. He might as well be in Illinois.

He flexed his arms, resituated the knapsack on his back and grimaced as his joints popped. Both legs, tight and stiff, wobbled, and his back screamed from the weight of the makeshift pack. The only relief would be a yip-yip followed by furious face licks. But there was no yip-yip and no kisses.

"Okay, Tim. What now?" He studied the landmarks. Brick townhouses, Diana's Flower Shop, a Phillip's 66 he swore he'd never seen before. He recalled little about stopping and curling up in the bushes, because he had been so exhausted, mentally and physically. And hadn't he cried himself to sleep? He thought so. His vow that he was no crybaby was like the Gerries saying they weren't drunks.

Modest homes, weathered but clean, shone in the moonlight. Children's toys lay scattered on every lawn, the newest trends in playthings more unfamiliar to him than the landscape. A go-kart made Timmy's itchy fingers tingle, but he had to stay focused.

"Okay, Tim, which way?" He would have to be his own best friend now. He glanced at his watch – 2:40 a.m.

Eenie-meenie-miney-mo. He pointed in each potential direction as he recited, *if it hollers make it pay....* When he finished, *and you are not it,* he promptly set off down the street that ran past Phillip's 66. The street signs meant little, because he had never heard of either of them. Then it occurred to Timmy. *Go in, bonehead. Ask for directions.* The nearest shelter, halfway house, or soup kitchen would be good. He no longer intended to avoid them, and it would be his mission to find one as soon as possible. No matter how much money he had folded into his jacket or stuffed in his Levi's, he would save it for what mattered. Splurging for an occasional lunch was one thing, but now it was time to search for help. *Real* help.

He walked into the convenience store, waited in line while people paid for gas, bought beer, and chose lottery tickets. By the time he got to the counter, there were a million things on the racks that made his mouth water.

"Excuse me, ma'am, could you tell me where the nearest soup kitchen is?" Timmy kept his eyes low. His stomach growled at the mere mention of food.

"You hungry, darlin'?" The plump sales lady lowered her head to look Timmy in the eye. Her dimples were deeper than Sam's. A flap of her smock covered her nametag, but he bet it was something friendly like Meg or Frannie.

"Yes, ma'am," he whispered. He didn't want any of the other customers to hear. He glanced around but none seemed to be paying attention to him at all. The invisibility cloak still worked.

"I tell ya what, I'll write down directions to St. Michael's while you grab yourself a couple of doughnuts. I was about to start boxin' them anyway. New ones are cookin'." Her warmth melted the ice around his heart.

"Thank you," he stated simply, but stood rooted to the same spot. He wanted one but didn't want to appear greedy. Having all that money in his pack made taking a handout feel wrong. She sensed his hesitancy and came from behind the counter to box two jelly, one glazed, and a cake doughnut. Timmy's eyes beamed like headlights.

While she drew him a tiny map, he couldn't resist the cake doughnut. It melted on his tongue and filled his mouth with such heaven, he thought he had died and gone to it. He fought the urge to buy a cappuccino, but he knew he would look like a hustler if he whipped out his roll of cash. Instead he savored the last bite and before he could swallow it, his Phillip's 66 savior pushed a small carton of milk across the counter. She had even opened it for him.

This time it was Timmy's turn to grin. A real one, though his eyes were filled with grateful tears. Before he left, she told him her name was Debbie and if he needed anything at all to come on back and she would help him. She pointed him to the nearest bus stop and then buttoned his coat all the way to his chin. By the time he left the store, she had bagged two more pints of milk and stacked them on top of the box of doughnuts. He thanked her again and told her he wished he had met more people like her. And he meant it.

Timmy turned his face up to the moonlit sky and whistled twice, just in case, but headed on not expecting a response.

He didn't get one.

Debbie's directions mapped out exactly which way to go, but it was quite a hike. And the idea of catching a bus seemed too final – his terrier's high-powered nose wouldn't be able to sniff out his trail if he did that.

His stiff legs began to cramp with the brisk pace, but he willed it away and continued to walk. He studied her map and realized he would have to keep track of which direction he was heading on each street. It would be easy for him to get turned around. He couldn't help but laugh at his inability to tell north from south without a little help from the sun. Or a giant landmark or large mass of running water.

Some street kid I am.

For about an hour, the narrow houses were mirror images of one another. Only the numbers changed. The owners got as creative as possible with their tiny front yards. Lawn ornaments, whirligigs, and bright pink flamingos stuck into the ground.

But everything else about the fifteen to twenty homes could have been photocopied and planted in front of each. Same toys, same cars, same flags. United States flag on top, Ram's beneath it, and Cardinal's flying third. There was an occasional Blues flag. Timmy bet the order changed depending on the season.

By the time he reached the end of the street, he squinted at the street sign then turned right. It was what the directions indicated, but the second he peered down the road, he knew he had gotten turned around. He had seen all of this before, maybe forty-five minutes ago. Somehow he had gone in a circle.

The crickets continued to chirrup, street lamps buzzed, and cars headed to homes he could only dream about. But Timothy Ryan Weaver, four months into a street sentence, didn't care.

For a fresh start, I sure am havin' trouble gettin' anywhere.

Chapter Thirty-Five

By six a.m., Timmy was ready to drop. But with directions from another convenience store clerk, he finally felt on the right track. The December sky shone with a yellow glow, as the sun threatened to peek over the horizon. He headed in the direction his updated map showed and hoped he'd find it soon. If not, he planned to curl up in some brush and catch a little sleep. His legs ached and he knew he needed to rest. It had been hours since he had last stopped.

He saw Highland Street and knew he was exactly ten blocks away. All he had to do was stay on this street and continue straight ahead. But ten blocks loomed like ten miles. His throbbing legs, aching head, and heavy feet needed a break.

"Skippy, if you come runnin' up to me right now, I'll give you a granola bar." Timmy turned circles, waiting for his buddy to appear. Instead, he heaved another sigh. His mutt would have long since returned to Brookline and the box looking for his boy. He would think Timmy had abandoned him. And he had, hadn't he?

Barely able to chew, he stood on a sidewalk in front of a convenience store and ripped open a cinnamon granola bar. He took the last sips of a Gatorade, satiating the physiological demands, but nothing could ease the pain in his heart.

"I don't wanna look like a desperate runaway," he announced to the crickets. He pulled the pack off his back and retied it, anxious to inspect the contents but too tired to take the time. All that cash, his bottle caps, ball cards, and miscellaneous belongings were all he had left. "Ah, Skippy," he mumbled, unable to stop the tears. Angry that he had allowed himself to cry more times than he could count, Timmy stomped down the road oblivious of the pain.

Constant, side-splitting stitches screamed in opposition,

but Timmy lumbered on. He could no longer see the map through his tears, so he didn't know if he was still on track. The only thing he did know was that he was beyond exhausted.

"I can't keep going," he muttered to the trees and anything else that would listen. Talking out loud seemed to be his new normal.

When he looked up, he couldn't believe his eyes.

The Virgin Mary, mother of Jesus, stood before him, beckoning with open arms. The sign read *St. Michael's,* and Timmy believed it was Heaven. He nearly sprinted to the doors but was too exhausted to open them.

"Hey, let me get that for you," an elderly man said. Timmy's head swam, like he was in a dream. Everything blurred, and then his legs noodled. He collapsed before the man could catch him.

"Son?" The man, bald on top with only a row of snow white hair around the sides, had green eyes flecked with blue – *like the Gulf of Mexico.* He remembered it from when he was eight and went to Panama City Beach. The man's wrinkles had wrinkles, and Timmy wondered for a split second if the man might be God.

The hand on his back suddenly panicked him. "I – I...please don't, I mean..." but Timmy's brain couldn't form an answer. His brain couldn't wrap around where he was, why he was there, or why God wanted his pack of stuff.

"It's okay. Come on in. Are you thirsty? Hungry?" God opened the door to St. Michael's, led him into a foyer, and called for Father Myers. The stained glass caught the lights and sprayed Timmy with a rainbow of color.

Seconds later, water trickled down his throat and seemed to spring his vocal cords free. The man held the water bottle out to him in case he wanted more.

"You okay, son?" The nice man Timmy knew couldn't be God shooed him into a small kitchen. Luscious smells made his stomach rumble.

"Thanks, mister," he said, his throat raw from screaming for Skippy the day before and inhaling the cold wind for endless hours. "Did I pass out?"

"You'll be okay," God consoled, sounding a little too much like Max on the day the old man had found Timmy lying on a cot in a shelter.

The eerie similarity opened the dam, and before Timmy could stop them, the tears unleashed. Tsunami Timmy bawled in God's arms for what felt like an eternity. A man in all black, except for a white square of cloth at his neck, stooped in front of Timmy and smiled.

"What's your name, son?"

Timmy swiped his face – tears and snot smeared his jacket sleeve. He made out the man's face through the blur of tears and tried to answer. His tongue stuck to the roof of his mouth, words not getting past his aching throat. Opening and closing his mouth, he knew he had to look like a begging baby bird. Or a starving fish.

"Let's get the young man some soup, Father Myers," an angel's voice suggested. If Timmy hadn't known better, he would have guessed it was Debbie from the convenience store.

"Would you like some soup, honey?" the angel asked. Even though his stomach hurt, the idea of hot, fresh soup made it growl again. "I'll be right back."

"Can you tell me your name? Or where you live?" Father Myers scooted next to Timmy on the bench.

His chest heaved with fresh sobs. What could he say? Certainly not the alley, since that wasn't really an address. And it also wasn't home. He started to say 4320 Catalina Avenue, but the words died in his parched throat. A Granville Auction sign from a fuzzy night three and a half months earlier reared its ugly head.

Timmy couldn't think. He mumbled that he didn't have a home, and the Father draped an arm over the boy's shoulder. The older man didn't push him to answer.

"And Skippy," Timmy managed in broken, heaving sobs.

"Who's Skippy, son?"

"My dog." A new sob made him hiccup.

I'm sorry, Skippy, he wanted to wail like a baby. But the sheer thought of his best friend made him cry harder. Leaning against Father Myers' shoulder, Timmy continued to bawl until he thought he might throw up.

Instead, he fell asleep, no longer bothering to claim he wasn't a crybaby.

Chapter Thirty-Six

Timmy jerked awake, covered with sweat, and tried to retrieve the nightmare. He threw back the covers, rummaged through his jeans' pocket, and pulled out the newspaper clipping to read it again.

Officer killed, family found slain, youngest child missing, believed kidnapped.

Slain. He weighed the unfamiliar word – one he didn't need to look up to figure out. But he didn't understand it, not really. *Why did they die? Why didn't I? Why did those jerks chase us?* Lying in a strange bed, Timmy's brain rattled with the questions to his past, his precarious future.

Father Myers had tucked him into a small bed in an upstairs room that served as guest quarters when visitors came to the shelter. The room, warm and cozy, had the softest bed he'd ever laid on. The Father told Timmy they could talk later, when the boy was ready.

Ready for what? He didn't know what the man wanted to know – too much of it lay in a confusing wasteland for him. How was he going to explain that to Father Myers?

Mrs. Hammons left a bowl of delectable smelling soup on his bedside table, trying to coax him to eat earlier. He sat up, ignored the emptiness clawing at his brain, and started in on the soup. He barely came up for air until it was gone.

*I gotta know...*but an obstacle loomed between him and That Night. No matter how hard he tried, he couldn't get past it. The hole in his heart wouldn't allow it.

Skippy. How could he leave his best friend behind to suffer the wrath of Billy and the Gerries? Without his boy or Max, the terrier wouldn't stand a chance. Timmy flipped on the small lamp and squinted at his Tigger watch.

My God, I've slept all day. It was almost eleven p.m. But he knew what had to be done. As much as he hated to, he gathered his things, repacked his bundle, and tiptoed down the back stairs of the shelter.

He intended to find the closest bus stop. The plan put a bounce in his step. *I have one family member I can save.* With renewed resolve and a mission, Timmy pushed the front door open as quietly as he could. St. Michael's had been a brief haven, but he couldn't be saved until he did a little of it himself.

He breathed in the bitterly cold December air. Rested but sore, he set out for a bus stop, and found one fifteen minutes later. He checked the schedule and sighed. He'd missed the ten forty-five, and the next one wasn't for nearly forty minutes. He wrapped his coat tight around his neck, velcroed it for maximum warmth, and set off walking. Get some distance and then catch a bus somewhere along the way. No point in sitting and waiting. Skippy needed him.

Brookline bound, he hoped he could do it without any of the Gerries spotting him – he couldn't risk what they might do to him. He'd seen them beat the crap out of bums who stole from them. Timmy pictured Billy ranting, throwing things, trying to exert his authority over the rest of the Gerries.

As he walked, the worry played second fiddle to the long-suppressed memories tapping at his tired brain. The trauma of losing his parents felt funny, tinted around the edges like someone had faded them, and added shades of yellow and gray. He tried to organize them in his head, retrieve them in whole chunks while he journeyed to find his best friend. But for the first time in a few days shy of four months, Timmy didn't want to remember. Not yet. Not until he had Skippy safe at his side.

A few of the clips stirred his certainty that he was bad – the acrid smell of gunpowder and something else pungent. *Blood maybe? I smelled both for days after, didn't I?*

He burrowed his head in his coat and lumbered on. He covered nearly twenty blocks when he stopped to rest, near a bus stop, to wait for daybreak and running buses. His legs were too tired after yesterday's marathon. After a little rest, he woke to an orangish yellow horizon. It brought a smile to his face, the prospect of a fresh new day.

Timmy climbed onto the first bus, smiling as he sat to watch the sunrise. After he transferred three times, he finally recognized streets along his food route. Getting fidgety at being so close to the Gerries, and worrying about them seeing him, he slid lower in his seat.

I'm comin', Skippy.

He hopped off the bus with plenty of cushion, about seven blocks away, and heard someone shout, "Hey, kid!"

A blip of panic evaporated when he saw the guy waving. "Hey, Vinnie, how's it hangin'?" Timmy returned the waved. Half a block later, he whistled sharply for his terrier mutt, hoping he was within hearing distance for the hearing-enhanced. A not-so-friendly pamphlet-passing fanatic scowled at a woman giving him a wide berth.

"God frowns on the pretentious!" he called after her.

Big word for a freak who looks like he hadn't moved for four months – same damn flyers.

"Let the Project save you! Buy a pamphlet and you too will see the light." The sun made the beggar squint, making him look even more sinister.

"The Lord is my savior," Timmy stated simply as he walked by.

"Yes, He is." The swindler furrowed his brow. Timmy thought the guy was trying to figure out where he knew the kid from.

"But He can't solve all my problems, mister, I gotta do that myself."

The man glared at him. Timmy smiled and for some reason, it reminded him of Sam making crowd noise with his hands after an awesome catch. Timmy could see his brother's dimpled cheeks and how his mom used to pinch them and say how doggone cute he was.

Then without warning, he could see his mom thrown to the

pavement and kicked, a gruff voice growling, "Shut the fuck up." The pain of that August night returned with a vengeance, a bright, electric pain inside him. The smile died, and it was all he could do to put his hands on his knees and suck air.

Out of desperation and frustration, he let out a shrill *get your buns over here right now* whistle that he knew Skippy would recognize.

Still no response. He knew he couldn't cover their entire morning routine, exhaustion and a heavy heart wouldn't allow it. But if he walked the area around their major haunts, even circled close to the alley, he prayed Skippy would hear him. Sometimes it was selective, but surely a night spent without his boy had made his mutt miss him.

When he finally neared Dexter Avenue, he forced himself to rest. Familiar gas stations where he had cleaned-up and stores with iron bars across the windows and doors – he was back in the land of the invisible. His home *After*. Not exactly Mayberry, but it had been his neighborhood. He was only a few blocks from Brookline and the alley. Tigger told him it was nearly noon, so if he timed it right, the geezers would nap and he could search for Skippy. No telling where the mutt was. The schedule had been thrown off.

Theirs too, though. He couldn't let his guard down. The Gerries had over two thousand reasons to still be on the lookout. And Cooter would feel betrayed. Timmy had done him wrong the worst way possible. Feeling guilt wash over him, he jogged past a Texaco he'd visited many times to use the restroom.

He let out a sharp whistle before slipping inside for a quick drink and a potty break. When Timmy came out, he looked around hoping maybe Skip would just be there.

No dice. So he continued another block toward Brookline, his heart thrumming in his ears. The anxiety squelched thoughts of his family. He had to be on his toes for Billy, Ralph, Cooter, or even Vernon. Any of them could be fiddle-farting around, as they put it, and see him. He gave a sharp whistle and stopped to listen.

Yip-yip-yip suddenly rang out behind him.

"SKIPPY!" Timmy turned, dropped to his knees, and bawled like a baby. "Ah, Skip," he moaned as his scraggly terrier vaulted into his arms. All fifteen pounds of him. Relief knocked Timmy over just as much as the mutt did, and the two of them were something right out of a Disney movie.

"God, boy, you scared me! I missed you so much." Timmy hugged, rough-housed, and petted his dog furiously.

Skippy wriggled free, gave a few more licks, then ran a circle around his boy. *Let's go play!* his wagging tail coaxed. He had no idea Timmy had traversed miles of St. Louis, left him behind, and then back-tracked just to reunite with him.

Not a clue and Timmy didn't care. He wouldn't lose him again. He slipped the collar he had made from the church's pillowcases around Skippy's neck and then tied twine to complete the homemade leash. He reached down and hugged his dog fiercely again. Skippy squirmed against it at first, but Timmy held firm.

"Sorry, Skip, but until we get settled, I don't wanna lose you again, okay?"

Skippy wagged that he didn't have a single problem in the world with sticking close or having his very own leash. Maybe it even made him feel protected, like he belonged to his boy for good now. Timmy supposed it might be a dog's dream to have a collar, no matter how ghetto it looked. A canine's prayer of escape, not so different than his hope of living in a real home again.

Timmy considered returning to St. Michael's, to explain to Father Myers that a boy and his dog were like peanut butter and jelly. But then a different option occurred to him, an early vision he'd had a hundred times during his first weeks After. One easy phone call, something he'd told Max he wanted to do. The old man terrified him into reconsidering, knowing how dangerous it would be for them and him.

All that was a lie.

Fireworks sizzled in his stomach as he and Skippy left the area of invisibility for the last time. Energized by his decision and overcome with the relief, as he made distance and headed toward a phone booth he remembered seeing, the fragmented memories of the article and of That Night flooded through him.

He cried as he walked. But Mom, Dad, and Sam were with him now. And he savored the memory of them, blinded by tears.

That Night. Those guys... The sharp pain of remembering jabbed him in the ribs, making it hard to breathe.

As soon as he reached a gas station, he had to write all this down in his little journal. *Don't let it slip away again. It'll swallow me if I do.*

It took less than ten minutes to see a convenience store – two more blocks. Had he been in that one before? It was too clean, too brightly lit for his homeless taste, but now it didn't matter. The force pulling him brought bile into his throat. *Let the force be with you.* God, didn't he love those movies.

In a perfect world, I'd be on Christmas break, vegging on the couch, and maybe watching one of those movies. That thought took him back to holiday breaks of the past. Sam had basketball practice almost every day, driving Mom crazy that it kept them from vacationing over Christmas break. Several of her friends spent the two weeks skiing or hitting the beach. Instead, she chauffeured his brother to and from school in her self-proclaimed Mom Mobile Limo Service. Dad called it Tori's Taxi, never ceasing to make us giggle. Timmy played multiple sports and took part in activities that warranted heavy chauffeuring, but nothing like the demands of a high school basketball team defending its state championship title.

A year ago at Christmas – *the last one with my family* – his parents broke the trend and took a cruise over the holidays. They sailed the day after Christmas and left Sam and him with the Kruschavens – to try out his new bike and Sam's Game Cube. Plus, Sam had a teammate with a license, so Mrs. K wouldn't have to tote him everywhere.

Mom and Dad got to get a tan while Sam and I spent two weeks being pampered and treated like royalty. Sam stared at Mrs. Kruschaven for ten days telling me that she kicked Cameron Diaz's butt any day of the week and twice on Sunday.

The memory evaporated and Timmy returned to the notion that he could stomach a piddly two-week Christmas break. The idea of crawling out of bed, showering, and scrambling for the school bus two minutes before it was supposed to be there sounded cooler than a chocolate sundae with nuts and a cherry on top.

School would be back in session in a week and a half. What he wouldn't give to be there, too. But without Mom, Dad, and Sam to roust him every morning, he couldn't imagine what it would be like. School was part of that other world, Before.

Did he want foster parents? Or to live in some kind of group home like Max had described? He didn't know, but he just couldn't deny himself the chance to find out.

What could be worse than no home at all?

Chapter Thirty-Seven

I can do this. It's one phone call.

But before crossing the road to the convenience store, a police cruiser pulled into the parking lot for gas.

Crap. His determination had bloomed into the size of one of his famous campfires, but he couldn't handle the stress of a confrontation with the law. Timmy tucked his head into his jacket and veered west – any store would do, as long as it had a phone.

Calling them seemed like the most logical thing in the world. The Max-instilled fear, along with months of doing the worst of the worst, had slowly killed the idea. But not anymore. How would he explain all of this to them? What would they say? He didn't know – he would cross that bridge when he jumped off it.

When he turned the corner out of the police cruiser's sight, Timmy ran. God knows he had done that before. He slowed after just a few blocks, stopping in a neighborhood of run-down cars, snot-nosed kids without shoes, and smells not too different than the alley.

Sam would have called this the hood. But Timmy knew it wasn't a true hood. He had been in the slums and this wasn't even close. He understood now how perspectives changed with life experience.

"Let's rest for a sec, Skip. I bet if we head that way, we'll find a gas station real fast." He pointed across a dilapidated park, complete with a rusted merry-go-round and graffitied slide.

Skippy stood on all fours, nosing in the pack for his bowl.

"You hungry, boy? Thirsty?" He rummaged for the paper sack holding the few things he had brought from St. Michael's. He pulled out a ham and cheese sandwich and split it, tearing Skippy's into bite-sized pieces. He poured water into this buddy's dish.

Once they polished off their breakfast, he continued to refill Skippy's water bowl. He suspected Mr. Skippy had sprung a leak.

"You drink like a fish, Skip."

The dog wagged but never stopped inhaling the water in his dish. Timmy shook his head but brimmed with love for his best friend.

How could I have done this without you, Skip? Having his buddy with him soothed the ache a little and gave him the strength to carry out his plan.

"Okay, boy, let's get poppin'. I'm ready. How 'bout you?" He realized he'd been stalling. Calling them was a no-brainer, but the actuality of it caused butterflies to erupt in his belly.

Skippy raced across the vacant lot next to the sad-looking playground. Timmy tried to read the graffiti, but the symbols made no sense.

"Yo, pretty boy, where'd you get that awesome scar?"

Timmy's stomach clenched around the sandwich he'd just eaten. *Dammit, why didn't I go around this shit-hole?* His street sense was already waning with the escape plan. Just because he was trying to leave his street life behind didn't mean he didn't still look the part. Instinctively, he traced the inch-long scar beneath his left eye.

"C'mere, blondie," a snaggle-toothed boy beckoned. The near-green, broken teeth reminded Timmy of Ralph's mouthful of rotten stubs. The kid, a couple of years older than Timmy, sat astride a bike much too small for him. The scene reminded him of one of his nightmares about tattoos and bikes.

"Back off, Jack," Timmy warned, rubbing the outline of the blade he'd stuffed in his front pocket. He was conscious of the bills in front of it and thought about just yanking it out for intimidation.

You want this blade, asshole? I knew it wasn't retired. A rush of adrenaline made his fingers flutter. Skippy growled, his hackles bristling.

"Who you callin' Jack, *Jack*?" Spittle flew from the kid's nasty mouth. He was classic trailer trash – a concept he'd learned from the Gerries.

"You, fuck face. Now back the hell off or you'll wish you never saw me." Timmy's voice, edged with a hatred he knew came from months of street survival, had deepened in the past few days. Having the prospect of a real life made him more dangerous than this piece of trailer trash could fathom.

Trash Boy balked at the bite in Timmy's voice but sauntered toward him, spying the roll on his back. Skippy growled louder, more serious. He tugged the pillowcase leash from his boy's hand, and Timmy obediently dropped it.

"That dog's gonna get gutted if he comes any closer, pretty boy."

Timmy inspected the freckled, dirt-matted face. The strawberry blond hair had gone so long without shampoo, he had the worst case of cradle cap Timmy had ever seen. And he had seen it several times on his own head – the near permanent brown splotches of oil and dirt. Max scrubbed Timmy's head once until it bled in places. The washing before the ball game belied his own past months of survival.

As they studied each other, Timmy couldn't tear his gaze away from the scrawny teenager's expression. Cold, hopeless, flat eyes stared with no fear. Maybe Timmy wasn't the only one who had lived a tough life. The depth of that stare told him that Trash Boy could tangle with him any old time over whose life had been worse.

He retracted his earlier conviction that any home would be better than no home. Especially since he didn't know what Trash Boy called home.

Maybe he doesn't have one.

Just before the punk could get close enough for Timmy to smell him, really catch a whiff of the permanent body odor, he yanked the knife from his pocket and punched the blade to life.

Trash Boy didn't even blink.

Real fear crawled into Timmy's belly, clutched his groin, and he wondered if he had a battle on his hands he couldn't win. Trash Boy had more than just years on him, but also five or six inches and at least fifty pounds. No matter how skinny the grimy adolescent looked, Timmy's diet hadn't exactly promoted muscle and bone growth.

"I ain't kiddin' about your mutt, fuckhead. I'd love to grill him up for my kid sister. She ain't had dog meat in months."

Timmy whistled for Skippy to stay back, but his terrier circled, understanding the threatening posture. Skippy smelled the fear and hatred better than he did. "My step-daddy'd love to have a crack at you." Trash Boy cackled, grabbing his own privates in crude gesture he'd seen the Gerries do a time or two when competing for the biggest kahunas.

Oh, shit.

Skippy crouched and before Timmy could blink, the terrier lunged and nipped at the scum's left calf. The guy's eyes went wide, but not a sound came out him. Timmy knew the bite had to sting like the dickens, yet the guy didn't so much as flinch.

Timmy needed to shift the cash from his shoebox to another pocket. The small stack in the box, the bulk of it still safe in his two front pockets, wouldn't survive a tussle.

"What the hell you want from me? I'm homeless, fuckhead. A street kid, you know? Like I ain't got no home so I don't have a lot to lose, got it?" Timmy sneered, thinking if he appeared reckless his aggressor might lay off.

He didn't.

"I wanna show you to my step-daddy," he repeated, and Timmy felt chills run down his back.

"I can give you money, if that's what you want. Just leave me alone, okay? I'll call my dog off, and you can just let us be on our way." The blade trembled in his right hand, his left on the bungee cord of the make-shift pack.

"What kinda homeless kid has money? Unless you a

hustler. My step-daddy'll *really* like that. Nice tight ass. Um, um. He's gonna love a taste o' you."

Timmy shuddered visibly this time. He pulled a few bills from his front pocket, cringing at the idea of giving up some of his cash. But sixty or eighty bucks was small potatoes compared to what Trash Boy would get if he swiped the knapsack, or worse – got to his front pockets.

Trash Boy's eyes locked on the money and held on like a badger to prey.

"That's gonna be mine, shithole." Trash Boy eased closer – fifteen or twenty feet separating them. Timmy used the only trick Max ever taught him that he felt would work.

"Fuck off!" Timmy screamed and scattered the bills with a ruthless pitch. He ran like a chased jackrabbit. Skippy yipped at his heels, and the two of them looked like escaped convicts racing through the slummy neighborhood. Just as he thought he was getting some distance, his pack, already unreliable and shoddy, suddenly came loose and spilled cash and bottle caps everywhere.

Timmy cast a terrified glance over his shoulder and saw Trash Boy pocketing the thrown bills and scrambling to chase him.

"Shit!" Timmy dropped to his knees, scraped everything into a pile, and threw it all back into the shoebox. He covered it with the pillowcase, his heart thumping like crazy.

"AHHHHHH!" Trash Boy yelled and then pummeled him. Scarred, dirt-crusted fists belted Timmy from all angles.

His nose splattered blood when a punch landed dead center. The second blow smacked him in the chest and sucked the air out of him. Trash Boy landed a strike to Timmy's mouth, a tooth popping loose and blood streaming down his throat. His tongue went immediately to the cut on his lip to measure the depth of the wound. A fist connected with his ear, gut, and chest. Dirt flew around their scrambling bodies, flying in Timmy's mouth and eyes. He couldn't see.

And then the volley of blows just suddenly stopped. Timmy scrambled to his feet and saw Skippy clinging desperately to the maniac's hamstring, blood dripping from his terrier's teeth.

"GET OFF ME!" Trash Boy screamed and flailed, trying to get hold of the elusive mutt holding tight to the back of his leg. He finally yanked hold of Skippy's scruff and jerked him loose.

Timmy didn't hesitate. He dove at the guy and jabbed the knife so deep into the pit of the guy's belly, he had to twist to pull it back out.

Trash Boy's eyes found his, and they both froze.

Like a syrupy moment in time, a greasy hand grabbed Timmy's collar, getting blood on his prized sweatshirt. Skippy squirmed out from beneath the collapsing kid who gurgled something and then swung a lame fist still clutching a lone twenty-dollar bill. Skippy growled, backing out of kicking range in a low retreating stance.

"It's okay, Skip." Timmy's voice trembled, but to prove his point, he shoved Trash Boy backward. The older boy fell, clutching his stomach and moaning for help. Timmy twirled his head surveying the park – not for help but to see if anyone had seen or heard anything.

Witnesses. It was always important to scope for witnesses. He saw none, and the same old guilt pulsed through him. *Bad...I'm bad.*

He slowly and deliberately collected all the bills, bloody or not. There were a few in Trash Boy's pockets, but Timmy wouldn't risk getting that close. Skippy circled the groaning teenager now belly crawling toward his bike.

"You shoulda left me alone," Timmy hissed. He watched Trash Boy creep away like a coward. In a different world, he would've left and not thought a thing about the loser crawling in the dirty lot beside a nasty neighborhood no kid should ever have to grow up in. But the new improved Timmy couldn't.

"C'mon, Skip!" He hurried across the park, ran down a street toward a convenience store on the corner. To the right of the entrance, pay dirt. Instead of the call he'd planned to make, he punched 911 and shielded himself from potential customers. He felt the immediate swelling around his mouth, nose, and left eye. He had to look like a boxer in a short TKO bout – the losing end of it.

Wrong.

"I – I want to report a kid in a park who I think might've been hurt...stabbed maybe." He grimaced. *How would I know that unless I did it?*

The lady pressed for information. "Where are you?" she asked more than once.

Instead of answering, he explained where he'd seen the kid, and that no, he didn't know him.

"Is he breathing? Can you still see him?" she prodded.

"Please, just send someone! I was walking through the park and found this kid bleeding, begging for help!" He slammed the phone into the cradle, then darted around the side of the store to breathe, to collect himself, and re-tie his pack. Before anyone could arrest him or kidnap him for a step-daddy, he and Skippy made like mice and scampered. By the time he heard the sirens, they'd gotten six blocks south, found an alley with a dumpster, and hid behind it.

When am I ever gonna get a chance to escape all this shit? But a lingering guilty conscious made him wonder if he was just inherently bad.

Maybe I brought all this on myself.

This time, there was no question that he'd committed a crime, self-defense or not. Cops would yank his butt to juvie so fast his head would spin. The cash, the blood, the blade. He wasn't kidding anyone. If they saw him now, he would be toast. Even Skippy had blood matted on his head and scruff. Timmy was sticky with it – his face and hands felt like he'd played with honey. His left eye had matted shut, his top lip so swollen he couldn't close his mouth, and his nose felt lopsided. He traced his scar and wondered if that eye had a target around it.

Pulling Skippy close to his chest, they hunkered behind the huge metal bin. It was chilly out, but not nearly as cold as Timmy felt on the inside. More to cover up the blood than anything, he slid his arms into the sleeves of his coat, closing his eyes in relief that he hadn't lost it from around his waist in the scuffle.

"OPEN YOUR EYES, YOU LITTLE SHIT!" The back of a hand hit my left cheekbone hard enough to rip it open. It connected again and again, didn't it? Wait...it was a ring. A ring on one of the fingers ripped through the skin on my left cheek.

Timmy defied the voices from That Night, squeezing his eyes shut. The smell of gunfire so acrid, he felt the burn in his nostrils again. A rat skittered behind them making him yelp and sending Skippy into a tizzy. Timmy held his mutt's muzzle praying for the rat to get and for his dog to get a grip.

"Hush, Skippy," he whispered.

Tucked safely behind the dumpster between two run-down garages, he pulled out his shoebox and inspected his stuff. Ball cards, bottle caps, and all but forty dollars, bloody or not, was safe. A layer of dirt sifted to the bottom of the box. He was lucky to have come through no worse for the wear – aside from his face, throbbing hand, and a piercing pain in his ribs. He recounted the cash three times, dividing the bills and tucking all of it safely into different pockets.

"Skip, you saved my life." Timmy thanked his dog by hugging him and pulled out the last of the water. "I'll getcha some more, boy, I promise."

I've just gotta lay low. I don't wanna end up like Max. But I can't go into any stores lookin' like this. Water would have to wait for a bit.

When the second volley of sirens faded, he crawled out from behind the dumpster to see if the coast was clear. He wiped a splotch of dirty blood off Tigger. Nearly thirty minutes had passed. How long did it take to get a kid in an ambulance and study the crime scene? He and Skippy headed south, away from sirens and crime scenes.

I can't solve all my problems by stabbing people.

He didn't have the skills to survive, to weather this on his own, he knew that. His one option, the only one that made sense, would hopefully allow him to retire the blade.

Put up or shut-up.

And put-up he would, if he intended to have a chance at the life he wanted to live.

"C'mon, Skippy. We've gotta find a phone."

Chapter Thirty-Eight

"Can you break this and give me quarters for the phone?" Timmy held out a five-dollar bill, leftover from his last convenience store purchase. When he glanced down, he realized it had a rust-colored spot on it. *Oh, crap.*

The clerk, Mike according to his nametag, stared at Timmy. The guy's eyes narrowed – even though Timmy had cleaned up, the blood on the stretched collar, swollen nose, already blackening eye, and split lip did little for his efforts to blend in.

Timmy must look like Trash Boy to Mike.

The cashier had been pulling cigarettes from a box to stock, stuffed the stack in his hand into their slot, then set down the rest. This time he studied Timmy.

All I need is two freaking quarters. He needed one for the call and a second in case he chickened out. He knew himself well enough to prepare for that possibility. Itchy feet would transfer to itchy fingers.

Timmy stood frozen, ready to make the call but hating the judgment in the guy's eyes. If he only knew what the kid had been through, the clerk might uncurl his lip and erase the disgust from his face.

"Whatever your game is, kid, it ain't workin'...." Mike took the five, put it in the drawer without inspecting it, then handed Timmy the ones and four quarters.

"No game, just surviving. Thanks," Timmy mumbled, then hurried outside before he lost his nerve.

Judge not, asshole. He'd heard the Gerries quote the Bible verse a million times and liked the sentiment. But he marveled how few people embraced it. The continual roadblocks chipped away at his resolve. But poised in front of the payphone, his heart hammering, he recited the numbers he'd dialed by heart his whole life. Brent's and Scott's numbers, too similar, jumbled for a second in his brain. While Brent's parents were awesome and treated him like family, the Kruschavens had not only been a second set of parents, they'd been his mom and dad's best friends.

A second family.

Hope.

Fumbling with the quarter, his hands trembling hard enough to drop it if he wasn't careful, he pushed it into the slot. The *chuh-ching* made it final and sent his heart into hyper drive. Skippy sat near the corner of the building staring at his boy.

"Here goes nothin', Skip." He inhaled and exhaled slowly one last time to calm his jangling nerves. Punching the numbers as he'd done a million times in his Before life, he rehearsed the spiel rumbling in his head.

The phone rang once. His heart thudded in apprehension. The second ring sent terror blendering his stomach. By the third, full-blown panic set in. He slammed the phone into its cradle.

Itchy feet, itchy fingers. He knew he'd need more than one.

"I can't do it, Skippy. *Shit*!" He hit the phone with the heel of his hand and wiped the nervous sweat from his forehead. His eyes, already blooming purplish circles from the blow to his nose, gave him a raccoon mask. His nose and black eye throbbed, but he didn't care.

Skippy whimpered at his boy's outburst, his tail flipping nervously. *Yes, you can,* the wag seemed to say.

"Dogs can't talk, Skippy, so *shut up*," Timmy snapped, regretting it immediately. "Sorry boy," he mumbled.

Skippy's tail wavered but resumed thumping the concrete with the apology.

"*God, why can't anything ever be easy*?" Timmy shouted, and beat the Plexiglas surrounding the payphone.

A lady leading her toddler son into the store glared at him.

She stopped. She cased him from head to toe long enough to trigger embarrassed splotches to bloom on both of his bruised cheeks. He suppressed the urge to hiss something rude, but swallowed it. She scowled and reached for the door.

"Sorry, ma'am." He dropped his gaze and hung his head in shame. He refused to be like Trash Boy or the Gerries.

The lady's contempt evaporated immediately, replaced by an expression of true concern.

"Honey, are you okay?" She pulled her toddler son close to her, resituated him in her arm to rest on her hip.

"No, I'm not. My life is a mess, and I have just one phone call to make that could, *could* solve everything, ya know?" *Why am I telling her this?*

She smiled and nodded like maybe she did. Her sympathy eased the frustration a little.

"But I don't have the ba – guts. It's just been so long, I mean, what're they gonna say? They probably think I'm dead anyway. It doesn't matter. I can't do it." Tears sprang to his eyes, and four months of pent-up frustration flooded through him. Self-pity threatened to consume him, something he'd never craved before.

"You know, son, the best way to meet a problem head-on is to run it by someone else. I know just the person for you to talk to." She head nodded at a flyer taped to the convenience store window.

Gulping the self-pity, he tried to read through the tears. She pulled down the page-sized poster and placed it in his hand. "Call this young man, honey. He'll help you, I promise." She caressed the boy in her arms, whispering in his ear around a tiny St. Louis Cardinals' cap.

Timmy ached to thank her but couldn't speak.

Big Brother's
of St. Louis

Mrs. Mahoney's Home

Big Brothers
of America

When you think no one else can

314-555-Help (4357)

Ask for Jeremy Gardner
he has a direct line to God

"My son." She paused and glanced at the little boy in her arms. "My older boy, he's seventeen. Got in a lot of trouble and ran away. Now he's in his last semester at Ritenour High and about to graduate. He's enrolled in college." She wiped a tear Timmy hadn't noticed until then. "We owe it to *that* young man." She pointed at the piece of paper in Timmy's hand. She smiled in spite of her tears.

Timmy read the poster, searching for the name at the bottom. *Jeremy*.

"Call him," she repeated, and disappeared into the store before he could ask any questions or thank her.

Without hesitation, he dropped the back-up quarter into the slot and dialed. He was too desperate for help, too eager for answers. And it was a heck of a lot easier to call a stranger than a loved one who had become one.

"Mrs. Mahoney's, how can I help you?"

...when you think no one else can...

He paused, his throat sticky with uncertainty, then asked for Jeremy Gardner. A hand over the mouthpiece muffled a shout that brought another voice to the phone.

"Yo, Jeremy here. Whatcha know?" Young, not much older than Sam. Same energy.

Timmy, distraught and at his wit's end, couldn't help but smile. "Uh, not much. But a lady just gave me your flyer at a gas station. She said you could help me. The flyer says you can help me." Emotion globbed in his throat, in his chest, in his brain.

"What's your name, kid?" Jeremy's tone was easy, non-judgmental. That helped.

"Timmy." He tried to swallow and added, "C...can you help me?"

"Whoa, just cut to the chase, why don'tcha. Well, that all depends on you." The no frills attitude appealed to Timmy but intimidated him, too. "Where are you right now?"

"Um, at the convenience store on, um, I'm not sure what street. Oh, God." Panic laced through him. *I'm gonna be stuck in a time warp because I never know where the hell I am.*

"Look around you and tell me what you see." Jeremy rustled paper on the other end.

"I went through Ruth Park to get here." Leaving out the details of that trek, he added, "I see a flower shop, a big intersection just a street away, and there's a sub shop right before it."

"Okay, perfect. Now, look at the phone and tell me the number. The prefix will help me."

Timmy didn't really understand what the guy meant but read the number to him, hoping he could miraculously be there with the snap of his fingers. The prospect of help eclipsed the swarm of emotion inside him.

"You want me to come get you, or do you just wanna talk?"

I want you to save me from myself, from using this knife again, from spending another night out here alone. But he hesitated, knowing that wouldn't make sense.

"I – I don't know. Where would you take me?" He envisioned a demon foster mother lurking in a house waiting to feed him a diaper, thrown-up hotdogs, or banish him to the basement – the horrors of a young adult book he'd read in the library in October, early enough to parallel Max's description of the system.

"Back here to Mrs. Mahoney's." He went on to tell Timmy a little about the program, about Mrs. Mahoney, and about taking baby steps. "I was a street kid, Timmy. Lived four years hustling, stealing, doing what I had to do to make ends meet. You can't even imagine –"

"Yes, I can," Timmy interrupted, and silence fell on the other end.

After an uncomfortable pause, Jeremy asked, "Are you homeless?"

Timmy let the question hang in mid-air for a minute. Paranoia needled his insides. If he told Jeremy, would the guy call DYS and send Timmy there? Had he already said too much and they could connect him to Trash Boy? Would Mrs. Chapman come drag him away and get on to him for running away that day?

"Yes," came limping out of his mouth, barely a whisper. It was his first admission to anyone who could do something about it. He hadn't been ready to talk to Father Myers. That conversation would have taken place at the breakfast table had he stayed.

Maybe that's really why I ran.

"Tell you what. I'm gonna figure out which store that is, okay? Shouldn't be hard, but it might take me thirty minutes or so to get there. Afternoon St. Louis traffic is gnarly, so don't panic if I'm not there too quick. Might even be an hour. Can you wait that long?"

I've waited four months, he started to say. All kinds of comments lingered, but instead he gave an obligatory *sure* and hung up.

"Skippy, we have about an hour to decide whether to put up or shut up. What's it gonna be?" The phrase sounded good in theory, but here he was again contemplating the pros and cons of tucking his tail and running. *Itchy feet.*

Skippy seemed to know what his boy was saying, because he walked to the side of the building, turned three circles, and curled up on the concrete. Either he wanted a nap in the worst way, or his best friend just gave his valuable two cents worth.

"You're bossy," he told Skippy, whose tail thumped a decisive *yep*. He joined his dog around the corner and out of sight. It felt good to rest and even better to hide. Note to self: Ask Skippy's opinion more often.

"I'll get us somethin' to drink. How'll that be?" But Skippy's eyes were already blinking, half-mast, and then closed. Maybe some hot chocolate would be just the ticket, though he wasn't as cold as he'd been just an hour ago. *I'll rest a minute then wash the blood off my sweatshirt and air-dry it a little.* The quick cleaning job before breaking his five didn't keep him from looking like a juvenile delinquent, and that wasn't the first impression he wanted to give Jeremy.

He peeled it off, tucked it in his roll, and put his coat back on. Exhaustion swept over him, so he leaned his head against the building with Skippy's resting on his leg. As his eyes closed, he couldn't ward off the dream that threatened to consume him at St. Michael's. But that August night had been waiting for him since he'd read the article.

And no matter how much it terrified him, it was time to remember.

Chapter Thirty-Nine

August—Four Months Earlier

We hurried to Gate D's sea of chairs to wait for Sam's plane. I patted my Nike pullover's front pouch pocket – the prized baseball cards I itched to share with Sam. Mom complained that I shouldn't be wearing the new windbreaker. Aside from the August heat, it was for school. But it was unseasonably cool, a manageable upper 70s by the time the sun was setting on our way to the airport, so her argument was lost on me. The main reason she gave, Dad and I both knew, was because I wouldn't give up.

"When's it gonna get here?" The clock hadn't budged since the last time. 8:50. Darn near my bedtime. But picking up Sam trumped the school night routine.

"Have patience, Timmy. Read a magazine." Mom turned the page of hers and shook her head.

Nearly thirty minutes passed before the plane taxied in. A few people came barreling through the door. A man straggled in pulling his suitcase on rollers, a woman holding a sleeping baby, and several ordinary-looking passengers. When Sam finally swaggered out, he looked exactly the same except cockier. I don't know what I thought, but I expected some kind of transformation. I was a little disappointed.

"Hey, squirrel face," he eventually said, after Mom and Dad let go of him.

"I gotta show you, Sam, they're just so totally cool!" I pulled out the ball cards, fanned them so he could see them, but with the best one hidden on the bottom. I really wanted him to get the full effect.

"Hey, you got 'em! You never said anything on your postcards, so I wasn't sure. I forgot to ask." Sam ran his hands through his hair, that had gotten a little longer. Mom would take care of that. She hated when it came over his ears.

"I didn't wanna tell you, I wanted to *show* you." I was brimming with excitement. I displayed the cards like I had a twenty-carat diamond ring. Mom and Dad grinned, knowing how proud I had been to get them.

"Whoa," he said as he inspected them.

Fernando Tatis, J.D. Drew, Willie McGee, Ray Lankford. And Mark McGwire. Prime condition rookie cards. All autographed. Sam stared at the Big Mac card then back at me. Below the signature, I had asked Mr. McGwire to write *For Sam*. For a second, I thought I saw a tear in my macho brother's eye.

"This is yours, Tim. You don't want me to have this back, do you?" His voice sounded funny. And I was about to burst with pride.

"We'll talk," I said, like a hustler ready to wheel and deal. I took the cards and tucked them back into the front pouch of my windbreaker. He had called me *Tim*. Nobody else may have noticed, but I sure did.

"Man, I can't believe you got 'em all," he admitted, his voice full of awe. "We may hafta talk some smack about that Big Mac card, Timster."

I grinned from ear to ear. As much as I loved the card, I knew Sam would frame it and put it on his wall. Then we could both enjoy it.

Mom and Dad took over by asking a million questions about his trip. While they talked, we made our way down to the baggage claim, collected Sam's two suitcases, and trudged to our SUV. All of us were beat.

"I still can't get over you gettin' that card signed," Sam repeated, shaking his head.

I beamed. "I'll hold on to it for you." And my smile never wavered. I was on cloud nine. We packed into the Cadillac Escalade, Mom and Dad up front, Sam in the middle row, and me all the way in back. Because Sam and I always bickered in the car, they made the rule to separate us last spring – preventative measures, Mom called it. Room to lounge, he and I called it.

Within fifteen minutes, we were on I-70 headed home. Sam bantered on and on about the trip to Mom and Dad, so I sat back and listened. I knew I wouldn't get a word in anyway.

"What's that jerk doing?" Dad kept glancing into his rearview. Mom told him to slow down, as I turned to see what they were talking about.

"You see it?" Sam pointed to a beat-up Chevy merging onto the highway with no head-lights on. He was coming up on our right with only a little more road to merge into traffic.

"Honey, let him over," Mom ordered. Dad slowed a little, unable to get over because another car was in the lane beside us. The Chevy slipped in front of us. Dad flashed his brights at the clunker. I spun around in my seat and watched a convertible, also without its lights on, come onto I-70 behind us.

"Robbie, don't flash your lights at them. I've heard you're never supposed to do that."

Dad sped up. *No one does road rage better'n me,* he liked to say, even though Mom always popped him on the arm when he did.

"But he doesn't have his headlights on. Moron." He revved the Escalade's engine – almost as a threat for the slowing car to get out of the way.

"Pass him, Dad. Show that piece of junk who's boss." Sam had a little driver's aggression in him already, even though he was six months shy of practicing it legally.

"But this other car won't get outta the way. I'm boxed in." Dad sat up straighter to get a better look at the car beside us.

"Slow down, Robert." Mom had the edge in her voice we knew meant business.

Dad let up on the accelerator, but so did the Chevy. The convertible beside us seemed to be keeping pace and showed no sign of passing.

"Should I just pull over and let them pass?" Dad glanced at Mom then back at the car. My heart thudded in my chest.

My dad can beat up your dad, I told Scott once.

Dad slowed, trying to let them pass. But the clunkers did the same. When they wouldn't go on by, he eased the Escalade to the shoulder.

Before he got completely stopped, the car in front slammed on its brakes making our Cadillac bump it in the rear. For ten agonizing seconds, we sat still – no one said a word. Every nerve in my body now at attention. The convertible sat beside us like an escort and then car doors slammed.

I won't look.

"Shit. Tori, do you have your cell?"

"Yeah. But don't you dare get out of this car, do you hear me?" She fumbled in the floorboard for her purse.

Before Dad could answer, the shouting guys fired shots into the sky and yahooed. Each held a black pistol, held high in the air, then leveled it at our windows, sideways in their hands.

"Yeah, c'mon outta your Es-ca-lade, Mr. Rich Man. I wanna take a ride in that bad boy. You can leave the beauty queen in there." They cackled, and the guy I glanced at had hold of his crotch.

All of us froze. Dad punched the auto-lock button and threw the SUV into reverse.

"Shit. I'm not stickin' around to find out what the hell *that* meant." Dad roared backward for five or six seconds, slammed on the brakes, then whipped back onto I-70. He swung as wide of the two cars as he could and tore off down the highway.

"GO!" Mom screamed. She punched in numbers while Dad raced down I-70. The speedometer already topped ninety miles an hour.

My stomach dropped, panic leaping like a bullfrog into my throat.

"God, what are these idiots doing?" Dad watched the cars

in his rearview mirror. "They're comin', Tori. And they're comin' *fast*. Call 911, Tori, *hurry*."

"I am...it's ringing. Jesus, Robert," Mom muttered. "I'm scared." She glanced back at us. "It's okay, boys. Your dad'll get us out of here."

I hope. I turned around in my third-row seat listening to Mom tell someone we were being chased. I felt vulnerable in the back of the SUV, like the thugs would target me since I was closest. I climbed over the seat, landing almost on top of Sam.

"He's catchin' up, Dad," Sam said. "He's gotta be floorin' it to gain ground in that old thing."

"I see him, Sam. It's all right, sit back. Everything'll be fine. You boys buckle up. Now. Tori, tell them we're nearing exit, um –" Dad jerked his head around trying to read signs. He told Mom the exit and she repeated it to the emergency operator.

"Yes! They're not just tailgating us, they're *chasing* us!" Mom closed her eyes, then told the 911 dispatcher her name, address, and telephone number.

Just send help! We're not at home!

Mom turned all the way around to inspect the car tailing us. I peeked over the back of my seat again and watched the clunker creep up on Dad's bumper. My heart beat faster the closer it got. Within seconds, I could barely see the front end. I unbuckled my seat belt and stood up on my knees to get a better view. My heart hammered in my chest.

"GET THE LICENSE PLATES, TIMMY!" Mom screamed, panic now raising her voice an octave.

I felt a thud, then the Escalade veered sharply to the left, sending Sam into the side wall and me into the floor.

"Hold on!" Dad slowed for a split second, then hit the gas hard.

I scrambled back into my seat but twisted to see that the Chevy had rammed us – I made out the bent license plates and rattled the letters and numbers to Mom. The front grill, now mangled, seemed to be snarling. The long convertible hovered just behind it.

"Dad, they're motioning to each other...and laughing," I told him. While I watched, the one holding up the rear came roaring up beside us. The old convertible had four or five guys who thrust their fists in the air and threw things at our SUV.

"Skip this exit and go straight to the police station, Robert." Mom's voice was laced with fear. She held the cell phone to her ear. "Yes, ma'am. We're exiting now."

"I'm tryin'. Where's the closest police station?"

"Highway 94 – North. *Shit!* I lost my signal. Goddammit!" Mom hit a button hard enough on her Nokia to knock it out of her own hands.

Fear gripped my throat. *I would have to eat soap for week for those words.*

Dad skipped our usual turn-off like Mom asked but then exited quickly onto highway 94, a small highway that we only took to a seafood restaurant *up north* as Dad always put it. But the operator was guiding us to a police station. We were now headed into foreign territory.

The Cadillac's back end fishtailed as he made the turn, but Dad straightened it out and floored it. Within seconds, we were flying. I tried to crane my head to read the speedometer, but Dad was in the way. He was willing to go as fast as he had to in order to lose the two cars – that terrified me. Stomach acid stewed my half-digested dinner and made me want to gag.

"Robert, hurry." Mom whispered, trying to get the 911 operator again. Her hushed voice made my bladder threaten to release.

"Mom?" I wanted to know if someone was answering her call, but I couldn't get it out.

A jolt made us all scream. Dad jerked the wheel to straighten the SUV and rattled off several cuss words he never used. He gripped the steering wheel tight enough to whiten his knuckles. He whipped the Escalade onto another exit ramp leading us to a lighted thoroughfare, a major four-lane street that somehow made me feel more comfortable. A red light twenty feet ahead made Mom groan.

"Yes, HELLO!" Mom screamed into the phone, and Sam nodded at me. *Help is on the way.* He seemed to be holding his breath.

I reached down and held my privates so I wouldn't pee my pants. I glared at the hateful cars chasing us and imagined what I would do if I had super-human powers. Because for the first time in my life, I really wanted to hurt people.

Tell them to hurry, Mom! Panic gripped me in a way I had never known. Things smelled funny, my head felt foggy, and the cashew chicken I had eaten for dinner was about to revolt.

"I can't just run this light, I can't see who's comin'!" The Cadillac slowed enough for Dad to see the intersection, and our two pursuers closed the gap again. We heard whooping and hollering, and I wished the two old cars would crash into something, anything—now.

Mom rambled as fast as she could. "Yes, ma'am, and I – we have two cars chasing us, with guns. And – and—" Mom took a deep breath and tried to continue. She held her head like it hurt, but for some reason she couldn't talk.

"Dad, look." Sam tapped Dad's shoulder. The guys in the beat up convertible waved pistols without a worry in the world, and two of them were pointed straight at us. On either side of us, like bookends, were the two vehicles. A Chevy Impala, Sam blurted, on our left. And I'd given the tags on the Plymouth convertible on our right, full of guys screaming at us. The five guys thrust fists into the air. One flipped us off while we stared. Three white older teenagers with stocking caps on, a younger black kid, and one dark complected guy with a net-wrap on his head. We couldn't hear exact words with our windows up and air-conditioning on, but their high-pitched squeals sent shivers down my spine. Terror had a fist around my chest. I couldn't figure out why they seemed so thrilled to be chasing us yet pissed at the same time.

"Th – they've g...got a *lot* of guns," I managed, fear sucking my insides like a vacuum.

All three cars accelerated when the intersection cleared, the three of us drag-racing down the four-lane street. Within a mile, one of the lanes disappeared and as traffic came, the Chevy fell back and slipped behind us.

Get back, you assholes!

"Mom?" Sam grabbed her by the arm, watching the souped up Chevy swing out to our left. I turned to see what he was staring at. The car made no move to pass or fall back. But I understood that it was in the wrong lane. What would it do if a car came heading straight for it? I was about to ask Sam when Mom shushed us before we could even talk. It was like watching a strange game of Chicken.

"It's – it's in the wrong lane. Mom, Dad...wrong lane." My head pounded, like the time I got so sick I couldn't go to school for three days. I held the seat but couldn't really feel anything. All the noise and chaos faded, and I couldn't hear anything. My ears hummed. Panic had officially swallowed me in a bubble.

"Boys, sit back and buckle up. You too, Timmy. NOW! Please tell me there's an officer in the area," she said, this time talking to the faceless stranger who couldn't seem to help us.

I wanna be home. Please leave us alone...please. I squeezed my eyes closed.

The Escalade's back end swerved, veered onto the shoulder, then whipped back and crunched metal, jolting my head against the seat behind me. Metal screeched against metal, like fingernails on a chalkboard.

Mom screamed, then shouted, "NO, I mean, *yes.* How the hell should I know? They've got FUCKING GUNS!" Mom's hands trembled, nearly dropping the phone. "I DON'T KNOW!" She whipped her head to see on either side of us.

"What's she saying, Tori? What's *wrong?*" The tiny lines on Dad's forehead were deeper than I'd ever seen them.

Everything's wrong! Bile came up in my throat, but I

wanted to spit it at *them.*

"Crossroad, Robert, what's your next crossroad, she wants to know. I'm so lost. There's a police station, but she wants to know if we're close to – what road?"

Please, somebody save us. I gripped the bulge in my pullover's pouch, the closest thing I had to a good-luck charm.

"Can't you just send someone down this road? And *hurry.* We tried to stop and – and these two cars full of guys. They pulled guns on us. They – they shot at us, for God's sake. *Please.*"

Dad shouted out a street name, and Mom repeated it into the phone. "Please, is there someone in the area? They're trying to run us off the road. You have to help us. Hurry! Robert!" Mom was having two conversations at the same time, both in a panicked voice I didn't recognize.

A split second later, the Escalade jerked and threw me into the floorboard at Sam's feet. *Ah, God.* I threw up in the floorboard, wiped the spittle off my mouth, and heard Dad cussing for Sam to get a better look. Mom was still jabbering on the cell phone, but I hunkered in the floorboard trying to pray it away. Sam jumped from side to side to update Dad on what each car was doing, nearly kicking me in the head in the process.

"The Chevy's only got two or three guys in it, I think, Dad. Not sure...windows are dark." Sam tugged me back on the seat and barked for me to buckle up, his face pinched in a funny expression. I forced myself to stare straight ahead, desperately wanting to ignore the Plymouth, the Chevy, and the guys in them. Fear clawed at my soured stomach when I realized Dad was making no effort to slow down for a stop sign fewer than twenty feet away.

"Noooooo," I moaned, as food rolled in my belly. It was only a matter of time before it joined the rest of my meal in the floorboard.

Dad flew through the intersection. Sam and I whipped

around to see the Chevy less than two car lengths behind us do the same. I frantically dropped onto my butt and closed my eyes again. Not watching made me feel better. The roaring engines and squealing tires like strange music in surround sound around us.

We're gonna die.... I held my breath. *Please, Dad, get us out of here. Please.*

"Shit. GET OFF ME!" Dad yelled, as if the beat-up car could hear him.

Sam unbuckled and jumped into the back to spy out the rear window. We raced toward a busy intersection and this time Dad had no choice but to slam on his brakes, the Escalade skidding to a complete stop.

"GET OUT OF MY WAY!" Dad honked his horn to get the attention of everyone at the stoplight. He hit the button and lowered his window and shouted to anyone who could hear. "HELP US! THEY'RE CHASING US!"

Dad's wild expression set my heart ramming in my chest, and for a moment, I had an idea what a heart attack felt like.

Silence in the Escalade was shattered by Mom's barking into the phone. "WHY CAN'T YOU HELP US?"

Dad put his hand on her leg and I saw that his hand was shaking. Sam groaned and mumbled, "We're back by the airport."

God, why are we always heading away from home?

"WOOOHOOO! Wanna play, mother fucker?"

All of us jerked to the left to see the stocking capped gang in the convertible laugh. I ducked as low as my seatbelt would allow. *Why am I hiding?* For a second I couldn't breathe.

"Make them stop, Dad," I mumbled. He couldn't hear me, but it made me feel better to say it.

"Just stay here, Robert. Don't let them chase us. Just stay." Mom relayed the intersection to the 911 operator.

Yeah... The gang wasn't willing to do anything with all the people around, but horns began to honk, long blares of impatience.

We sat for an eternal few seconds. So did the convertible. Cars whipped around us – yelling, gesturing, still honking – oblivious that we were in a fight for our lives. When a car passed between us and them, Dad floored it. The Escalade's power, the V-8 Dad had been so proud of when he bought it, caused the tires to squeal. I sat up and peered over out the window to my right. The pursuers couldn't match the surge but caught up too fast with crazy driving, passing in wrong lanes and even running a car off the road.

I jerked my head toward Sam behind me, desperate not to watch any more. "Where are the police, Sam?"

"I don't know, Tim, I don't know." He spun in his seat tracking both cars and barking their locations to Dad with each maneuver.

Dad shouted, "If they don't do something quick, Tori..." Dad gripped the wheel with both hands, as we blazed past other cars like they were standing still. I wanted to scream at them for not helping us.

"An officer where?" Mom listened for a second, then gave Dad a street name. "Go, Robert...turn here! Now! An officer is waiting to intercept them."

Horns honked in a rhythm, as if speaking to us in some strange code. All the noise echoed in my throbbing head. *Make them go away, make them go away, make them go away....*

"We're almost to Stewart." Dad barked for Mom to tell the operator. He slammed his palms on the steering wheel, cussing that we were in a death grip. "I'm doing seventy and can't shake them. What the HELL do these guys *want*?"

His tone sent Sam and me from side to side, trying to figure out what the cars chasing us were doing. They flanked us and squeezed our Escalade in a metal fist. Sam tugged me to jump over the seat into the back row with him. *Oh, thank God,* I wanted to tell him. But an invisible fist had hold of my throat. He grabbed the seatbelt and motioned for me to fasten it.

"DAD!" I screamed, because I saw it coming first. Dad slammed on his brakes and went into a locked skid. Our SUV couldn't swerve because the cars gripped us in a vise.

A police cruiser with lights flashing headed right at us, the Plymouth directly in its path. The two cars hugged us in a brutal game of chicken. The cop car went into its own skid, but never had a chance. It turned sideways and teetered like it might flip.

It all happened in a millisecond. I braced myself against the seat in front of me right before my seatbelt nearly yanked me in half. The last thing I saw was a passenger in the Plymouth being catapulted like a football headed toward the uprights.

My head slammed against the seat behind me – *ahh, God!* – and rattled my brain. Funny smells clouded my head. Stars flashed all around me. I could smell gas, but strangely I couldn't feel anything.

The Escalade finally came to a stop as the shattering glass, crunching metal, and cracking plastic ended. All the chaos, the night filled with screams, colliding cars, and sirens stopped as quickly as it had started. The suffocating silence seemed eternal.

Am I dead? Sam? Mom? Dad? I tried to call out to them, but fumes choked me.

I undid my seatbelt and swiveled my already aching head. Glass from the side windows sprayed all over us in small diamond-like pieces. They sparkled in the street light that loomed over us. Everything was twisted and broken. Our windshield had splintered into spider webs. Every inch of it cracked, but it held its shape in one mass. I could hear distant shouts outside our SUV. Angry voices circled around our smashed Cadillac like a hungry pack of wolves. A police radio crackled for the officer's 10-20.

I tried to locate the voices, but I couldn't see any of them. I prayed policemen had corralled the assholes before they could get to us.

"Get the hell away from my family!" Dad shouted, followed by more glass smashing.

Get the policeman, Dad! He'll help us!

I couldn't tell where they were – behind the convertible on our left, Chevy Impala to our right? Our sandwiched SUV was filled with smoke, burning my eyes and creating a haze I struggled to see through. I couldn't see Sam, couldn't sense him anywhere around me. I gagged, praying I could suppress the cough building in my chest. Frantic for relief of the pressure on my pinned legs, I rammed my shoulder against the battered back hatch. It barely moved.

I gotta have air. The deployed airbags smelled like blackened marshmallows, stinging my nostrils. I thrust myself against the door, finally wedging it open enough to suck air.

"Get back in your mother fuckin' Es-ca-lade, dog," a strange voice taunted. For a second, I froze, thinking he was talking to me. The guy spoke English but with a deep Spanish accent.

Dad was somewhere right outside the mangled passenger door – I used an umbrella to pry the hatch open enough slip out, falling to the ground. I gulped the fresh air as it hit my burning face. Where was Mom? Sam? My body throbbed – something had to be broken.

"Yeah, old man, hop back in and drive your prime piece of shit to the bank." Lots of laughter to the right of the Cadillac followed. I didn't get the joke. I squatted next to the rear bumper of the Escalade and poked my head out – *where are you Sam? Mom?* I watched through the missing back window and had a clear view through absent side windows of a short thug with a stocking cap, a sneer on his face, and bad acne scars. He grabbed Dad by the collar and shoved him against the wrecked SUV. The jolt made me jump.

Let him go! I gritted my teeth and clenched my fists, but fear cemented my feet in place.

None of the five young guys, most only a few years older than Sam, matched my dad's size, except an enormous goon leaning against the battered Chevy. From where I hid, I could only see the left side of the man, but he had enough muscle on just that side to bench press my dad. I shivered. I couldn't take my eyes off all his tattoos.

Static crackled, the pop preceding an inaudible radio call somewhere in front of the Escalade. *The police car!* I craned my head to see how clear it was between my hiding place and the cruiser.

"Whaddya think, Ray? Whose turn is it? Let's just do these fuckers and get the hell outta here. This asshole thought he could just run us off the highway, and it'd be no biggie. Is that it, asshole? Why didn't you just give it up like a good little boy? Look, Zeke!"

"Well, well, well," someone else said, maybe Ray, but who could keep up? I couldn't see several of them.

My head thumped making it difficult to think. I reached up and felt another cut on my forehead and on my neck. My whole body ached, and I just wanted Mom and Dad to hold me and make everything go away. Make *them* go away.

"Shhhh, Timmy, don't jump – I'm right behind you."

"Sam!" I whisper-shouted, and crawled over to my brother hunkered down behind the Plymouth. The Maybe Ray Guy and my dad started shouting on the other side of the Escalade, but I couldn't focus enough to make out what they were saying. "Should we g – go *help?* May – maybe the cop can help us." I stared at the crumpled St. Ann police car pancaked to the front of our SUV. *Oh...my...god.*

Sam studied my face for a quick second, then whispered, "He's dead. I tried the radio, too, but couldn't get it to work. I think we gotta make a run for it."

"Rolo, where's JD? I'm cappin' you, fucker, if *anybody* got hurt, you got it?" A loud *whack!* made Sam grab me. We scrambled underneath the Escalade when the gangbangers wandered around the back of the Cadillac toward the Plymouth convertible.

I tried to calculate how many of them there were – three of the Chevy's guys slipped out of the crunched car and brushed glass off their jeans and shirts. We twisted so we could see more. A trio in stocking caps had on button-up shirts only fastened at the collar. The shorter, black guy hovering in the background seemed younger, a bottom of the totem poler. Two more slid through the shattered windshield and dropped to the ground groaning. I couldn't figure out why all the glass had shattered in their car and not ours.

"I'm scared, Sam." My voice quivered, no matter how tough I tried to sound.

"Just hush, Timmy. I'm thinkin'." Sam closed his eyes, let out a sigh, then seemed to be measuring the space between their location and the open field on the other side of the Chevy.

I tried to see the street behind us, the small houses that refused to open up and help us. They sat silent and dark. *I hate you! All of you!* The wreckage blocked potential traffic from any direction. But for now, the streets were empty. Front porch lights had popped on all up and down the road, but not a soul came out to help. Most of the lights had blinked off almost as quickly as they came on.

What's the matter with these people? Why aren't they helpin' us?

I reached for Sam's hand, then cringed when someone screamed, "We killed the mother fucker! Score points for a dead pig!"

Several guys cheered. A *Bang!* made me jump. A few others laughed as they inspected the point of impact with the police car.

"Check for JD, Speed, and Rolo. If those douchebags took off runnin', I'm kickin' their asses." The darker, taller guy standing face to face with Dad pointed for the lanky in the blue shirt to get a move on.

"Sure, Ray, I'm on it."

Ray moved in closer to Dad's face, then turned so Sam and I could really see him, a strange top lip that gave him a permanent snarl.

They're too many of them to keep track of.

"C'mon, Zeke." Blue Shirt motioned for the gargantuan WWF wrestler who followed him around the back of our SUV searching for their friends.

"OH GOD! NOOOOO!" one of them screamed, followed by an animalistic howl.

I jerked around just in time to see Blue Shirt shouting and scrambling to something on the ground in front of the Plymouth.

"YOU KILLED MY BROTHER! Not J.D, goddammit, you *mother fucker*!" He pulled a smaller body into his arms and fell to the pavement between the convertible and our SUV. He cradled the broken frame like a doll. His agonized cries ripped through me, no matter how much I wanted to hate him. *And now he's pissed. One glance to his right and we're doomed.*

Ray yanked Dad's collar, already bloody from cuts he got in the crash.

"Eat this, old man!" he hissed, and shoved the muzzle of a black revolver into Dad's right cheek. Dad bucked against him, tried to grab the gun, but two of the Chevy guys grabbed an arm and threw my dad against the battered passenger door of the Cadillac.

I couldn't stand it. I tried to squirrel away from Sam's grip.

One of them whacked the butt of a pistol across the side of Dad's head.

"STOP IT!" I shrieked, and shimmied out from under the SUV to help my father.

"NOOOOO, TIMMY! Get back here!" Sam yelled after me.

"Get your butt in the car, Timothy Ryan Weaver – NOW! You too, Sam!" Mom's voice, high-pitched and hysterical, skewered my already sick stomach. A hand must have covered

Mom's mouth, because whatever she tried to add came out muffled. I never saw her or who held her hostage.

Before I could get to Dad, an arm clothes-lined me – smacked right into my throat and dropped me to the pavement. Pain exploded in my neck and rocketed through my head as it thudded on the pavement. I gagged and coughed, down on all fours trying to get my breath and ease the piercing pain in my Adam's apple.

"Get that shithead, Shaun, and him, too!" Ray pointed at Sam. But Ray turned his attention slowly and menacingly back to my father.

Shaun yanked my brother around and got him in a choke-hold. The black guy flipped me over onto my back, squatted, and pressed his knee into my chest.

"Give that little runt to me!" The WWF look-alike jerked me to my feet. "I'm gonna earn mine." He grinned, but the smile didn't touch his eyes.

During the chaos, Blue Shirt never stopped crying.

"You killed my brother," he moaned. "Not JD. You killed him!"

But you chased us....

They didn't care about that. All they saw was how we had hurt them.

"Speed, I'll do this rich asshole for your brother, for JD." Ray called out, as if he wanted to console his friend or shut him up.

The kid in the blue shirt, Speed, set his brother down, stomped around the back of our Escalade, and stopped two feet shy of Ray and Dad.

"Yeah, you do that rich prick, Ray." He sniffled, his voice deeper from crying. "Make him *suffer*. He killed my baby brother. Blast his fucking head off!"

"You're going to kill us for what *you've* done? It was the cop car that caused the – " Dad's voice cracked, broken off by a sharp blow to his temple with the butt of Ray's gun. Ray slammed it against Dad's forehead over and over until I felt my knees go weak.

Please stop. Oh, God, please... My head spun from the terror that was suddenly our life. I gulped, trying to get air past the lump lodged in my throat. *Stop!* And then I finally found my voice. "STOOOOOOOOP!"

Mom shrieked, running toward us, toward Dad, but Speed caught her. He gripped her throat in his right hand and squeezed, almost lifting her off the ground.

"Please," she gurgled. She turned to Sam and me, her expression lost and unfocused. Then her gaze locked on mine, a pleading in her eyes that I wasn't sure I understood.

"Finish her, Dante. Your turn!" Speed shoved Mom like a rag doll into Dante's waiting arms. When the black kid caught her, he gripped her tightly and licked the side of her face with such exaggerated slowness, I could see the trail of spit glisten in the streetlight.

Dante grappled with Mom, then backhanded her *hard* with his left. My head throbbed. I wanted desperately to close my eyes and make it all go away. But I gaped at them, an acidic taste burning my throat.

"JESUS! ROLO'S DEAD!" another guy shouted. "You killed Rolo, you fuckin' murderers!"

"You sonuvabitch," Speed hissed. He cocked his head, pulled Dad off the ground, too weak to stand on his own, but he still managed to resist. "You killed a mother fuckin' *kid!*"

"We – we were just trying to go home...you chased us," Dad moaned, sounding weak and tired. I cringed at the tone, because on some level I understood.

He's given up.

"Screw this." Speed rammed the gun into Dad's teeth, busting his lip. The guy pried my father's mouth open with the barrel. Dad jerked his head away, blood now streaming from his top lip. Two of the younger guys had grabbed tire irons and jumped on the hood of our Cadillac. They started smashing the already shattered windshield, beating metal and anything they could reach. The sheer volume of noise overloaded my brain. The loud report of a gunshot jolted me like a lightning bolt.

"NOOOOOOOOO!" I yelled. Sam's legs gave out from under him. Mom screamed, a howl so piercing it made my legs noodle. I convulsed, jerking and thrashing to get free. Zeke held me in a death grip, but I pummeled him with everything I could muster. Another gunshot ripped through the night.

Don't look, don't look, don't look.

Lights warbled. Sounds faded. Time stopped. All the screaming, even Mom's agonizing cries melted into the dark silence that swallowed the night. Shaun held Sam by the hair, but my brother was limp. His wobbly legs no longer supported him.

Not my Dad. What have you done to my daddy? The world blurred, and I felt my own body go limp. I saw – *don't look* – but tried not to see Dad crumpled on the pavement.

The massive guy's tattoos shimmered and shook with every twitch of his muscles. He held me against the Cadillac, refusing to let me fall. I was fixated on the tattoo on his left arm. His light skin seemed even paler next to the blood red heart and detailed greenery of curling vines. A pearl-handled knife pierced the heart, producing the drip-drip-drip that dotted the length of his bicep. The color and finely sketched drawing amazed me. All the droplets so red, too real. I stared harder to make sure they weren't. I couldn't bear to look anywhere else.

"YOU KILLED MY HUSBAND!" Mom wailed. She swung blindly, and my eyes blurred as she slapped, hit, spit on anyone within reach, still pinned by the throat. She kicked, writhed to scratch his eyes, and drew blood. The hand around her throat let go to protect his face, and she raced to Dad.

I watched her hover over my dad's limp body and something snapped. My world went black. I couldn't breathe, I couldn't think, I couldn't stop screaming.

When my throat clogged, I gulped. That's when I heard it. Sirens wailing in the distance. The nearby police radio crackled again, someone over the airwaves shouted *Officer down!*

I squeezed my eyes shut as hard as I could, trying to make this horrible movie end. *Daddy...*

"OPEN YOUR EYES, YOU LITTLE SHIT!" The back of a hand hit my left cheekbone hard enough to send blood and snot spraying through the air. It connected again and no matter how hard I flailed to stop it, I couldn't. A ring on one of the fingers ripped through my cheek, sending a rocket of pain to punctuate the tear. I screamed, scratched at the arm, but couldn't see through the blood seeping into my left eye. Mid-howl, something hard smacked my head right above my left ear. Stars erupted, making me collapse, upright only because the massive arm wouldn't let me fall. I cringed at the strange odor I'd smelled earlier when my head whiplashed upon impact during the crash.

"BITCH!" Ray jerked Mom to her feet. He ripped her shirt open with his left hand and held a pistol to her head with the right. I yanked and flailed, anything to get to my mother. I couldn't figure out why Sam lay crumpled on the ground next to me, not moving, not doing a damn thing to help.

Shaun lifted his foot and stomped on the small of Sam's back while I watched. The crunch of my brother's spine ripped through me. The sound knifed through me, and the world tilted, warbled, greyed.

Oh, God, oh, God, oh, God....

I couldn't breathe. But Zeke held me so I couldn't look away. I closed my eyes in a panic as Shaun pressed a small silver pistol to the back of Sam's head. "That's for JD and Rolo, you pissant." The loud report drove another dagger through my brain. A trickle of urine slid down the inside of my leg.

"Oh, God, no, please. MOM!" I cried, but as I turned to find her, Ray had hold of her hair, shoving her face into Dad's bloody chest. He shouted, spittle flying from his angry mouth, but I couldn't understand the jumbled words.

I didn't even realize I was screaming until Zeke smacked me again with enough force to wrench my neck. More stars erupted, but I continued to howl until my throat went raw.

I won't look. If I don't look, none of it will be real and we'll all be in the Escalade driving home, going too fast down 270 and Mom'll crank the radio to some dumb song. I'm still asleep. That's it. If I just close my eyes, I'll wake up and none of it will be real. That's it, I'll close my eyes and – and....

Ray got down on one knee, pulled Mom by the hair, and whispered something in her ear. A little louder he said, "Eat this," and spit on her. He squeezed her throat until she gasped, then rammed the revolver into her mouth. Someone beside me snarled, "Do it!"

He did. The sirens from two different directions echoed in the distance but couldn't drown out the sharp gunshots that sliced through my heart.

Mom, Dad, someone, wake me up. I...want...to...go... home.

Before I could control it, I collapsed against Zeke's chest. The world disintegrated, out-of-focus. But Zeke shook me, slammed me into the Cadillac. I gagged, dry-heaved until my eyes watered. Zeke stepped back, to avoid my puke. But nothing came out.

"Ah, no you don't, little boy. You ain't checkin' out on me yet."

My brain tried to fold in on itself. I saw flashes of Mom cooking, Dad yelling at the Chiefs to kick some ass. I tried to pull Sam up in my mind, but he just kept lying on the pavement like a forgotten toy.

Oh, God, Sam. Mom, Dad, please help me.

Zeke held me out by the scruff like a master offering a bone to his mutt.

"Open 'em, you little pissant. Look whatcha done to my friends." The revolver bloodied my lip as Zeke tried to shove it in my mouth. I whipped and jerked and kneed him hard in the groin. Ray shouted for him to hurry the hell up. The whirring sirens were getting closer. *Why're they taking so long?*

When the massive man turned to tell them he was coming, to give him a minute, he grabbed my jaw.

"You see this, you little pissant?" And with that, he shoved my face in front of his expertly drawn tattoo. The pearl-handled dagger, the blood.

I didn't answer. I *couldn't* answer.

"I'm gonna earn my tag, you little prick, and I don't give a shit if you're 8 or 80. I *earned* it. And you can't take it from me." Zeke pointed to his tattoo, just above the handle.

Earn his tag? I didn't know what it meant, but I knew it wasn't good.

He flailed me around like a rag doll, held me in front of him, and ran the gun hand down the side of my face. He turned toward his buddies and in that split-second, I bit his firing hand as hard as I could. I felt my teeth break through skin and crunch past it. I tasted his blood, and he howled in pain. He dropped me and grabbed his wounded hand.

I thumped to the pavement and felt gravel bite my skin. That same sense of time stopping, shifting happened as I rubbed my temple. I'd been clubbed too many times to count. I could smell matches, like when Dad grilled and a match didn't light. I tried to raise my head but the dizziness layered everything, duplicates of the world overlapping. Then I saw it, like a hundred-dollar bill in the middle of a pile of pennies. Laying right beside me was Muscle Man's gun.

I refused to worry about whether I could aim or fire. I grabbed it and gripped it with my trembling hands, my brain swirling with the possibility of what I meant to do.

Zeke glared down at me and laughed, a snort that sounded like a cough. One of the guys told him to quick dicking around. He kicked at my hand but missed as I scrambled back against the Escalade.

"Leave me alone, or I – I – I'll shoot. Please, just leave me alone, I want my mom. You killed my mom and my dad and Sam, and I swear to God, I swear to God, oh, God, please don't make me." I tried to keep the gun from wobbling. Zeke reached for me, and I flinched.

Muscle Man yanked me roughly by the hair and grabbed for the gun, but I waved it out of his reach. I swung it in front of him and pulled the trigger. The force of the shot bucked my hand so hard, what was aimed at his chest blew half of Zeke's face off. His teeth splintered, his nose disintegrated, and blood sprayed all over me. As his massive body collapsed, I heard his buddies screaming, running, shouting for someone to grab the little shit with the pistol.

I got my gun, I heard Ray yell, but I couldn't orient myself or be sure. Hands grabbed at my feet as I kicked at them, and I fired blindly five or six times.

They let go. Sirens got louder. I heard more screams. As I crawled sideways, my back against the Cadillac, I continued to pull the trigger until the shots were a strange *click—click—click.*

The police cruiser's radio blared, "Shots fired! Shots fired!"

I rolled onto my belly and crawled under the Escalade and shimmied to the other side but then considered staying under it. Sirens echoed loudly off the houses, right on top of me, beside me, around me.

"THIS WAY!" Ray shouted. Someone was screaming in pain and it gave me a sick rush of victory. One of them yelled, "I'll cover! Run, *goddammit!*" Three or four loud POP-POP-POPs, then feet shuffled, a cop shouted for them to freeze, then the sound of running, pounding pavement.

I scampered out from under the Escalade, on the field side of the chaos, the mangled mess of metal, and wavered. I knew I had shot at least one of them, besides Zeke. I could tell by the screams of pain. I just wasn't sure who. Zeke's huge body lay crumpled beside another one.

Oh, God. I did that...I killed them. I – I....

I tried to keep my eyes from straying to where I knew Mom, Dad, and Sam lay.

I could hear grunts, cops shouting for cuffs, and one of the guys bolted back my way.

"The open lot, quick! NOW!" More the pounding feet that fade on the far side of the Escalade. A nearby patrol car's radio called for back-up, officers in need of something, the ebbing sirens swallowing every other word.

"Hands up, asshole!" A voice shouted.

"Fuck you!" One of the guys answered, and a volley of gunshots hit the SUV side mirror, shattering it.

That jolt was all I needed. I scampered to my feet and jackrabbited into the dark night, away from the crash, away from my family, away from my life. I sprinted, praying for something to hide behind, barely able to see through my one eye. The other was swollen shut, and my brain threatened to do the same.

That's when I saw it. A storm drain yawned half a football field away, down a steep slope.

Hurry, hurry, hurry, rambled through my head, keeping pace with my pounding heart and throbbing legs.

Oh, God, what have I done?

"STOP!" Another voice ordered. Before I could worry they were shouting at me, more gunfire erupted. I zigzagged my way across the field, toward the storm drain. My head throbbed, my eye pulsated, and the harder I ran, the more I hurt.

More flashing lights swirled the sky, sirens echoing all around me. Car doors slammed back at the scene. *What did I do?* Gunpowder burned my nostrils, but confusion swirled my aching head.

I'm gonna earn my tag, you little shit.

He didn't.

But I did.

I stumbled over a clump of grass, a clear view of the drain so close I could imagine the smell of the mucky water. I righted myself and dashed the last ten feet.

Freedom...I'll be safe there. They can't arrest me if they can't find me.

When my foot clipped a rock, I rolled, flipped over, and landed at the bottom of the drainage ditch, slamming my ear on a rock.

Everything went black around the exploding stars in my head.

A foot stomped on the small of Sam's back... Mom hunched over Dad's limp body...a hand squeezing Mom's throat until she gasped, then a revolver rammed into her mouth....

"No," I moaned, my forehead grinding into the ditch's pebbled ground as I tried to lift my head. *"NO!"* Jumbled scenes jumped out of a focus, a TV losing reception.

The more pain I felt, the less real it all seemed.

I can make it all go away.

With the last of my strength, I raised my neck and slammed my forehead into the filthy concrete.

***

When I came to, I couldn't lift my head. Everything about me hurt. Nausea rolled in waves through me, pain stung in places I didn't know I'd injured, and every muscle throbbed. Cuts on my face thrummed with the beat of my heart, a dull echo. My hair felt sticky in places, and a lump had erupted like an egg on my forehead. I traced it with my fingers, but I couldn't quite touch it. *Who did this to me?*

You know what you done, you little shit.

"No," I moaned, and managed to crawl into the pitch-black storm drain and nearly came unglued when tiny feet skittered behind me. But my head and neck hurt too much to turn and look. Whatever it was scampered the other way.

I was pretty sure I'd be scared if I ran into me in a storm

drain.

I curled up, hugged my knees, and begged the world to stop rotating. Instead, I waited – for time to pass or life to end.

I didn't really care which.

Part IV

Changes

Chapter Forty

In another world, a horn honked, people shouted, and a dog yipped. City sounds. Another yip.

Skippy.

A head nudged my hand. It took a concerted effort to center myself, to return to the convenience store, the flier from the lady, the phone call, the article, my past. Then slowly, I came up for air, squinting in the afternoon sun. Because the nightmare had taken me so deep, I was drowning in memories of my past. Tears had dried on my cheeks, dampened my coat, and my throat had swollen to the size of a peanut. I gasped for air, anxious for oxygen to clear my brain and make the excruciating ache in my heart go away. The December air bit at my damp skin, so I tugged my jacket's collar as high as it would go.

Skippy crawled into my lap, sensing his boy needed him. *You're all I got, buddy.* I tugged him tight to my chest, to feel his heart beat against mine. I couldn't express to him how thankful I was for his unconditional love. The annoying horn blared again, and I wanted to tell the jerk to shut up. My head throbbed from crying, dreaming, dying that slow agonizing death for the second time.

And watching my family die.

I turned to see a beat-up Ford Escort, the driver standing with his door open and a right hand smacking the middle of the steering wheel.

The phone call.

"You Timmy?" he called, when he saw me poking my head around.

"Are you Jeremy?" My voice sounded like I had the worst cold of my life. I sniffed hard, trying to clear my nose and my head.

"The one and only!" He beamed, his teeth so white it

reflected the late afternoon sun.

Jeremy Gardner was nothing like what I expected. He was barely taller than the car he stood next to, likely shorter than me. His blond ponytail had sprigs of wild curls trying to escape. His pock-marked face declared a battle lost with acne, and he had two deep scars chiseled across his forehead.

Awesome scars. I imagined rivers could flow through the one that traced from above his right eye all the way across and into his hair. The smaller, shallower one etched from dead center between his eyes, above the left brow to the dangerous area of his temple. I wanted to touch them.

"Come on. Let's go grab a bite." He waved me over, the smile still natural and welcoming.

My body ached even though I didn't think it had been that long. Tigger showed that only an hour had passed. *Long enough to watch my family die.*

Skippy tugged impatiently at my jeans.

He squeezed her throat until she gasped, then rammed the revolver into her mouth and pulled the trigger.

I gagged, the memory so close I could taste the vomit, the blood, the airbag dust.

"Skip, give me a sec." I craved human contact, needed it for my sanity, but I was nervous thinking about having a conversation about me. And my head still swam with That Night.

"Cute mutt. He yours?"

"Through thick and thin." I tried to smile, to shake the after-images. I gathered my stuff and set it carefully among the junk in Jeremy's backseat. "He can come, can't he?"

"Don't know why not. They may not be too kosher with it at Subway, but they'll be cool with it back at the ranch. Let's cross that bridge when we come to it. Mrs. Mahoney loves dogs." He stood next to his car, still not getting in.

Someone's foot stomped on the small of Sam's back. I braced a hand on Jeremy's car and wobbled.

I'm sorry I couldn't save you, Sam. Tears stung my eyes, and Jeremy waited, not saying a word.

I slid into the passenger seat, and Jeremy hopped in and nodded. "First day of the rest of your life, Timmy. Today. Tomorrow. One foot in front of the other." With that, he zipped out of the parking lot and I felt a ripple of uncertainty.

I had just left the gas station with a total stranger. I allowed myself to be treated to a sweet onion teriyaki sub, my favorite from Before. Jeremy loaned me a jacket when he saw the blood on my collar. He didn't even ask about it. He told me he had cream for the cuts on my face, and I wished he had some for my heart.

While we ate, Skippy got full reign of the Escort's back seat while we dined. I shared superficial details about my life on the streets. I told Jeremy about the Gerries, the burn barrel, my daily route to the Arch, and searches for food. I gave a shortened rendition of Max finding me.

"Found me at a shelter a few days after...well after," I said, then hurried past the comment.

When Jeremy asked, "After what?" I shook my head. A gesture that meant, *Give me some time for that one.* And he didn't press. I knew he got it. His patience, his long pauses, his warm eyes that didn't judge, didn't push, didn't let go.

After we ate, I told Jeremy I would pay him back.

"In more ways than you know, kid." He laughed. I didn't know what that meant, but when we hopped into his car to rejoin Skippy and headed for "the house," as Jeremy called it, I mulled over the possibilities. Before me knew it wasn't a threatening comment. After me wasn't so sure.

The drive felt eternal, and I marveled at how far he had come to get me. We were venturing close to my world of old when we took a Chesterfield exit.

"Okay, Timmy, here's the plan. We're gonna give you a room, then tomorrow we'll talk about a plan of action, okay? I know it's almost Christmas and there'll be lots of emotion with that. We'll deal with the rest in a few days, okay?" He turned onto a vaguely familiar street. I was pretty sure I went to a haunted house in the area last Halloween. The weirdness of the day, coupled with reliving That Night, made my head swim.

"Sounds good," I answered, though I hadn't understood all of what he said or meant. Jeremy pulled into a driveway, and I stared at a house so huge and old, I thought it could be a castle. He chuckled when he saw my reaction and helped me gather my things. I picked Skippy up, thinking that might be more proper and less messy in case he got too excited and peed on the floor. It occurred to me that I didn't know if Skippy was housebroken. He never peed in my box, but there wasn't a lot of room for him to hike his leg.

When Jeremy opened the door, I smelled cookies baking, heard Christmas carols playing on the radio, and twinkling lights brought tears to my eyes.

"Timmy! Dinner's in thirty minutes. Did you finish your homework? If so, go wash up and come set the table." The memory sucker punched me, a fist to my chest, and I heaved to get air.

"Go slow, Timmy. Only a few kids are home, so you get to ease in."

I felt Jeremy's hand on my shoulder and stepped carefully into the huge foyer. A giant archway led to an enormous living room with couches, overstuffed chairs, a recliner, and a great big TV in the corner. A massive pine Christmas tree blinked in the far corner. The opposite bricked wall had a fireplace with a mantle filled with stockings. Names glittered across the top of each, but they were too far away for me to read.

"Hey there, boys." A heavy-set lady pulled a tray of cookies from the oven. "I'm Mrs. Mahoney. But everyone calls me Mrs. M. You must be?"

"Timmy, ma'am," I answered softly. I liked her the moment I saw her. She was round, cheerful, and resembled a lady I had seen in the movie *Misery* over at Brent's earlier in the summer, except happier. She cupped my free hand in hers and welcomed me to her home. When she smiled, lots of little wrinkles spread around her eyes.

"This whole house is yours?" I gawked, turning a circle to take it all in, awed by the idea.

"Well, yes it is, Timmy. And who might this be?" She reached out and kissed Skippy right on the nose. His ecstatic tail let me know he liked her very much, thank you, and we could just stay here forever. Right now, I agreed. But visions of evil foster mothers kept drifting back to me. Evil things could be wrapped in pretty packages, Max once told me. A guy couldn't be too careful. But seeing the tinsel draped down the stair railing, the tree decorated with popcorn strings, balls, and various other ornaments brought my defenses to an all-time low.

"This is Skippy, ma'am, and I think he likes you already."

"Well, dogs are a good judge of character, Timmy. Did you know that?"

"I knew Skippy was." I smiled, then I blurted, "Wait, no, he didn't like me at first."

They laughed, tousled my hair, and I suddenly felt the shattered pieces of my life begin the long process of mending. Jeremy took me up a million stairs to my room on the fourth floor, the attic he called it. It was small, with golden wood floors and furniture. It smelled good, like Lysol and Pledge, scents from my past. A twin bed lined the far wall, a chest of drawers across from it with a TV on top, and clothes strewn everywhere. A dresser still had all kinds of personal odds and ends on it.

"You got a bathroom up here that you share with just two other kids, one girl, one boy. It's just the three of you on this floor now. Haley's two doors down, and Benji is right next to you." Jeremy gathered the stuff on the dresser as he talked and dumped it all into a trash bag.

"Who was in the room before?" I asked, while patting the bed to see if Skippy would jump on it. He did, then promptly turned a zillion circles in the middle of the pillows and plopped into a nest he had created.

Make yourself at home, Skipmeister.

"Um, Michael left today," Jeremy started slowly and seemed hesitant to share more. And he didn't. He plucked clothes from the back of a rocking chair and off the floor like it either ticked him off that whoever was in here hadn't gotten a chance to do it himself or that the clothes were there in the first place. I had only known him for two hours, so I wasn't exactly an expert.

"He get kicked out or what?" I knew I was being a nosy, but I wanted to know if it was commonplace to get booted from Mrs. M's.

"His father came and got him, Timmy. Kind of in a rush. His dad isn't exactly a nice man, and he didn't appreciate us interfering. If you see any of this you want, help yourself. He's not coming back for it." A dark cloud fell on Jeremy's face, his scowl so intense, the words on the tip of my tongue evaporated.

Interfering with what? I had overstepped my boundaries already, and Jeremy had no intention of offering more. Maybe I didn't know these people as well as I should've before agreeing to stay there.

"I'm gonna leave you alone, let you explore, and have some peace and quiet. If you find anymore of Michael's things, just set 'em on the dresser. You look like you could use some rest. You can shower tonight or in the morning – whichever you prefer. Remote's on the dresser. If you want to come down in a little bit for dinner, I can introduce you to everyone. If not, I'll run you something up to eat. First days are tough. Introductions can wait 'til breakfast. What time do you get up?"

I laughed, and Jeremy seemed to understand.

"Okay, how 'bout this. I'll wake you at eight. First night in a real bed might make it tough to get up, so I'll let you sleep in. I'll have Mrs. M save breakfast for you." He winked. "Someone will run a sandwich up here in a bit, unless you change your mind and want to come down. No pressure."

"Thanks, Jeremy." I picked up the remote, needing something to do with my hands. A sudden bout of nerves made my feet itch.

"No problem, Timmy. She won't mind."

"No, I mean, thanks for everything. I – I can't even imagine what I was gonna do."

"I'm glad I could help. There's only one question I'm gonna ask before I leave you alone, okay?"

I swallowed. "Okay."

"How long did you say you were on the streets?"

"Three months, three weeks, and five days. Or six. I – I'm not sure. These last two or three have been a blur."

My memories seemed to have found their place, like my brain had been a jigsaw with a bunch of missing pieces. I had them all gathered now, I just needed to start sorting them and fitting them together.

It was like I could look at the whole picture for the first time since That Night. No more jaunting into the past because I felt safer there with Mom, Dad, and Sam. I hoped I could build a puzzle that included them.

"Wow," was all he muttered and started to leave the room.

"Hey, Jeremy?"

"Yeah?" He stood in the doorway looking back at me. I still marveled at his scars.

"What's today?"

He laughed. "It's Wednesday."

"So five days, not six."

"Christmas is Saturday. Is that what you were wonderin'?" Jeremy's smile was warm, and I felt like I could tell him anything.

"Yeah," I mumbled, and then he left.

Alone in the room, I took it all in. I wouldn't be on the streets for Christmas, but I wouldn't be with Mom, Dad, and Sam either. It boggled my mind that so much had happened in only a few days. After so many carbon copied days, in a matter of 72 hours everything had changed.

A tiny twinge of guilt for Max pulsed through me. I made a note-to-self: *Write Max a letter*. Quick on its heels came a surge of rage at how he lied to me and manipulated me, using my family the way he did. I tore up the mental note to self.

Skippy scratched and resituated himself, pulling the bedspread so he was half covered. My Skippy had obviously spent time on a real bed. I felt a pang of loss for him, wondering what had sent him to the streets.

But thank God it had.

I explored the room, opening drawers, inspecting potential hiding places for my baseball cards, the bottle caps, and my cash. But for the time being, I stuck my box under a pillow and settled back to flip through channels. A task from my past that I had loved with a passion, one I seldom really got to do because Sam always took charge of the clicker.

"Go ahead and watch your boy stuff, Timmy.*" Stephie's pony tail flipping me off as she threw the remote control at my feet.*

Stephie Kruschaven. Hadn't she inspired much of my quest for freedom? I landed on a channel showing reruns of the original *Star Trek* series.

"Ah, c'mon, Timmy. We don't wanna watch that crap. Mom, make him turn it. This is why we don't let you use the clicker." Sam threw a pillow at me.

A lump swelled in my throat as I flipped it just to make Sam happy – whether he was there to appreciate it or not. I thumbed past one of Mom's favorite law shows, then a sit-com on a comedy channel that was even before my time, and when I landed on *Independence Day,* Sam's favorite movie four summers earlier. He'd gotten the movie for Christmas that same year.

That was all it took to open the floodgates. I turned over and buried my face in the soft, freshly washed pillowcase and let the tears come.

For nearly ten minutes I cried, and listened to President Whitmore tell his motley troops that July fourth would no longer be America's day but the whole world's. A memory of Sam reciting the line by heart brought on the second wave. I bawled like the baby I claimed not to be. And I didn't care. When the soul-swallowing emotion finally passed, I found a movie channel and sniffled through some dumb old movie about fraternity guys having a food fight. At least that one didn't have ghosts reciting lines from it.

No clanking while old-timers tossed or crushed empty cans. None of the constant honking, shouting, or arguing of Gerries hogging the barrel fire. An odd sense of nostalgia swept through me. Strangely, I thought I might miss them eventually.

The channel guide scrolled names of Fall shows unfamiliar to me. *I've got a ton of catching up to do.*

It didn't matter what I chose at this point. Halfway through the first show, I fell asleep. And for the first time in three months, three weeks, and six days, not a single nightmare chased me there.

Chapter Forty-One

A light tap at the door startled me, and Skippy came alert in one fluid motion. He jumped down, yapped at the intruder, and turned to wag me out of bed.

"It's okay, boy. It's probably just Jeremy." I slid out from under the thick comforter, hustled to open the door, then dove back under the covers. The hardwood floors chilled my bare feet. I was used to sleeping in several pair of socks, but Mrs. M had taken all of my street clothes to wash them. Or burn them, she had teased.

"Hey, sleepyhead. Feel good to sleep in a real bed?" Jeremy sat on the edge and tugged at the covers and played like he was going to expose me to the chill of the room. One thing I always loved about my before life was sleeping in a cool room wrapped in fluffy blankets all the way up to my ears. A small pleasure I had forgotten.

"Whatimisit?" slurred out of my sticky-with-sleep mouth.

"It's nearly eight-thirty. Mrs. M saved pancakes for you. Your choice of homemade syrups. She makes a killer blueberry syrup. Anyway." He paused like he wanted to add something else, but instead added, "We'll talk when I get back."

"Where're you goin'?" Meeting all the house's residents without Jeremy made my nerves jangle.

"You'll be fine. Get that panicky look off your face. Most of the rezzies are at work, on visits, or prospecting. I'll explain all that to you later. Mrs. M just has you and Haley for breakfast yet. Haley just got here day before yesterday, so you two might have a lot to talk about, bein' the newbies and all." He stood and headed toward the door.

"Rezzies?" My head was reeling. Everyone was already up and gone? Another newbie who might have something in common with me? *I doubt it.*

"Residents...or roomies if you prefer. But once I referred to a few teenagers as *kids* and about got my head snapped off." Jeremy let out a laugh, an infectious sound that eased Timmy's worries.

"All good?" He held the doorknob in his hand but waited.

"All good." I let out my breath, not aware until then that I was holding it.

"Awesome. I'll see you this afternoon. Relax, eat breakfast, take a look around. It'll make you feel better." With that, Jeremy was gone. A little of the dread seeped back in. I had so many secrets. I didn't know what to hide, share, or simply avoid. I *knew* I wouldn't share anything about my knife-related incidents. Not now, probably not ever.

I sifted through some of the clothes Jeremy told me I could use. I tugged a University of Missouri at St. Louis sweatshirt over my dirty hair, suddenly feeling too gross and unpresentable.

In my past life, I bathed every night before I went to bed. That way I could wake up and fly. In the past three months, three weeks, and six days, waking was not the problem. But flying had taken on a whole new meaning.

I plucked a pair of Fruit of the Looms, a tattered pair of too-large jeans, and tip-toed down the hall to the bathroom. I locked the door behind me and inspected the supplies. Jeremy had said I could use what was there.

Suave shampoo, Irish Spring soap, and Crest, though there wasn't an extra toothbrush. I knew my finger would do better than what I'd been using. I couldn't even imagine how good having clean teeth would feel. I pulled a washrag from a shelf for my bath.

I ran the water so deep, I nearly overflowed it when I stepped in. I soaked for ten minutes before beginning the slow process of washing the months of grime off my body. No matter how many times I had cleaned up in bathrooms, there were parts of me that had been neglected so long, one bath might not be enough. But it would be a start.

Max and the Gerries made gross jokes about "crotch rot," and as much as they talked about it, I knew it was a serious problem for some of them. I didn't know whether I had it or not, but every time I scratched my privates, the old men chanted *crotch rot, crotch rot, crotch rot.*

After scrubbing my hair, soaping up all over, and rinsing carefully, I was one big wrinkle. The bath water had turned a rusty brown, so I let much of it out and ran fresh water, not as scalding as the first fill, but I got it as hot as I could. I laid my head back while the water ran, relishing the luxury I had taken so for granted Before.

When I could no longer get the water warm enough, I got out and dried myself, then finger-combed my blond mop. *God, I need a haircut.*

Hair removal – isn't that what I teased Sam about after his football buzz?

I dressed quickly, then traipsed down the four flights of stairs noisily enough that Mrs. Mahoney would hear me coming. Skippy bounded ahead of me. Prior to my street scavenging, directions hadn't exactly been my strength. I couldn't remember where the kitchen was, so I hoped someone would intercept me, greet me, anything to keep me from having to hunt around.

And greet, Mrs. M did. I was swooped into the kitchen, placed at the head of the table, and given the five-star treatment. Sam used to say the sick Weaver got the five-star treatment, so I guessed nearly four homeless months counted as being sick.

A fleeting image of Sam crumpled on the ground sucked the air out of the room.

"Timmy, you okay?" Mrs. M put a warm hand on my shoulder. I looked up at her through a thin film of memory, and nodded. I couldn't speak. An after image of Sam catapulting me onto the couch made me smile, the tears brimming. Emotion seemed to be on the edge of every thought. I swiped at my eyes, feeling like a baby my wounds were too tender to care.

"Laughter through tears is my favorite emotion," Mrs. M said, smiling so big, her dimples and wrinkles multiplied. "Good movie. Very quotable."

I must've seemed confused, because as she led me to the kitchen table and pulled out a chair for me, she whispered, "*Steel Magnolias.* My favorite movie."

Before I could tell her how much my mom loved it too, she had set a plate in front of me that made my senses swoon. The smell of bacon, the sight of syrupy pancakes, the luxury of buttered grits – my fork hovered over each, not sure where to start. When I sprinkled a little sugar on them and scooped a bite of grits, she laughed and applauded.

"Finally, someone who loves grits as much as I do." She set a glass of orange juice in front of me, then busied herself at the sink. When she wasn't looking, I drank it in one long blissful swallow. Sam and I used to joke that OJ tasted best when you drank it all at once.

I let out a soft belch, apologized, then took equal opportunity bites of pancake, bacon, and grits, rotating between the three, not sure which was more heavenly. I savored the syrup on my tongue, chewed the bacon slow enough to let the taste fill my mouth, then followed it with a creamy bite of buttery grits. Mrs. M said nothing, but twice refilled my glass.

"Slow down," she whispered, as I chewed a mouthful so big I could barely close it.

I lowered my fork and realized I had been hovering over the plate like a starving mongrel. My face reddened, but I managed a smile.

You all would like Mrs. M. It felt good to talk to them, now that I remembered and knew why they hadn't come back for me. The agony of thinking about them was lined with a wonderful glow of love. But a quick flash of anger flared at Max for lying, for pretending to be family, for taking advantage of me.

I hid my anger by sipping the juice, then finished the last bites.

Overwhelmed by her kindness, but not quite able to talk, I nodded through grateful tears. I wasn't sure why they kept coming this morning, but Mrs. M must have understood. She gave my shoulder a soft squeeze and whispered, "You're welcome."

Rubbing my noticeably distended belly, I let out a long burp. "Excuse me," I blurted, embarrassed again that I couldn't suppress them. Sam would've given that one a 9 out of 10. It didn't rattle windows, but it definitely rivaled some of Dad's. I suspected breakfast would require a few bathroom visits, but it had totally been worth it. I drained the last of my orange juice as Skippy slurped the last of whatever was in a dish on the floor by the refrigerator.

"Good grief, Skip, have some manners." I chuckled, not exactly full of manners myself. Skippy looked up at me, his tail wagging ninety miles a minute. With a rush of love for him, I patted my lap and he ran and leapt into it so fast he almost knocked me over. I gave him a fierce hug, then didn't kid myself that his lavish kisses weren't really his attempt to wash the syrup from my chin.

"I tell you what, Timmy. Because you haven't really been shown the ropes, I'm gonna let you off easy this morning. I'll wash, you dry, and Skippy can supervise. How does that sound?" Mrs. M rubbed Skippy's head, then held a dishtowel out to me. The gesture warmed me – accepting Skippy was another step in accepting me.

"Sure," I happily agreed. Chores. It had a nice ring to it. I could actually do something to earn my keep. *Hadn't I said as much after I left the alley the other day?*

I stood next to her in the enormous, old-fashioned kitchen and felt the world go fuzzy.

"Grab the flour, Timmy, and Sam – you get the chocolate chips." Mom ordered us around while we giggled. Then she

got testy when we wouldn't be serious. "Get moving, boys, or I'll eat them all myself."

The memory made the world swim out of focus again. I tried to stare at the high ceilings, the neat decorations on top of the cabinets. Greenery vined across antiques, giant antique-looking jars, and a variety of china plates. Mrs. M had succeeded in a homey atmosphere that made me ache for home – my *real* home. Knowing I couldn't march into my house on Catalina flooded me with a mixture of emptiness and anger.

"Robert, you're hanging it crooked, good grief." Mom supervised the whole remodel, with Dad following her orders because he said he knew better than to not. Sam and I mocked them, but the wallpaper turned out awesome. Less than a week later, Sam tripped me, and I splattered grape juice all over it. That spot never came clean, but he and I thought the spot gave it character. Mom scowled when we told her we had broken it in.

"Timmy, are you okay?" Mrs. M bent down in front of me, but I couldn't make out her face.

"Yeah." I laughed out loud. Mom tried to get Dad to re-do that section. Instead, he bought her an expensive wine cabinet to put in front of the spot. Mom had thanked me once she got over being mad.

"What's so funny?" Mrs. M cocked her head and pushed the graying hair out of her eyes. She finished washing the first plate, rinsed it, and handed it to me.

"It's hard not to think of my parents and my brother in a house like this." It surprised me that the words came so easily. Being in a real house with a real person cooking made it hard to stay street savvy.

Max told me that a homeless person losing street smarts was more dangerous than fencing without a sword. I laughed at the time, but now I got it. And it frightened me. I knew it was possible I could be back in a box by the weekend. Hard questions might reveal to them that I deserved to be in jail, not in the attic. I might not miss peddling at the NFC Championship game after all. Or my first homeless Christmas.

"This old house might remind you of a lot of things. I grew up here, and my folks used it as what they would now call a bed and breakfast. They let people come stay here for a small fee, and the boarders would sightsee, spend time in the city, then come spend the night here. It was cheaper than a hotel and gave them a sense of home. Daddy was a carpenter. He built stuff out in the workshop. I'll show it to you later." She handed me another plate.

"I'd like that." I continued drying, trying to stay focused on the dishes.

"Oh, Robert, that – that's um, how do I say ugly *in a nice way?" Mom covered her mouth, smiling but grimacing at the same time. But Sam and I thought the assembled boards did actually resemble a picnic table. Dad raised the hammer in the air in a salute and dubbed his product "Chez Weaver." Mom teased him that it was a table, not a house, but the name stuck. When we ate at it, we had to be careful, because there was such a slant, glasses couldn't be filled within an inch of the top. We couldn't set anything on the gaps either, or they would wobble. Dad never attempted to build anything after that. To tease him, Mom bought three different types of levels to put in his stocking that Christmas. We never laughed as hard as we did that Christmas morning two years ago.*

"Memories coming back easy now?" Mrs. M asked, smiling warmly at me.

"Yeah," I answered, my voice husky. I knew I hadn't been a crybaby for most of the four months, but I had been having serious trouble making good on that claim for the past two weeks.

Everything about this place reminded me of home.

We finally got all the breakfast dishes finished. I counted eleven plates in all, so there had to be at least nine of us in the house. I couldn't be sure if Mrs. M or Jeremy had eaten or not.

After that, she took me on a formal tour.

Upstairs, in a room directly underneath mine, I met Rico, a younger dark-complected boy who didn't have much to say. Mrs. M explained about the disappearance of his mom and how he'd been living by himself for three weeks when a neighbor came over to borrow flour. The elderly lady freaked out, brought the nine-year-old to Mrs. M's and a week later, they found his mom's body in an East St. Louis crack house. The Division of Family Services was currently trying to find Rico's relatives.

"That's sad. So he doesn't talk much?" I couldn't relate. My motor didn't have an off button most of the time. The Gerries once told me if I didn't find it, they were going to staple my mouth closed.

Mrs. M led me down the hall, showed me where the other bathrooms were, all the while I took in the smells of the house – hardwood floors, fresh-baked biscuits, smoky fireplaces. Skippy bounded ahead of us, sniffing in all the corners and worrying me that he might hike his leg on something.

"Not much. I know it's hard to hear things like that, but it's important that you all know where each other comes from. It builds respect for space. Rico's only been here seven weeks, so we're helping him cope. Be mindful of that, okay?" Mrs. M smiled at me, and I couldn't imagine doing anything on purpose to make her angry. Her round face, filled with soft wrinkles and wise eyes, warmed me in a way I'd never felt. Skippy came and jumped up on her – she bent down and rubbed his scruff, then he took off down the hall with a *click-click* of toenails.

"There's a new girl, Jeremy said, that just got here, too. Right?"

"Haley will be back in a little bit. She had to run a little errand. And never you mind about Haley – she's seventeen and much too old for you." Mrs. M cocked an eyebrow, but the corners of her mouth twitched.

We finished the tour in the Great Room. The rest of the house fascinated me – room after room with shiny hardwood floors, thick area rugs that Skippy insisted on rolling around on, and antique furniture. The house had been built way before central heating, and she never had the heart to install it, so baseboard heaters did the best they could, and occasional fireplaces were all blazing this morning. I wanted to stoke the dying fire in the Great Room just to wrap myself in the warmth of it, to enjoy the roasted feeling I had experienced on a daily basis as a boy.

"We have circle time every night, Timmy. It's our form of group therapy. When everyone gets home today, you'll be formally introduced, okay?"

I nodded, though the idea of formal introductions made my stomach flip. I shoved it out of my head, because seeing a home that could never replace Catalina Avenue had left me feeling empty in a way I couldn't describe.

Mrs. M left me to do her lunch preparations, telling me to help myself to the clicker. I plopped onto one of the couches and admired the huge Christmas tree in the corner. No matter how beautiful it was, it didn't compare to Weaver trees of my past. Sam and Mom fought about the snow he loved to spray all over everything, even the furniture, and Mom absolutely despised it. Sam always won because Mom knew what every mother knows – Christmas is all about making kids happy. She'd said that more times than I could count.

The year after Chez Weaver was built, we brought home a tree so lopsided, Dad had to tie it to keep it upright. It fell twice on Christmas Eve. My Huffy bike was my big gift that Christmas, my last real Christmas. We had started a trend of jokes about our family leaning to the right, though Mom insisted she was a Democrat. Sam had to explain that one to me.

Skippy hopped into my lap, turned a circle, and settled in for a nap. I scratched him and hoped the flashbacks would ease a little, instead of assaulting me every five seconds.

By the time Jeremy got home, I had retreated to my room, straightened the borrowed clothes, and watched an episode of a cool show where remote control cars bash into one another.

A small tap on the door startled me. Jeremy stuck his head in and asked if I could make time for a chat.

"You know how it goes, Timbo. No time too soon to wind the watch."

In that instant, he reminded me so much of Sam, I couldn't speak.

Shaun lifted his foot and stomped on the small of Sam's back while I watched. The crunch of my brother's spine ripped through me, as painful as a knife to my gut.

Oh, God, oh, God, oh, God...

The crack of the gunshot that...that...

"...if you want," someone said, then a hand on my back made me jerk away and shriek. I felt my front pocket for my blade, my protection, but the denim was smooth and flat.

I gasped, unable to catch my breath or get the burning smell of gunpowder out of my head.

"It's okay, Timmy, I'm sorry." Jeremy crouched down beside me on the floor, where I had dropped, doubled over and rocked back and forth while I waited for the world to right itself. I swallowed hard to keep my breakfast down, the stench of airbags and burnt rubber making it impossible to breathe. I squeezed my eyes shut to block out the memory of someone bashing Sam's head against the concrete.

Being in the alley was easier. This is too hard, I can't do it. I've gotta get outta here. My itchy feet scared me. I wanted this, I *needed* this. But I wasn't sure I deserved it.

"You okay?" was the first question that broke through the fog.

"I think so." My voice sounded full of snot again, and there was a girl standing behind Jeremy staring at me. She held a glass of water and extended it when I looked at her.

"Here...take a sip. I'm Haley, and – and I didn't mean to intrude, but I heard Jeremy in here scrambling around, and I thought I could help."

At first, I thought she was an angel – blonde hair, blue eyes, tall. She could have been my mother at seventeen.

"Hi." I took the glass and gulped, praying for it to wash the visions away. I could smell her perfume on the glass. *Hi? I sound ten.*

"It could be all the food you ate. Mrs. M said you oinked." Jeremy chuckled.

How could I tell him that no, it was the remembering that made me want to vomit? The brother I worshipped kept getting shot, right after some asshole slammed his skull to the ground so many times it nauseated me to think about. And my mom and dad were murdered by gangbangers who didn't give a shit about anything except an image or a damn tag on their tattoo.

I shuddered, then the rage started in the pit of my stomach. Jeremy sent Haley away and pushed Skippy out of my face. The mutt thought he could cure cancer with a few kisses, and most of the time, it was true.

"Feelin' better?" Jeremy gave me space, settling back on my bed.

"Yeah, I think so. I wasn't sick – it – it was ghosts, you know?" I surprised myself again by sharing exactly what I was feeling.

"Ah, and do these ghosts have names?"

Here it was. The Q and A I knew would come. He had described the program at Mrs. Mahoney's, and I was relieved it didn't sound anything like the Division of Youth Services. I heaved a window-rattling sigh and settled in to share what I could. I didn't plan to give up my life history, but I could tell him a little.

"Sam," I said simply.

"Your brother? Sister?"

"Older brother. He would've been a sophomore in high

school." I hesitated. "At Marquette."

"But he's not? You're using past tense." Jeremy watched my expression stiffen. "You don't have to share if you don't want to, Timmy, but I can only help if I know enough. Okay?" Jeremy cocked an eyebrow, an expression that deepened the scars and made him look funny.

"Sure." A stalker sensation tapping at the door to my heart went away but only with some effort.

"Did Sam die?"

Wow. Talk about cut to the chase.

I opened my mouth to say yes, but my throat had shriveled around the word. I nodded instead. My chest tightened and the room swam out of focus.

"Sorry," Jeremy said softly. "Tell you what, why don't you share with me what you can. That way I don't hit any quicks."

"Fair," I mumbled, and tried to settle the ghosts.

He studied me. My calloused, scarred hands, and battered face. The fight with Trash Boy had me looking eerily the way I must've after That Night. I had inspected my black eye, split lip, and swollen nose after my bath, and they were beauties. But I wished they could see the cute Timmy Weaver.

"I don't know where to start. I already told you about Max. He's in County. That's why I left. I actually had a pretty decent set-up with him. I had one of the best boxes on Brookline before I left. I bet Billy took it though." I stopped myself when I realized I was rambling. It helped that Jeremy understood that part of my life, that he had served street time, too.

"Do you remember what happened to put you out? Single Mom? Drugs? Sam get into trouble?" Jeremy forgot his suggestion to let me share what I could.

"What? Oh my God, no." The questions almost made me laugh, except everything was tinged with anger. Jeremy and I both glanced down and saw that I had balled up my fists.

"Sorry. I don't mean anything by it. Most of my prompts come from a place of experience."

"It – it was nothin' like that," I snapped, trying to suppress the anger. It came too quickly, too easily because it had been a powerful ally until yesterday. Could I admit to Jeremy what I had done in the vacant lot to Trash Boy? *Not yet, maybe not ever.*

Jeremy sat silent on the bed, me sitting in the middle of the floor suddenly vulnerable and uncertain. Skippy sat beside me, sensing my tension, his head on my arm.

"I just figured a lot out in the past few days. It's all been sort of...sort of gone. Lots of stuff I couldn't remember. It's weird, but..." I took a deep breath and then let out a long sigh. "I'm trying to figure it all out."

Jeremy's brow furrowed. It didn't make much sense. I had been homeless for exactly four months, but I just now figured it out? I wouldn't believe me either.

"Well, I want you to feel ready to talk, so I won't push. When you're ready, okay?" He stood, and a wave of guilt blanketed me. "Lunch around 12:30...if you wanna come on down in a few, I'll give you the lowdown on chores and stuff before we eat."

"Thanks, Jeremy." I felt like an immature brat saying *I've got a secret and I'm not gonna tell you – na-na-na-na-boo-boo.*

He patted my shoulder and left me with my guilt and confusion. Now that I remembered the past, the tricky part was dealing with it so it wouldn't consume me. Only then would I be able to consider the future. That thought swirled like a tornado inside of me.

Chapter Forty-Two

"Who the hell are you?" A scrawny black kid about my age stood at the entrance to the Great Room with his chest puffed out. I sprayed a little more Pledge and wiped it across the second shelf of the book case.

After the chat with Jeremy, I had come downstairs so he could give me the inside scoop on house rules. He showed me the Chores List tacked to the side of the refrigerator. Mrs. M had scribbled my name over Michael's, and I'd gotten half-finished when the boy, maybe ten years old, confronted me.

"I – I'm Timmy, who the hell're you?" I stood straighter and had at least four inches on the shrimp. But he had the muscles of a normal teenage boy, not those of an emaciated homeless kid. His dark corn rows glistened and chocolate eyes blazed. I felt like Skippy when strange dogs came up and sniffed his butt.

Where's my protection, Skip? So much for having my back.

"Erik, and you ain't s'posed to cuss. Mrs. M don't like it, knowwudImean?" Erik walked around behind me like he was measuring me, sizing me up. He finally held out his hand, balled into a fist. "With that beat-up face, I reckon you ain't as tough as you sound."

I didn't know how to respond, so I didn't do anything except flex my muscles.

"You think you're hot shit, or what?" Erik grabbed my arm, held it, and closed my hand, then he bumped his fist against mine.

"Oh, god, I'm stupid. I get it." I pushed my fist into his again, just to show that I understood. I really did feel dumb, but I wasn't going to give Erik the satisfaction by saying more.

"That's a PIB. Gotta get you in-the-know." He lifted his chin, and I felt his butt-sniffing again.

"PIB?" I asked, before I could stop myself.

"Geez, you really don't know shit. Pound it brother...guess you're too white to get it." He snickered, then added, "What happened to your face, homie?"

"Erik...whoa. Timmy's had a rough few days. He doesn't need any crap from you. Go check the list on the fridge and get on your chores. *Then* the two of you can get acquainted." Jeremy turned Erik by the shoulders, pushed him toward the kitchen, then winked at me.

"Aiight, dog, I'm goin'. Yo, Punchin' Bag, I hope the other guy looks worse, knowwudImean?" Erik snickered as he pushed through the swinging door into the kitchen.

I let out my breath and wondered if meeting all the kids would make me feel like the runt of the litter.

"Erik is as straight-forward as they get. But they're all gonna run you through the wringer a little. Your cute face covered in cuts and bruises is gonna make you an easy target. Don't take it personal – just remember that you're fresh meat, okay?" Jeremy handed me the dust rag I had dropped.

"Okay." I grabbed the Pledge and resumed dusting, trying to make sense of the introduction. Jeremy told me not to sweat the small stuff, but I couldn't tell him that it might seem small to him, but for four months on the streets, my face was all I'd had. And teasing never sat well with me either – that was Sam's doing.

At the lunch table, Erik admired my shiner, the scar on my cheek, and all the nicks and cuts. He gave my scar a thumbs-up, asking if the girl had a name. He insisted any dude capable of that had to be defending his lady. When the cloud changed my expression, he apologized with a quick, "My bad."

His slang confused me, but I was learning.

"Okay, boys, grab your PBJs and some milk." Mrs. M motioned for us to come to the counter to get a plate.

While I snarfed my first half and washed it down with icy milk – a delectable taste from my past – Erik filled me in on the *real* rules of the house.

"You know whatcha gotta do, don'tcha? The gist of this place, I mean?" Erik's face was thin, but his cheekbones were like round balls when he grinned. The corn rows were always neat and in place, but his eyebrows needed a little braiding of their own.

I nodded, even though I didn't have a clue.

"All of us gots a story, but all of us got to find our destination, knowwudImean?" Erik nibbled his sandwich. "It's part of your *plan*, homie. You'll have to come up with three potential goals – somethin' like DFS, long-lost relatives, the lottery. You get the drift."

By the time I finished my second peanut butter and jelly sandwich and a third glass of milk, I had most of the important details. The house was like a gas station, a rejuvenating point on the road to recovery. The program helped troubled or abandoned kids make the transition into foster care or to relatives and how to move toward a future.

"Hey, boys, I'm here to offset all the testosterone." Haley be-bopped into the kitchen, patted Mrs. M on the back, and proceeded to make her own sandwich. "You feelin' better, Timmy?" She turned and studied me while she smeared peanut butter on a piece of bread.

"Yeah, I'm good. Thanks." That's when I realized who she reminded me of – Morgan, Brent's older sister. Sam had crushed on her for two years, almost as long as he'd been admiring Scott's mom. He would be falling in love with Haley. I felt a little giddy around her myself, and I hadn't decided if girls were worth all the trouble yet or not.

"Haley, you and me would make a killer couple. You sure you don't wanna cohabitate?" Erik leaned forward and gave her an exaggerated wink.

I understood Erik's sentiment. I didn't know why she was here, but she seemed too perfect for anything to ever go wrong in her life.

"Erik, control your hormones." Mrs. M shook her head, stifling a grin. "Timmy, Haley here's a good example of what kind of options you want to consider. And she's only been here a couple of days."

"Well, I'm lucky. I'm seventeen, so I could just get a job and my own apartment. But I also have grandparents in Arizona and my best friend's family in St. Peters. I'm considering adopting them." She flashed perfect white teeth and sat down at the table with us.

Mrs. M laughed. "I like that – *you're* going to adopt *them.*"

What would I do? I was obviously too young for my own place, and I didn't have a single relative that I knew of. A vision of Max hovering over my cot at the shelter brought a flash of anger, but it evaporated with weight of worrying about my options. My grandparents had died before I was born, and I was too old to bank on adoption. Most agencies didn't list kids over eleven. It was possible, but in my mind I couldn't imagine someone deciding, *Hmmm, I think I'll bring home an eleven-year-old today.*

I continued to consider my choices while everyone talked. I chatted with them, but my head swam as I finished my last gulp of milk. I lightly touched the spongy swelling in my check and under my eye. Could I leave all the violence behind me?

When Jeremy came in and nabbed a sandwich, the buzz of activity turned up a notch. He told me about the other older residents, two who worked full-time while going to school.

"How old are they? As old as you?"

"Me? You kiddin', kid? I'm twenty-six. Damn near old enough to be your daddy," he teased.

I couldn't believe it. *Twenty-six.*

"Wow. I thought you were like nineteen or twenty." I tried to picture Sam, and Jeremy didn't seem that much older.

He laughed. "It's the ponytail, huh?"

"And the pierced eyebrow. I didn't know older people did that." Others at the table laughed, as Jeremy busted into a goofy grin.

"Hey, kid, twenty-six doesn't exactly qualify me for cheap meals and movie tickets."

"I know," I added, my cheeks flushing.

I still hadn't gotten the nerve to ask him about the deep scars across his forehead. I guessed they might have a little to do with his street-life, but tact kept my tongue in check. Twenty-four hours hadn't exactly been ample time to delve into everyone's secrets, though I had learned some about most of them.

"So, you gonna add a chapter to the Mahoney Anthology?" Haley asked as she cleared the table.

"Eventually." I grinned. "But I'll need more than a chapter."

Erik smirked, claiming my humor didn't amuse anyone that much. I countered that he couldn't be the self-proclaimed angry black boy if he continued to laugh all the time. Jeremy added that the shrimp – less than a year younger than me – had "little man's syndrome." Erik scoffed, but stifled a grin while he did it.

I could tell that Erik and I were going to be friends. We had a bazillion things in common. Everything he liked, I liked. He and I planned to stay up and watch Blair Witch later, because he told me it was totally wicked. I didn't know what the heck it was, but I didn't care. I enjoyed his company and liked the idea that I was making a real friend.

Haley had said she might join, since she'd rented it for everyone to watch. I grinned like a goof, even though I'd vowed I would never froth at the mouth the way Sam did over Mrs. Kruschaven – a Sandra Bullock look-alike. *Yuck*, I had said, *She's like my mom*. And when he whistled every time I mentioned Morgan, I waved him off in disgust. Girls were too much trouble, I told him. But he kept telling me that would change. Haley Crenshaw might be proof of that.

We spent the afternoon finishing chores and chilling by the

fire. Around 4:30, my heart started to pound when Jeremy starting manipulating furniture in the Great Room. The fire crackled and I wanted to enjoy it, but that would have to wait. The idea of "group therapy" had me as nervous as a cat near bath water.

"Okay, gang. Let's make introductions formal." Jeremy motioned for each of them sitting in the circle, some in easy chairs, others sharing couches, to take their turn. Each did, and a few even leaned forward or crossed the circle to shake my hand.

I heard the names, but I knew I would never remember them all. I was just too darn nervous. When the conversations started, I heard Philip, the high school senior whose family kicked him out for a drug incident, talk about the rejection. Tears sprang to his eyes. He waved his hand to indicate that he was finished, he couldn't talk anymore. Erik was quick to chime in, to insist that nobody knew hard times like his. He began baring his soul and my feet tapped wildly. If it went counter-clockwise like this, I was next.

His words buzzed, but I had stopped listening when he went into detail about his "moms" and what he had to do to live with her again.

"Come on, Tim. Your turn," Erik quipped. "We've all laid it out. If I can share about my crack head Momma, I think you can give us a taste."

My heart started pounding. I knew my expression had to show my discomfort, but I figured they all wanted to know my story bad enough not to bail me. It was part of the healing process, Jeremy said in a voice so hushed, I thought maybe I imagined it. I pretended not to hear him.

"C'mon, homie. It's no biggie, we all gotta purge, knowwudImean?" Erik slapped my knee.

Silence blanketed the room like a heavy snow. It reminded me of a time when Mrs. Blankenship in second grade asked me what six plus seven was, and I just couldn't think. It felt like ten minutes passed before she asked someone else. Sitting in the Great Room, I felt the same hot spotlight and the answer was a heck of a lot tougher than thirteen. Even Jeremy watched me, probably trying to decide whether to bail me out. He didn't, and my face flamed hotter as a result.

Don't look at me! I wanted to scream. Hadn't the Gerries made me feel the same way? The pressure made my stomach hurt, so I did the one thing I knew to do. I sprinted up the stairs taking two steps at a time – all four flights – and then slammed the door as quickly as I could. I wished it had a lock, so instead, I plopped on the floor in front of it.

Screw them and their spotlight. I was better at begging than talking. The old Timmy loved the chance to talk about himself, but the not-so-improved street-me didn't. At least not about what had split me in half. I was just coming to terms with all of it myself. Each member of the group downstairs had grown comfortable with their past, like coming to terms with shoes that didn't fit anymore. Theirs were all long-term, falling apart situations. But mine had been an all-of-a-sudden tearing apart. The shoes didn't fit because all that was left were the laces, too fragile to hold me together.

Barefoot would be better than accepting what Ray and his Blades' assholes had done. When I was sure no one was coming to yank me back to the circle, I curled up on the bed next to Skippy who had raced up the stairs with me. I turned on the TV and flipped to an old show on the Sci-Fi channel that I had once lived for. Watching Mulder and Scully helped me remember the good about my life, wrapping me in a warm blanket of memories Before.

When someone tapped on my door later, I pretended to be asleep. Skippy jumped up and stared at me, curious why I didn't answer. After one last try, the visitor left, and Skippy returned to my side. He sighed, and I wanted to bop him for making me feel guilty for not answering the door.

He sure was bossy for a mutt.

Chapter Forty-Three

"Dinner's ready, Tim," a voice mumbled through the door.

"Not hungry." I shot back. I couldn't face them and didn't know how to tell them I wasn't a baby. I even considered packing my things and hitting the road. *It wouldn't be the first time,* an ugly voice mocked. *Screw Christmas.*

Skippy stared at me as if to say *Fine for you, Daddy, you may not be hungry, but what about me?* The minute he'd heard the H-word, he had a one-track mind. I sat on the edge of the bed trying to decide what to do. I couldn't let Skippy starve, but my ego was at stake. I wanted to tell the mutt to suck it up, he'd certainly gone longer without eating. Much longer. The high-life had changed his mentality way quicker than it had me.

Mrs. Mahoney's voice floated like an angel's through the door.

"Here's a plate for you, dear. And a bowl for Skippy." She shuffled quickly away. My eyes filled with tears again, and I furiously rubbed them away.

I opened the door and thanked her, apologizing for not coming down. She turned on the top step and smiled.

"You know, Timmy, everyone has their crosses to bear, but doing it alone only makes it heavier. Erik feels horrible for pushing you, but I think he really likes you. You and him are a lot alike, and I think he's pretty excited to have a friend here. Most of the boys are several years older or quite a bit younger. He said you two were supposed to watch a movie together later. Are you still up for that?"

Screw Erik, I wanted to snip, the anger always hovering. But then the more I thought about it, I decided maybe spending a little time just vegging in front of the TV might be okay. Less threatening with just Erik than in a circle with everyone staring at me.

My therapy was beginning, even if I couldn't do group,

Mrs. M helped me realize there were other ways to mend.

"I'll think about it," I compromised. But I wouldn't make any promises.

"If you want dessert later, I've baked a cake. It's Rico's ninth birthday today. Come down if you want. We'll cut it around nine o'clock, when everyone has gotten home." She turned to head on down the stairs and called over her shoulder. "If you don't come, I'll save you a piece."

I glanced at the alarm clock by my bed. It was six-thirty. Erik had said we'd watch the movie at ten. I had a few hours to eat and get my bearings straight before I had to decide. I picked up the plate Mrs. Mahoney had left – fried chicken, mashed potatoes with gravy, and green beans. Beside it there was a giant glass of milk and a small brown bowl of wet dog food for Skippy.

"Whoa, boy, no wonder you like her so much. Canned dog food. You're eatin' high on the hog, aren'tcha?" It was a favorite saying of Max's anytime I scored big.

He wagged that *yes, he liked this lifestyle just fine*. I felt the same when I took my first bite of fried chicken, chewing it slow and letting the flavors roll around my mouth. I moaned, and Skippy glanced up from his bow, his tail doing the moaning for him. It rivaled my mom's, complete with washing it down with milk. I'd had more milk today than I'd had in four months total. When you begged for dinner, it wasn't exactly kosher to request a drink. I was lucky if I drank anything with meals at all. City parks with water fountains provided most of my daily beverages, and when they shut them off in the winter, I resorted to bathroom faucets.

I remembered once when Louie, an Italian cook, gave me a cup of wine with a plateful of linguini.

"Kids in Italy and France start drinking vino at birth, you know? Enjoy, boy, enjoy!"

I didn't really like the taste, but I loved the way it made my head dizzy and warm all at the same time. I could see why Max liked the feeling so much, but if one tiny cup of wine did it to me, why did he have to drink so much? The memory made me wonder if I would ever call Max. The jury was still out on that one.

After savoring the fried chicken dinner, I licked my fingers until I thought I might be removing skin. Then I started feeling bad for not helping with the dishes. I swallowed my pride and hoped it would settle well with all the food I had just eaten. The stomach cramps weren't nearly as bad as some I'd had, but I knew I needed to stay close to the bathroom.

"Let's go, Skip. I can't bail on my duties. It wouldn't be fair. I don't want 'em to think I'm a freeloader." I slipped into the kitchen, washed my own plate in the sink of sudsy water, rinsed it, and placed it in the drainer. Four of them were still at the table, but no one said a word to me. I appreciated that more than they could imagine. I picked up a washrag and wiped a counter clean that Haley hadn't gotten to yet, and she smiled. I grinned nervously.

At seven o'clock, I knew all of them would gather on the three couches, two chairs, and bean bags scattered on the floor to watch TV in the Great Room. There was a system for what shows were watched when, because anyone could go to their respective rooms at any time if they preferred something else. I admired their organization and how strictly everyone adhered to it. If only it had been that easy with Sam and me. Sometimes we would argue just for the sake of arguing. Kind of like Scott and Stephie.

The group settled in for a sit-com marathon. I was stunned when *Friends* came on, and I had seen it. I'd never cared for the show when Mom watched it, and the irony that I had actually seen the episode nearly sent me into hysterics. Everyone kept saying and doing things to crack me up, and I found that I loved their attention. That kind anyway. It had been a long time.

"You're easy to crack up, Timmy," one of the older boys

said. I couldn't remember his name. *Philip? Andrew?*

After sit-coms, everyone insisted we watch *ER,* then we ate cake, laughed, and bonded in that Great Room. I knew it was called great because of its size, but I figured everyone would agree it wasn't the only reason. When Erik and I left the comfort of that room, it was like leaving warm covers to tread through a cold house to pee in the middle of the night.

"What're they gonna watch?"

"Ah, they watch the news every night at ten. Haley and Todd are really into current events and staying up on things, as they put it. *Blair Witch* will beat the heck outta anything they watch. Haley rented it yesterday, and I've seen it three times already. Scared the crap outta me the first time."

"Seriously?" I chuckled. There were some movies I'd watch over and over, but in one day? I'd usually agree about the news, but I made a quick "note-to-self:" *watch the news in bed tonight.* It would feel good to get caught up on the world.

Mom and Dad had always turned on the news at ten o'clock. They didn't watch much television, except Mom's fixation on *Law and Order* and Dad's sports, but they always caught the news.

"Hey, I'm real sorry about earlier," Erik said, when we were finally alone. I had hoped he would just leave it be, but I appreciated the apology. I tossed him my remote, happy that we had chosen my room. I wasn't ready for a sleepover, even if it was just a few doors away.

"That's okay."

"You think your story is so different, homie? I mean, no disrespect, man, but we all been there, done that, knowwudImean?" His face was serious, and much darker when he wasn't smiling. I suspected he had the whitest teeth I'd ever seen.

And I didn't know what he meant, not humored by his run-together expression this time. I doubted any of them had their brain shut off after watching their family get murdered. Then get swindled by an old man to live in a box, eat what they could scrounge from dumpsters, and kill when his hand was forced.

A crack mother might not be the best life, but at least you have one.

"Sure. I'm just not ready to talk about it, knowwudImean?" I tried to smile, to tease his favorite phrase. I loved his slang but I hated the way he called everyone his *homie*. He said it was from some movie he had just seen, but I thought it made him sound like a drug dealer. And that image didn't fit Erik at all. He looked more like the little kid on *Independence Day* than a gangbanger. And I would know.

"You ain't never gonna be ready if you block it out, Tim. I'm just lookin' out for ya, knowwudImean? C'mon, homie, you gotta accept who ya are. It's awright to feel sorry for yourself, but we all been there, done that, knowwudImean?"

I forced a smile. I knew Erik didn't mean anything bad by it, but sometimes I thought his message got lost in his lingo.

"Yeah, I know. You're a rocket scientist, Erik. But trust me, I ain't blockin' nothin' out. That's part of my problem. I blocked it all out for a long time. Now it's like kickin' my butt. I just need some time to get used to it, knowwudImean?"

He cackled at my mockery of him. He hit *play,* and we yelled at the idiots for going into the woods, Erik jabbering about this being real. I tried my best not to jump every time a stick cracked in the woods. Jeremy slipped in sometime in the middle and watched with us. Just having him around gave me the comfort Sam's presence used to. And without the teasing. With Skippy's warm furry head on my arm and Jeremy lying next to us, I felt safer than I had since I lived on Catalina Avenue.

When the movie ended, Erik slid off to bed barely able to keep his eyes open. My street life had turned me into a night owl. I was at peace with a full day off the street under my belt and a security net of four walls around me. Jeremy rolled off the bed rubbing his eyes.

"Hey, get a good night's sleep. Tomorrow's Christmas Eve. We'll have a heck of a breakfast in the morning. Mrs. Mahoney loves every opportunity to cook a spread. G'night, Timster."

One of the many nicknames my family, primarily Sam, used for me brought a flicker of pain, a memory lost. Jeremy saw it as he was leaving.

"Sorry. You sure have some serious ghosts, Timmy. I've never seen someone with so much turmoil. Most of us come here itching to share what's happened to us. Kind of a kid's nature to unleash, you know?" Jeremy's easy expression showed no sign of badgering, even though I felt the pressure.

Then something seemed to click. Jeremy turned and took me in with a look so understanding, I felt the urge to throw my arms around his neck.

"You feel guilty," he declared, then he repeated his revelation again as if he hadn't heard himself or he feared I hadn't heard him. "You feel guilty." He knew there was something deeper to my story, and I wanted to try to tell it.

I could tell you, but then I'd have to kill you, Sam used to say when I wanted to know his secrets. The thought, too close to home, made me shudder.

Then the words started to form, but nothing would come out of my mouth. I wanted to tell him everything, to spill it all, but I just couldn't. There was just so much baggage, I didn't know where to begin.

When the door closed and I heard Jeremy thump down the stairs, I slipped off the bed and retrieved my Ked's box. I sifted through my bottle caps, the baseball cards, fingered the roll of bills. Some were still speckled with blood – Trash Boy's blood. I shivered. Skippy licked my face to let me know he still loved me.

I couldn't believe two worlds could exist within a few miles of one another. That I could really be sitting on a bed in a home with people who seemed to genuinely care about me even though they just met me. Billy could learn some lessons from them.

After twenty minutes of going through my stuff, I put the lid on and motioned for Skippy to come on. We plodded down the stairs. It was after midnight, but I hoped Jeremy hadn't gone to bed.

I found him at the kitchen table reading the sports section. Mrs. M, sipping coffee across from him, had the front page.

"Hi." I placed the box on the table and slid it in front of Jeremy.

Mrs. M got up and left without a single word. She kissed my head and said goodnight on her way out, and I dropped into her seat.

When Jeremy opened it, I pointed to the folded article that I had laid on top. As he picked them up, he glanced at the baseball cards beneath them. *For Sam* stared up at him, but he unfolded the pages instead of acknowledging McGwire's face.

"Officer killed, family found slain, youngest child missing, believed kidnapped," he read aloud. "Jesus, Timmy."

He scanned the article, the pictures, and I could read the expression on his face. Disbelief. No one could imagine the road I had traveled. All our stories were tragic, but mine had the drama of a bad TV movie. No matter how much they said we all had in common, I knew better. It pissed me off every time I heard it.

"Go on, read it," I muttered, but I dropped my gaze unable to make eye contact. I studied the pattern of the oak table – the lines and swirls on one leaf darker than the others. But then Jeremy began reading aloud. I didn't want to stop him, but the words burned into me like a branding iron. *I didn't mean out loud,* I wanted to say, but he had already started.

"Sergeant Amos Thompson, 28, of the St. Ann Police Department was pronounced dead on arrival from injuries suffered in a crash with three other vehicles on Stanton Street in Northern St. Louis. A Ballwin family was found brutally murdered at the scene." Jeremy paused. I avoided his gaze, waiting for him to continue. I just wanted him to finish.

"Officer Kevin Rodriguez, one of the first to respond to the 911 call placed by a neighbor, said the nature of the crime was still being investigated. Each victim was shot with a high-caliber automatic pistol. Robert Weaver, 39; Victoria Weaver, 36; and Samuel Weaver, 15; all died of gunshot wounds and numerous blows to the head and body, probably post-mortem. The youngest Weaver, Timothy, was believed to be with the family at the time of the shootings. His blood was found at the scene; however, at this time, the child has not been found."

Jeremy sighed. "Damn." He took a deep breath, glanced my way, and continued. My heart, weighed down with guilt, raced with apprehension. Reliving that night made my stomach churn and my palms sweat. Hearing it out loud felt surreal.

"Two assailants, Shaun Holmes and Ezekial Cawdel, both known Blades' gang members, were pronounced dead at University Hospital, suffering from gunshot wounds. Two vehicles, witnesses say, pursued the family. A Chevrolet Impala and a Plymouth convertible forced the Weavers' Cadillac Escalade into an approaching police car responding to a 911 call by the Weavers." He paused and glanced up at me. "I've heard of the Blades. They're rough," Jeremy said. "What was your family doing in Blades' territory?"

"We – we were pickin' Sam up from the airport. He was getting back from – from a foreign exchange thing in Chicago. And they chased us way north, I think. I'm not sure. I'm not so good with directions." That was a bit of an understatement, but I was certainly in no mood to elaborate.

Jeremy took a breath and kept reading.

"Timothy Ryan Weaver, eleven years of age, has blond hair, blue eyes, and stands approximately four feet ten inches tall. He was last seen wearing a gray Nike windbreaker, blue jeans, and Adidas tennis shoes. He may be the victim of abduction and is believed to be seriously injured. If you have any information leading to the boy's whereabouts, please notify authorities immediately. The police are canvassing the area thoroughly in an effort to locate the boy." Jeremy scanned the last few sentences but read silently. His sigh said plenty.

"What kind of injury did you have?"

"Cuts on my face, bruises." I traced the scar on my left cheek. "I also had a pretty bad bump on my head, but...but that came later," I whispered.

"It sounds like they thought you were really hurt." Jeremy's eyes, warm and comforting, searched mine.

"When I bit him – Zeke. I bit Zeke on the hand 'cause he kept smacking me. He cut me with a ring, I think. God, it all seems like it happened to someone else."

Jeremy pulled the last page forward.

"Oh, God, Timmy. You printed the obituaries. Why?"

"I – I wanted to have.... God, I don't know. I was so sick when I saw it. I just did." But I did know. I wanted everything that spoke of my mom, my dad, and my brother. It was the last connection I had with them. The last moment in time we were all four together. When I read our names again, I didn't even realize what the two-inch article was. Our names in bold letters at the top didn't mean much to me. It wasn't like I had ever read an obituary before.

Jeremy read it slowly, quietly, as if delivering our eulogy. I felt like my heart was being wrenched out of my chest and through my throat. I couldn't swallow.

"Robert Douglas Weaver, age 39, Victoria Lynn Weaver, age 36, Samuel Jacob Weaver, age 15, and Timothy Ryan Weaver, age 11, are survived by their dear friends Michael and Sarah Monroe, Caleb and Laura Matthews, and Charles and Beth Kruschaven. The Kruschaven family has set up a trust in honor of the Weavers to help battle gang violence and increase awareness. If you would like to donate money or volunteer time, contact Mrs. Kruschaven at 555-9186." He paused, then added, "Wow, they thought you died." Jeremy looked up, as if a light bulb suddenly clicked on above his head.

I saw the look in his eyes and knew immediately what he was thinking. The idea of it brought back the butterflies from the day on the pay phone.

"Why didn't you ever call them? Weren't you close?"

"Yeah, you could say that." I grimaced. *Like one of the family,* I almost muttered.

"So why didn't you call them?" His eyes, though gentle, unleashed something inside of me.

"Max told me, he had me believing I would put them in danger. And...and I believed him, because I...I..." But tears clogged my throat. Then the dam broke. "Because I killed those guys. I held that gun, pulled that trigger, and blew that guy's brains out. And then shot again and again and again. The blood was everywhere. One of the guys hit me, dropped me, I think, but I don't remember. And...and...." The sobs hitched in my chest, but now the fury came unleashed. "Ray and Zeke and Speed, they...they...." I couldn't get air, the sobs robbing my lungs of precious breath. I felt the strangling clutches of Zeke's hands around my throat.

"It's okay, Timmy, I'm sorry. I gotcha'." Jeremy put his arm around my shoulders, but I shoved him away.

"I just kept shooting. One of them charged me, and I shot him. Then I just kept shooting, and I knew I had gotten someone else because I heard him fall, and they were all screamin'. I did bad things that night. And I...I ran. I couldn't save them. Mom, she...you should've seen it, Jeremy, she couldn't get him to let go of her. And Sam, oh, God, Sam's face was in the pavement, and they...they...." But the image of my brother's head being slammed into the ground broke a valve. The enormous pressure in my chest made it hard to breathe, and I bawled like a crybaby. But I couldn't stop. I heaved, I choked on the salty, snotty tears, and hitched as the sobs came too hard and too fast.

Snot fell in a string from my nose, and I wiped it away with my sleeve. I felt Jeremy's arm around my shoulder again, and this time I let it stay. He handed me a box of Kleenex.

"I stabbed a guy at a buffet, too. Only two or three weeks after. Then I threatened someone who tried to swipe my box around Thanksgiving. And just yesterday, or Tuesday, I don't remember, I stuck a kid by Ruth Park. I'm hardcore, Jeremy, they're gonna put me in juvie. The judge'll throw away the key. I'm a repeat offender, that's what Max said. Three strikes and you're out. And I don't wanna be out. Max said they'd put me in juvie, and that all those things I did would be held against me." I wailed, unable to control the pain ripping through my chest, tearing me apart inside.

I bawled like there was no tomorrow.

"To hell with Max...I don't know him, but I don't like him already. You were defending yourself, Tim. And I bet it's safe to say that survival required a degree of violence on your part or you would've been killed. I've knifed my fair share. Not to mention the guy's face I shoved a busted beer bottle into. He grabbed his own and did this." He pointed to his forehead. "No judge threw me in juvie, and I jumped that guy first. You did bad things, Timmy, but you did them because you had to. You're the victim, not the criminal. You didn't choose for them to murder your family. You didn't choose to be left without a home. And you sure as shit didn't deserve some old man filling your head with shit. Right? You're gonna need a lot of therapy, but you don't belong in a jail." Jeremy rubbed my back and handed me more Kleenex.

A weight suddenly lifted, and I laid my exhausted head against his arm. Skippy licked the tears from my hands and pushed his head underneath one of them so I would pet him. For the first time in forever, I thought of Trevor. Maybe he had been more Sam's dog than mine, but I wondered where he was, if he was still alive. Would he remember me if he saw me now?

When all the tears dried and five million Kleenexes lay scattered around me, Jeremy led me to my bed and said goodnight. He pulled the covers up under my chin and told me to sleep tight. I thanked him.

"We have a plan, Stan," he said with a wink and left my room.

Saviors come in all shapes and sizes, Father Myers had told me the night he let me in. I watched one of them leave my room so I could sleep, while the other curled up at my feet.

Chapter Forty-Four

"Oh, God!" I bolted upright in bed, bathed in sweat and panting as if I had just run a mile.

Skippy let out a sharp yap, ready to attack whoever had me in such a tizzy.

"God, Skippy, I dreamed we were bein' chased by the *Blair Witch*. Oh man."

Skippy wagged his tail with a *Yeah, whatever, Dad*, and laid his head back down.

"You're so clueless, Skip. But I sure love ya." That brought on a more excited wag, the kind that shook his whole hind end.

I remembered why I was so apprehensive. I forced myself to stay under the covers, hoping maybe Jeremy would forget the mission he had set in place for me. I imagined my freight train of a world hurtling into a future so uncertain, I couldn't slow it down quick enough to jump off.

Skippy's tail thumped on the comforter beside me when he saw my eyes open again.

"What're you lookin' at, you goof?" As usual, the mutt refused to answer, but I knew what he was thinking.

Get your butt up.

"But it ain't time to get up, is it?"

My pushy mutt just kept staring at me, and I knew he wasn't going to give up.

"Fine." I crawled out of bed. I pulled on my clean but tattered jeans and walked downstairs slow enough to gather moss. From the foyer, I smiled at the Christmas tree's blinking bulbs. I had risen before the sun, just shy of 6:30, and seeing the dark room sparkle made me want to curl up on a couch and stare at it for hours – anything to keep from facing today's job.

"C'mon, Sam, let's just take a peek. Mom and Dad won't be up for another hour."

"Jesus, Timmy, you'll ruin everything, and you know it.

Lay down with me for a little bit, then we'll go down."

"All right." I slipped under his covers and sighed. Didn't they know it was Christmas?

A wave of dizziness accompanied the memory, but I steadied myself by holding the edge of the couch. An ache settled in the pit of my stomach reminding me how vulnerable I still was. And how lonely. As strange as it felt, I missed Max.

When I heard the clank of silverware on plates, I shuffled through the kitchen door forgetting the anxiety I had felt only minutes earlier. A few of the rezzies were already sitting at the table eating.

"You're up early. Merry Christmas Eve, by the way," Mrs. M said, as she handed me an empty plate. "Help yourself, hon. Eggs, sausage, and biscuits. I'm making gravy right now, so be patient." I saw all the bowls, some with dents of food already taken.

My head spun. Mom used to make biscuits and gravy so awesome, Sam and I would eat until our bellies rounded like bowling balls. I smiled in spite of a heart that had been shattered and pieced together too many times to recognize. It was a wonder it was still beating at all.

Jeremy waltzed into the kitchen and acted shocked to see me up with the roosters, as he put it. He grabbed his own plate and heaped a pile of eggs on top of a biscuit. He crumbled three pieces of bacon on top and held it in front of Mrs. Mahoney like Max used to at the soup kitchens. "Please, suh, could I have some mo'?" Max used to slur. He explained that he was Oliver Twist, but I didn't know who that was. I just thought the accent he used was funny.

"It's not ready, Jeremy. Give me a minute, okay?"

"Sure, Mrs. M." Jeremy took his plate and plopped down at the table next to Haley and started eating. "Must have a reason to be down here so early," he said to me nonchalantly.

"Maybe I have places to go." I wanted to add that in the alley, I always got up this early, because the best handouts happened at opening time.

"You have time to eat first?" Jeremy's grin was contagious. "Or you leavin' us before you even get settled in?"

"What is this, another interrogation?" I returned his sly smile, managing a little sarcasm of my own.

He play-punched me on the chin, careful to steer clear of my nose, eye, and lip. The swelling had gone down, and the colors had toned down, now less purple and tinged with more yellow. Not as pretty, I thought. In another time, I would have boasted about the awesome bruises, a mark of durability.

Haley watched our exchange and furrowed her brow. "You already have a plan, Tim?"

"Sort of." I watched Jeremy smooth his wild head of hair. He had made every effort to tame it, and I wanted to know what it looked like without the ponytail. Tiny sprigs of wispy hair seemed eager for freedom. Several around his forehead had found it, too short to be restrained by the black band. "Maybe. But first I'm going to brush my teeth, get a job, maybe buy a car. Heck, I've got all day!" I grinned, but I saw Jeremy studying me.

Haley, Rico, and Erik cracked up. Haley had bed-head and told Erik and Rico they were lucky they didn't have to worry about their hair.

"Whatever. I gotta grease this stuff every day, dog. My scalp's sensitive, knowwudImean?" Erik stroked a hand across his head, then wiped it on a paper towel.

Rico added that his cornrows took hours, and he was thankful several of the girls knew how to do it. It helped, he said, or he'd sport a fro Monday through Thursday.

"Okay, funny guy, how about giving me a few minutes of your time after breakfast?" Jeremy asked, and I looked to make sure he was talking to me.

I need a whole bunch of minutes... Remember, Momma? How many do you think it would take to fix my heart?

"Okay." The butterflies in my stomach took flight, but

Jeremy's grin was bigger than the St. Louis Arch. That helped ease the anxiety a little.

"So, you gotta make your plan today," Rico blurted. "Sounds like you got options. That's good."

"Give the kid a break, Rico," Haley scoffed. "He can do it today or tomorrow. I did mine yesterday."

"So what did you decide?" I was curious what she had chosen.

"Well, I have two really serious options. I came up with four, but living on my own and going to a boarding school don't really trip my trigger. So I'm leaning toward living with my grandmother or Melissa's family. If they'll have me."

I envied her list of choices. I had two. I continued nibbling on my eggs, but the food started tasting funny, tainted by the anxiety swelling in my chest.

"Hey, Tim, don't sweat it," Erik chipped in. "They'll give you time. I mean, you come up with a plan, you work it out, maybe change your mind. Heck, I been here nearly six weeks. Course, my options are a little different than yours. They're waitin' for my mom to dry out and get into rehab. You got a mom, Tim?"

Food nearly sprayed from my mouth. I coughed and had to cover it with a napkin to keep from losing any egg. I liked Erik, but he kept me on guard.

A hush fell over the table, and before I could think of what to say, Jeremy saved me.

"Erik, you ever think that some stories are better saved for a fireside chat? Not everyone lays it out like you do."

They all chuckled, because Erik bantered all the time about the chaos and filth of his childhood. He made no bones about living a hardcore life. It was his badge of honor.

"Sorry," Erik mumbled as a rosy color quickly filled his dark cheeks.

"You'd think you would have learned, bonehead." Haley smacked Erik on the arm with an audible pop.

He rubbed the spot gingerly. "Well, me and him are tight, knowwudImean? I thought he might tell me now."

I listened as they talked about me as if I weren't even there. Mom and Dad used to do that to Sam and me, and we hated it.

"She's dead, Erik," I stated matter-of-factly and rose to take my plate to the sink. I couldn't wash it because I couldn't see the sink. I tried to wipe the tears away with my shoulder, but I couldn't and didn't want to make it any more obvious that I was crying. Through the blur, I managed to set the plate on the counter. But remarkably, saying it out loud didn't hurt any more than the bright flash of pain that pierced through me every time I thought it.

Saying the words didn't make it any worse, just real.

"God, Erik," Rico muttered. "You're a dog."

"Man, I didn't know."

"Now you do. Learn some tact, Erik, or you're gonna swallow that foot whole next time," Jeremy scolded. I hated hearing them ride Erik. I didn't want him to resent me for it.

By the time I could see to wash and dry the few dishes left in the sink, Jeremy helped put them away.

"Okay, you're dreading it, so let's do it. The longer you put it off, the tougher it'll be."

"Okay," I whispered.

He led me into a dining area just off the kitchen. I hadn't spent much time in it, because when everyone ate together, there was a larger dining room on the other side of the kitchen. This den-like room was rich with family heritage. Every space was filled with pictures of Mrs. M's children and more photos of grandkids. We sat near the head of the table, Jeremy sliding a piece of paper in front of me and laid a pencil on top of it.

"At least three viable, I mean, doable options. List them on the right," he instructed, and I stared at the columns he had drawn. At the top, it said *Timmy Weaver's Plan for Success*. I cringed at the sight of it. It was time to put up or shut up.

I picked up the pencil and jotted one option on the massive empty space, the absent future the blank piece of paper implied. I wanted to write it big enough to fill ten lines, but instead I neatly printed the words.

Foster care.

Images of Sarah Chapman, of the boys bickering in the nearby room made me consider erasing it.

"Um, I think maybe I can't, I mean...."

"Yes, you can, Tim."

It reminded me of the night before Sam left for his eternal end-of-the-summer trip. He had called me Tim several times that night. *Tim,* like I was old. That was the night he gave me the ball cards.

The next time I saw him – when we picked him up at the airport – I nearly busted a gut waiting to show him those cards.

The flash of a gun's muffled report exploded in my brain, and then echoed before it faded. I tried to unthink the image of a man grasping Sam's head and smashing it into the ground.

Bile rose in my throat.

I quickly wrote *Kruschavens* and then *Matthews.*

"One more," he said. "Do you have family? Aunts or uncles?"

"No. Max lied to me. Said he was my grandpa, but Mom and Dad told us the story of losing my grandparents before I was born. You said three...this is three." I pointed to the families of my fellow musketeers. The idea that I had missed out on four months of their lives made me ache.

Worse yet, they had mourned my death and moved on. What else could they think when my body was never found, but my blood was there? The logical conclusion had been drawn. Hadn't the article even said as much?

"Okay, I'll give it to you. That's three, but I think the choice is a no-brainer, Tim. Isn't it?" Jeremy watched my expression closely.

My mouth felt sticky, my tongue had swollen to twice its

normal size. How could I call someone I thought of as a second family and tell them, *Hey, I know you thought I was dead, but actually, I've been living just north of the city in the nicest box. And sorry I never called. Max told me not to. Didn't wanna get arrested and all that.*

"What is it, Timmy? What're you thinkin'?"

"Why didn't I call them? Won't they wanna know?" I imagined that phone conversation, and a slew of butterflies got in a squabble in my stomach.

"You tell me." Jeremy sat back in his chair.

"Uh, I forgot the number?" I attempted a smile, but it felt pasted on. My lame attempt at humor felt almost sacrilegious in light of the topic.

"C'mon, Timmy, think. What went through your head that first day, before Max found you and started feedin' you his lines?"

My brain swirled with the memories, trying to wake the sleeping demons from my past. I had been so scared, I remembered that, but why didn't I just go straight to a pay phone and dial 911?

Because I had been bad, that's why. My brain had snapped after I had murdered Zeke. And I'd wanted to, after what they'd done to my family. Even when I couldn't remember, I *knew* the police would just cart me away to prison. I had watched my fair share of *Cops*. I pulled that trigger and experienced anger unlike any emotion I had ever known.

It seemed stupid now, but what eleven-year-old understood the concept of self-defense? In a fist fight maybe, but not when your family had been brutally murdered and you had squeezed off a round into a gangbanger's head. And then several more into how many others?

But they deserved it.

"I thought I was bad. A criminal, you know? Because I wanted to kill them, I wanted to kill every one of them. If I could've gone back and finished them, I would've. I was covered with blood, and honest to God, I really thought I would go to jail for the rest of my life. I was so totally out of it, I had to have looked like a serial killer."

"Okay, so our logical choice is here." Jeremy pointed to my best friends' last names. They had written me out of their lives, probably gone to my funeral, and accepted that D'Artagnan had perished in battle. No matter how much they might have missed me, I was dead to them now.

"What do I say?" I couldn't fathom how I could possibly make that phone call. How did I explain? The minute one of them answered the phone and heard me say who I was, wouldn't they hang up thinking I was some cruel prank caller?

I shared my thoughts with Jeremy.

"Tell you what, I'll call them and explain the facts. I'll let it sink in, then I'll let you talk to them. How's that sound?"

The room pressed in on me, like a shaft with walls that moved in until the garbage is smashed, destroyed, and ready to toss out on the curb. I felt like that trash.

"Thank you." I could barely whisper. I worried that when it came my turn to talk, my voice might not work.

"Let's do it before you totally go noodles on me." He dashed into the living room, grabbed the cordless, and pulled a slip of paper from his jeans pocket.

"What's that?" My voice already had a tremor to it. "It's awfully early...not even quite 8:00 yet." I glanced at my Tigger watch. *7:45*. I knew Scott would be up, especially on Christmas Eve. Brent was the one who slept all day.

"It's the Kruschaven's number. Is that the one you wanna call? And it's never too early for something like this." Jeremy held the phone in front of him, ready to punch in the numbers.

"I could've told you the number," I muttered. "Ask for Beth or Charlie. They were like second parents to me." I trembled. Had he known all along what choice I would make?

He had the number in his freakin' pocket.

"Gotcha."

Next thing I knew, Jeremy Gardner was asking for Beth Kruschaven. My past and present were on course for a head-on collision. Someone else had answered – probably Stephie, only a week after our encounter at Union Station. *That was less than a week ago.* It seemed impossible. Or what if Jeremy had just spoken to Scott?

Aramis lives.

I ached to tell him that D'Artagnan was alive and well.

"Uh, ma'am, you don't know me, but my name is Jeremy Gardner. I'm a social worker and chapter president of the Big Brothers of America here in St. Louis. I have some really strange news I need to share with you."

Silence, so I knew Mrs. Kruschaven must be trying to figure out the phone call. Prankster or legitimate? I suddenly felt guilty for springing this on them on Christmas Eve.

"Yes, ma'am. Well, do you remember the evening in late August when the Weavers were murdered?"

I couldn't imagine what Jeremy was thinking, and the visions I was having of Mrs. Kruschaven on the other end, the waiting. It was more than I could stand. I stood and paced around the end of the table, my heart thudding in my ears. I couldn't even imagine what Mrs. Kruschaven was feeling.

"I know. I was just reading the article from the *Post-Dispatch*, and I also read the obituary. What you did with the donations, ma'am, that was really awesome." Jeremy fell silent again, this time nodding, waiting to talk in response to things Mrs. K was saying.

I remembered the Christmas break when Sam and I stayed with them while Mom and Dad went on their New Year's cruise. I wondered if she was still as beautiful as Sam thought she was. For an adult, four months wasn't that long, not like the dog-year feel for a near teenager.

I would giggle at Sam's drooling, but all I knew was that Mrs. K treated me like family, baked us cookies, made real Chex Mix in the oven, and went to the trouble to make fancy meat and cheese trays for football games on the weekends.

My mind had ventured into la-la land, and I missed part of the conversation Jeremy and Mrs. Kruschaven were having about my future. A phone call that could change my life and I had chosen to daydream.

"...I know it's hard to believe, Mrs. Kruschaven, but he's here. He's sitting next to me right now. Blond hair, blue eyes, and pretty ratty lookin', I might add." Jeremy's eyes clouded a little, and I panicked. I saw tears in his eyes, and I couldn't imagine what Beth Kruschaven had said to cause them. I gritted my teeth trying to suppress the anger building in my chest.

God, she's telling him she's already closed that chapter of her life. Max told me that's what all of them would do. They would go on, accept that I was gone, and not think another thing about me. Fond memories but the horror of our deaths would make us too difficult to think about, he had said.

"On the streets, ma'am. He's been homeless this whole time, fighting for his life. That's what brought him to us, to Mrs. Mahoney's here in Chesterfield. Would you like to speak to him?"

Time stood perfectly still. I watched my hand reach for that phone, but it seemed to belong to someone else. Then Jeremy shook his head. The brimming tears spilled and streamed down his face. I watched Jeremy cry as he held my future in his hands.

My heart ripped, shredded into a million little pieces. Rejection washed over me with such bitterness, I wanted to scream. Instead, I lay my head on the table and cried. Jeremy kept talking, but I couldn't hear a thing.

I was a liar now, too, because I really was a crybaby. Skippy whined at my feet, but I couldn't reach out to him. My life was crashing down around me. How much further could I fall? I wanted to scream, throw things, break anything I could find.

I choked on the emotion and tried picturing myself in a foster home. Would it be as nice as Mrs. Mahoney's or something out of a gut-wrenching novel?

I heard Jeremy hang up the phone. "She...she...." my throat

clogged with emotion and tears. I swallowed hard. "She didn't want to talk to me?"

That searing anger welled up inside of me, my fists clenched causing my fingernails to dig into my palms. I gritted my teeth and wanted to thump someone, throw something, break anything.

"She was crying so hard, Tim, she said she wanted to talk to you, but she just couldn't." Jeremy's voice was husky with emotion. I resented his tears. *What the hell are you so upset about?* My body wavered, my brain threatening to check out. I thought about rushing out the front door and never looking back. If I had my pack, it would have topped my new list of best options.

"Wh – what – di – did sh – she say?" My words hitched around the heaving in my chest. I could barely breathe, much less talk. I searched Jeremy's eyes. Why had this affected him so much?

His mouth began to spread into a huge grin, widening until I thought his whole face would be consumed by it. It wasn't the Arch-sized smile from earlier but close.

"She's on her way, Timmy. Said she'd be here in about forty-five minutes."

Chapter Forty-Five

Jeremy swiveled in the desk chair toward me, while Skippy and I sat on the edge of my bed.

"First, I'm gonna have a chat with her, Timmy. You can give her a hug and all that, but then I'm going to take her in the kitchen and just talk for a minute. This is a big step, and I don't want it to overwhelm you. There's a protocol to all this. I know that doesn't make a lot of sense to you, but it's kind of like re-introducing a prisoner to society. Sorry for the analogy, but you get what I mean."

"Yeah. But I will get to go with her, right?" I had showered, treated the cuts, but couldn't do anything about the jagged bangs and haunted eyes. How long would it take before the veil would be lifted and I could see the *real* me?

"For a while. But we need to take this slow. You're not going to just pack your bags and head off into the hills. Right now, you're actually a ward of the court, do you know what that means?"

"It means I don't belong to anybody. That I don't have any control over what happens to me and that I might as well be homeless again," I snapped. That ugly feeling roared inside of me. I wanted to scream that none of this was fair. I would've kicked dirt if there had been any available.

"Hey, Timmy, it doesn't mean any of that. But you don't have parents, so someone has to act as your guardian. For now, that's us, so don't snub your nose at it. We're not turnin' you over to just to anyone. That's the reason we're takin' this slow." Jeremy held my gaze.

"Whaddaya mean?" I furrowed my brow, ready to argue for myself.

"I mean you're gonna be pissed at the world for a while. I remember, because I was too. So we've gotta make sure you don't take all of this too fast. You'll have counseling, lots of time to get used to being a kid again. And you're gonna need it. It may seem like the most logical thing for you to go with the Kruschavens, but there's a lot more to it than that." Jeremy paused, letting it all soak in.

"How long?" Hadn't I waited long enough?

"I can't even make that guess. It'll depend on you and them. We still have to make sure this is the right fit for you."

"What's that supposed to mean? You think I need you to make my decisions? I've done just fine for four months without your help. What if I'd called them myself? I wouldn't have to go through all this crap!" I realized I was nearly shouting, the heat in my face surprising me. I felt instantly ashamed for what I had said but not for the sentiment. I *could* take care of myself.

"Whoa, Tim. First of all, you've always had someone to take care of you. Max helped you during those four months, and really, so did Skippy. Now, it's gonna be me and Mrs. Mahoney with some help from Erik, Mrs. Kruschaven, and your old friends. This is not gonna be easy. And if you had called them yourself, social services would still have gotten involved. Mrs. Kruschaven would've needed help to get you into school. And there's one small detail you may not realize." Jeremy stopped, stared at me long and hard.

"What?"

"You didn't die. Your parents had insurance, Mrs. Kruschaven said, and all that trust money. I mean, heck, kid, there may be an estate to be settled on your behalf. You'll want the courts on your side. We *will* have to go through the DYS system."

My head swam. I didn't want money. I didn't want to go through anything associated with DYS. And I sure didn't want to think about insurance, because I didn't understand it. I just wanted a home.

"Hey, Tim! You got company!" Mrs. Mahoney shouted up the stairs.

I jumped. *This is it.*

Jeremy stood, waved his hand for me to go in front of him. My heart thudded. I inhaled, tried to calm jittery nerves, then straightened my new Big Brothers of America T-shirt.

"You'll be fine." He rubbed my back affectionately.

The stairs seemed to lengthen as I stepped down them one at a time, extending like a hallway in a bad movie. I wondered if she would look the same. *Should I race up to her and hug her or be cool and wait for her to hug me? What if she sees me and decides she's made a mistake? Am I clean enough so the sight of me wouldn't send her screaming back to her car?*

The thoughts, questions, and uncertainties swirled around me as I turned the corner into the foyer. I regretted for a split second not wearing the nicer shirt Jeremy had offered.

My breath suddenly caught in my throat. My mouth fell open slightly but turned up quickly into a hesitant smile. I couldn't believe my eyes. It hadn't occurred to me that Scott might come, but he had. Aramis stood at least two inches taller than me, huskier, but the look on his face tore me apart.

Pity.

He tried to mask it, but I caught it before it vanished. But could I blame him? Wouldn't I have felt sorry for some homeless kid back in The Musketeer days? Before I could process it, absorb that my best friend was standing in front of me, Mrs. Kruschaven smothered me with such untethered emotion, I burst into tears right along with her. Scott wrapped his arms around the two of us, so we stood in a three-way hug for what felt like a blissful eternity.

"I don't even know what to say, Timmy," Mrs. Kruschaven started. But I held up my hand, stopping her.

"Please don't feel sorry for me. I don't want that, I just want—" Then I paused. *Don't lie to them.* "I don't know what I want, but not that."

Scott took a step back and sized me up. I felt an uneasiness between us, an awkward space filled with the four months he had lived and I had merely survived.

I furrowed my brow. What the heck did that expression mean? I could hear Mrs. Mahoney introduce herself to Mrs. Kruschaven and then Jeremy did the same.

"You're short," Scott finally said. Just like that, his first words after four months away from his best friend, and that was the best he could do?

"You're fat," I retaliated, and the two of us busted out laughing. Once the ice was broken, it was like time had never passed. He put an arm easily around my shoulder and squeezed my neck. I marveled at Scott's biceps, how buff he was and knew I must feel like a twig to him.

Don't bend me. I might break.

Mrs. Kruschaven wiped the tears from her cheeks and eyes, then took me by the hand.

"Timmy, we have someone who will really want to see you. Can we take him for a few hours?" She glanced to Mrs. M for permission, but it was Jeremy who piped in.

"Can we chat real quick first? Then he's all yours for the day, how's that?" Jeremy motioned her toward the kitchen and head waved Scott to come, too. Mrs. Mahoney held the door for them and smiled at me as she closed the door.

I stared, feeling like a child having a toy yanked from his grubby hands. I remembered once in second grade when the class had to vote for the president of some stupid play we were having. The teacher made Larry McElvaney and me wait out in the hall while the class raised hands in favor of him or me. I had that same feeling now, and wondered if the result would be similar. Larry won thirteen to ten. I spent the rest of that day trying to figure out who had voted against me.

"Hey, you wanna sit in here, or do you wanna listen? It's okay either way." Erik nodded toward the Great Room.

"Leave me alone," I grumbled. "I don't know what I want. Shit." Confusion swirled inside me like a tornado.

But Erik stayed in the entryway to the Great Room. He crossed his arms and leaned against the wall. I tried not to look over at him, because I could tell he wanted to talk. I just wanted him to go away so I could eavesdrop.

"C'mere." He pulled me by the arm to the wall next to the kitchen. He dragged two chairs from the dining room just off the foyer and plopped down in one of them. He tapped the seat next to him. I followed his lead and couldn't help but grin.

"You're sneaky," I whispered.

"Yeah," he said, and promptly flattened his ear to the wall. I did the same and couldn't believe how clearly I could hear them.

"...so if it's hard for him, what should I do?" Mrs. Kruschaven asked.

"Well, the key is to introduce everything slow. Don't expect him to be the same old Timmy. He's been through more than you or I could ever imagine. He's told me quite a bit, he's also read the articles that were in the *Post-Dispatch* a few days after the, uh, incident. Likewise, he needs to open up when he can. Don't push but don't be too passive either. You'll feel like you're walkin' on eggshells, but to break through, you might have to crack a few. But today, go easy. Be sympathetic but try not to be too emotional."

"I'm sorry," Mrs. Kruschaven said quickly. "I couldn't help myself. Bless his heart, he looks so small, so beat-up."

I choked back tears hearing her talk about me. I felt like a loser listening without her knowing. Erik seemed to know what I was feeling, because he pulled away from the wall, rubbed his ear dramatically like it was hurting, and smacked me on the shoulder.

Mrs. Mahoney added something but her voice was too soft to hear. It was almost as if she knew we were listening. Either that or I just felt guilty for doing it.

"Hey, look at Skippy," Erik said and pointed toward the couches. I turned to look and couldn't help but laugh. Skippy lay in the middle of a fluffy rug in front of the fireplace. But he wasn't curled up like a normal dog. Instead he lay spread-eagled on his back with his business hanging for everybody to see. His head lolled to one side with his tongue dangling between his teeth. Aside from the rise and fall of his tummy, he looked dead.

"You got one cute mutt. He's got more personality than most people, knowwudImean?"

"Yeah, I do. He's a ham is what he is." I smiled like a proud daddy and then stuck my ear back to the wall unable to resist the temptation. But I silently thanked Erik for the gesture. He didn't want me to hear anything that might hurt my feelings. Besides which Skippy was adorable. He liked this house-dog business.

"...so I might not. But yeah, you can talk about things. Just understand that he's got a lot of anger and guilt issues to deal with. He was there that night and survived it the best way he knew how."

"So how long can he stay with us today?" Scott's voice surprised me. It sounded like he really wanted to spend time with me, and that stirred my insides again. Even if he had pitied me for a split second, I had always been our leader. Would I ever be again?

Mrs. Mahoney answered Scott's question, but again I couldn't hear her.

"Here they come," Erik whispered frantically. He grabbed both our chairs, put them back around the enormous table in the dining room, and both of us rushed into the Great Room. Not knowing what else to do, we both suddenly dropped to the floor and started arm wrestling. It was more real than if we had plopped on the couch and twiddled our thumbs. The TV wasn't even on.

I made it look even more legitimate when they all came to the door and saw me whip Erik's butt by slamming his wimpy arm to the floor. His eyes went wide making him look a little like Buckwheat without the crazy hair.

"You're stronger'n you look, homie."

"I may be scrawny, but I pack some heat in these babies." I showed off my hard ball of a bicep.

"Hey, you two, sorry to break up the party, but would you mind if we stole the towhead?" Mrs. Kruschaven asked like she wanted Erik's permission. I thought it made him feel good.

"The what?" Erik raised his eyebrows in confusion.

"Towhead, you goof." I hit him on the arm. "Really blond hair is called a towhead."

"What a stupid name. Sounds like your foot's got a zit." Erik shook his head.

"Mrs. Kruschaven, Scott, meet Erik," Jeremy introduced with a laugh.

"God, I bet you two get along great. You got the exact same sense of humor."

I laughed at Scott's take on Erik, and I guessed it was true. Smart alecky with a flair for the one-liners. I hoped I could maybe come up with a few of my own to ease the tension I felt now. Otherwise, it was going to be an awkward day.

It beats the heck out of the last few holidays though, doesn't it?

I wanted to shout from the mountaintops that it did, it beat Halloween and Thanksgiving with a great big stick.

"Timmy, you ready? Six o'clock sound okay with you all?" Mrs. Kruschaven checked with Jeremy and Mrs. M. I nodded when she looked at me with the most sympathetic eyes I'd ever seen. Just looking at her made my heart ache for my family.

"We don't need to see his goofy mug until dinner. Use him and abuse him." Jeremy smacked me on the back.

Suddenly I felt odd, like a third wheel. I wanted to go with them forever, not be brought back and wonder when they would return.

"Thank you so much," she said to Jeremy and Mrs. Mahoney. Both shook her hand and told her to take care of me. Then Jeremy grabbed me and gave me a quick half hug, a sports hug, Sam would have called it.

"Hey, Timmy, are you hungry? It's only 11:00, but we can beat the rush." Mrs. K glanced at her watch the instant we stepped outside. I hoped she wouldn't feel the need to coddle me, and I almost wanted to tell her so. But the shy bug had bitten me.

"Um, sorta. I ate breakfast at 6:30." I wanted to add more, be conversational, but I just didn't know what to say. I wasn't hungry. My body was still adjusting to all the food.

"Well, let's go home for a bit, then we'll talk about lunch."

There was an odd pressure to fill the silence, afraid of what they might ask if I didn't. I climbed into the backseat of the same Lexus SUV I'd ridden in a million times. Scott rode shotgun but turned halfway in his seat so he could talk to me.

"Jeremy's pretty cool. And that Erik, he seems like a hoot. You like havin' someone as funny as you around?" Scott grinned. He had cut off his hair, but the smile was exactly the same.

"Who said he was funny?" I tossed back and couldn't help but grin at my comebacks. It had always been my specialty.

"Charlie will be so glad to see you, Timmy. He couldn't believe it when I told him. He's working a little today, but he'll be home pretty quick."

The Lexus pulled out into heavy traffic, and I remembered all the carpools Mom, Mrs. K, and Mrs. Matthews had always rotated with Brent, Scott, and me.

"Are you playing basketball?" I asked Scott, wanting to turn the attention away from me.

"Yeah. I'm not a starter though. We're not too hot either. You still fast as greased lightning?" Scott's easy manner felt comfortable, and I could sense his maturity. He had always been our loose cannon. Brent and I tamed the Tasmanian Devil, kept him out of trouble. Had someone taken my place? That thought had never occurred to me.

"Yeah, still pretty fast. You should see me and Skippy fly down by the Arch. We race the bikers sometimes." I caught myself before I went too in-depth. That world seemed so far away now, like a time that happened to someone else.

"Who's Skippy?"

"Ah, man, he's my dog. A terrier with a little mutt in him, too, but don't tell him. Been with me almost the whole time. He was the one loungin' in front of the fireplace, if you saw him." Talking about my sole companion of the past four months made me proud.

"You shoulda brought him." Scott asked if I wanted to go back. Maybe he sensed that my buddy might make me feel more comfortable.

"I don't mind," Mrs. K added, glancing at me in the rearview mirror.

"He'll be all right. He'll probably try to milk all the attention he can. Maybe you can meet him when we go back. But I warn you, he's a ham, and he's kinda bossy." I smiled, just talking about Skippy made the mood lighter.

Scott flipped on the radio and started bantering about his favorite new band, some alternative group I'd never heard of. But the chatter was nice, like the old days when we couldn't find the off button. Brent once said that Scott just had two speeds, *off* and *on*. There was no in-between. It was one of the things we had liked so much about him.

My heart raced when we drove by the Casey's store where The Three Musketeers had often performed – choosing sodas, irritating sales clerks.

We hadn't driven far. I knew when Jeremy had taken me to the Big Brother house that we had entered home territory. It had been a jolt. Now I felt like I was strapped in an electric chair. Mrs. K turned onto Bentley Street, coming in the back way – the next street would be Catalina.

Oh, God, my house. I'm gonna see my house.

I braced myself and felt Scott glance back at me. He finally turned and grinned.

"I can't believe it, Tim. You're really here," he stated

simply. "It's like a dream or somethin'. Dude, it's just so boss to see you."

"Yeah," I muttered, but my voice was barely audible. All the other encounters with places I had been before like Busch Stadium, the Dome, and the Arch couldn't compare. This was where I had lived, played, grown up. A flash of the morning I'd spied the Granville Auction sign in the front yard surfaced. I couldn't breathe as the Lexus steered left onto Catalina. Two small dark-headed girls toddled by on training-wheeled bikes. Tassels on the handles fluttered in the wind.

I remember the playing cards I used to put in my Huffy's spokes so it would flap-flap-flap down the street.

"You okay?" I could hear Scott, and I opened my mouth to speak, but the sight of my home, the house I had spent every day of my life before that August night, wouldn't let any words form. While I stared at it, an elderly lady opened the front door and hobbled toward the mailbox.

Get outta my house.

Mrs. K eased into their driveway, not caring a damn that some strange woman had stolen my house. I couldn't tear my eyes away. The flowerbeds in front of the bay window no longer had small, trimmed bushes but woodchips. Maybe flowers would sprout there in the spring. The black metal mailbox was now wooden. I ached to go inside, stand in my old bedroom, walk down the stairs I had stomped up and down for so many years. Did it look the same? I figured it probably didn't if the outside was any indication. Somehow that made it easier.

"Timmy?" someone asked as I stepped out of the SUV, emotions bombarding me like sand in a windstorm. I had to brace myself against the car until the dizziness passed.

"Scott, run in and get him, okay? I'm gonna stay out here with Timmy." Mrs. K put her arm around me, but I could barely feel her. The gray-haired woman pulling mail out of the imposter mailbox finally glanced my way. She smiled and waved.

Does she know me?

But I realized then that she was waving at Mrs. K, not me. My stomach rolled and my cheeks felt hot. These people moved on without me, even befriended the thieves who stole my house. Before I could stop it, my stomach revolted. I threw up my breakfast, heaving until nothing was left.

"Oh, honey, I'm so sorry." Mrs. K rubbed my back. I gagged and then spit the last of the bile out of my mouth.

"Who is *she?*" I pointed toward the old lady – that ugly anger that had ridden shotgun with me for four months hopped right back into my head. But I pushed it away, and then a sloppy tongue suddenly slobbered all over my right hand.

"TREVOR!" I shouted, dropped to my knees, and threw my arms around his enormous neck. He responded with long, swiping licks all over my face. Nothing could have erased my anger quicker.

His anguished whimpers let me know just how much he had missed me. *And Sam.* Trevor probably wondered where the heck we had gone, why his people had left him. A low moan came out of his mouth and I rubbed his head, kissed his nose, and nuzzled his neck. He still didn't stop whimpering.

We sure didn't want to leave you, boy. It wasn't by choice. I rubbed his head till I worried I might take off fur. I hugged him and held him until his whimpers stopped.

"Boy, he missed you...wow." Scott beamed. He reached for Trevor, but our yellow lab shoved his head back under my arm. He wouldn't let go of me. Tears glistened in my eyes, but Trevor was quick to lick them away. *Skippy is gonna think I cheated on him.*

"I've thought about him so many times. I wondered if he was okay and who took him in. I guess when you die, you assume everyone close to you does, too," I said without even thinking before I spoke.

"Oh, Timmy." Mrs. K wrapped her arms around me again. Any lingering anger melted into bitter tears, and I felt her body hitch. She held me, rocked me back and forth as both of our bodies shuddered with sobs. Note to self: quit claiming not to be a crybaby. That notion got tossed out the window darn near a week ago.

"Hey, Mom, company's comin'!" Scott shouted from the doorway. I didn't even notice he had gone back into the house.

I wiped my face and glanced up at Mrs. K who was smiling as if she had won the lottery.

"Timmy, you wanna play a little catch?" Scott suggested as he flipped a football a couple of times in the air. I had to admit some good old All-American fun sounded cool.

"Who's comin' over?" I felt like a secret was being told right in front of me, and I was totally clueless. But then I knew. *Duh.*

"You'll see," was all Scott would offer. Mrs. K grinned and rubbed my back again.

"You boys go play. I'll holler at you when it's time."

Time for what? Can't he just appear like a good Musketeer?

The two of us chatted endlessly while we tossed the ball back and forth. We didn't throw any long balls at first just so we could talk. I picked Scott's brain about middle school and our classmates. I had catching up to do. I was shocked to find out one of our classmates had been killed by a drunk driver only six weeks after my family was murdered.

"They built a really cool memorial for your family in front of the high school. Hey, when're you gonna go back to school?"

Go back? The idea added a level of stress I hadn't considered.

"Hey, Spook, heads up!" Scott launched a bomb, and I took off like a bullet. In my dead sprint, I grinned at the new nickname. He had laughed saying I was the first ghost come-back-to-life he'd ever known.

I liked it. In a bizarre way, I sort of *felt* like a spook. Mrs. K didn't approve, but in a strange way, it acknowledged what I had gone through. No dancing around the elephant, as Jeremy called what I'd gone through and how people would try to avoid talking about it.

"And Weaver makes a remarkable catch," I announced after doing just that. I had always had the hands and the speed. "Think I'll be able to make the team next year?"

"Only if you grow, Shorty," a voice behind me teased.

I whipped around and stared at a scrawny Athos. Brent Matthews hadn't changed one bit. I laughed out loud, unable to suppress it. Even I had an inch on him still.

It reminded me of how Mom kept telling Sam in seventh grade that growth spurts came late for boys, that girls developed sooner and to be patient. He had sprouted three inches from April to August before eighth grade, then another two prior to his freshman year. I suspected Brent would have to be more patient than that.

"You callin' *me* short? Wow, you're a dwarf then."

We hugged fiercely, clapped each other on the back, and spent the next two hours catching up. I remembered a comment Max made about kids being resilient. I had looked up the word at the library, and even though I understood it, I hadn't really bought it then. I hadn't felt very resilient. But now? I believed it. I was living it.

"Lunch, boys!" Mrs. Kruschaven stood on the front porch and pointed at a BMW pulling into the driveway. Mr. Kruschaven hopped out.

My heart hammered. "MR. K!" I ran toward him, feeling like a kid again. He hadn't changed a bit – thin, wispy brown hair, smile lines so deep it made him look like he was squinting. He lifted me off the ground as he hugged me.

When he set me down, he stared at me, shaking his head but smiling the whole time. "God, Timmy, it is so damn good to see you, son." He held me at arm's length, studying me. "You need some meat on your bones – and I might have just the thing for that."

Seeing Mr. K brought on a whole new slew of emotions. So much like my dad – similar hair color, same age, almost identical height. It felt eerie to be held by him. If I squinted, I could pretend it was Dad. The wave of sorrow made me wobble. He pulled me close again and held me.

"Charlie, you owe me seventy bucks, my man. Any guy who doesn't bet on his own team deserves to lose his money." Dad held up his beer and toasted, but Charlie was laughing too hard to lift his glass.

I remembered the many Cardinals' wagers, and the friendly competition between our two dads. Brent's parents had been friends, too, but not like the Kruschavens. We'd celebrated every Thanksgiving together since I was old enough to remember.

"Well, are you hungry?" Mr. K led me to his sedan and opened the back door. "Check it out." He nodded toward a box, and I peeked inside.

"Ah, man, Chinese!" No matter how unsettled my stomach was, I couldn't pass this up.

"Not just Chinese. Cashew chicken, hot and sour soup, and egg rolls." Mr. K stared at Timmy, tears welling in his dark eyes. The show of emotion caused me to tear up too.

"C'mon, Spook, let's eat," Scott ordered and took my hand. I felt like a child again and quickly pulled my hand from his.

"Hey, people'll think you like me." I still had a lump in my throat, but the urge to laugh outweighed it. *God, it feels good to be here.*

"Well, I do." He winked, putting his arm around me. "Can I kiss you?"

"Oh, God, get off me, butthead. I already got a boyfriend...C'mon, Trevor!" The three of us laughed, while Trevor wedged between us, keeping me as close as he could. Brent joked that he felt left out and he wasn't one for any threesome. He had needs and just couldn't share. Scott added that he'd never been dissed by a dog.

"Well, I don't know about that, son…I saw that Mitchell girl you were sitting with at the football game this fall." Mr. K let out a bark of a laugh, and we howled right along with him.

"Charlie…don't be mean." Mrs. K shook her head, and I suddenly remembered just how much fun the Three Musketeers used to have making scenes.

I punched Scott on the arm. "A girlfriend? I'm gone for four months, and you already got a girlfriend? Brent, we'll find you someone so you don't feel left out. How about Erik? He's cute, got a great smile, and I bet he'd be okay dating a shrimp." I high-fived Scott, who liked the joke enough to repeat it.

"Dating a shrimp! Ha!"

Brent smiled, said okay, and we marched inside to eat.

The Kruschaven home was exactly the same, except their thirty-inch TV. was now a massive big screen that filled an entire corner of the living room. There was a big red bow on the corner, so I assumed this was their family Christmas present. They did one big thing for the family every year. I thought it was a cool tradition that I'd often suggested to Mom and Dad. They reminded us that their big present was a vacation with one another…away from the kids. Sam and I would feign heart attacks, like they could possibly want time away from us.

I shoved the memory aside and blurted, "Wow!" I admired the TV, but Scott pushed me toward the kitchen.

They pulled out all the containers, and Mrs. M handed me a plate. I poured some hot and sour soup into a small bowl, then scooped chicken chunks one at a time, spread them on my plate, and then doused them with sauce. A memory flashed of Max pouring too much of my sauce on meatballs Skippy and I had scrounged out of the trash. And then how he had bartered them for a bottle.

Was it possible that was only a week ago? I shivered. Just thinking about it reminded me how cold I always was. And angry. And hungry. And tired. And lonely.

Slowly, I was slipping back into my skin. It was a nice fit.

We sat at the bar instead of going to the dining room, and I was glad. We struggled with chopsticks, making all of us laugh, and ate our first few bites in silence. I savored the first taste of the oyster sauce on my tongue. Mrs. Mahoney had served some delicious meals, but none of it held a candle to cashew chicken. I chewed slowly, let the flavor fill my mouth, and finally swallowed it. I had the fleeting thought that I had died and gone to heaven, but I knew better. If that were true, I would be with Mom, Dad, and Sam. Could they see me? Were they happy I was back with the other half of our family? I hoped so.

When we finished, I felt odd and a little out of place. Through our silence, I had visited the past and felt detached from the present. It would take a minute to regroup.

"I'm stuffed," Scott said, sliding off his bar stool.

"You're already fat," I jabbed, and everyone snickered.

"You need to get fat." Mrs. Kruschaven felt of my ribs. I liked how maternal she was being with me. It made me ache and warmed me all at the same time.

"You need to eat, short stuff, or you're going to be a midget all your life." I threw a fortune cookie at Brent and worried this might be a soft spot with him. Brent had always been the sensitive one.

"Bite me," he said, grinning. I made a quick note-to-self: *don't tease Brent too much about his height.*

Mrs. K shooed us outside, telling us to go play. I knew from the looks exchanged between Mr. K and her that they wanted to talk about me.

"Thanks for lunch, Mr. K. It was awesome." I beamed, feeling that confused happy sorrow again. The coupling of happy and sad might be my new normal for a while.

"Ah, Timmy, you're welcome. It's just so good to have you back." He half-hugged me again.

"I feel kinda bad, Timmy. It's two o'clock. I'm worried

you're not going to be hungry for dinner." Mrs. K finger combed my hair, then kissed me gently on top of the head.

"Ah, you know how Chinese is, Mrs. K. I'll be hungry in an hour," I said. Then a vicious memory slapped me in the face.

Oh, Tori, it's Chinese food. Zero calories. It'll wear off in a minute. I gasped for air and closed my eyes praying the cashew chicken would stay still in my stomach. The image of Dad pinching at Mom's nonexistent love handles made me stagger.

"Timmy, are you okay?" Mrs. K was staring at me as I opened my eyes.

"Yeah," I whispered. "Lots of ghosts." I swallowed a few times, amazed I was able to share so much. Brent and Scott opened the back door to the huge deck and steered me outside.

"We'll take care of him, Mom. Will you flip on the radio?"

I took a deep breath, willing the memories to give me a break. One of the guys led me to the bench where I plopped to my butt.

God, I feel like I'm in a time warp. I stared at Brent and Scott, then inside at the two people Mom and Dad had shared everything with from Friday night happy hours to Sunday brunch.

I felt the chill of the December wind, but already, it meant something totally different. *I don't have to sleep in it, so it doesn't seem as cold.*

My head started to clear as music started playing a song I didn't know. We wandered to the deck, chairs covered just like the swimming pool.

I savored the fresh air and enjoyed being surrounded by music. The three of us rubbed our full bellies and chatted and enjoyed the easy pastime of listening to the radio. Songs played, we talked, and it seemed so comfortable to be sitting with my best buddies on Christmas Eve.

"Hey, I love this song!" I shouted as an old Aerosmith tune came on.

"Yep, good song, but we gotta get you caught up. We'll

work on that." Brent nodded, jabbed me on the arm, then started singing.

"It's only been four months...how much music could I have missed?" I was always the classic rock fan, repeating Dad's assertion that sixties and seventies rock hadn't been topped yet.

"Dude, there's at least ten more boy bands." We cracked up. I could picture us sitting in Scott's living room with paper and pen taking a quiz as each new song played on the radio.

The three of us were singing at the top of our lungs when Mr. and Mrs. K stood in the doorway grabbing their throats like we were gagging them. Scott threw the Nerf football at them, but we must have sounded hysterical. Mr. K didn't miss a beat – he plopped into a lounger and broke out singing right along with us.

"Hey, where is everybody?" a girl's voice called from inside the house.

My heart raced.

Stephie.

"Your favorite person is here, Tim." Scott punched my arm, but that wasn't what I was worried about.

Had she recognized me at Union Station? That seemed like a century ago.

Seconds later, Stephie stood in the sliding glass doorway staring at me, her mouth open wide enough to catch a small bird.

"Timmy?" She was truly shocked by the sight of me. My crude haircut and bruised face certainly added to the effect.

"Hey, squirrel face," I teased. And then Stephanie Kruschaven did something that couldn't have shocked me more. She rushed past her mom to hug me. I hesitated, then embraced her with a sincerity I never knew I felt.

Her parents joined us on the deck. "Sorry, sweetie. You were at Carrie's, and we didn't have a chance to tell you. And it didn't seem like the kind of thing you left a message about." Mrs. K brushed the hair out of Stephie's eyes.

She stepped back to inspect me. I did the same. I couldn't believe how much she had changed in just four months. I wondered if she thought the same about me.

She demanded answers. Between her parents, Scott interrupting with details, and my explanations, she suddenly got the funniest look on her face when I mentioned how much time I had spent at the Arch.

"I saw you," she stated simply. "I couldn't believe it was really you, but boy it sure shook me up. I convinced myself I was seeing things. But it was you, wasn't it?" She gawked, her mouth still hanging open. She glanced at her Mom and Dad who seemed confused. "I saw him last week."

"Yeah, it was me... Seeing you sort of woke me up." I started to say more and stopped myself.

"Wow, you met with a mean wall sometime between then and now." Her sympathetic expression genuinely touched me. I figured I was probably dirtier then, but I hadn't encountered Trash Boy yet.

The four of us sat out on the Kruschaven's deck and reminisced. We talked about everything from school to what happened that horrible August night. I wouldn't avoid it anymore, but I told an abridged version without my participation in the violence. I even answered their questions about the days After the best I could. We cried, we laughed, and we planned, sparking the already growing hope in my heart.

It was the best afternoon of the new phase of my life, better than any other in the past four months and sixteen hours – it only needed a terrier friend to make it perfect. As perfect as it could be without Mom, Dad, and Sam.

"Do you get to spend Christmas with us tomorrow? You've gotta."

I stared at Stephie. *Is this the same girl who vowed never to talk to me again?*

"I – I sure hope so."

But no matter whether I did or not, the offer warmed me in

a way Stephie Kruschaven couldn't imagine. I felt my heart leap a monumental hurdle in my healing process.

On the way back to Mrs. Mahoney's, I didn't say much. I didn't need to. I had spent the afternoon with the Musketeers, eaten Chinese with my parents' best friends, and witnessed a transformation more astounding than Dr. Jekyll morphing into Mr. Hyde – once a cucumber, now a friend.

I smiled – I had proof that miracles really did happen.

Part V

New Beginnings

May 2005

St. Louis Post Dispatch Special Feature—Marquette High School Graduation

St. Louis teen gives new meaning to survival

Today marked an ending and a new beginning for a Chesterfield teen once listed as missing, his face on posters distributed all over the city, and ultimately presumed dead.

Timothy Ryan Weaver, 18, graduated from Marquette High School today with a future, a new family, and a human-interest story the potential subject of an award-winning novel.

Marquette's graduating class was addressed by their valedictorian, salutatorian, and then Weaver, the classmate many once mourned.

Five years ago, August 27, 1999, Weaver's family was slaughtered in a gang-related crime in northern St. Louis. The then eleven-year old escaped, but only after shooting two of the men responsible for his family's deaths. Weaver retreated to the alleys of the city, and when he was manipulated by a homeless bum, Weaver lived among them for four months, surviving with sheer will and the help of his canine savior, Skippy.

Of the time he spent homeless, Weaver admits, "People felt sorry for me at first. I was little, cute, and that scared the crap out of them. If this can happen to a middle-class kid, no one is immune." But the newness wore off, he says, and he resorted to violence to survive. When probed about the specifics, Weaver generalizes by saying he "did what he had to do."

He addressed his classmates and promoted the program he helped create with money he made selling t-shirts during the Rams 1999-2000 Super Bowl season. Weaver touched hearts and tugged heartstrings.

"A lot of people endure tragedy and many of them do it with more grit than I did. I'm just a kid who suffered and had lots of help overcoming it. Many of you would have been able to do the same, but because of Jeremy Gardner and Mrs. Mahoney of Big Brothers of America, I won't be a statistic. Instead, I'll be their poster boy."

During his speech, classmates called out heartfelt sentiments, some from what Weaver calls his "musketeers." Scott Kruschaven, Brent Matthews, and Erik D'Angelo, a boy Weaver met at Mahoney's Rescue Mission, make up their version of Dumas' quartet. One shouted, "All for one," bringing about cheers and tears from many in the crowd.

But in researching Weaver's story, his most notable sidekicks have been his dogs. Weaver was adopted by Charlie and Beth Kruschaven in 2001, and also adopted Skippy, Weaver's terrier mutt acquired on the streets, as well as Trevor, the family dog left to fend for himself after the tragedy in August 1999. Both dogs were subjects in Weaver's speech.

"What really got me through was the spirit of my family. They're the reason I'm here today. My dad would have insisted I wear his gown, my mom would have made me get a haircut, and Sam would have teased me for still being a towhead. He would have been off at some big-name college, probably too busy to come to my graduation. And Skippy. I can't begin to make anyone understand how special he's been in my life. And to come back and find Trevor waiting. It's like having part of Mom, Dad, and Sam with me."

Weaver also promoted the new Save the Streets Program he helped back through donations, now facilitated by Jeremy Gardner and Mrs. Mahoney's Rescue Mission.

"That August night, my life ended. I was so alone. I had nowhere to go. But that doesn't have to happen to anyone else. Not if they know about Mrs. Mahoney's Rescue Mission. With Jeremy Gardner and Mrs. Mahoney, their new program means no one will have to do what I did if they know they have options."

Timothy Ryan Weaver accepted a scholarship to attend the University of Miami. He plans to study sociology and business finance. Kruschaven and Matthews plan to enroll in the same school, while the other musketeer, Erik D'Angelo, is applying to a fine arts school in Ft. Lauderdale.

The four plan to rent a house that allows pets.

Amazon Super Store
Ballwin, Missouri
April 3, 2026

"Mr. Weaver, would you sign my copy?" I handed him the book, and he took it – his eyes as blue as any ocean I'd ever seen, his sandy blond hair neatly cropped.

"Absolutely. What's your name?" His pen hesitated, poised above the inside page of the hardback.

"Stefanie, with an *f.*" I was star struck. I'd seen him on TV – Ellen, Oprah, The Late Show. But up close and personal, he seemed like such a regular guy. The scar just below his left eye made him rugged. I'd heard how he had gotten it. Now I would finally get to read about it. The idea made me giddy. I'd never met an author before, much less the most famous Marquette graduate ever.

"Well, Stefanie-with-an-f, that's a mouthful. Do your friends just call you *F*?" He smiled at me. My face reddened, all the way to the tip of my ears. I wanted to turn to Molly and say something, but she was already prodding me in the back.

"Yes, I mean, *no.*" I bit my lip. *So much for acting more mature.* "It's just Stefanie." I started to say more, but stopped before I made more of a fool of myself.

He wrote something in a flurry and signed his name. "I have a very dear friend named Stephanie. We go *way* back. Introduced me to my wife, matter of fact. Here, enjoy. And you might consider shortening your name." He flashed a huge smile, and I understood why my fellow seniors were crushing on him.

"Thank you, Mr. Weaver. I...I will." I half waved, stepped to the side and waited while Molly got hers signed. *I will?* What a dork.

I finally had his book. *Wow.* The cover had bottle caps all over it with the title written using one of them. *Fifty Cents for a* was embossed just over a Dr Pepper lid. Opening it to read the inside flap, I wanted to skip to the dedication, but I refused to mess up the grand design. I knew quite a bit about the story, from Mr. Weaver's visit to our school and his talks on TV. It had been highlighted when the autobiography first came out a week earlier.

On the streets of St. Louis, a boy loses his family, his home, and his dignity. This true story of Timothy Ryan Weaver's quest to survive as a homeless kid will take you from Brookline Avenue to Catalina Avenue – two sides of one of the most violent cities in America and opposites ends of the world.

Timmy, the victim of brutal gang violence, survives a horrifying night by fighting back, but in his efforts, his life is shattered. And so is his soul. An inability to remember is the catalyst that ultimately sends him to old Max, who claims to be his grandfather.

Feel Timmy's anguish as he searches for life, defies the odds, and remembers when change *meant fifty cents for a Dr Pepper. One hundred eighteen carbon-copied days proved to Timmy that nothing would ever change again. But with the help of a three-inch blade and a fifteen-pound terrier mutt, Timothy Ryan Weaver* would *change and overcome the cruel obstacles to unravel the mystery of that horrible August night.*

I flipped to the back jacket. I studied the author photo when he was eleven beside a current picture. I glanced over at Mr. Weaver chatting with a pony-tailed man with fancy forehead scars winding like a crazy river.

"Look," Molly said, and tapped my book so hard she nearly knocked it out of my hand. "Isn't that so cool?" She pointed to the writing below the picture.

Timothy Ryan Weaver lives in Chesterfield, Missouri, with his wife and four-year old terrier, D'Artagnan. Fifty Cents for a Dr Pepper *is his first book. A portion of the proceeds will go to Mrs. Mahoney's Home for Children, the*

American Cancer Society in memoriam of Mrs. Francis Mahoney, and the Inner-City Movement to Stop Gang Violence.

Mr. Weaver is currently at work on his second book.

"Yeah, that's really neat."

"Well, Greg Munson's little sister goes to kindergarten with Stephanie Kruschaven's son, Ryan. She kept her last name, you know. Anyway, Greg said the next book is about Max and the Gerries – what made them drunks and stuff. He's going to track Max all the way up until he died." Molly nodded like what Greg said had to be gospel.

"Mr. Kruschaven died?" I raised an eyebrow, trying to irk Molly because she always had trouble telling a good story without getting her pronouns mixed up.

"Huh? *No!* Are you messin' with me? When *Max* died. Man, sometimes you're really hard to talk to. Didn't you see Mr. Weaver on *Good Morning, St. Louis* when he talked about Max? It was sad." Molly furrowed her brow like the thought of it might make her cry. "Greg says Ryan and his sister are best friends."

"They're five, Molly. Everybody's best friends in kindergarten. They're babies." I shook my head, amazed at what a ditz my own best friend could be. I turned to the front of the book and read the dedication before Molly could ruin it for me.

It takes many people to tell a story, especially one as hard as this one. My best friends, Scott, Brent, Erik, and Jeremy, were instrumental in so many aspects. But the real hero in my survival was Skippy – without him, this story would never have been told. Without him, I would've never survived to tell it.

I only wish dogs could live in human years – and not have to end after only sixteen. He gave me so much. And I know when I see Mom, Dad, and Sam again, they can admit what I've always known was true – Skippy was really the reincarnation of the three of them.

I blinked back tears, knowing Molly would tease me. I cried at Hallmark commercials, so it wouldn't surprise her. I turned back to his autograph, the inscription. *Stefanie with an F, Enjoy my story and always be open to change. Timothy R. Weaver*

Change or not, I planned to ask Greg Munson myself if Ryan Kruschaven was really in kindergarten with his kid sister. Or if any of what Molly said was true.

Some kids had to grow up way too fast. Others had trouble doing it at all.

Other books by Barri Bumgarner
Available on Amazon B&N.com
Kindle and Nook

8 Days
Slipping
Dregs

About the Author

Dr. Barri L. Bumgarner, the author of two thrillers and one young adult novel, is an Associate Professor and Education Department Chair at Westminster College, a liberal arts college in Fulton, Missouri. The author of *8 Days, Slipping*, and *Dregs*, Barri has also published eighteen short stories, over thirty poems, and hundreds of articles, both academic and teacher-education focused.

Barri was recently on a Dateline episode, "Before Daylight," sharing her research on her true crime project about the conviction of Steven Rios for the murder of Jesse Valencia. To learn more about the project, visit: https://www.**facebook**.com/**BarriLBumgarner**

When she isn't teaching or writing, she loves to travel, watch sports, read, spoil her furry kids, as well as create and play with all things digital.